City of the Damned

By Kay Marrie

For my beloved

Jacket art: Kailey Reidel

Instagram: kaymarrie__

TikTok: kaymarrie_author

ISBN: 979-8-9910836-0-7

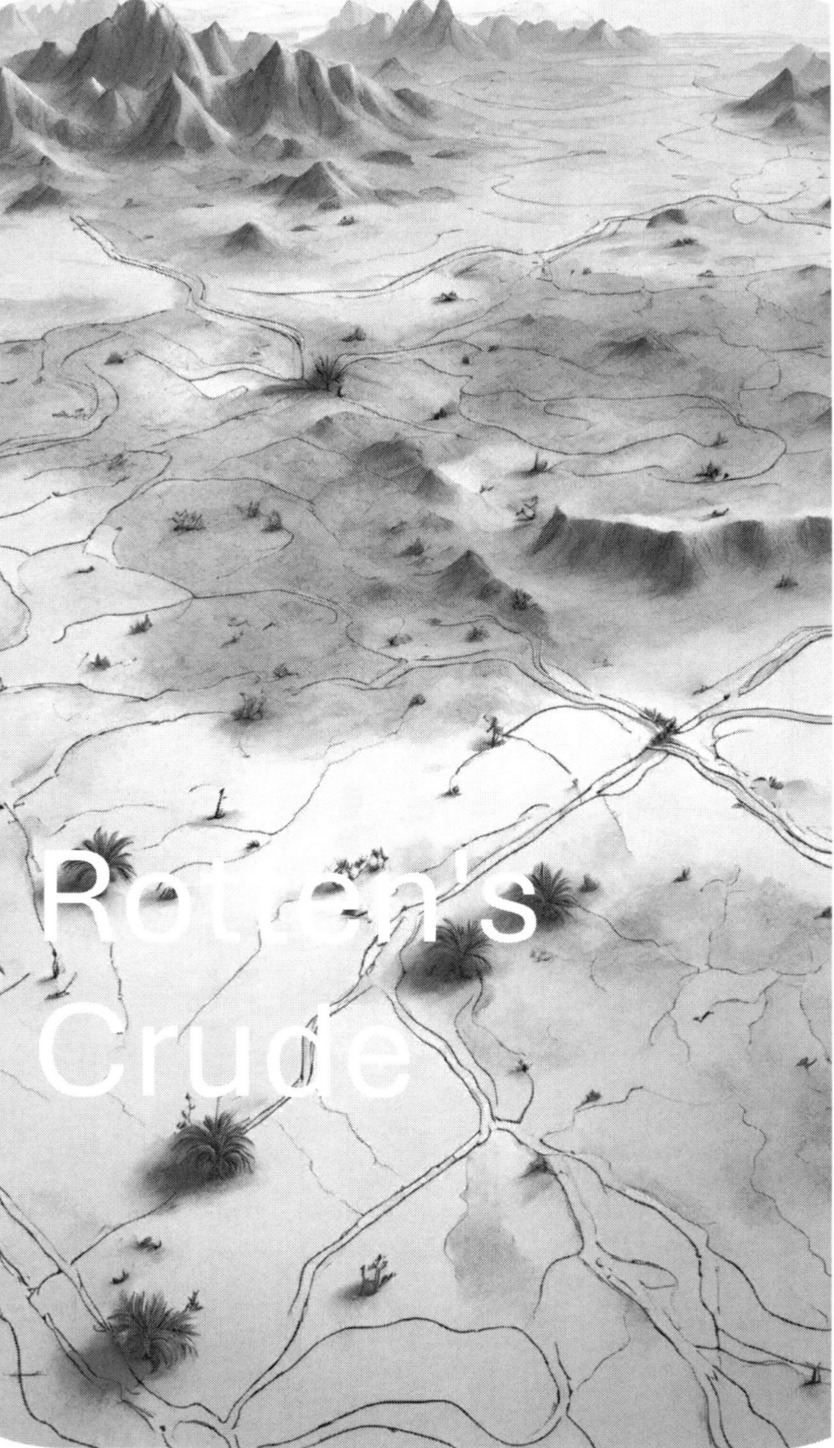
Rotten's
Crude

Prologue

DESTI ANDERSON GREW UP AFTER THE rapture. After millions of lost souls were left on a desolated Earth. The planet was now plagued with disease, famine, and demons. With every society, rebirth happens. Desti was born in the Land of Mors (Land of Death) and knew no other reality. Her faction kept the demons out and the people alive, but at what cost? What was the point of living in a world where love was forbidden? Was it worth it? If you were to break the rules, the demons would demand a blood sacrifice.

Desperate for deliverance from the clutches of her Hell, Desti and her best friend Tate Mitchell decide to sneak out of their faction, and explore the forbidden cave system, Rotten's Crude, to search for the lost Lux. Legend has it that *he who finds the Lux shall hold the power of the angels, able to cast away the evils of the world and deliver the people to the Kingdom of Light*.

Desti and Tate grew up hearing about the myths of the Lux. It's what brought them close together and gave them something to hope for. Now grown up, they search for the mysterious Lux to break their faction free of the clutches of the demons. With growing desires, tension between them threatens to tear everything apart.

Their time is running out. They are almost twenty-one. Once someone turns twenty-one, they can be offered to the demons and receive the *mark*, promising their soul to the demons forever.

1: The Dust Storm

OUTSIDE, THE WITHERED DUSTY AIR HAD PICKED UP its speed, blowing through the desolated town like a hurricane. Shards of tiny glass sand crystals shot through the air.

No one would dare go outside in a storm like that. Desti had her cheek resting on the palm of her hand as she gazed out the cracked window in her classroom.

She imagined the world to be different. Beautiful and lively. Like before. *What was Earth like before*? *Before the rapture. Before the people were left to suffer under the control of the demons.*

She heard stories of vast cities filled with people, free to do what they pleased. Free to go to a movie. Free to go shopping. Free to love. *What was it like to love anyway*? Her thin strands of auburn hair dangled in front of her face. She blew out a huff of air from the corner of her lip and pushed the strand off to the side.

The sounds of the classroom were muffled by her mind swirling into her imagination. That's where she could escape. Desti hated her reality. To live controlled by tormenting demons. To live in a world plagued by disease and famine. Her whole reality was to survive. That was it. *What kind of life was that*?

Memories of her childhood flushed through her like a rushing river. There was no love, not from her parents and certainly not from her teachers. The children of the city of Mors were to obey and conform, forced to school as soon as they were able to sit and listen and forced to stay until they were old enough to be shoved out into this desolate world, using them as a slave tethered to this forsaken wasteland. She had grown up with most of her classmates, seeing them across the hall or around the city. Even though she didn't talk to them much, she still enjoyed the occasional head-nods and half smiles. It was difficult to make friends here. There was too much control. Too many eyes watching to do such a thing. That was why Desti loved her friendship with Tate. He was her secret best friend— since they found each other one day as children. Ever since then, he was her person. Suddenly she felt something hit the back of her head.

Desti glanced down at her desk and found a crumpled-up ball of paper. She looked to her left. She quietly mouthed, "what is it?" Next to her, Tate was doodling in his raggedy notebook.

He pointed to her desk and silently mouthed, "read it." She smiled. Desti glanced at the front of the class to make sure the teacher wasn't paying attention. The last thing that she wanted was to get sent to the Master. Everyone feared being sent to him. Desti heard stories of kids being sent to him. If they came back, they would come back torn and tearful, and no one would ever speak of what happened in the Master's chambers. She held the paper ball in her right hand. Her fingers played with the tiny rips from the corner of the note as she opened it up. *Tate's handwriting is the worst,* she thought. A slight giggle escaped her mouth. Desti held the note down in her lap and carefully glanced down to read what it said.

This class is lame. Want to skip next?

Desti rolled her eyes. She wasn't the type to skip class. She couldn't be. Not with who her parents were. *Would they find out? How would they punish her this time?* Desti lifted her cotton sleeve and touched the leftover scars from her last punishment. She closed her eyes just for a moment. She recounted those times.

The people who were sent to punish her. You could get punished for anything in the city of Mors. She thought of Tate too. *What would his parents do to him?* He didn't talk about his punishments much. Maybe it was too painful. Desti had an old Bic pen lying in the corner of her auburn desk. She glanced up one more time to make sure that the teacher wasn't looking and wrote back.

No way. I don't want to be punished. Where would we go anyway?

Desti crumpled up the note into another withered ball and tossed it through the bottom side of her desk, landing the note right by Tate's scuffed-up Converse. Just as he leaned down to pick up the note, Desti sucked in a huge gasp. Tate froze midway past his desk, his hand almost touching the dirt floor, when he glanced up to a tapping on his desk. Desti sat in her chair paralyzed, and the only thing that she could move was her shaking leg. The teacher, Ms. Clyde, stood over Tate, with her ruler set on his desk. Time froze for a moment. Desti sat there counting the moles on Ms. Clyde's face. She traced them with her eyes, connecting them like a connect-the-dot picture. Her leathered wrinkled skin reminded Desti of the butchered skin that would hang out to dry down at the bazaar. She had one black hair that stuck out from her chin, which didn't match the rest of her ice-gray hair. Every kid was terrified of Ms. Clyde. Suddenly, Desti snapped out of her thoughts as she heard a rasping growl that exuded from her putrid mouth.

"Tate. What have you got there boy?"

Ms. Clyde stood tall above Tate's hunched-over body. Desti sat back in her chair with her hands cupped to her mouth. *Please don't see it.* Tate glanced out of the corner of his eye and locked sight with Desti. She knew that her face said it all. *Don't let her see the note. Make something up. Create a distraction. Something.* She and Tate had been friends for so long that they didn't even need to speak to know what each other was saying sometimes. Tate slightly shifted his foot until it was covering the note. Luckily, he had a pen already in his hand, and with a clever reaction, he sat up, placed his pen on his desk, and replied, "Ms. Clyde, I was just grabbing my pen. I must have knocked it off my desk." His face was confident. Poise. Desti admired how he could put on such a façade like that.

Ms. Clyde stood still, with her arms crossed over her chest. She tilted her chin toward the ceiling. Her thick black chin hair stuck out like a bristle brush, drawing all the attention to her underwhelming face. Desti waited for her to respond. *Did she see it? Will she punish us?* Tate never broke his focus, not once. Ms. Clyde responded with a deep grunt and then turned around. Desti watched every step that she took back to the front of the classroom. Simultaneously, Desti and

Tate pushed out a huge exhale of relief. She looked over at him with a hidden smirk and whispered, "That was a close one."

There was an old clock that hung on the chipped-painted wall. Just above the door. It looked as though it had gone through a fire. The glass had black stains on the inside and seamless cracks that decorated the exterior. Desti would listen to the ticking to soothe her boredom. Her mind didn't pay attention well to the material taught in school. *Obey your demons. The history of the rapture. The forbidden rules*. It was an endless cycle of depressing literature that every kid was forced to endure growing up. That's how the demons wanted it anyway. They wanted the people to herd like sheep and breed like rabbits. They were creating a new world, which was what Ms. Clyde taught the class. A world where the people obey their demons. More people for them to eat or enslave.

It had been one hundred years since the rapture happened. Since eighty percent of the world's, population disappeared in a fraction of a second. Desti twirled the strands of her hair around her finger as she thought about those lessons. *What was it like? At the beginning of the Era of the Damned*. Ms. Clyde started at the beginning of the school year teaching about the beginning of the Era of the Damned. It was a blood bath for the humans and a feeding frenzy for the demons, but she didn't need school to teach her that. Stories of that time fluttered around like insects, scaring people into submission since childhood.

Desti recounted seeing the horrendous drawings of demons in her classroom. They all looked different in some way yet shared the same essence to them. What covered their bodies was thick, slimy skin that was usually charcoal black or rusty brown. Their physiques were massive compared to humans. Ten feet tall would make anyone human look minuscule. But the worst part about the demons was their horrid growl. With sounds that ripped through the air with their razor-sharp mouths, emanated the evils from the depths of Hell—or so she heard.

She thought a little too long about the unspeakable terror that it must have brought to their victims. Desti had never seen a demon in the flesh. Demons didn't slither their way into the cities anymore. They had their offspring keep watch. Desti and Tate always played a game, where they would guess who was a Cambion and who wasn't. It was difficult to tell these days. They mostly looked human. She heard that they imbued themselves into the cities to control the people. *Ms. Clyde must be one,* Desti thought. By this point, Desti had daydreamed the rest of the class period away. She glanced at Tate, His emerald, green eyes glimmered with the slight ray of brutal sunshine that shined down through the shroud of smoke outside the window.

Judging by the sun, half the day had passed by. Desti watched Ms. Clyde stride her way back to the front of the room, balling her fingers into fists and slamming it hard on the desk. Everyone jumped. Silence was immediate as Ms. Clyde took control of the classroom. And even though Desti's room was the room assigned to young adults— in their last years of training— the looks and postures that everyone had made them look young again. Like a scared child in the presence of a monster. Even Desti was afraid of Ms. Clyde.

"You have twenty minutes. If you are back even one second late, you will be sorry," she grumbled.

Tate immediately turned toward Desti and said, "come on, lets get out of this room and stretch our legs." She smiled and nodded. That sounded like a great idea. Way better than being cooped up in an old, dusty classroom, cluttered with depressing history books and propaganda.

"Gladly," Desti said as she stood from her chair. The rest of the classmates had dispersed to wherever they go on their breaks. Sometimes Desti and Tate would just walk the perimeter and talk. Other times they would find somewhere to sit and eat a snack. She guessed today was a sit outside and ponder kind of day.

Tate took a seat on one of the steps outside and patted next to him. "Sit."

Tendrils of his hair flew like spilled ink in the air. The wind blew heavy and fast from the dust storm that was rolling through. Desti loved her best friend's hair. She had always joked about how he was the one blessed with *good* hair. She ruffled her fingers through the flowing strands and then sat down, pulling in a deep breath. Tate was silent, but his eyes glimmered with something more than just gazing. He was curious about something. Desti could tell by the way he was looking at her.

"You are staring again. I can tell when you have something on your mind."

"It's nothing…" he trailed off.

"It's not nothing. What is it?" Desti leaned closer until her shoulder brushed his. He was worried. But about what?

"Your parents…" he cleared his throat and continued. "Your parents—what is going on with them? Have you noticed anything unusual?" His voice was hesitant which was unlike him.

"Tate, you know how my parents are. My dad is an abusive alcoholic, and my mom is just absent. Why are you asking about my parents?" Desti placed her hand over his, tilting her chin slightly.

"I just—are you okay? I mean at home…when I am not there. Do they hurt you?"

Even though his eyes were only filled with compassion, his words cut through her like venom. She had never thought about how terrible her home life was. It just was. But that was something she didn't talk about much. Everyone in the city of Mors had a horrible life. In a world where couples were forced together purely for mating purposes by the ruling demons and love was forbidden, it was kind of rare to have a loving family dynamic, and if someone was lucky enough to have loving parents, they sure as Hell wouldn't make it known. That could easily get you ripped away from them or worse. She was sure it existed somewhere, but unfortunately, she was dealt a shit hand at that.

Desti traced her fingers across her battered arm, images of her recent beatings now flooding her mind and said, "my father hasn't hurt me in a few days. But you know how he is. I just need to stay out of his way, obey the rules, and then I should be fine." She waited for Tate to respond but Tate was still silent. "I'll be okay. I promise."

Before Tate could respond the sound of a bell chiming broke his focus. Desti glanced back and said, "our time is up. Come on," and held out her hand.

As she was making her way up the steps and back inside, she noticed one of the classmates sprinting from the distance. "Where does he go all the time. I see him sneaking around."

Tate looked back. "Who? Brandon?" Desti nodded. Tate leaned in closer, his voice now a mere whisper and said, "I think he is up to something. But you didn't hear it from me."

With only two minutes left, Desti began to run back to her class, fearful of what would come if she were late, but thankfully she had made it just in time. She took a seat and the last one to come bolting through the door was Brandon, panting and sweaty. Close one, she thought as she watched him sit in the back of the classroom. He was next to some other people Desti had seen around. By the look in their eyes, they all seemed to share some kind of secret friendship. Probably how she and Tate have. Desti yearned to be able to befriend more people, live a normal life, but she knew that was wishful thinking.

Another brutally boring hour slipped by of Ms. Clyde's lecture; the different types of demons that roam the Earth ever since the Beginning of the Era of the Damned. Some could only hunt at night, and others, well, they could seek their meals any hour of the day, however those kinds were rare and didn't bother the town much. She had heard this lecture before when she was little. Her mother would tell her demon stories before going to bed and it would give her terrible nightmares. *Don't ever let them smell your blood,* she had said.

Suddenly the alarms sounded, reverberating a cacophonous blare of splitting loudness through the halls. Desti jolted forward and covered her ears with her hands. She then sat back in her chair and looked over at Tate as he cracked a smirk from the corner of his lip. She silently mouthed, "Why are the alarms going?" Tate glanced around, watching the rest of his classmates doing the same, and focused back to Desti and mouthed, "It must be some kind of drill," as he shrugged his shoulders.

The alarms usually never went off unless there was something serious like a breach in the city. Ms. Clyde stood from her chair. The screeching echo forced a piercing sound through the classroom. "Out in the hall, now," she yelled. Her tone was infused with a potent, and almost palpable sense of intimidation. One by one, each student gathered their belongings and ran out into the hall. Desti thought they all looked like a herd of sheep, huddled together, doing whatever they were told. That's how the demons wanted it, right? Desti grabbed Tate's arm and squeezed it tight. She glanced over at him, and through the resounding alarms said, "don't you dare lose me in this." His fingers grasped onto hers and squeezed tight. "No way in Hell," he mouthed back as they followed the sea of panicking students. The frenetic energy in the halls was intensified by the chaotic array of flashing lights and frenzied screams, which seemed to further escalate the fear imbued in the air.

As Desti passed by the decrepit and grim covered window, she sucked in a ghastly gasp, as her eyes met a horrifying sight of the raging dust storm outside. The swirling tempest of shards of sand propelled forward, casting a sense of helplessness to the city. She squeezed Tate's hand as it rested on her arm. "What is this?" she asked.

"It must be some kind of storm."

Tate stepped forward and placed his hand on the glass of the window. The sea of students behind them had faded away into another corridor, leaving Desti and Tate alone. "It's no storm like I have ever seen before." said Desti. "Maybe it's the demons, trying to get into the city." Desti shot a look of fear and annoyance at Tate. "No way," she said. "The demons haven't come this far into the city in years. Since we were kids. They don't need to anymore. At most, they will stay at the perimeter."

Desti followed suit and stood almost face to face with the window. It felt cold to the touch. Like burning ice on her skin. A rush of adrenaline shot through her nerves. *Could it be? A demon?* She knew that she had a look of fear in her eyes and even though Tate didn't say it, she knew he felt the same. The emerald green in his eyes had been engulfed by the blackness of his pupils. A foul smell suddenly crept its way down the hall, smelling like a mixture of hot breath and rotten flesh. Desti threw her hand over her mouth and nose, and involuntarily gagged from the potent odor.

"What is that smell, Tate?"

Tate had done the same. His perfectly symmetrical face was covered by the placement of his hands. There was confusion in his eyes. *Tate always knew everything. Why does he look confused?* He replied, "I'm not sure, Desti." His voice was muffled through the cracks of his fingers.

Suddenly, a roar of echoing screams pierced through their conversation. Desti jumped back and hit the wall behind her. Tate had swiftly turned around, facing the door that led outside. As Desti rubbed her shoulder, she asked, "is that coming from outside?" *What is happening out there?*

Tate stepped forward and started to push the doors open. "Tate, wait! You don't know what is out there." Desti screamed. She reached out her arms and just as she felt the cotton fibers on his jacket touch the tips of her fingers, he was yanked outside into the whirling vortex of the storm.

"Tate!"

Without a thought in her mind, Desti leaped for the doors and pushed them open.

All Desti could hear was the mixture of distant screams and the ringing alarm. She covered her face, holding her bent arm above her mouth. Her eyes squinted tight as she tried to search through the shroud of the storm. "Tate!" she tried to yell. Her tiny voice was being drowned out by the cacophony around her. In the distance through the blanket of sandy gusts, she saw silhouettes moving around. *What is that? Is that Tate?* Just before she stepped off the ledge of the stairs, Desti was tugged backward and pushed into the brick wall. Almost too afraid to look, Desti slowly turned her gaze to her side and immediately exhaled a sigh of relief.

"Tate!"

She wrapped her arms around his neck. "Where did you go? What happened?" She pushed herself off and stepped back. Tate's midnight black hair danced crazily in the gusty winds. He reached out his hands and grabbed her arms firmly. "Shhh." He held his finger to his mouth. "I think there was a breach." Desti's eyes shot open wide. "A breach? Like demons got in?" There was silence just for a moment.

"What else could it be?" he replied.

Desti had never seen a demon in the flesh. They didn't come to torment the city anymore. They were too busy ruling the outskirts of the desolate world. *Why would they come here*? She thought. Her eyes were big and locked onto Tate's. "But why would they come here? I thought—" she trailed off.

It was Ms. Clyde stopping around the corner of the building. "Desti! Tate!"

They both stood still in fear. Desti sucked in her breath and held it in her chest. Her arms hung down her side and her feet forward. With every heavy stomp, Ms. Clyde's boot sent a rumbling thud through the ground. "What are you two doing over here? Get out in the field now."

Ms. Clyde stood in intimidation as she waited for Desti and Tate to make their way out into the field. Desti opened her mouth. "But—" A snarling screech escaped Ms. Clyde's mouth as she screamed, "now!" Tate reached for Desti's hand and pulled her forward, trailing behind Ms. Clyde.

They were led into the chaos of the sandstorm. The shards of sand hit their skin like glass bullets being shot through the wind. *What is going on? Where is she taking us?* Desti's mind raced with overwhelming thoughts. She looked over at Tate. He looked so calm, she thought. Tate was always great about never showing his true emotions. He had to be tough, growing up in the city of Mors.

Ahead, Desti saw her classmates standing in a line in the center of the dusty plane. They were all arrested in motion, as if they were a line of motionless sculptures. Desti tugged Tate's hand, pulling him to a swift stop. He turned around and locked eyes with her. "Tate, I don't have a good feeling about this. What is this?" she cried. "Don't worry, we will be fine. Follow me and stay quiet." Tate gave Desti a nod and kept his pace following behind Ms. Clyde. Desti followed Tate and stood still next to a girl at the end. It was her friend Nash. She crossed her arms behind her back and silently questioned what was going on.

Ms. Clyde approached the front of the group, poised to enforce her intimidation onto them. With a snarling screech, she shouted, "there seems to have been someone who broke a rule." A unanimous gasp rippled across the group. *Broken a rule?* Desti thought. *Which rule?* There were many rules enforced and shoved down their throats since birth. Desti racked her brain trying to think of which one Ms. Clyde could be talking about. *Thou shall not disobey their demons. Thou shall not go past the city boundaries. Thou shall not love. Was it that one?* Breaking the rules was unheard of. No one broke the rules. The punishment for doing so meant torment and suffering. If they were lucky, they would be sent to the Master. The last time someone was punished by a demon was ten years ago. Desti never witnessed it, but she heard the tales growing up. She squeezed Tate's hand tight. Holding onto him gave her a sense of comfort. *He will protect me,* she thought.

The nerves that rushed through her body sent her legs into convulsions, her knees almost buckling under the stress. Nash stood beside Desti. Her eyes were bloodshot red, as if she had been crying. Desti elbowed Nash in the arm. "Pssst. Nash. What is going on?" she whispered.

As Desti locked eyes with Nash, she could feel desperation and hopelessness in the look in her eyes. *What is wrong?* She wanted to ask, but her eyes said it all. Without any words being spoken, Desti knew that Nash was in fear. *Fear of what though? Is she the one getting punished?* Ms. Clyde's unnerving voice broke their focus once again. "We live under the protection of the Master, but to get his protection, we must obey the rules. I am sure you all know the rules." Once she finished, Ms. Clyde glared upon each student in that line. Her eyes were soulless. Evil. *She must be a cambion,* Desti thought. Anyone with that much hatred in their life must be an offspring of a demon. There was no response. The silence was a blanket of anxiety, muffling anyone's courage to speak up. Ms. Clyde paced back and forth, in front of the students. The shards of sand struck her like pins, and yet she didn't flinch once.

Suddenly, a horrifying unearthly growl roared through Desti's ears, followed by the stench of rotten flesh. Desti held her breath. The smell was too wretched to breathe. She glanced at Tate. He seemed to be holding his breath too.

She wondered if he was scared. His face didn't show it. Desti studied the details of his pointed features, trying to get a sense of what he was feeling underneath. But nothing. The energy in the air shifted, catching the attention of half the classmates.

Through the vast wall of the storm, there appeared a shadow coming from the distant horizon. *What is that?* Desti stepped back and tripped over a rock. Her natural reaction would be to run. Run far away from whatever *that* was. But Tate tugged her back into place. He must think that she would be better off obeying their orders. The palms of her hands profusely sweat as she stood there paralyzed with fear.

Ms. Clyde had hunched down to the ground and bowed her head. The dark figure from the horizon slowly came closer and closer until it was standing a few feet from where she was kneeling. Desti sucked in a gut-wrenching gasp. "That's a—" Her whisper faded off into the wind. She couldn't even finish saying it. *Demon.* The fear that ravished her body overwhelmed her senses, evoking a shroud of sheer terror. She dug her fingers into the side of her khaki pants in a fearful tick. There was total silence. Not a single student spoke up, and yet Desti knew what everyone wanted to say. *Please. Not me. I didn't do it.*

The demon's grotesque physique was dark gray with mottled scaly patches of skin that writhed and pulsated oozing puss. Its eyes were massive. Black as the depths of Hell and pierced right through anyone who dared to stare. Desti couldn't bear to look it in the eyes. She turned her head slightly to the side and focused her gaze to the ground beside it. The worst part about the demon was not its horrendous appearance, but its foul rotten stench. She wanted to gag. Wanted to run away.

Desti recounted the pictures of demons that she grew up learning about. She knew that they were ugly, but nothing could have prepared her for the shift of energy that they emitted. She could feel it. Feel it sucking every ounce of joy, courage, or hope she had buried within. She wanted to drop to the ground.

Desti glanced to her right. It seemed as though she wasn't the only one feeling the way she felt. Nash was shaking with fear. Desti could sense it. She wanted to reach for her. Comfort her, but she didn't' dare draw attention to herself at that moment. A blanket of silence held everyone still. What else could they do anyway? If they run, they for sure would be hunted down and eaten. Desti wanted to run so badly. She yearned to escape the unknown terrors that were lurking ahead.

She was shaking. Shaking from the pain and from the fear. *What is this? What is going to happen?*

Ms. Clyde stood up from her kneeled position and seemed to be communicating with the demon. Usually, the demons didn't use their voice to speak, but instead injected their horrifying voice into your mind. Desti squinted her eyes. She expressed confusion and curiosity. *What are they talking about?* She thought.

Ms. Clyde turned toward the line of terrified students and started down at the end farthest from where Desti was standing. Desti cupped her hands in front of her body and squeezed her fingers tight. One by one, the students stood face to face with Ms. Clyde. So close that her bristled chin hair could have stuck them in their eye. She was whispering something. Desti leaned slightly forward. *What is she saying to them?* She was close now. Only a few students away. The heavy beating of Desti's heart felt as if it were going to throw her to the ground. There she was now. Ms. Clyde stood face to face with her. Desti could smell Ms. Clyde's hot, musky breath protruding from her tongue. She whispered, "was it you girl?" *Was it me? What is she talking about?* All Desti could muster up to say was, "I don't know what—" she trailed off. Cut off by a powerful grunt from Ms. Clyde. She was no longer face to face with her.

Desti glanced to her side. *Tate,* she thought. She watched as Tate stood in his position strong and confident. He held his chin high and had a look of complete confidence in his eyes. He was asked the same question and he responded with a forceful, "no Ms. Clyde."

Was that it? Is this over? Desti racked her brain questioning herself. She was sure everyone else was too. Ms. Clyde stood about five feet from the group and yelled over the whistling gusts of wind.

"Someone has broken one of the forbidden rules. And it seems that no one wants to come forward and confess."

The demon stood high behind Ms. Clyde. Its eyes radiated the feeling of despair and hate into the air. *Which rule? Who would be so stupid to do such a thing?* Desti's fingers reached for Tate's for a sense of comfort. Since they were children, she had always gone to him when things got tough.

His finger locked with hers and they twisted into a knot. She glanced down just for a moment before her focus was snatched by Ms. Clyde vulgar tone. "Since no one wants to confess. One of you will be sacrificed until the true offender comes forward." In that moment, it was as if the blackness of the world around her swirled into her mind and engulfed her sense of reality. A silent gasp escaped the clutches of her teeth in reaction to the absurd threat of Ms. Clyde.

There was a unanimous sense of desperation and fear that swept across the line of students. Their heads turned from side to side, glancing at each other, trying to see who it could possibly be. Desti saw tears forming in the corner of Nash's eyes. She wanted to cry too. She wanted to drop to her knees and give up, but she didn't. Not with how she was raised. Her parents would tell her, "*If you cry, I will give you something to cry about*." She learned to hold it in. Bottle it up and push it way down. Desti lost her focus on Nash and looked forward as she saw Ms. Clyde step to the side. Desti could tell that everyone felt that something was about to happen. The air became thick and heavy, weighing on her chest like a blanket of lead.

Suddenly, in a fraction of a second, the demon had lunged its massive body forward, reaching for the group. Its two-inch claws latched into Nash's flesh, tearing through her shirt, and puncturing her skin. Nash belted out a blood-curdling scream and tried to reach for Desti but before she touched her hand, the demon expelled a guttural growl and slithered away, dragging Nash into the darkness of the forbidden wastelands. Desti threw her hands up to her mouth, covering her face. She wanted to scream. Wanted to cry. *Nash*, she thought.

The agonizing screams slowly faded away into the storm until they all stood there in total silence. No one spoke a word. They were too terrified to do anything. Tate had reached for Desti's hand, but she pulled away, too scared to draw any attention to herself.

Ms. Clyde began walking back toward the school and yelled, "inside. Now!" Like a herd of sheep, each student followed Ms. Clyde back into the school. Tate led the way. His walk was tall and poised. Desti tilted her head and observed every step he took. *How is he feeling right now? Is he okay? Because I am not okay.* Tate made it back to the front entrance doors and turned back and glanced at Desti. He didn't say anything. She wondered what he was hiding behind his perfect face.

The golden flakes in his emerald, green eyes shimmered with mystery. He looked at her, stern and serious. "Desti, we need to talk." *Talk? Talk about what? What could he possibly need to talk about right now?* Desti exhaled. Her breath was shallow. It was as if all the fear and trauma that she had just experienced was weighing on her chest. "Tate, what is it? Does it have to do with—" Desti was interrupted by the pressure of Tate's finger shushing her mouth. "Not here," he said.

At the school there weren't many places to hide out at, but Tate and Desti always found a way. "So, I guess I am skipping my class after all," Desti joked while being tugged around the corner of the building. There was an old storage room that connected to the backside of the gymnasium. It never got used anymore.

Her school was withered away from years of apocalyptic weather. The stone brick walls would crumble with the slightest touch and half the building was pieces of debris. That space wasn't needed. Not anymore.

In the city of Mors, there was only a population of three hundred and ten people. Desti remembered learning about her city. *Mors*. It meant death. The City of Death. All the cities that existed now were just like the city of Mors. Broken and full of prisoners. Desti felt Tate gently shove her into the storage room. She immediately coughed from the stale dusty air that surrounded her. "Tate, what do you need to talk about right now? If they find us, you know what will happen." She glanced up into his eyes. She had stared into his eyes for years and they were always so— calm. Confident. But not this time. She tilted her head to the side and scrunched her face. In his eyes, Desti for once saw fear and guilt. "Tate? What's wrong?"

2: Legend of the Lux

TATE STEPPED FORWARD INTO THE SMALL DUSTY closet and shut the door behind him. The only lights were the beams coming through the cracks and holes in the wall. Desti could see the tiny dust particles swirling around him like dancing miniature tornadoes in the air.

The touch of Tate's fingertips on her arm sent chills down her body. *He is acting weird,* she thought. "I think they were looking for me." Desti perched her lip in confusion. "What do you mean they were looking for you?" Tate exhaled and tilted his chin down. "The broken rule. I think they were talking about me." Desti sucked in a gasp. Her hand rested forcefully on her hips. "What the Hell does that mean? What did you do?" All the possible scenarios flashed through her mind. *What rule did he break? And when?*

Desti boiled up a feeling of anger and confusion. Tate paused for a moment and then explained. "I went into the Wastelands. I think someone must have seen me and reported it." Desti's eyes grew big, and her cheeks flushed with red. She wanted to slap him across his perfect face. "You went out of the city boundaries? Do you know how stupid and dangerous that is?" Desti began pacing back and forth. Her feet kicked up the layers of dirt on the ground. "When did this happen?" she asked. Tate was silent for a moment. Since they were kids, they did everything together. *How could he not tell me?* For once, Desti could hear the nervousness in his voice. "I went about a week ago."

A huff of annoyance escaped Desti's chest. "Why? Why didn't you tell me?" She crossed her arms across her chest. Her finger picked at an old scab on her elbow.

"It's complicated. I was looking for something." *What could he possibly need to look for out there?* She didn't say that. Instead, she composed herself and tried to be more understanding.

"What were you looking for?" she asked.

She could see the hesitation in his eyes, as he rolled them. "I was looking for clues."

Clues? "Clues for what?"

Tate paused for a moment. This wasn't like him. They did everything together. Told each other everything. They were best friends. *Why didn't he tell me about this?* Tate's chest began to rise and fall heavily. *He must be nervous.* "I was trying to find clues to the whereabouts of the legend of the Lux."

Desti rolled her eyes and dropped her mouth. "The Lux? That is just a fairytale. It's not real." She searched her mind for memories of the stories about the Lux. It was supposedly the power of the angels. The Light. *But it wasn't real. Right?* Tate grabbed ahold of her arms and squeezed tight as he leaned in closer. "I don't think it's a fairytale. I think it's out there. I found something while out in the Wastelands." Before Desti could respond, a burst of bright light blinded them as the door to the storage closet swiftly opened. Desti threw her arm up to cover her eyes. She blinked away the spots in her eyes until she could see.

To her disgust, there was that familiar snarling voice she despised. "Tate and Desti. What are you two doing in here?" Desti's eyes held open big with a blank stare. Tate too had nothing to say. She cleared her throat and wiped the sweat on her palms on the side of her khaki pants. "Ms. Clyde. We umm—" Tate jumped in. "Ms. Clyde. We were just trying to escape the sandstorm. It got pretty crazy out there and we couldn't find our way to the entrance."

How does he do that? Desti thought. Tate could always think of clever things to say on the spot. Desti didn't have that skill. Ms. Clyde let out a quiet grunt as she played with her chin. She glared them down until she stepped out of the doorway and held her hand out to the side. "Go on. Get out of here." Desti nodded her head, followed by Tate and they shuffled their way out of the closet.

The sandstorm had let up its intensity and now was just blowing occasional small gusts of dusty wind. The students from their classroom were roaming the halls and gathering their things out of their lockers.

"School must be out." Tate said while leaning into Desti's ear.

"I hope my parents don't find out that I skipped last class." Desti twiddled her fingers and picked at her nails in a nervous tick. The last time she skipped class, her parents had punished her. She caressed her covered scars underneath her sleeve as she thought of that moment.

The stampede of the students' footsteps roared through the halls. Desti could hear whispers flow through the air as she passed by. *What are they all talking about?* Tate must have seen her worried face and known what she was quietly questioning to herself. "They must be talking about the demon." Hearing that word sent shivers down her spine. *Demon.* It never gave her chills before when she thought about them, but after what she witnessed, it had a whole new meaning to her.

Desti clutched the sides of her arms and paused at the end of the hall. Her face felt sorrowful. Numb. "Tate? Did Nash die because of what you—" she couldn't finish her question. How could she blame Tate for the death of Nash? But was it his fault for going out into the Wastelands? She felt him take a step back. Desti turned around and saw the look in his face. It struck her like a knife to the gut. For once, he had a gloss to his eyes, as if her were holding back tears. "Tate. I'm sorry. I didn't mean it." She reached for him, but he pulled away. Tate shook his head and held up his hand to her face as he walked away. Desti stood there and watched as his body disappeared into the sea of students.

***

Desti had walked the path to her home alone. She and Tate usually walked together. In her chest, she felt the guilt of her question weighing down on her. The rocky pebbles that lay on the path were kicked to the side as she walked through them. She watched them as they rolled around like dust devils blowing in the wind. As kids, she and Tate found clever ways to play in their desolate town. There were no toys like how the world had before. Pleasure and fun were forbidden in their world. Desti glanced up at the smog filled sky. The sky was the color of burnt wood. Orange and brown. To her, it was pretty. She had known no other sky. Dark ashy smoke floated past the setting sun. The city was constantly burning something. It was part of their duties. On the outskirts of the city, a few miles from the borders, is where Desti and Tate's neighborhood was. They only lived a few houses down from each other.

Desti walked the path toward her home, pausing once she stood in front of Tate's. *Is he home yet? Should I go talk to him?* The sides of her fingers were picked to a point of rawness as she stood there, trying to think of what to do. She took a slight step forward and then hesitated. Maybe he wanted to be left alone, she thought. Desti turned around and continued down the path to her home.

Her neighborhood was a mixture of withered down houses and empty lots. There were no solid structures anymore. The bricks and wood that once held the houses together, were rotten and decayed. The surrounding vegetation was unkempt and overgrew the tops of their roofs. Desti didn't mind. The vines that grew onto her home made it easier for her to sneak out. Before the rapture happened one hundred years ago, Desti heard how the Earth's disasters destroyed cities all over the planet. In the city of Mors, they were hit by a wall of water reaching one hundred feet high. Learning about the time before always fascinated Desti.

She tilted her head up and watched as the last bit of sunrays fell behind the horizon. *I must get home.* The dark of the night enveloped the structures around her.

Desti took shallow breaths, careful not to draw attention to herself. It wasn't safe to be out at night. That's when *they* would come out. Her eyes glanced all around as she passed by each house. *Only a few more houses to go*, she thought. Desti clutched the sides of her arms, digging her fingers into her skin. Her mind delved into a whirlpool of fear and terror the closer she got to her home. This was the time of the foreboding realm, where the creatures of the depths of Hell would emerge from the crevasses of the Earth to hunt and feed.

The moonlight highlighted distant shadows from afar. The darkness around her seemed to grow thicker with every passing second. *Almost there*. By this point, Desti had broken the skin on her arm. Small hints of blood trickled down to her finger as she grasped herself tight. A slight gasp escaped her lips.

Blood.

Her eyes shot open. *They can smell blood*. Suddenly, there was a cacophonous echo of rumbling growls and screeches that came from the distant shadowed horizon. Desti's feet swiftly took off, sprinting toward the front door of her house. She could feel the creatures closing in on her. Their piercing screeches felt like jabs to the eardrums. Desti reached her hands up and cupped the side of her head. With every heavy breath she took, the louder the creatures became. She had run to the point of almost collapsing from exhaustion. Desti reached for her door and ran through, swiftly slamming it behind her. Her fingers clenched the cracks in the wooden door as her body leaned up against it, panting for a decent breath of air. Desti could hear the muffled growls and grunts just on the other side. Slowly, the creatures from the depths of Hell retreated from their hunt, leaving Desti standing there in complete silence.

"Hello?" The house was dark. Only the dimply lit hallway expressed any light. *Where is everyone?* Unaware of what was lurking around the corner, Desti took a step forward and was met with the brutal force of her father's calloused knuckles. Her nose cracked from the intense pressure and immediately began to gush. The crimson red blood cascaded down her face and through her trembling fingers as she held her nose tight. Desti belched out a searing scream of pain. Her knees hit the floor as her blood pooled around her.

"Dad? What the Hell?" she cried.

He stood tall above her crouched form. "You know the rules," he said. His fist was still clenched tight. Desti wanted to cry. She wanted to leap into Tate's arms as he held her against his chest.

"What did I do, Dad?"

He lifted his fist as if he were going to hit her again. Desti flinched and cowardly fell to the floor. "Don't play dumb with me Desti." His voice had a tone of hostility. Desti threw up her arm, covering her head. "Dad, I'm sorry. I won't skip class again." Her father grunted as he stumbled his way out of the hall and back into the kitchen to make himself another drink. Her silent sobs quietly echoed through the paper-thin walls. Even though she was an adult, living in this house made her feel as if she were a child, under the reign of terror from her controlling father. *Why does he care so much where she was or what she was doing?*

The brisk nightly winds blew its gusts through the old cracks in the house, creating a symphony of screeches and creeks. Desti held her nose as she ran upstairs to her room. She was raging with anger. "I should have known this would happen," she quietly told herself. Desti held up a dirty rag to the tip of her bruised face and glanced at herself in the mirror. Her eyes said it all. The desperation for a life worth living screamed at her as she stared at her reflection. *This is your life Desti.*

Tears began to burn as they gathered in her eyes. She huffed and threw her hands down. *You don't cry.* Desti was raised not to cry. Not to show emotion. They all were. But she yearned for something more. Something more meaningful than a life serving the will of the demons. She rolled her eyes. *That's impossible.*

She leaned forward into the mirror and lifted her head. The skin on her face was swollen and bruised. She reached her hand to her face and touched the tendered spot. A raging anger started to fester inside. It started with a hot tingling feeling in her chest. *I need Tate. He would know how to talk me down.* Desti turned toward her window, staring at the night sky. It was cold and black.

The smog that filled the air of the city masked the true beauty that lay above. Desti had only seen a few stars in her lifetime. Most of her life was spent under the same blanket of brown, ashy smoke.

There was a black leather jacket hanging on the edge of her dresser. Desti yanked it off the corner and threw her arms through. The blood had stopped gushing from her nose and now was only dripping the occasionally bloody droplets. She sniffed it back up and leaned forward. Just as she was about to climb out the window, she saw Tate's head appear from the bottom.

"Tate!" Desti accidentally yelled.

She immediately crouched down and covered her mouth. Tate threw himself through her opened window and landed his feet onto her floor. *How is he always so graceful?* Tate grabbed her hand and pulled her to sit down on the edge of her bed and as he saw her his hand reached for her cheek.

"What happened to you? Are you okay?" Tate held his hand on her face. She lifted her hand and held onto his.

"I'll be okay. My father. He—" she trailed off. It was shameful for her to admit that her father did that to her. Tate lifted his shirt and twisted to his side. "It's okay. Mine did too." Desti was looking at a massive laceration across his ribcage. "Oh my gosh. Are you okay?" He let go as his shirt fell back down. "I'll be fine. It is what it is."

There was a blanket of awkward tension. Desti could feel the unresolved tension from before. "Tate. I didn't mean what I said earlier. I am sorry."

Her eyes fell, unable to look him directly in the face. He didn't wait to respond. She thought he would just brush it off and not want to talk about it, but to her surprise, he agreed.

"You were right, Desti. Nash is dead because of me."

Immediately she glanced up and gazed right into his eyes. She saw sadness. Guilt. The words that she wanted to say wouldn't come out. *It's not your fault. Don't say that.* But it was. Her mouth fell slightly open as she listened. Tate's eyes had a seriousness to them. Desti knew that look. That was the look of Tate when he was about to do something very stupid and dangerous. He grabbed her hand.

"Desti, I never got to tell you what I found out there."

She leaned in closer. "What did you find?"

Tate reached into his pocket and pulled out a small piece of paper. It was brittle and burnt around the edges. He held out his hand and read it to Desti.

"He who finds the Lux shall hold the powers of the angels and cast—" The message was cut off. Desti grew

annoyed as she shoved his hand down. "And cast what? This is what you went into the Wastelands for?" Desti stood from her bed and paced across her bedroom floor. The thick layer of dust that covered the hardwood sprung up as her feet kicked around.

"Desti, do you not realize how big this is? This is the first ever found evidence or reminiscence of the Holy book."

Tate grew passionate and stood up too. He reached for Desti, but she was reluctant to accept his touch. She couldn't bear to lose him to something so idiotic. "Do you realize how dangerous that was. If you got caught—" she couldn't bear to say it. The thought of losing her best friend hurt worse than her bloody broken nose. She threw her hand to her face as she muffled her silent sobs. "It's just a piece of paper Tate. How do you know that is the real thing? We don't even know if the stories are true." Tate grabbed her hand and forced her eyes upon him.

"Because I have faith Desti. I don't want to grow old in this demon infested world. I know the stories are true. They must be."

She could see sadness in his eyes. There was more to it than he was showing. "Why are you so passionate about this all the sudden? What happened to make you want to go search for the Lux of the angels?"

As the final tones of her voice echoed to a silence, a palpable hush enveloped the room and a stillness descended upon them. Tate exhaled. *He is holding back.* Desti leaned forward and grabbed his hand. "What is it? What are you not telling me?" Tate's eyes stared at the floor. He only did that when he was avoiding something. "I overheard my parents talking to someone."

Desti jumped in. "Who?"

"I don't know but they were talking about giving us up to the demons. Something about our souls being forever theirs when we turn twenty-one." Desti sucked in a small breath of air. She had heard stories of that happening. Parents would deliver their offspring as a sacrifice and in return, they would be rewarded with riches.

"Are you sure that is what you heard?"

Tate's eyes were serious. "Yes, I am sure."

Desti blinked away a left-over tear from her eye and threw her hand to her chin. "And you don't know who your parents were talking to?" Tate shrugged his shoulders. His midnight hair almost blended in perfectly with the darkness of the night. "I don't know. But since they mentioned your name too, I think it could have been your parents."

That would make sense. Desti pondered for a moment. Her whole life she grew up in a broken family.

Unloved and beaten as early as she could remember. "My birthday is in about a month. And yours is a few weeks after that." Desti said. She had twirled her auburn hair around her finger to the point of it knotting up. She pulled her finger out from her hair and cupped her hands.

"I can't believe this. I mean I know my parents are awful, but I didn't think they would be like, offering me up to the demons, awful."

Desti aggressively paced back and forth. She glanced over at Tate as he calmly sat on the edge of her bed. "If this is true, then we need to do something to stop it Tate." She threw her hands in the air. Tate held up the piece of paper in his hand and said, "this is why I went to the Wastelands, Desti. This is how we stop them."

Desti had never been to the Wastelands before. To her knowledge no one she knows has, until now. The Wastelands were where the demons and creatures of Hell roamed freely. It was rumored that you could hear the screams of tormented souls from the depths of Hell echo through the night. There was nothing out there except hungry people-eating creatures and dry dusty canyons. The thought of being out there terrified Desti. She gulped as she thought of how vulnerable they would be.

"What about the demons Tate?"

A slight chuckle escaped Tate's mouth as he shrugged his shoulders. "They mostly only come out at night to feed. They are attracted to the smell of blood. Just make sure we aren't bleeding and that we stay quiet."

Tate was always so fearless. Nothing scared him growing up. That was what Desti loved about him. He was always there to push her out of her shell and into new adventures. Desti bit her lip as she pondered. *I don't know*. She was hesitant at first, but the thought of possibly being sacrificed on her birthday sounded even worse.

"Okay. But we need to come up with a plan before we just head out there."

Tate embraced Desti with an overly joyful hug, crushing her arms to her side. "Tate, I can't breathe." She whispered.

He let go and glanced down. "Sorry. I'll see you at school tomorrow. We will talk then, okay?"

The howling gusts of wind blew through Desti's opened window, blowing around the dust and sand on the floor. Tate leaned over the edge and dropped, disappearing into the night. Desti threw herself on the bed as a storm of emotions swirled around in her mind. Feelings of anger, fear, and excitement tore away at her conscience. *What are you getting yourself into Desti*? She closed her eyes and let the darkness take control of her mind until she was in a deep sleep.

3: The Hostile One

THE MORNING SEEMED TO HAVE COME TOO SOON. Warm sun rays beamed through the ashy smoke above and into Desti's room. She lay there still, on top of her covers and still in her clothes from the night before. The sound of her father stomping around downstairs rumbled through the floor. *He must be going to work.*

She sat up and propped her body on her elbow. Desti reached her arms high above her head in a cat-like stretch and let out a boisterous yawn. She had almost forgotten about her broken nose until she lifted her hand and accidentally swiped her face. *Ouch.* The mirror across from her bed was cracked and old. Tate had found it in a pile of trash at an abandoned house and gave it to her as a gift. It was her favorite piece of furniture in her room because it had meaning behind it.

Desti stepped forward and stood still in front of it. Her body looked thin and frail under her leather jacket and khaki pants. She leaned forward and tilted her head to the side. The tips of her fingers grazed her bruised face as she pushed on her tender skin.

"Great, I have a black eye," she said as she threw her hands down to her side. Desti rummaged through her empty drawers, searching for a clean pair of clothes to wear. The people of the city of Mors didn't have much. Most of their clothing and household items were things found in the trash of the dead ones around them. Desti only owned two pairs of pants.

"Where are they?" She frantically twisted around looking beneath her bed and behind the chair in the corner of her room. Her auburn hair whipped around her like electric bolts. "Ah ha. There it is." Intricately shoved under the corner of her bedside desk was her other pair of pants. She gleefully smiled as she shook off the dust from her denim jeans and slid her legs through.

***

The heat from the brutal sun was picking up intensity as it lifted high above the town. Desti's father had already left for his daily duties, so she didn't need to try to sneak past him while leaving her home. Desti's mother was still soundlessly sleeping in her room. She didn't usually wake up until later in the day anyway.

Every morning, Tate would knock on Desti's door and walk with her on their way to school. And so, she sat down at her kitchen table and waited for Tate to come knocking. A few minutes had passed and Desti had finished her one piece of stale bread. Thoughts of her conversation from the night before crowded her mind. *Your parents are going to sacrifice you. How could any parent sacrifice their own child?* She thought.

Even if they were abusive and unloving, there had to be some compassion deep down inside. Right? The blood-stained ground was still fresh and filled the surrounding air with a smell of potent metal. Desti stared at her blood. She had been through worse. The scars up her arm still felt fresh to the touch. She pulled her sleeve back down and pushed those memories away.

A gentle knock at her front door snapped her right back to reality.

"Desti. Are you up yet?" It was Tate.

Desti grabbed her brown bag with her few pieces of paper and a pen and reached for the door. As she glanced down, she carefully stepped over her pool of blood and stepped outside.

"Tate. Hey. How'd you sleep?" Tate didn't answer.

He was stuck in a daze staring at her face.

"Oh my, Desti, this looks bad. Are you sure you are, okay?"

He reached to touch her face but then pulled away. The skin around her eyes was purple, blue, and swollen almost shut. "I'll be fine, Tate. I'll put a cold rag on it when I get to school. Okay?"

"How's your side?" she asked. "Oh yeah, I almost forgot." He lifted his shirt and twisted. Desti stared past his chiseled core and looked only at his tender red cut.

"Does it hurt?" she asked.

She wanted to touch it. Something about his wounds lured her in. She wanted to be there to fix him when no one else would. *He would do the same for me.*

The Earth had no beautiful weather anymore. They were trapped in an endless cycle of sandstorms and musky air. It was difficult to breathe and sometimes caused pain in the lungs. Desti coughed as she covered her mouth with her arm.

"You good?" asked Tate, smirking from the corner of his mouth.

Desti playfully shoved him on the shoulder.

"I'm fine. Stop asking. You know how this air gets to me."

The walk to school was like any other day they had had. The brutal heat baked them under the blanket of ashy smoke. Desti looked over at Tate. Her eyes flickered with hues of green and gold.

"Do you ever think of what it was like—before?"

He shot her a look of confusion. "Before? Like before the rapture, before?"

She picked at her shirt and plucked the cotton fibers from her chest. "Yeah. Like what life was like back then.

I heard that the sky was blue, and the ground was green."

Desti twirled her arms in the air and closed her eyes. Imagining the Earth before its destruction gave her a place to escape to. To feel free. When she opened her eyes, she glanced over and noticed Tate staring with a permanent soft smirk on his face. She stopped in her tracks.

"What? What is it? Why are you looking at me like that?" Tate never looked at her like the way he was now. *Why is he looking at me like that,* she thought. She waited for him to respond, and finally, he did.

"I wasn't— you're just cute when you talk like that." She felt a warm rush go to her cheeks.

"Like what?"

There was a fuzzy feeling in her chest. A flutter of electrifying currents ran through her body and as she waited for Tate to reply, he just simply smiled and kept walking.

The school was only a couple hundred feet away. Desti rolled her eyes once she made it to the front gates.

"Here we go again. More learning about how to serve our demons."

She reached for the door as Tate expelled a sarcastic, "woohoo."

As they entered inside, the energy in the air felt different. It felt heavy. Like there was danger lurking around the corner. Usually, her classmates would be conversing among themselves, but not this morning. Desti and Tate glanced around with a confused expression.

"Where is everyone?" she asked.

Tate scrunched his eyebrows and leaned his body until he was looking down the hall. "I don't know. Maybe they are already in class."

He took a small step forward and walked toward the dreaded classroom. In the air, there was a distant aroma of a putrid stench. Desti threw her hands to her face and through the cracks of her fingers, her muffled voice yelled, "ugh. It stinks Tate. What is that smell?" Tate plugged his nose with his two fingers and shook his head.

Once they stepped foot into the classroom, it was as if Desti had been transported into a different reality. There her classmates were, in their seats. Yet, there was something off about the energy in the air.

The sea of students exhibited a state of hypnotic stupor as they all sat there in a disconnected, expressionless state. No one glanced up at Desti and Tate as they walked into the room. Desti sucked in her breath. Her eyes narrowed with confusion. *What the Hell is going on?*

When she looked over at Tate, she noticed the same perplexed look. Ms. Clyde stood at the front of the class, in her usual black and gray cotton floor-length dress. *It was probably to cover her hooved legs,* Desti thought. Her hunch back protruded from her spine, twisting her into an even more intimidating form.

Then there was that snarling voice Desti despised so much. "Desti. Tate. Glad you could make it today. Please take your seats."

Silence enveloped every ounce of her body. She wanted to speak up. She wanted to ask *what the Hell was going on?* But she couldn't. Not to Ms. Clyde. Desti sat at her same withered auburn desk, which sat in the back left of the classroom. Tate's desk was adjacent and a few feet away from hers. There was a presence in the air that held her down. Evil. She could feel it to the core of her bones. Tate glanced back, looking through the layers of his jet-black hair. The gold flakes in his green eyes shimmered just slightly as the light from the window shined through. Desti wanted to reach for him. Wanted to just touch his fingers. *He would give me comfort,* she thought.

Suddenly a boisterous crack of Ms. Clyde's' ruler breaking on the desk in the front of the classroom echoed around her ears. Desti threw her hands up covering the sides of her head.

She leaned forward and saw Tate had done the same, but no one else seemed affected. *Why is no one moving?* She silently questioned herself as her eyes nonchalantly glanced around. Her focus was stolen again by that wretched voice.

"We seem to have a little problem here class."

With every steady stride, Ms. Clyde's heavy weight rumbled the broken dirt and wooden floor. "Someone here has broken a forbidden rule and has yet to come forward."

Tate's eyes grew big. Desti's too. *Is she talking about Tate?*

"It was a sad thing, what happened to Nash." Ms. Clyde stopped and slammed her fists down onto the desk and yelled, "But I will sacrifice every single one of you until the offender comes forward. Today there will be two of you fed to the demons of the Wastelands!"

Desti's body quivered with anxiety and her shallow, erratic breaths caused her to feel tingly all over. She glanced at Tate. He sat still. Poised, as usual. But there was a look in his eyes. She could see it. She knew that look. *Please Tate, don't do something stupid.*

To her utter dismay, Desti sucked in a horrid gasp as Tate stood from his desk and yelled, "it was me Ms. Clyde. I snuck into the Wastelands."

Desti wanted to scream. She wanted to slap him across the face and yell *shut up*! But she didn't. Instead, her body was paralyzed. Paralyzed with regret and with fear.

There was an eerie unanimous shroud of whispers that danced around the room. The students had seemed to break out of their daze and glanced all around. It was as if Desti was living in a complete nightmare. But it wasn't a dream. She was just living in a perpetual Hell on Earth.

Ms. Clyde had walked over to Tate until she was towering over his body. There was a low and continuous hum coming from her chest.

"Follow me boy."

Without hesitation or resistance, Tate followed behind Ms. Clyde. He glanced back at Desti and locked eyes with her. She could see what he wanted to say. *I'm sorry. Please forgive me.* He was silent though.

Desti never cried. She couldn't. Since she was a child, her parents taught her that it made her weak to cry. They would punish her for it, but at this moment she didn't care to hold the tears back. The dam that held her tears in place, broke free as she wept passionately at her desk. She stood up, reaching for Tate's hands.

"Tate! What did you do?" She tried to catch up with them as she screamed, "Tate. Please! Ms. Clyde, where are you taking him?" The door slammed shut in Desti's face.

4: The Master

THE WEIGHT OF THE WORLD CAME CRASHING DOWN ON Desti. Her hands were placed on the window of the door, and she hung her head and sobbed. A warm feeling festered in her chest. Her eyes opened, bloodshot and fuming. Desti turned around and yelled at the students behind her.

"What is wrong with all of you? Where is she taking him? Someone, please answer me!" Desti wept helplessly at her classmates, but she was only met with a blanket of blank expressions.

I need to get out of here.

With all her strength, Desti shoved open the heavy door and ran out into the hall. Tate was nowhere to be seen.

"Tate!" she shouted.

The trembling in her hands rattled up her arms. Her arms flailed up and down in a frantic panic. *Where did he go?* Across from the class was the bathroom. Desti lunged forward and ran inside. Her fingers grasped the edges of the cracked porcelain sink as her tears splashed into the rusty drain below. It was too much to bear. After what happened to Nash the day before, the fear of losing her best friend ravished her mind.

There was an old broken mirror that hung just above the sink. It had a film of white muck, which probably hadn't been cleaned in years. Desti glanced up and gazed at her distorted reflection when something caught her attention. Behind her in one of the stalls, there was something written on the walls.

What is that? She squinted her eyes and then turned around. It was a message. Desti lifted her arm and wiped away her tears and pushed open the stall door. The message was written in a blood-red medium. She tilted her head as she read it.

He who finds the Lux shall hold the powers of the Angels and cast away the demons back into Hell.

"This is what Tate was talking about." Desti reached out her hand and gently grazed her fingers along the wall. The message was simple yet had a sense of power to it. *Maybe he is right? But how do I find it? Where would I begin?*

Suddenly, the sound of the bathroom door bursting open shocked Desti and made her jump. She took her sleeve and wiped the message until it was just a red smudge and swiftly stepped out of the stall and shut the door behind her. The heavy beating of her heart fluttered in her chest.

If she got caught even reading that, she could be sent to the Master.

"Desti?" A soft voice echoed around the corner.

Desti knew that voice. "Laura?"

Desti walked around the corner. It was her friend Laura. Desti ran up to her and grabbed her arm. "What the Hell was everyone doing in class? Why did you all look like mindless zombies?" Laura's expression fell to a somber look.

"Ms. Clyde told us that if we moved, she would feed us to the demon."

Desti rolled her eyes in annoyance. "She just took Tate. No one did anything about it. Do you know where she took him?" There was desperation in the crackle of her voice. Something that Desti never had. Her entire life she grew up to be strong, unbothered by pointless emotions. But this was different. It was Tate.

Laura's hands fell until they were holding Desti's. She looked her in the eyes with a serious note. "Desti. Ms. Clyde took him to the Master."

A ghastly gasp escaped the clutches of Desti's chest as she stepped backward. "No. She can't. The things that I've heard—" Desti trailed off. She couldn't even finish the horrific details of the stories of what happens in the Master's chambers. Her bloodshot eyes began to tear, burning down her swollen bruised face. She grabbed Laura's hands again. "Where is the Master's chamber? Is it here in the school?"

Laura shrugged her shoulders. She couldn't even look Desti in the eyes. "I'm sorry Desti, I don't know where his chamber is."

"Do you know of someone who might?" Desti desperately asked.

Laura glanced up with a glimmer in her eyes. "Yes. The old house off Mayberry Lane. There is a woman there who might."

"You mean where Crazy Joan lives?"

The entire town knew who Crazy Joan was—rumored to be almost ninety years old. She was the closest living human to the Era of the Damned. The people of the city didn't bother her much. She was always rambling about nonsense.

"Yes."

Laura shook her head and was abruptly left behind as Desti sprinted out of the bathroom, yelling, "thank you!" She didn't care that she was going to be skipping another day of school. Her father could give her one hundred black eyes and she would still do I again to find Tate.

***

The city of Mors was a town about the size of Las Vegas, except instead of wonderous buildings and beautiful scenery, they were left with what was left after the destruction. No buildings stood tall anymore. The glass on the windows had been shattered to dust and the concrete on any structure had become overgrown with wild vines.

The ground was dusty and dry, making it almost impossible for vegetation to thrive, besides the occasional potato farm. They were surrounded by canyons and desert for miles until the next desecrated town.

There was a constant pungent smell that hovered in the musky air, and through the dark sky of smoke was the brutal sweltering sun. It really was Hell on Earth.

Desti had never seen a beautiful city before. She had only heard stories growing up. *Were they even real?* It was hard to believe anything anymore. Desti's tangled hair blew in the fogy gusts of wind. She coughed as the smoke filled her lungs.

She was now miles from her school and had walked almost to the neighborhood on Mayberry Lane. The sweltering sun now hung high in the blood orange sky and beamed down a brutal heat. Desti wiped the salty sweat droplets from her head and kept forward.

Unimaginable thoughts invaded her mind as she walked. Tate being tortured. Tate being eaten alive. What was happening to him? Was he scared?

On the outside, Tate never seemed fazed. Never worried or frightened but Desti knew that it was just a façade. She knew the real Tate. He would flinch if he heard a noise coming from the dark. Desti wrapped her arms around her chest and closed her eyes as she pretended to hold him. *I'm here Tate. I'm coming. Don't worry.*

Desti was now turning on Mayberry Lane. No one dared to explore the street of Mayberry Lane. The houses down there were rotten and decayed, littered with carcasses of demons and their victims. An overwhelming stench of decaying flesh swarmed her senses. She involuntarily gagged from the smell and threw her hand over her nose. "Oh my. That's gross."

There was only one house that still stood in that neighborhood, and it was the last house on the street. No one from town would dare visit it unless it was dire. It was rumored that Crazy Joan lived off the carcasses of the rotting demons that littered her street and if you crossed her, she would feed you to her pigs.

Desti never got nervous. Not like this. But this was different. She picked at her fingers more and more the closer she got to Crazy Joan's home. *There it is.* There Desti stood. At the edge of the curved driveway. Her silhouette stood small compared to the size of Crazy Joan's house.

On the ground, there was no grass, just dry dust and sharp rocks that covered the front yard. The windows were boarded up with only small cracks being left for some sunlight. Desti stepped forward to the front door. Blood red, it stood tall in front of her. She cleared her throat and lifted her hand. With three hard thuds, Desti waited for an answer.

It seemed as though she had stood there for hours, waiting for an answer. Just as Desti was about to turn around and give up, a creak from the door opening stopped her in her tracks.

The door had cracked slightly open, only leaving a thin sliver of darkness visible in the home. An old crabby voice answered, "Who is it?"

Desti's throat got tight as she gulped. "Uhm—" She stepped forward. "Excuse me? Are you Miss Joan?"

Desti held her hands to her chest as she twiddled her fingers. The voice was sharp and harsh, sending Desti into a flinch every time she heard her speak.

"Who's asking?"

The wind was blowing in vigorously now. Desti's strands of hair whipped her skin as it blew around her face. "My name is Desti. I was hoping I could come inside. I have some questions."

Suddenly the door slammed shut in her face. Desti was immediately consumed with the feeling of futility and self-doubt. *I'm never going to find him*, she thought. She felt a sensation of profound disappointment. Tears splashed on the hard ground as she began to turn away, when suddenly she heard the door open one more time. She paused, opened her eyes and when she turned around there stood Crazy Joan in the middle of the doorway.

Desti had never seen someone so old before. In her world, people were lucky if they lived to be fifty. Crazy Joan's face was marked with an array of wrinkles, lines, and blemishes. Her hair was white as snow, and she stood about four feet high. A brown wool cloak hung over her hunched back and dragged the floor. She reminded Desti of characters from old stories she would listen to growing up.

"What is it that you want, young lady?" Crazy Joan snarled.

Desti's finger picked at her pants as she thought of what to say. "I would really like to come inside and talk. If I may."

There was a long awkward pause. *No? I can't come in?* she wanted to say but kept her thoughts to herself. Crazy Joan stepped aside and waddled her way back into her dimly lit home as her voiced trailed behind her. "Come in then."

The smell protruding from her home was like a wall of rotten carcasses and spoiled milk. Desti threw her arm up over her face, trying not to gag.

"Did something die in here?" she asked.

Crazy Joan didn't answer. Only a slight grunt escaped her chest. She led Desti to a seating area. There was an old tree stump lying in the middle of the room and a pile of rocks with a wool blanket thrown over it. Crazy Joan swayed her arms over it said, "sit."

Without hesitation, Desti scurried her way over to the tree stump and plopped herself down. The last thing that she wanted to do was upset the village crazy lady. Desti cupped her hands in her lap and began to talk.

"Miss Joan. I don't want to take up too much of your time, so I will be quick. I need to know where the Master keeps his chamber of punishment." There was a glare of suspicion and confusion coming from Crazy Joan.

"Why in Hell would you be needing to know that girl?"

Desti's palms were sweating at this point. *Should I tell her the whole truth? Will she turn me in?* An array of conflicting thoughts swirled around in her mind, making it difficult for her to think of the right answer to say. Desti leaned forward. *I might as well tell her the truth.*

"My friend was taken to the Master. He did something stupid and now must be punished."

There was a constant pungent odor of gas fumes and rotting flesh. Desti clutched her face as she tried not to cough. Crazy Joan stood up from the pile of rocks and walked across the room, using an old wooden cane to balance on. "Your friend must be very stupid to do such a thing."

Desti sighed and hung her head in shame. "Yes. He must be. So please tell me you know where I can find him. I must go after him."

Crazy Joan twisted around and slammed her cane on the table beside her. "And you would be even stupider to do such a thing girl."

At this point, time was running out and Desti was desperate. She stood from her seat and landed on her knees, begging for an answer. "Please. I know it's stupid. I know I will probably regret it, but I can't just not go after him. He is my everything." Desti never cried, but there she was, shedding tears for Tate.

"Ahh. Young love. I was in love once. That will get you sacrificed to the demons you know." A silence enveloped the room. Desti glanced up with her eyebrows scrunched.

"I'm not in love. He is my best friend. I just want to help him."

"Very well stupid girl. But first, I want to know what your friend did." Crazy Joan sat back down on the pile of rocks and placed her cane in between her withered knees.

"He—" Desti stood from the floor, brushing the dirt and dust from her pants. "He escaped into the Wastelands. Went searching for something called the Lux." Desti froze in fear as she heard Crazy Joan suck in a gasp.

"What did you say girl?"

"Uhm. He went into the Wastelands searching for the Lux."

Crazy Joan stood from her spot and inched her way over to a side table at the far end of the room. *What is she doing*? Desti thought Crazy Joan could be doing anything. She could be grabbing a knife to kill and eat her or grabbing something to tie her up with.

Desti wanted to run out of there as fast as her legs could carry her, but something held her down, imprisoning her to the stump that she sat on.

Suddenly the drawer slammed shut and there stood Crazy Joan, holding a red leather book in her hands. She shook from old age and her hands were decorated with blemished spots.

"What is that?" Desti asked.

"It was my mother's." The book was just as big as the palms of her hands. Desti sucked in a breath as she reached for it.

"Is that—" she trailed off.

It couldn't be. Could it really be the Holy book?

"My mother lived before the rapture. She lived in the world when it had meaning to it. Life. She was a holy woman, but unfortunately made a terrible mistake," said Joan.

It was as if Desti was in a total trance, staring at that book. She had only heard stories about it. It was forbidden to even speak of the Holy book. It was embroidered with gold lettering and was smooth to the touch.

"Your mother left you the Holy book? I thought that it was just a myth." Desti's finger just barely touched the edge of the red leather before she flinched and pulled away.

"Yes girl. She refused to let the demons rule her. After she had me, she became rebellious. Stupid. It got her killed. Sacrificed to the demons."

There was no emotion in her voice. As if she had been robbed of feeling anything for so long. Then again, Desti thought about it. She didn't feel anything for anyone either. No one except Tate. That's how the world was now. Cold and heartless.

"Can I please hold it?" asked Desti.

She reached for the book again but this time, didn't flinch away. All her life she had heard the forbidden stories growing up of the Holy book. They would whisper in her ear about the power it held. She never expected that she would see it in real life. Sometimes Desti would question even if the stories were true. *The power it held.*

Those words resonated with her. *Does it really hold power? Does that mean that I will have power?* Crazy Joan placed the book into Desti's cupped hands. It was as if she didn't even know how to hold it. *I can't believe this.*

Her fingers gripped the edges tight as she analyzed every inch.

"Why are you showing me this?" she asked.

Crazy Joan sat back down on her pile of rocks and expelled a monstrous huff. "It's been a long time since I have met someone who even thought about searching for the Lux of the angels. When I was young, my mother would talk about delivering us to a better place. Breaking us free from this foul world." Crazy Joan spat on the floor. She took a deep breath in and continued her story. "She saved her Holy book. Hid it from the demons and left it in my possession after she passed."

Desti held onto it tight. She clutched it with passion and fear and held it to her chest.

"She told me that one day we would need it, to deliver us from the clutches of Hell and send those vile creatures back to where they belong."

There was silence. The air stood still and only slight gusts of wind coming from the outside could be heard rustling the dry twigs in the front yard. Desti was speechless. She wasn't prepared for all of that.

She stepped forward and held out her hand as she tried to pass the book back to Crazy Joan.

"No dear. You keep it." Joan struggled to sit up straight. "My time is almost up. Maybe you can find the power within."

A sense of shock enveloped Desti. *Me*? she thought. *The girl who can't even stand up to her own father, is going to somehow stop the demons from ruling?*

"Miss Joan. I don't think I can—" she was interrupted by the whack of Joan's cane hitting the floor.

"Nonsense girl. Don't ever give up hope. It's the only thing they cannot steel from you."

"Thank you."

A softness came over Desti. Her eyes gleamed with a sense of hope. Something that she never had before. Miss Joan reached into her pocket that was sewn to the side of her cloak and retrieved a small silver chain. Her frail hands shook as she leaned forward and stretched out her arm.

"Here girl. I want you to have this. It was my mother's."

There it dangled between her fingers, shimmering with every slight twist. Desti froze. *It couldn't be*. She reached out her arm and Miss Joan placed it in her hand. "Is this a cross?"

There was a soft smirk across Miss Joan's face.

"Yes dear. May it bring you protection on your journey."

Desti was speechless. It was forbidden to even draw a cross, let alone carry one in your possession.

"Thank you so much. I will keep it safe."

Desti stood up to exit the room, but then paused. "I almost forgot. So, do you know where the I can find Tate?" A low rumbling chuckle reverberated from Miss Joan's chest. She leaned on her wooden cane and stood up, slowly shuffling her way over to her window.

"What you seek my dear is past those ridges. You shall find what you are looking for, but be warned, you probably won't make it out alive."

Desti peered out the small crack in the window. And there it was. Nestled within the rugged rift in Earth's crust stood the vast canyon of Rotten's Crude. Rumored to be home to unfathomable creatures from the depths of Hell. No one would ever dare enter Rotten's Crude. Not if their life depended on it. Desti sucked in and held her breath in her chest. *Of course, he must be there,* she thought. The metallic shimmer fluttered between her fingers as she nervously twiddled with the cross.

"I will be fine. I've outrun demons before."

"Not demons like this honey."

5: Rotten's Crude

THE AIR THAT SURROUNDED THE CITY HAD AN absence of moisture, leaving Desti's skin feeling cracked and burned. There were no clouds in the sky. They rarely ever showed up. The sky was replaced with a constant smog that enveloped that air, blanketing the people of Mors with its heavy musk. The brutal sun was now a few hours from setting behind the horizon. Even then it felt as though Desti was being cooked alive. She lifted her arm and wiped the sweat that was beading off her face. She had walked miles from Miss Joan's house by now. With every step, her feet felt more like lead and dragged behind her. Desti's throat burned. Ached for just a drop of water, but nothing was going to stop her from finding Tate.

The edge of the city was outlined with piles of debris and decaying bodies. It was where the demons would come to feast on those who broke the rules or ventured too far. Desti threw her hand over her nose to avoid the rotting smell. There was a cacophony of buzzing insects swarming the pile of rotting flesh ahead. *I should probably find a weapon.*

In the rubble of the pile of debris, Desti found a broken metal pipe with a sharpened edge. She swung it around trying to get a handle on it.

"This will do."

It brought her mind back, recounting the days when she and Tate would play sword fight with each other. She could still hear Tate's prepubescent voice. *This is how I will fight a demon. He-yaw!* She smiled. As she gripped her fingers tightly around the rusty metal, she gave it a few swings through the air. "I've still got it."

Desti was now walking through the pile of rotting corpses and entering the forbidden Wastelands. As she glanced down, her eyes met with the soulless eyes of the demons. They were black as coal and even when dead, sent chills up her back. Most of them looked like humanoid snakes, covered in scaly leather skin. *Thank goodness they are dead.*

Behind her was the silhouette of the city, radiating with a warm orange glow. She glanced back one last time. It was beautiful from where she was. Something broken and damaged yet it had beauty to it.

The sun was now setting above the horizon, creating a magnificent red color in the sky. The air now faded to cool. Desti closed her eyes and breathed in through her nose. She was past the border and now entering the forbidden Wastelands. She had no idea what kind of dangers were lurking ahead.

Going to the Wastelands was something that Desti always thought about as a kid. In school they would imbue it in her mind that if she were to go out there, she would die. That there would be swarms of demons waiting to rip her body limb from limb and eat the flesh from her bones. In every direction she glanced. The city of Mors was now miles away and ahead, was open wasteland, but no sight of any live demon. *Maybe the city put the dead carcasses at the edge to scare us away from going out here.* Desti lifted her finger to her chin as she pondered. *It could have been a scare tactic set to control the people.* Her fears about the unknown dangers of the Wastelands dwindled away, but having no fear could come at a cost.

As the horizon fully engulfed the last bit of warm golden rays, the velvety blue darkness enveloped the surrounding land. A palpable sense of discomfort crept over Desti. Her nerves rang with an eerie sense of dread. Every rustle of a twig blowing in the wind was amplified in the vast stillness of the desert. The very atmosphere itself seemed as if it were bracing itself for what has yet to come. Desti tried not to be scared. She was fearless. Right?

Sporadically, her head darted all around her, scoping out the empty plane ahead. She reached into her pocket and pulled out a box of old matches that she had saved from a night of scavenging. She was told that sometimes the demons were afraid to come into the light, and so she tore the bottom half of her shirt off from her body, leaving just her bellybutton exposed. She wrapped her shirt around the metal pipe and lit a match. Within seconds, a burst of flames engulfed the fabric and illuminated the area around her. She blew out a sigh of relief thinking, *that's better.*

About a few hundred feet ahead, was the beginning of the vast canyon system. It towered over the land, as if it were touching the stars. Desti's eyes traced upward until she was staring at the night sky. For a moment, the beauty of the stars captivated her focus and brought her mind to a place of peace and serenity.

Memories of her and Tate swarmed her mind of the time when they were kids, staring at the night sky. Chills began to ravish her body as the crisp night air dropped to freezing. With every gust of wind hitting her body, it felt like being struck by an icy whip. Her body tensed from the discomfort. *I need to find shelter.*

Desti's eyes tried to look past the banket of darkness, searching for anything that could provide her comfort and safety. She almost gave up hope until she noticed a small cave embedded in the side of the cliff.

Oh, thank goodness. Desti's homemade torch was almost burnt to nothing and the light that was providing her protection from the ravenous creatures of the night was diminishing. Her heart heavily skipped a beat, knowing that her lifeline was about to be gone. There was only about a minute of light left, and so she took off, sprinting toward the cave ahead.

Her breathing became loud as she forced the air from her lungs. Making noise out in the Wastelands was a sure way of being hunted, so she forced her hands up to her mouth, pushing as hard as she could to keep any sounds coming from her. Once she reached the small cave, she dropped to her knees in exhaustion, gasping for a full breath of air. The air out in the Wastelands felt different. There was no smog or constant clouds of smoke like there was in the city of Mors. She had never experienced a clean breath of air until now. Desti rested her back to the back wall of the shallow cave, facing the opening toward the night sky.

As her panting became less intense, she slowed her breathing, closed her eyes, and relaxed. Desti's overwhelming fatigue took control of her consciousness, succumbing her to a deep slumber.

***

Hours slipped by as she lay there dreaming. Her face was soft and expressionless. By this point, Desti's torch had completely burnt away and left her in total. darkness. Suddenly the slight sounds of grunts and snarling gradually grew louder until it jolted her from her sleep.

Desti shot up with a rush of adrenaline and sat in complete fear. Her heart felt as if it were going to pound out of her chest. *What was that*? She didn't move. Her body sat still like a statue as she listened to those inexplicable sounds.

With every passing second, the noises grew closer and louder. Desti sucked in her breath and held it in her chest. The sounds of the claws of the creature scraping against the rocky terrain echoed around her.

They were walking right outside the cave. A tremble began to rattle through her. *Can they see me? Smell me?* Thoughts of the creature ripping her to pieces invaded her mind as she sat there completely helpless.

Quietly, she gripped her metal pipe that was sitting next to her. Her hand slowly started to feel around the rugged back wall of the cave, searching for anything that could help her. The snarling was now right out front of the cave entrance.

All hope was lost as she accepted that it was going to find her, when suddenly her hand pushed through a hole. Her eyes jolted open. *Is this a way out*? Stealthily, Desti scooted her body to her left until she was now entering a small crack in the cave wall. It was a tight squeeze, and barley big enough to fit her petite body.

As she pushed herself through, her metal pipe ricocheted off the rocky ground, echoing a cacophony of alarming ringing. *Oh crap!* The creature belted out a screeching snarl and sprinted into the cave. Desti pulled her body through falling onto her back just before it could reach her. She reached into her pocket and pulled out her matchbox and lit a match.

Desti froze with terror as she sat there face-to-face with the demonic creature. Its hideous elongated head had tight leathery skin stretched across it and its sharp, jagged teeth dripped with acidic saliva. Its eyes were black as coal and too large for its face. Her eyes traced its horrendous appearance up and down. It reached out its two-inch clawed paws, swiping through the crack, trying to snatch her leg.

She scooted back just before its claws could grab ahold of her. Small sharp pebbles jabbed into her hands as she shuffled her body farther into the crack in the cave. *What do I do now*? Desti couldn't help but to feel helpless as she sat there trapped. *Tate would know what to do.* Tate always knew what to do. Desti reached her fingers into the box of matches and counted the remaining ones with her fingers. *One. Two. Three. Four.* She had four left. Out in Wastelands, four matches could mean life versus death, and so she shoved the box back into her pocket, conserving the rest for another time. At least she was safe at that moment. The creature was too large to fit through the crack, and so she decided to wait it out.

***

Dawn soon came.

At first, the darkness of the night still clung to the air, but the shadows of the night were soon cast away by the warm orange glow that illuminated the sky. The creature had retreated and crawled its way back to whatever hole it escaped from, giving Desti a feeling of relief. The gentle sun rays beamed through the cave and into the crack that she was hiding in.

She closed her eyes for a moment, embracing the warmth on her skin. *I made it,* she thought. All her life growing up, it was imbued into her mind that no one could survive the Wastelands, and yet there she was. Alive. Desti pulled herself up from the ground and scoped out her surroundings.

Behind her, she could see down another cave system. The sunrays illuminated the path, allowing her to see far in. It was as if it went on for miles. As curious as she was, she decided to explore the system to see where it would lead her.

She grazed her hand along the rocky wall, as her fingers bumped over the rough texture. Every step was taken with stealth and caution. One by one and one in front of another. The creatures and demons of Hell were known to live underground. Desti thought about, *what if this was one of their tunnels*?

In her other hand, she gripped her metal pipe tight, ready to swing if she must. It felt as if she had walked for miles down this cave and now the light from the sun was no more. Desti was engulfed by the darkness that surrounded her. For a moment she panicked. *What do I do*? She only had four matches left. If she used her matches for this, then she would leave herself defenseless if they were needed in the future. Her eyes popped open with an idea. She pulled out a small pocketknife from one of her back pockets and cut off the bottom half of her pants and wrapped it around her pipe. She made sure it was secured tight and then pulled out a match, lighting it up. A breath of relief pushed out of her lungs as the darkness was shoved away from the light coming from her torch.

The crack that she had crawled through was no longer visible. She was now deep into the mountainside. With nothing but her, the silence was the loudest thing around. Every breath and every heavy beat of her heart was amplified by the total silence. But suddenly a noise broke her focus. It sounded like an echo of screams and music coming from the end of the tunnel. *What is that*?

Desti's mind raced with horrifying thoughts. How could she not, with what kind of world she lived in? She crept forward, carefully stepping over anything that could make noise. There was a warm red glow ahead, bending around the corner. The screams grew louder. Desti began to tremble. She lifted her hands to her mouth and muffled the shallow breaths escaping from her teeth.

She had crept her way to the end of the tunnel, which was a ledge hovering above a vast opening. Down below she saw the horrors that she wished she didn't hear. The room was surrounded by fire pits and at the center was a stone table. There was a naked man laying on it, tied by his wrists and ankles. She could hear his cries for mercy.

"No! Please! Please, I will do anything!"

Tears burned her eyes as she crouched down, hearing his sorrows. *What is this?* As horrifying as it was, she couldn't look away. Her body lay flat on the stone ground as she peered her way over the ledge.

It was as if the air was sucked out of her lungs the moment, she saw *It* walk into the room. *What is that*?

It stood tall. Taller than any human she had ever seen before. It looked human and yet had so much evil to it. The cold black eyes, the pointed claw-like fingers, and a sharp smile. She sucked in a gasp. Immediately, it dawned on her.

A cambion.

She watched in horror as the creature-like man strode his way over to the guy on the table. His snarling laugh echoed off the walls. It gave Desti a twisted feeling in her gut. She clenched her stomach tight.

"Please let me go. I can give you something."

The man begged and pleaded but the cambion wasn't fazed.

"Let you go? And why would I do that? I'm starving."

His voice echoed with evil. He grabbed the man's left leg and with incredible force, yanked down hard, and ripped it from his body. Desti heard terrifying screams and gargles coming from the man as he endured the agony of being ripped to pieces.

The cambion ate away his thigh until there was nothing left but bone. Blood pooled from the man's body and filled the surrounding ground. *Oh my God.* She held her hands to her mouth and silently sobbed. Tears ran down her face and through her fingers. The taste of her salty tears collected in the corner of her lips. Her focus once again was captured. The dying man gathered enough energy to let out one more cry for help and with a large breath he said, "Master, please. Just kill me now."

The name swirled around in her mind. *Master.* Growing up, she was always taught about the Master of the city, and how he would punish those who broke the rules, but she had never seen him. She didn't even know what he was supposed to look like. Sometimes, she even questioned if he was even real. But now, seeing this, it is as if her worst nightmare had come to life. Ravished by total fear, Desti started to shake. *Is Tate next? I need to save him, but how? How do I get us out of this?*

The situation was too much to bear. An overwhelming sense of doubt succumbed to her. Desti raced in her mind trying to think of a way to save her best friend. She didn't even know where he was or even if he was alive.

Her face recoiled with disgust. She couldn't bear thinking of Tate being eaten alive. She returned her focus back to the cambion. He continued to eat away at the dead man lying on the table, ripping him limb from limb like a wild animal. Desti lay there in silence for what seemed like hours, just waiting for something to give her a chance to get down there.

Suddenly the cambion exited the cave through an opening across from her. *This is my chance.* Desti crawled her body over the ledge until she was dangling by her hands. There was a slight hole beneath her feet, and so she used that to support her weight as she climbed down. Once she reached the bottom, a sense of confusion swept over her. *Where do I go now*?

There were five openings in the cave. Desti's eyes darted from each one trying to figure out where she should go. The opening all the way to the right was where the cambion went. *Not that one.*

With no sense of direction, she randomly chose the opening farthest to the left. There were small torches that lit up the pathways, illuminating her surrounds with a warm orange glow. Moisture droplets collected on the cave walls, creating a cacophony of hushed echoes as they hit the ground. With one foot in front of the other, Desti tip-toed her way as far as she could go.

There was a turn ahead. Desti stopped in her tracks for a moment. Unsure of what was around the bend, she questioned if she should even keep going. She closed her eyes and bowed her head. *I have to. Tate needs me.*

Her eyes opened, and when they did, it was as if something had changed within her. She pushed forward, peering around the corner. It was another room, dimly lit by a handful of lit torches hanging on the walls. She was surrounded by metal cages lined up like jail cells. She gasped.

"Tate?" Her voice sounded like whispers through the wind. Soft and quiet.

Most of the cells were empty, but down toward the end, there lay a man, raggedy and beaten. Desti sprinted forward. "Hey. Are you okay?" There was no answer. She tried one more time, but this time slightly louder. "Hey! Wake up." Desti could hear the man groaning as he lifted his head from the cold stone ground. His face was bruised and bloody. "Are you okay? What's your name?" she asked again.

"What?" The man groggily question-ed.

"I said, are you okay?" He rubbed the side of his head and sat upward. "I think so. Who are you? Are you here to get me out?"

"My name is Desti. I'm looking for my friend. Tate. Have you seen him?" The man shook his head from side to side in a frantic reaction. "No. No. No. No. I can't help you. He will punish me." Desti rolled her eyes. She slammed her fists against the metal pipes and yelled, "he is going to eat you anyway! If you tell me where Tate is, I will break you out." There was silence for a moment. She knew that he was pondering. "What does your friend look like?"

"He has jet black hair and green eyes. About six feet tall and is probably wearing a leather jacket." Desti cocked her head to the side as she analyzed the man. The look in his eyes said that he knew who she was describing. He was hesitant. Desti slammed her fists one more time. "Come on!"

"Alright. Just be quiet please. He will hear you." He took a deep breath in and said, "your friend is probably being held in the preparation chamber. It's where they go before their punishment."

Desti's eyes shot wide open. She knew what that meant. *He is next*.

"Alright, I told you what you wanted. Now please, get me out." Desti searched around her looking for anything that could help. There was a broken piece of metal in the corner of the floor. She picked it up and thought, *this could work*.

Desti shoved the sharpened tip into the keyhole of the lock and twisted firmly. She heard a crack and to her surprise, the lock opened and dropped to the ground.

"I did it."

The man raced out of the cell and rushed Desti with a hug. "Thank you. Thank you."

"No problem. Now show me where the preparation chamber is."

6: No Way to Escape

THE CAVE WAS COLD AND NARROW AND REEKED OF A potent rotten odor. Desti knew that smell. It was the smell of rotting flesh. It was probably the leftover bodies that the Master had eaten.

The man in front of her led the way as he crouched down and walked with a limp. "Hey. What is your name?" Desti whispered. The man stopped and glanced back, whispering back to her, "my name is Elijah."

"Well nice to meet you, Elijah." She cracked a soft smile. His head turned forward again. They were coming up to another opening to their left.

"It's up here," his voice echoed. *How does he know where to go?* She could have questioned him more, but truthfully, didn't have the strength to. Instead, she let her feet lead the way, one foot in front of the other. But once she looked up— he was gone.

Elijah disappeared around the corner and so Desti picked up her pace, running after him. As she made the turn, she stopped in her tracks in total shock. Her eyes burned from the tears collecting and dripping down her cheek. She couldn't bear to witness what was in front of her.

"Tate? Oh my God. Tate, please."

Her sobs wailed from her chest as she ran over to Tate. He was chained to the wall. One rusty metal cuff per wrist and ankle. His body was bloody and beaten. She saw fresh drips of blood still pouring from a wound on his head. Her hands shook relentlessly as she grasped the sides of his face. His blood seeped between her fingers.

"Tate. Wake up. Please." She cried like she had never cried before.

This was her best friend. Her everything. Suddenly, she felt Tate lift his head, and when his gaze looked up, she was staring into his magnificent green eyes. "Desti?" She leaned in and held his head to her chest and cried, "yes. I'm here. I found you."

Desti swiftly looked over to Elijah. "How do we get out of here?"

Elijah looked stunned. Like a deer in the head lights. He threw up his hands and shrugged his shoulders. Desti fiddled with the sharp metal object that she had found earlier until she had a good grip on it. She shoved the tip into the keyholes and one by one, popped off Tate's cuffs. Tate's body lay limp over her shoulders as she held his arm and helped him move.

"I'll find a way. Just move."

Desti walked past Elijah and continued down the dark path. Elijah followed closely behind them.

The maze-like caverns twisted around for miles beneath the Earth's surface. Desti had dragged Tate far into the Earth, not knowing where she was headed. There was a sweet musky scent that emitted from the cavern walls and the air around felt moist and cool.

Desti could no longer hear the distant screams or music coming from the echoes of the punishment chamber. "We must have walked like five miles. Elijah, does this cave open up, or lead anywhere?"

She looked back. Elijah crouched down for a moment. "I don't know. This is as far as I've gotten."

Desti laid Tate against the wall and sat beside him. The last lit torch hanging on the cavern wall passed a few hundred feet ago. There was very little light left from where they were sitting.

"Okay. I have a few matches left. We have no more torches ahead and we don't know where we are going or even if this is leading us somewhere." Her voice sounded defeated.

Desti placed her head in the palm of her hand. Elijah let out a small chuckle. "What's so funny?" Desti shot him a sharp look.

"Nothing. It's just—we are totally screwed. We're never going to get out of here."

His laughter soon turned to fear. Desti could hear the whimpering in his voice. "Don't say that. We can't give up. We just need to keep moving forward until we find something."

She too had succumbed to a feeling of doubt, but that didn't faze her. There was no other choice except to keep going. Desti leaned forward and ripped a piece of Elijah's shirt from his body.

"Hey. What did you do that for?" Desti was silent. She wrapped his shirt around her metal pipe that was in her back belt loop and lit one of her matches. "See. Now we have light. This won't last long, so we need to hurry."

The cave ahead was soon engulfed by the flaming light. The vastness of the rocky terrain seemed to go on forever. Desti lifted Tate over her shoulder and dragged him forward. Elijah took the other side of Tate and helped support his weight.

Tate was in and out of consciousness. The blood from his head trickled down his cheek, staining his skin a deep red. Desti had dragged Tate for about twenty minutes, following the diminishing flame of their torch. She stopped for a moment.

"Elijah. I need you to go as far down as you can and tell me if you see anything."

Elijah looked scared, but the fierceness behind Desti's eyes forced him forward. He nodded his head.

His hands caressed the uneven walls, feeling for any opening. Desti could see his body slowly get engulfed by the pitch blackness ahead.

"Anything?" she yelled.

At first there was no answer. Just the sounds of her heavy breathing. Just as she was about to lose hope, Elijah answered, "There is another opening to the left."

Desti popped her eyes open in relief. Her torch had about another ten minutes left of light, so she picked Tate up by his arm and helped him walk. Tate's slight groans broke Desti's heart. She couldn't bear to see him so broken. "It's okay Tate. We are going to get out of this. I promise."

Elijah had disappeared around the corner before Desti could catch up.

"Elijah. Wait."

There was a slight glimmer of deep orange glowing from the opening. *Light.* She proceeded with caution and peered her head just around the bend. There stood Elijah, still as a statue. He had a look of total fear in his eyes.

As Desti crept forward, she too realized what was so terrifying. The cave opened into a vast room and in it, were hundreds of sleeping demons. Their bodies littered the ground, looking like black leather rocks. She could see them breathing. The room was filled with a musky horrid stench and the sounds of the creatures grunting almost made her want to throw up.

She carefully and quietly placed Tate on the ground, leaning against the wall. "What do we do now?" she whispered to Elijah. Elijah was frozen. Desti gave him a slight nudge to break his focus. He slowly turned toward her and shook his head. Desti held her finger over her mouth and locked eyes with Elijah. She knew her eyes said it all. *You better not make a sound.*

The cavern opened to about three hundred feet long and one hundred feet wide. She scoped the area for any passageways. To the right, there was nothing but a stone wall. Desti traced her eyes over every sleeping demon until she was scoping the other side. In the far-left corner, there was another opening to a tunnel. *There. That's our way out.*

Elijah peered over Desti's shoulder. She turned toward him and pointed to the far-left opening. Tate had slowly gained some of his mobility back. He leaned forward and tried to pick himself up from the ground. Desti rushed over to him and held his arm around her shoulder.

"I think I found a way out, but we have to walk past demons. I think they are sleeping, so we need to be very quiet." Desti's lips almost brushed against Tate's ears as she whispered to him. He looked up at her into her eyes. Desti had never seen that look before. *What is this look?*

His eyes locked onto hers, soft as silk. It pulled her in. Mesmerized her just for a moment.

"Hey. Let's go." Elijah's voice broke her focus.

"Right. Come on." She grabbed Tate's arm as they stepped their way into inevitable danger.

***

The corpulent fiends sprawled across the stone ground, completely enveloping every inch. Their grotesque and unsightly features instilled a sense of repulsion and terror into Desti. She covered her mouth with her free hand, trying not to gag from the sickly smell. Her footing guided Tate and Elijah behind her, slowly and carefully stepping over the demons' massive claws. Only a few more steps were left until reaching the opening. She wanted to sprint for it.

Being secluded in that cave surrounded by those infernal entities sent a shock wave of fear through her veins like she had never experienced before. It took all the strength she had to keep her pace slow and steady.

Just as Desti had cleared the final obstacle, she waited at the entrance for Elijah to make that final step. Tate stood next to her, leaning against the cavern wall. Elijah lifted his foot and leaned his body forward in an attempt to pass over the last demon, but to Desti's dismay, he slipped and fell right onto its mottled body.

She gasped and almost fell backward in shock. Suddenly there was a horrifying cacophony of infernal growls rumbling through the room. She watched as the massive dark bodies began to lift from their slumbers.

Oh shit.

She turned to Tate and held out her hand. "Run."

Desti and Tate took off down the hall, followed by Elijah.

"Guys wait!" he screamed.

She could hear fear in the crackling in his voice. "Elijah run!" she yelled.

There were dimly lit torches every few hundred feet guiding their way. The labyrinthine tunnels served as a twisted and tortuous maze, disorienting Desti with every turn. "Where do I go?" she screamed.

The horde of fiendish unholy beings were relentless. Elijah ran with all the strength he had. Desti glanced back and could see a demon catching up to him.

"Elijah! Behind you."

Elijah turned around and within a split second, the demon that was slithering behind him shot out its razor-sharp tongue, piecing Elijah's leg. His screams reverberated through Desti's ears. She didn't look back. She couldn't bear to see another person being eaten. When all hope was sucked out of her, she finally turned around one more corner, and when she did, she almost dropped to her knees.

Sunlight.

"Tate, that's sunlight! Hurry!" Desti and Tate clawed their way up a mound of boulders and slipped their bodies through a small crack above them. The radiant beams of sunrays blinded her as she broke through the Earth's ground. She gasped as she crawled from the cracks.

Tate.

Desti turned around and yanked Tate upward as hard as she could. She screamed from her chest. Completely exhausted, their bodies lay there on the ground, tangled and limp. Desti grabbed her metal pipe from her back belt loop and firmly gripped it in her hand. There was a noise coming from the darkness of the hole, and so she lifted her head in terror, thinking that the demons were going to follow her up to the surface. But, to her surprise, Elijah's hand shot through the hole, and he clawed his way out.

"Elijah!" Desti rolled over and ran over to him. His body felt heavy like lead, and she almost dropped him to the ground. Just as his feet cleared the cave, the snarling beasts of Hell screeched and growled, clawing at them through the crack. Desti could see the look in his eyes. "Don't worry. They can't fit through there. We are safe."

7: The Unlucky Ones

DESTI, TATE, AND ELIJAH WERE PANTING HEAVILY. They had just done the impossible and escaped a horde of rabid demons. They all lay on the ground, with their arms sprawled across their chests. Desti glanced over and watched the rise and fall, as if they were in complete synchrony.

"Tate? You, okay?"

Tate had now full gain of his mobility. He sat up and looked over at Desti.

"Yes, thanks to you."

The blood that dripped from his head was now a dried dark red streak down his face. "Yeah Desti. If it weren't for you, I would have been eaten." said Elijah.

Desti propped her body up. The scorching sand burned the tips of her fingers as they dug in. "We need to find water and maybe something to eat."

Tate glanced all around with furrowed brows. "Yeah, and where are we going to find that our here?"

Around them, were miles of vast empty wastelands. The desert was a harsh place to be. Water was scarce and almost impossible to find, and food had to be whatever insect or animal you would so luckily stumble upon.

"We can't give up Tate. There must be water somewhere." Desti looked over to Elijah. "Do you know where we are?" Elijah's head tilted back as he closed his eyes. He let out a large exhale from his chest. "Not exactly, but I know which direction we should go in."

Desti realized that she had never asked Elijah where he was from. Her hair whipped across her face as she endured the harsh gust of the desert winds. "Elijah, I never asked. What city are you from?" Her question was sincere, but Elijah jolted back as if she were a threat. There was silence for a moment. He looked hesitant to answer her. "Did I say something wrong?"

"No. I'm sorry, I just don't usually tell people where I am from."

"Well, I did just save your life, so I think you can trust me," she answered.

The sand was now becoming too much for her skin to bear. She stood up from the ground and brushed off the dirt from her clothes and said, "come on. We should keep moving. You can tell me all about where you are from on our way." She cracked a peculiar smirk from the corner of her cheek and held out her hand to pull him off the ground.

Tate stood on his own. He seemed to be healing quickly from whatever injuries he sustained. Elijah led the way, north of the hole they crawled out from. Desti looked back. The city of Mors was no longer visible along the horizon. It was now just an empty desert and canyons.

We just have to keep moving forward. We can do this.

Doubt tried to push its way into her mind. She couldn't help but wonder if what they were doing would be worth it. You would never be able to guess what she was thinking. Desti wore her facade like armor. Covering up her true feelings deep down inside.

She walked right next to Tate, following behind Elijah. Their arms swung in synchrony. They used to match each other's rhythms when they would walk as children. It was a game that they would play, but now, Desti didn't need to even try. She and Tate were so aligned in everything they did, that it just came naturally.

Her eyes focused down, on the swinging of his arm. Slowly she traced up to his elbow, then his shoulder, until she was looking at his face. When her focus turned up, she locked eyes with him. He was staring right back at her. Their gaze locked onto each other. She studied the green and gold specks in the iris of his eyes. His prefect nose and jawline. *How come I've never noticed him like this before*?

No words were exchanged. They didn't need to speak at that moment. *I see you. I need you. I want you.* Desti never looked at Tate this way before. This was a new feeling that sent a shockwave of confusion through her veins. Tate reached his hand slightly toward her until his fingertips touched her hands. She sucked in a shallow breath as she felt an electric rush of goosebumps rise on her body.

His touch satisfied her in a way that she didn't even know it could. She wanted to reach back. Hold his hand to her chest, but she didn't. She pulled her hand away and ran up to Elijah to hear more about his life story. "Hey Elijah. Wait up." Tate kept his pace the same, trailing a few feet behind them.

"So, you never answered my question before. Where are you from?" She turned toward him as her feet crossed sideways, still walking forward. Elijah softly chuckled. "Alight. I'll tell you. I was from the city of Ignis."

"Oh. The city of Fire?" Desti turned her feet forward again and matched the pace of Elijah. He answered back, "right. The city of Fire." His face fell soft and sorrowful. Desti knew there was more to his story.

"You said were from the city of Ignis. Do you not live there now?" Elijah glanced up at the radiant sun and lifted his arm above his head. "I grew up there, but I left a few years ago." Desti cocked her head to the side.

Left? No one just leaves their city unless there was a good reason. "Why'd you leave?"

"You sure are testing my trust today," Elijah joked.

Desti kept her gaze on him, begging for an answer with her big green eyes. "Alright. All right. I left after my parents were killed and then I joined the Resistance." Elijah's voice carried just enough for Tate to hear. He stepped forward, shoving his body between them.

"Resistance? What Resistance?"

Desti too was shocked. She had never heard of a Resistance before. No one would ever dare to do such a crazy thing. But then again, she and Tate weren't much different. She narrowed her eyebrows as she listened. Both Desti and Tate stared at Elijah until he kept going.

"Alright you guys. The Resistance is a group of us, somewhere out here in the Wastelands. I heard stories of it growing up. I was sick of how we were treated in our city, and I wanted to put a stop to it, so me and a few friends snuck out one night to search for it."

"And you found it?" asked Desti.

"Oh, we found it. I joined and never looked back. That was about two years ago." Elijah's dark brown hair was sticking to the side of his face. Desti watched droplets of sweat glide down his cheek as he spoke.

"What? Do you guys like kill demons or something?"

she couldn't help but to dig more out of him. She had never met anyone who was actually resisting against the demons of the world. Elijah stopped for a moment. His head was down. Desti and Tate waited for him to respond.

"Yeah, we kill them all right. But our mission is much larger than that." Elijah picked up his pace again, stepping even quicker now. The crunching of the sand beneath their feet sounded like brittle bones breaking. Around them were vast canyons on both sides, reaching miles high above them. Elijah kept forward and steadily fast, leaving Desti and Tate trailing behind him. "What do you think by when he said that their mission is much more than just killing demons?" Tate looked over at her. "I don't know."

"Should we tell him why we are out here?" There was a glimmer of hope that sparked inside Desti. Something that she rarely ever had. But her sparkle soon diminished when she saw the look in Tate's eyes.

"We should keep this to ourselves until we know that we can trust him."

Desti had been so caught up in rescuing Tate and running from demons, that she realized she hadn't even told him about Crazy Joan and what she gave her. Desti reached into her pocket and felt the coldness of the cross necklace touch her fingers. In the other pocket, the leathery texture of the Holy book fit perfectly in the grasp of her hand.

"Tate, I need to show you—"

Desti was interrupted by Elijah yelling. "it's up here!"

Tate took off running, following Elijah.

"I guess we'll talk later," Desti whispered to herself.

Elijah had disappeared around the bend of the canyon. Desti was staggering behind, inhaling, struggling to keep up.

"Tate! Wait up!" Desti ran around the bend and stopped in her tracks. There stood Tate towering over Elijah's limp body. Desti sprinted forward.

"What happened to him?"

Tate turned around with a puzzled expression and said, "I don't know. He was laying on the ground when I caught up."

Elijah looked as if he had just dropped to floor in a split second. His body shivered as if he were exposed to extreme cold. Desti reached her hand out and touched his clammy skin.

"He's burning up."

She grabbed his face, squeezing his cheeks between her hand, trying to get a reaction out of him. "Elijah. Look at me. Wake up." A ponder swept over her. *What could have happened? What is this*? Tate kneeled next to her.

"Didn't he get bit by one of those demons?"

She shot a look of realization at him. "Tate, of course! Quick, check his body." Elijah's clothes were raggedy and torn, as if he had found them in a pile of trash. He wore navy blue jeans, ripped with holes, and a worn-out Metallica T-shirt. As Desti's fingers lifted and studied the skin under his clothes, she had a quick moment of curiosity sweep her mind. *What is Metallica?*

"Desti, why'd you stop? Keep searching." *Right.* Her fingers lifted the shirt over his abdomen, and then went to search his pants. She still hadn't found anything yet, but then she gasped once she saw it.

"Tate. I found it."

Desti took out her old rusty pocketknife from the back of her pocket and sliced open a slit on the side of Elijah's pants. His leg oozed a green and white puss and was bubbling with an acidic foam.

"His skin looks infected. Tate what do we do?" It looked as if Elijah's skin was becoming necrotic around his wound. The flesh of his skin was a mixture of black and purple. Desti went to touch the foam oozing from his leg when Tate yelled out, "Desti don't!" She stopped. "Why? What's wrong?"

"I think it's venom. Don't touch it. You don't know what it would do to you." Desti pulled her hand back.

She didn't know what to do or how to help. The brutal sun rays felt as if it were cooking them from the inside out. She so desperately yearned for a sip of water. Her eyes searched the horizon for anything that they could use to help their situation. Defeated is what she felt. *Why did we do this to ourselves*?

"I don't know how to help him Tate. He's going to die if we can't clean his wound."

There was a heavy feeling weighing on her chest. She barely knew Elijah, and yet, she was sad to see him dying in her arms.

"Tate, you need to go find some water." Tate stepped back, almost angry. "Water? Where the Hell am I going to find water out here?" His arms stretched out as far as they could.

She looked up and said, "we have to at least try. *We* need it too, Tate. I haven't had water in almost two days." Immediately Tate changed his demeanor. Desti was right. Without water, they too would not last much longer.

"Please Tate. Go look for something. I'll stay with Elijah." Desti watched as Tate ran off through the canyon to search for anything that could help them. Elijah was shivering. His skin was pale and clammy but was searing hot to the touch. Desti sat next to him and held his head in her lap. "It's okay Elijah. I won't let you die."

Desti couldn't understand why she cared so much. People died all the time in her world, but something was changing. Heartlessness and obedience didn't have to be the way of life out here. In a sense, she felt free, and this freedom ignited a new Desti to come to the surface. She slipped her arms out of her leather jacket and placed it next to her. The sweat that pooled under her clothing dripped from her sleeves and splashed onto the dusty terrain. She kept her body leaning forward, keeping her shadow strategically placed over Elijah's face.

Out on the desolated terrain, it was rare for clouds to appear. The world had been scolded to a crisp, leaving only a small chance for shade to come. But Desti pleaded for a miracle. The heat was too much to bear.

A wave of nausea hit her stomach like a ton of bricks. Desti clenched her stomach and hurled over. *Oh, this is not good. Where is Tate*? Hours had seemed to creep by as she patiently waited for Tate to return. With every passing second, Elijah and Desti grew weaker and weaker. The skin on her body was now boiling to the touch, and yet she felt flushed and cold. She knew what her body was going through. Heat exhaustion.

"Don't worry Elijah. Tate should be back soon." To keep herself from passing out, Desti rocked back and forth and hummed a lullaby to keep her mind focused. Elijah was barely breathing. His chest rose just lightly with every shallow breath.

The wind was picking up speed, blowing sharp shards of glassy sand crystals onto Desti's skin. She squinted her eyes and raised her arm to cover her face. *We need to get out of here*. Desti glanced all around, searching for anything that could provide them with some shelter from the brutal winds. *There!*

Ahead, Desti noticed an overhang embedded in the canyon walls. "I'm going to move you. Okay?" Elijah didn't respond. He lay there motionless. Desti shoved her arms under his armpits and with all her strength, she yanked him over to the overhang. Once she made it, she leaned against the stone wall and closed her eyes, slipping into a hypnotic sleep.

The western horizon was soon filtered by intricate sun rays descending in the sky, casting elongated shadows that stretched for miles across the rugged canyon. Above was filled with fiery red and strokes of orange, as if it were painted in the sky. The thick musky air carried a soft hint of desert brush through the wind and the distant echoes of the rustling of drifting leaves hummed through the narrow passageways. Desti only had maybe an hour left of daylight protecting her and Elijah.

Desti was suddenly seized by an intense surge of panic that coursed through her entire body. She sat up in a frantic urgency, glancing all around. *What time is it*?

Her mind was invaded with a flood of unsettling thoughts, dragging her into a confused and fearful state.

She leaned over and shook Elijah. "Elijah, wake up. It's almost dark."

Every muscle in her body quivered with a sense of dread. There she was alone, stranded in the Wastelands with a boy she didn't even know, and Tate was nowhere to be found. *How could this get any worse*? She shot her focus to her left, staring off into the distant horizon. *What was that*? In the distance, Desti heard bloodcurdling howls reverberating through the canyon. "Elijah, please wake up. Where can we go? We aren't safe out here."

A sense of helplessness struck Desti in the chest, causing her to curl forward. She knew that without proper shelter, they were just waiting to be the demons' next meal. Only a small sliver of sunlight shone through the canyon, illuminating the last bit of land that she sat on. Desti threw her head back in frustration and closed her eyes. *It's over,* she thought.

But then there was that familiar voice that she loved so much. The voice that could break her free from any terror that clouded her mind. Desti sucked in a slight gasp and opened her eyes.

Tate.

She could hear it in the distant yelling, "Desti!"

Desti shot up from her seated position and ran toward the voice calling her name. She waved her arms above her head yelling, "I'm here!"

Ahead was a wall of fog seeping through the canyon valley. Desti stopped for a moment. There was a silhouette appearing in the distance, through the fog. Suddenly, Desti sprinted forward toward the wall of fog and embraced Tate in a passionate hug.

"I thought something must have happened to you." Her head rested on his chest. She felt the rise and fall of his heavy breathing and heard every heavy beat of his heart. It was music to her ears. Tate held her tightly in his arms as he wrapped his biceps around her. He looked down and said, "I would never leave you." She looked up at him in his golden-green eyes. The thought of looking away was too much to handle, and so she didn't. She gazed upon him in a beautiful silence, only speaking with her eyes. Tate suddenly lost his focus and stepped back.

"Come on. We must hurry. I found something, but we need to beat the night." Tate glanced around with a confused expression. "Where is Elijah?"

"He is over there. I'll bring you to him." Desti pulled Tate toward where she and Elijah were sitting, underneath the shallow overhang. Elijah was pale gray and almost blue in the lips.

"Oh, shit Desti, he doesn't look good. Is he still alive."

Desti kneeled down and touched his head. "Of course, he is Tate. He just needs some water. Did you find any?" She looked back up at Tate. His silky black hair fluttered in the gusty wind. There was a sparkle in his eyes. Desti knew that look. The look of Tate when he had good news.

"I found something better. But we need to leave now. Come on. I'll show you." Tate held out his hand and helped Desti to her feet. "You take his left arm and I'll take his right arm."

As they carried Elijah toward the wall of fog casting through the canyon, their footsteps pounded down on the dusty ground in a frantic rhythm. Desti glanced back and saw the wall of the impending darkness looming ominously behind them. "Hurry Tate!" Her muscles burned with the strain of her exertion and her lungs ached from her ragged gasps of air. Desti, Tate and Elijah were soon engulfed by the shroud of uncertain fog. A somber shade of deep blue crept over the blazing fiery sky, and soon engulfed the land, surrounding it with a cold and oppressive shroud of eerie darkness.

8: Survival of the Fittest

AS DESTI MOVED FORWARD THROUGH THE CLOUDED canyon, the ethereal wisps of moisture seemed to swirl around her like a whirlpool. The darkness had fully enveloped the land, and so each step was taken with such caution, only to be guided by the faintest glimmer of the moonlight.

"Tate. I can't see anything. Where are we going?"

Desti clung to the back of Elijah's shirt, terrified that she would be separated with a simple slip. The howling echoes from afar grew louder in her ears.

"Just trust me Desti. Keep moving forward and don't stop."

Elijah's feet dragged behind him as his body lay limp between Desti and Tate's arms. There it was again. An eerie wave of hisses and growls echoed from behind. Desti's eyes shot open.

"Okay, tell me you heard that." She looked over to Tate.

"I heard that. Just keep going and don't look back."

A rush of adrenaline and fear pumped through her veins. Desti could only see a few feet in front of her. "Tate, where are we going? We need to find shelter now."

The stampeding of the hooved claws scratched the path behind them and picked up its speed. Desti and Tate picked up their pace and began to run as fast as they could. "They are right behind us Tate!" Her voice quivered with dread. *I don't want to be eaten*. Images of her and Tate being ripped to pieces by the ravishing demons invaded her mind. She shook her head and shook them away, keeping her fast pace.

"Were almost there!" yelled Tate. There was a glowing light in the distance just slightly above her head. *What is that*?

Suddenly, as if it were a simulation, they broke free from the wall of fog and were running straight through an opened gate. Desti collapsed to her knees, dropping Elijah to the ground. Behind her, she felt the rumbling of the gate slam shut in her chest. Loud scratching from the claws of the demons pierced through her ears. She would never get used to their unsettling screeching. She clenched her shirt in discomfort and confusion. With every heavy breath, she tried to gather the energy to speak. "What is— going—on?"

An army of armed men rushed forward, holding a collection of spears and swords toward the gate. Desti's froze, trying to figure out what was happening. As she sat there curled on her knees, her fingers tightened in the dirt. Tate was to her left, picking himself off the ground.

"Tate. Where are we?"

There was a permanent soft smirk smeared across his face. The kind of look that would make anyone question it. Desti tilted her head to the side and asked again, "where are we Tate?"

Suddenly, she was interrupted by a raspy voice coming from behind her saying, "You are in our camp. We are the Resistance." *Resistance?* She looked over to Tate. "Like the Resistance that Elijah was talking about?"

The women stepped forward, barricading Desti with her feet. When Desti looked up, there was a hand reaching down in her face. She placed her hand in the woman's and was lifted from the ground. The ashy dust particles clung to the cloth on Desti's clothing as if it were afraid to let go. She brushed it off with her hands and refocused her attention to the woman in front of her.

The woman stood tall above Desti and had vibrant orange hair and pale freckled skin. Half of her head was shaved, leaving the other half a frizzled mass. Desti's eyes traced her features until she snapped herself out of it.

"Thank you, I'm sorry for just intruding like this. My name is Desti."

She waited for just a second. Intimidation was not something Desti had ever felt before, and yet there she was feeling as if she were shrinking in the presence of her. "My name is Tess. I'm glad you are here. Come on, I want to show you something."

Desti's eyebrows narrowed with question. *What is going on*? She looked back and saw a few guys with spears lift Elijah into their arms and drag him off to another part of their camp.

"Elijah. He's hurt. He needs medicine."

Desti felt the urge to run over to him, but was interrupted by Tess saying, "don't worry, he will be taken care of." As she watched Elijah disappear into one of the tents in the distance, she refocused her attention on her surroundings.

It was like a small city embedded in the canyon. Above, were hundreds of glowing balls of light, decorating the camp like stars in the night sky. To her right, there were small huts sporadically placed along the valley and to her left was something that looked similar to the bazaar back home. People were selling hand carved spears and knives from their booths. An aroma of something cooking enveloped the air. Desti closed her eyes and inhaled. "What's that smell?" Tess pointed to her left and said, "over there you will find our local market. Go on, check it out."

Tess stopped in her tracks and stood strong, crossing her arms behind her back. Desti hesitantly stepped forward. There was a woman at one of the booths standing in front of a lit fire. She had speared scorpion roasting above an orange flame.

"Is that a scorpion?" Desti asked. Tate approached the table and said, "that smells great. Can I try one?"

Back in the city of Mors, their main source of food was potatoes and beans. Desti grew to love the blandness of their food. It was all she had known. She thought about eating the scorpion. Her body quivered with disgust as she shook her head. "Are you really going to try that Tate?"

He smiled. He always got a rise out of making Desti uncomfortable. It was his way of enlivening their melancholy life. "What? Does it gross you out?" he said while picking up one of the scorpion skewers. Tate opened his mouth and tilted his head back, slowly gliding the crispy scorpion body onto his tongue. With a swift crunch, he began munching down on it. Desti threw her hand over her mouth as she involuntarily gagged from disgust. "Oh, that's gross Tate."

"It's not that bad. Better than I was expecting," he said while still chewing on the tail. Tess approached Desti's side and stood next to her.

"Would you care for some soup then?" The sound of soup sent flutters to Desti's chest. *Soup*. She closed her eyes and imagined the warmth running down her throat. Desti lifted her arm and grazed her hand down her neck, lost in thought. Tess cleared her throat, snapping Desti out of her trance. Desti giggled and nodded, "yes, I would love that. Thank you."

They were almost out of the bazaar and entering where the living quarters were. Desti turned around and yelled, "Tate! Come on!" He was licking his fingers as he finished his last bites of the scorpion.

"Yeah, I'm coming."

Tate caught up with Desti and Tess, slightly trailing behind them. Desti had so many questions swirling around in her mind. *Where do I begin*? She leaned closer to Tess and asked, "how did you all survive out here? I thought no one could survive out in the Wastelands."

Tess smirked. Her freckled face wrinkled with a peculiar expression. "You've survived, haven't you?" She was right, but Desti wouldn't consider her situation surviving. More like mere luck. Desti twirled her hair around her pointer finger.

"Well technically yes, but that was just luck. How do you have a whole community out here? What do you do about the demons?" They were approaching a burgundy tent. Tess stuck her hand through the cloth slit and lifted the pathway open. She nodded her head and said, "after you."

Desti ducked under the curtain and ended up walking into a fortress. "Woah. What is this place?" She was surrounded by dozens of people. People who looked like they could kill you with a single look. There were long wooden tables stretched far across the back. *Must be their dining area,* she thought.

Beside the dining area was what seemed to be their sleeping corridor. Small cots stacked upon each other and sprawled out for half of the area. Tate followed behind Tess and immediately looked blown away by the elaborate details of the place.

"Woah, Desti. Check this out." He ran over the wall to his left and snatched a silver sword from a mount and began to swing it around. Desti giggled as she covered her mouth.

"Tate, put that down before you cut someone's leg off."

He rolled his eyes and set it back down. Tess had walked ahead toward the table in the back. She waved her hand, ushering them to come forward and follow her. Desti and Tate took a seat across from each other and waited for Tess to join them. A glass of water glided down the hardwood surface right into Desti's hand. She hadn't seen water in days. Her throat ached for a simple quench. Desti tilted her head back and gulped down the glass of water in a mere second, wiping the excess drips from the corner of her mouth.

"Thanks. I needed that."

As Desti finished her water, Tate too was given a glass. He followed suit, chugging down the ice-cold refreshment. Tess sat down next to Desti, one leg on each side of the bench. She slid a bowl of soup to Desti and cupped her hands, placing them on the table.

"So, you must have a lot of questions for me. I too have some of my own." Desti slurped down the warm broth and vegetables. It had been a long time since she had a bowl of soup. Once finished, she wiped the excess drops from her mouth.

Desti spoke first. She was never a shy individual and had no problem speaking her mind. Her body turned slightly toward Tess as she took a breath in. "First, I would like to know how you have survived out here. And how did you manage to attract so many people to your Resistance?"

"The word of our Resistance has traveled like an ember being carried through the wind. Spreading its flame across the land, igniting a light within those brave enough to join us." Tess took a sip of her drink, cleared her throat, and continued. "It started many years ago, just as a secret conversation between two lost souls. The destruction of this planet can push anyone into a state of desperation. And that desperation was the beginning of our resilience and our hope to give us back our freedom."

Tate was silent as he listened with full attention.

"So, all these people here are here because of rumors of your existence?" asked Desti.

"Isn't that how you got here?" asked Tess.

Desti leaned back. Tess wasn't wrong. She refocused her attention and said, "well, we found you by accident. Or at least Tate found you." Tess shot a side look at Tate. She lifted her finger and wiped her lip.

"Ah, I see. Your friend here is the true seeker." There was tension in the air. In Desti's chest she felt something festering, like a storm brewing inside her. Tess locked her gaze on Tate and gave him a flirtatious smirk. Desti never knew jealousy before. She never experienced it until now. But at that moment, she wanted to throw herself across the table and drag Tate far away from Tess. *Why am I feeling this way? We are just friends.* She tried to reason with her emotions and tried to shove them far down.

Desti cleared her throat to interrupt their intense stare. Tate had a hue of pink covering his olive complexion. He lost his focus and turned his attention to Desti. "What did you say?" he asked. "Nothing I was just about to say something to Tess." Tess slowly turned her head, with a slight smirk peering from behind her finger. She lifted her eyebrow and said, "yes?"

"You never told me how you are able to keep the demons out. How do you stay safe from their attacks?"

Tess dropped her hand back on the table. "Right. Those glowing orbs you saw coming into our camp. They protect us. It protects our camp from any of those things that crawl out from the Earth." She spat on the floor as she finished.

As disgusted as Desti was, she didn't react. She leaned forward, narrowing her eyebrows. "Light? How'd you get that? Don't you need to have power? I thought power was only given to demon-controlled cities."

Tess stood up from her seat, avoiding the question. "I have some questions of my own." She paced back and forth. "Like how you just so happened to be alive out there in the Wastelands, untouched and somehow Elijah was the one who got injured."

Desti had been so preoccupied by the explosion of her curiosity, she had completely forgotten about Elijah. She gasped and stood from her seat.

"Oh my God! Elijah. Is he okay? He needs medicine. His leg is infected."

Tate arched his head back, insulted by Tess's tone. "What do you mean Tess? Are you trying to accuse Desti of something?"

Suddenly the realization hit Desti in the face. *She is accusing me*. Her eyes lit with fiery anger. Rage began to build up from her legs and into her chest. "I am the one who saved Elijah from the Master's prison. He would have been eaten if it weren't for me. How dare you accuse us of doing something to him." Tess sat back down, quiet, and unbothered. "We will see soon enough. Why don't we ask him ourselves?"

Tate stood up as well. His hands still rested on the wooden table. "I would like that. When can we see him?"

"Woah." Tess threw her hands up. "Slow down. Not just yet. He is still recovering. Tonight, you can rest here and tomorrow I will take you to Elijah." She pointed over to the far end of the tent and said, "over there, you will find a bed, clean clothes, and a blanket. Please see yourself to it, and I will find you in the morning."

Desti nodded her head and held out her hand for Tate to follow. He grabbed her hand and walked as she guided them to the beds.

As the distance between her and Tess grew, she glanced back one time, only to lock eyes with Tess in an incredibly uncomfortable stare. The softness of Desti's lips brushed Tate's ear as she whispered to him, "I think she doesn't trust us."

And by the way Tate slightly nodded his head, she knew that her feelings were valid. He cupped his hand over her ear and whispered back, "I know. Don't worry. We have nothing to hide."

They reached their beds, a simple twin bunk bed styled cot. Desti grabbed her pair of black cotton shorts and white tank top that were laid out for her and held them up to her body.

"Hey Tate, does this outfit look cute?" she playfully asked as she twirled around the floor. Tate exhaled a small laugh. "You always do. Now go get dressed. We need to rest."

Desti turned her body around, hiding behind the backside of the cot. She pulled her new clean shirt over her body and slipped her legs into her shorts. Tate did the same. His arms lifted and tensed as he yanked his old shirt off. Desti couldn't help but stare at his chiseled abs. The details of every line and quivering muscle drew her in, as if she were being pulled into a different realm.

In her stomach, a fluttery tingle tickled her. She placed her hand onto her stomach as she quietly inhaled and held her shallow breath. Tate threw his dirty shirt onto the bed and in that moment Desti jolted her head in the opposite direction, hoping that he didn't notice. She couldn't figure out what was going on with her. *We don't look at each other like this. We never have*. She tried to reason with herself silently.

The past few days had been so chaotic and so stressful, she realized that she never got to ask Tate about what happened to him in the Master's chambers.

"Tate?" His eyes gave into her. His focus was only on her. "Yes?" Desti patted against the bed, inviting him to sit down. "What happened to you? When you were taken away." She was almost scared to ask. The stories she had heard growing up about the Master were terrifying and gruesome. She couldn't bear to hear about Tate's suffering, but she had to know. She had to.

Tate looked down, almost as if he was ashamed to speak it. "When Ms. Clyde took me, she shoved me through a door, and then all of the sudden I had fallen onto a boulder." His voice quivered. "It was dark and cold, and then I realized that I wasn't at the school anymore." Desti seemed confused. "Tate, I think you were pushed through a portal. I didn't know that those existed." He nodded. "I think so too. It has to be the only explanation."

"But how? How is that possible?" Desti searched her mind for a logical explanation. She was a critical and logical thinker. Portals weren't real, were they? Her eyes glazed over as she asked Tate the question that she had been avoiding.

"What happened to you down there with him?" She reached for Tate's hand. Sadness enveloped his eyes. "When I fell into the cave, the first thing I remember was the horrible sound of his chuckling. I can't get it out of my head. It was as if he was laughing at my misery."

Tate clenched his hand around Desti's and continued. "He grabbed me and dragged me to this room. He and his demons took turns tearing away at my soul. They stripped me of my bravery and pride until I was nothing but an empty shell. They broke me. I didn't even know that I could be broken."

A quiver of goosebumps ran over Desti. "I'm so sorry Tate." She stared into him. Past his eyes and into his soul. *I'm here. I'm with you.* "If you hadn't gotten to me when you did, I don't know what would have happened to me."

"He was going to eat you. I watched him tear away a man, limb from limb and eat the flesh from his bones. I knew you were next. I—" the pain of her recounting that was too painful. She hurled forward in a silent cry. One single tear splashed along her leg. Tate held her to his chest. The rhythm of his heart gave her comfort.

She inhaled. Embraced him. Embraced the warmth of his skin and the smell of his scent. Suddenly she snapped out of her thoughts, being guided backward by Tate's hand on her shoulder.

"What?" she asked.

"I said, let's go check out what they are up to over there."

Across from where the beds were, sat a group of young adults, who looked to be about in their early twenties. Back in the city of Mors, Desti didn't have many friends. She only grew close to Tate because they lived so close to each other and shared the same classes growing up.

History of rapture, farming, the hierarchy of Hell. It bored her to death. She fiddled with the bottom of her shirt in a nervous tick as Tate shoved her closer to the group. Desti wasn't surprised to see Tate walk up in such a sanguine way. He wore his confidence like a cheap bottle of cologne.

Overbearing and intrusive.

The two girls that were sitting the closest to him glanced up and smiled. "Come sit," they said, while waving their hands. "You too," said one of the guys toward the back. Desti was a fake-it-til you make it kind of person, and so she shoved down her resistance and approached the group with her façade of confidence.

Tate sat in between two of the females and Desti sat across from them next to the guy who waved her over. "My name is Matt. Nice to meet you," he said while holding out his hand. His short brown hair stuck up like spikes coming off his head.

Desti glanced at Tate and then back to Matt. She grasped his hand firmly and shook it. "Nice to meet you too. I'm Desti." Tate was introducing himself to the two girls sitting next to him. Clara and Tilly, Desti heard them say. Matt leaned forward with his arms resting on his knees.

"So, you guys are new I'm guessing. Where are you from?" Desti looked to Tate for reaction. She gave him a slight nod which said, *answer him*. Tate cleared his throat and leaned his body forward, reaching out his hand to shake Matt's hand.

"I'm Tate. We are from the city of Mors." A sonorous gasp rippled through the group, making Desti's confidence curl within her. She looked confused, and even more so couldn't understand their reaction to Tate's answer.

"What's wrong? Why do you all have that look?" asked Desti.

Tate too had a curious expression smeared across his beautiful face. Clara was the first one to break the silence. She sat up straight and said, "oh it's nothing really. We just have never met anyone from the city of Mors before."

Tilly jumped in after Clara and said, "yeah. People don't usually break out of there easily."

Tilly tilted her head and locked eyes with Desti and asked, "how did you guys break out of the city? The city of Mors is one of the most locked down cities around. Your Master is supposedly like a High King of Hell." All of this was news to Desti. *The hardest city to break free from. Where did they hear that?* Desti was even more confused now than when she was coming into the camp.

"I don't know where you heard that. I pretty much just walked out." Desti focused on Tilly and asked, "and you? How'd you guys escape your city?"

"Oh, you know, with lots of preparation and stealth." Tilly took a sip of her drink and Clara slapped her on the hand. They both exerted a cacophonous giggle that sent a shock of annoyance through Desti.

"Why was that funny?" Desti rolled her eyes. She wasn't used to typical girl behavior.

"Oh nothing. I think I've just had too much of my tea," said Clara while hurling over in a slump. Desti glanced over to Matt to her right. His lip curled into a soft smirk and held up his cup.

"Want some tea?" *Tea? What kind of tea?* She shot a sharp glare at Tate. It wasn't smart to take things so willingly, but Tate seemed to have no care in the world as he held a permanent smirk across his face, lifting his eyebrows and shrugging his shoulders. His eyes said it all. *Why not*? Desti mimicked his lifted expression. *Why not?* Maybe she was being too up tight. Too cautious. A sigh pushed from her lungs, and she shrugged. "Okay, I'll have some tea."

Matt stood from his seat. Desti watched him walk across the room to where the kitchen was. There was a large countertop with a pot of something, cooking over an open flame. Matt took a ladle that was hanging above and scooped some of the drink into two cups, stumbling his way back to the group.

"Here you are Desti." He leaned forward and handed Desti her drink, almost stumbling on his own two feet. "And here you are Tate. My new friend." Tate gave Desti the side eye as Matt smashed his cup into his.

A unanimous "Cheers!" reverberated around the group. All but Desti and Tate seemed to know what that meant. Quietly Desti mouthed, "cheers?" and shrugged her arms. He too was clueless to what the group was doing.

Clara and Tilly seemed to be lost in another world, slumped over on the couch. Tate scooted closer to Desti and Matt and asked, "hey man. What is in this tea? It's pretty good."

Desti took her first sip. The warm steam tickled her nose as she inhaled the floral aroma. It tasted sweet like black licorice. Desti had only eaten licorice once in her life, to even know how to make the comparison. A memory of when she was a child, celebrating her birthday with Tate played in her mind. He was the only person who had ever given her a gift. She didn't have many but those few sweet memories of her childhood felt like a distant dream now. Desti refocused her attention on Matt as he took one more sip and said, "it's a small mix of a few things. Our scavengers found a nice batch out on their runs." Desti took another sip. A shiver fluttered up her shoulders as she said, "mmh. It's so good."

The moon shone high above the canyon valley, beaming down milky streams of white. Through the small rips in the canopy, the rays peered through, illuminating the tent above them like a splatter of stars in the evening sky. And as Desti was caught in a trance, studying the glimmer of the stars, a gentle touch from Tate took her mind right back to him. All her worries, doubts, and reservations soon melted away until she felt as if her body and mind were completely weightless, freeing her from the burdens that held her down. The room suddenly exploded with color. A wave of ecstasy rushed through Desti. *Woah.* Desti expressed a permanent smile across her face and began to giggle.

It seemed that Tate too was beginning to feel the effects of the tea. His eyes narrowed and cracked a soft smirk from the corner of his lip.

"Do you feel it?" asked Desti.

Tate nodded his head in slow motion and replied, "oh I feel it."

A warm, tingly sensation rushed through Desti. She leaned back on the couch and grazed her hands over her neck. She inhaled slightly and closed her eyes. The gentle touch of Tate's hand on her arm broke her focus.

She opened her eyes. As Tate grazed his hand down Desti's arm, leaving only his fingertips gently touching hers, she bit her lip and exhaled. *We shouldn't be doing this. I shouldn't enjoy your touch this much.* The forbidden rule hung in her mind like a shroud of disappointment. Love was forbidden. Lust was forbidden. Touching like *this* was forbidden. The ones who ruled their cities were the ones who had a say in who would be paired together— strictly for breeding purposes. They needed obedient workers, and when that failed, they needed their food. Desti recoiled slightly from his touch. She knew it was wrong for her body to want it, but right now, it was almost impossible to resist.

"Follow me," he whispered.

At this point, Matt was practically passed out on the couch, slumped over a pillow with half his body hanging off the side. Tate grabbed Desti's hand and pulled her up from her seat.

When she stood, she felt like a weightless balloon, floating in the wind. She stumbled over her feet as she followed Tate over to their beds. All her suppressed emotions exploded to the surface. The sweet scent of Tate trailed behind him as he walked. Desti inhaled, savoring the rustic, earthy aroma trailing him. She loved everything about him. His braveness, his powerful demeanor, but the best thing about him was his loyalty to her.

She studied the details of his body upward, watching every flexing muscle as he walked. Desti sat down first. It was quiet for a moment, and her mind had shifted to somewhere else. Tate reached his hand for her arm.

"What are we doing Tate?" she asked. There was a somber tone to her voice. She looked over to him. "Why did we leave the city? Was life really *that* bad?"

She hated life back in the city but at least she knew that they were alive. Out here were so many uncertainties about her survival, taunting her, leaving her empty inside. *We shouldn't be here,* she wanted to say but it was as if she were fighting something. An invisible force that kept pulling her in.

A wave of electric current rushed through Desti. Her lips started to tingle. The tip of her tongue glided across her top lip, and as she finally stopped trying to fight that invisible force, she let go, lifting her hand to her lips. Her eyes drifted back to Tate. The golden flakes in his irises shimmered from the milky moonlight above. *He's beautiful.* His eyes could drift her away from any negative thought. There was a gentleness to them. Passion.

He reached for her hand and gently pulled it back down and said, "this is most free I have ever felt. Thanks to you." Their gazes locked. *Does he mean that*? Desti didn't give herself enough credit at times. She had almost forgotten about saving Tate from the Master. The thought of losing him was like a knife to her heart. It was unbearable. He was her best friend. Her everything, but was there something more?

Desti questioned silently in her mind, *is there more to us?* That phrase resonated with her. She was lost for a moment in the magical realm of her mind, feeling an array of ecstasy and euphoria, when the gentle touch of Tate's fingers guiding her chin forward broke her focus. His eyes said it all. *I want you.* She had never thought of him more than a friend. Not until now.

The soft texture of his lips invited her in. The tension in the air pulled her forward, embracing every ounce of him. Her mouth slightly opened as she passionately leaned into him and caressed his lips. Their tongues danced with the momentum of their breathing. Heavy and slow. She wrapped her arms around his shoulders. He tightened. She felt the flex of his muscles underneath her trembling hands. Her soul belonged to him.

The reminiscence of the forbidden rules got lost in the passion between them. "Tate, what are we—" she tried to speak but was abruptly stopped by Tate lifting her up around his waist and twisting her onto the bed.

"Shh," he whispered. She inhaled and bit her lip. Tate gently kissed down her neck, while his fingers traced the curves of her unexplored body. A slight moan escaped Desti's throat as she embraced his touches. The warmth of his skin touching hers felt like a gentle touch from the sun. Comforting. Inside, she exploded with pure ecstasy. She tightened her thighs as he kissed his way down farther. Desti clawed at the bed and arched her back in pure pleasure. In her whole life, she had never felt anything so good. She wanted him to keep going but—

"Tate we can't. Stop."

Desti rolled over and pushed Tate to the side. He was panting heavily, staring at her with a confused expression. "Why? What is wrong?"

"We can't. It's forbidden."

Tate went to reach for her, but she pulled into herself. "Don't. You know it's forbidden." That gentle glimmer in his eyes faded. Desti hated the fact that she caused that, but she couldn't risk it. It was too dangerous. Besides, she still hadn't made up her mind if she trusted these people or not. "We are here on a mission. We shouldn't let ourselves get— distracted." Desti slipped a glance at Tate's exposed abs. His shirt must have slid up when he was kissing her. He pulled it down and opened his mouth to speak but—

Suddenly, the voice of someone familiar burst into the tent, startling Tate and Desti from their erotic pleasures. Tate jumped back and Desti sat up, trying to fix the tangles in her hair.

"Hey Desti? Tate? You guys over here?" The frizzled orange strands of hair poked their way around the wall first, followed by her body.

"Over here," said Tate.

His words sounded as if they were being muffled by his overwhelming euphoria. He slumped over on the bed. "I see you've met Matt." Tess exhaled a small chuckle. Her fingers rested on the wall beside her.

"Go easy on that stuff. It'll make you do some crazy things." Desti lay back on the bed almost passed out. Her arm lay halfway across her chest.

"Okay, Well I will just see you two in the morning I guess." Tess turned around and left their small room. Tate crawled over to the bed and lifted himself up, plopping his body right behind Desti. She could feel the rising of his chest as he took in his breaths. Their legs intertwined and bodies curled up. She had slept next to him before but now things felt different. She should have shoved him away or made him go to his own bed, but the energy to do that didn't surface, so instead she just laid there until they both fell into a deep slumber.

9: Everything and More

IN THE WASTELANDS, THERE WERE NO ALARMS OR sirens that woke you up from your sleep. Not like how Desti would sometimes wake up before school. The city of Mors was more like a concentration camp, molding the people into perfect working soldiers into complete obedience. Sending children off to school until they were adults. They had to learn obedience and when that didn't stick, they learned consequences.

Desti's mind raced with intrusive thoughts of the days leading up to her escape. *Nash. Ms. Clyde. The Master*. There were so many uncertain scenarios that could be happening, and she wouldn't even know it. *Are they coming after us?* Desti slowly cracked her eyes open, only to be blinded by a stream of sunlight beaming through one of the rips on the top of the canopy.

She groaned and sat up. "Oh. What time is it?" she asked, while rubbing her eyes.

Tate was still half laying on her bed. *What happened last night?* The night before was seemingly a blur. Only being recounted as bits and pieces that didn't seem to match up. "Tate," she whispered.

Desti shoved her toe into his side and pushed him. "Tate. Wake up." The warmth of his side rolled onto her legs as he started to succumb to waking up.

"Oh, I feel like I got hit by a truck," he said.

Usually, his hair was beautifully styled with a lifted swoop, but this morning, his jet-black locks hung in front of his face, brittle and dry. Desti glanced down and saw Tate half-dressed and then looked at her half pulled down shorts.

"Did we—" Desti trailed off. *No, we didn't. I put a stop to it.*

Tate swiftly jumped in and said, "no way. I don't think so." A soft blanket of awkward silence enveloped over them. *Does he remember everything? Does he remember the rejection?* The last thing she wanted was for her to hurt him in any way. She was hurting too, because her body was yelling for her to let go and let him be with her, but her mind was the one holding her heart hostage. *We are just friends. We can't be together. It's forbidden.* She tried to reason with herself, but the sight of Tate's exposed muscular physique made it difficult for Desti to shove those urges down.

"Here, put this on," she said, while throwing him a shirt.

The ground was still cold from the brisk desert night air. It felt good on her bare feet. She stepped up and said, "I'm going to get some water. Do you want some?" Tate involuntarily mumbled, "yeah," as he held his head.

What did we drink last night? she questioned, rubbing the aching side of her head as she walked toward the kitchen to grab some water from the well. Soft chattering echoed around the camp from the other residents waking up.

There was a certain ambiance in the room, almost as if the people of the camp were under a spell. Desti held her glass of water in her hand and froze in the middle of the room. As if she were connecting the dots, her eyes jumped from one person to the next until she was facing toward the entrance of the tent. Standing at the center, tall and intimidating, was Tess.

Her vibrant orange hair almost glowed under the bright sunlight from outside. "There you are," she belted.

Desti almost dropped her cup of water in startlement. She pointed to her chest. "Me?"

Tess approached with a twist in her step. "Yes. If you don't mind, I will wait right here. Go get dressed and grab Tate too."

It was as if Desti was under a spell too. She nodded her head and shuffled her way back to Tate. Slamming the water down on the side table, she said, "Tate, Tess wants us to go with her."

He had just finished throwing on some clothes, a cotton T-shirt and black cargo pants. He stood up and threw Desti a pair of pants to change into.

"Here. Now you get dressed and I'll go see what she wants." Desti slipped out of her shorts and into something more tactical. She slid her small pocketknife into the right leg pocket of her pants just in case. *You can never be too prepared.* Desti threw her hair up into a high ponytail, whipping her bronze mane around as she walked with a swift pace. There Tate was, standing next to Tess. *She is awfully close to him,* Desti thought.

There that feeling was again, boiling in her chest. *Get your hand off him,* she wanted to say, but instead walked up with a smile and said, "alright. I'm ready. Now, what did you want to show us?"

Tess's eyes hid something. It was deep, but Desti could see it. There was no reason to yet, but for some reason, Desti didn't trust her. The bright sunlight blinded Desti as she exited their tent.

"Oh my, that is bright," she said while lifting her arm over her face. Everyone looked like simple mirages in the distance. She squinted her eyes and tried to stay focused. *Where did they go?*

Desti had fallen slightly behind, getting blinded by the beaming rays above. It was brutally hot. The sweltering heat caused her body to leak a constant stream of sweat from her face and neck. That was something that Desti never could get used to. She hated the desert air. Hot and dry. It was as if she were being cooked alive.

Desti inhaled a large breath of the musky air and glanced around one more time, looking for Tate and Tess. Her eyes skimmed over the market to her side and then past the tents along the other side. Dozens of moving heads in black clothing bounced around making it almost impossible for her to spot Tate. But then, she saw that beautiful mane of jet-black hair.

There he is.

Desti took off, leaving a trail of dust particles swirling in the path behind her. "Hey. Wait up!" Tate and Tess stopped and turned around.

"There you are. I almost couldn't find you," said Desti while gasping for air.

"I thought you were right behind us," said Tate. Desti gave him a sight nudge in the arm. "No. You should have walked slower."

The wind had an incredible force, blowing around her hair- like whips. Desti tucked the loose strands of hair behind her ears and asked Tess, "what are you showing us Tess?" She didn't reply. Tess turned around and ducked under one of the tents, disappearing into the shadows. Desti rolled her eyes. Tate's lip curled a little smirk as he shrugged his shoulders. "After you," he said, while bowing his body. "Ha-Ha, very funny," Desti said with a sarcastic tone. She went in first.

Tess was ahead speaking to one of the soldiers. The way they carried themselves sent a shiver down Desti's spine. These were people that you wouldn't want to cross, she thought.

Along the perimeter of the tent where, what looked like, medical beds carefully spread out. Most of them were empty, draped with tan linen. But then, someone caught Desti's eye. *Elijah*. Elijah was sitting up at the very last bed. She would recognize his short auburn hair anywhere.

"Tate, it's Elijah." Desti left Tate where he stood and ran over to Elijah. She didn't understand why she cared so much about him. She barely knew him, but something drew her over there.

"Elijah! You're okay." An overwhelming sense of relief swept over her body, leaving her feeling weightless from all the stress that surrounded her. Tate called out Desti's name, but it was as if his voice dispersed through the thick air, only barely reaching her. "Elijah. Oh my God. I can't believe you are okay. I thought we were going to lose you."

The color of Elijah's skin was still pale gray, as if all the blood had been drained from his body. Desti placed her hand on his and felt a slight twitch. He looked over at her and said, "Desti. I will be fine. Thank you for saving me. Both of you did." She smiled. "What happened to you?" Elijah tried to sit up but groaned from the weakness of his body. "When the demon got me, it injected venom into my leg. I would have been dead if we didn't make it here when we did." A slight chuckle pushed from Desti's chest as she said, "we all would have been. You probably don't remember but we were being chased by a horde of demons. I thought we were going to be food." Before Elijah could respond, the smooth voice of Tate saying, "Elijah. Glad you are alive," interrupted.

"Thanks. I appreciate that," said Elijah.

Tess had finished speaking to the guard and glided over to Desti and Tate. Her bright orange hair bounced with every heavy step.

"Good. You found Elijah." Desti twisted around when she heard the raspy voice creeping behind her. Tess placed her body close to Tate's and held her hand gently on his shoulder.

"This is what I wanted to show you. I had a very long conversation with Elijah, and it seems that my assumptions toward you were wrong. Thank you for getting him out of the Master's chambers Desti."

It felt good to be appreciated. Desti couldn't remember the last time someone, besides Tate, thanked her for anything. She cleared her throat. "Uh— of course. He helped us as well. We were a team." She glanced over to Elijah, curling her lip.

"Okay, so now that we have established that you aren't here for ill intents, maybe we could get more acquainted. What do you say?" asked Tess. *Do we have a choice?* Desti wanted to ask, but she didn't. She had been holding back a lot of her true feelings lately. Instead, she politely said, "sure. Lead the way."

Desti leaned into Elijah's ear and whispered, "I'll come back to check up on you." He gave her a nod and slightly reached for her fingers, but she pulled away, not glancing back as she followed Tess out of the tent.

Desti played with her fingers as she asked Tess, "so how did you find this place?" Her eyes squinted as she tried to blink away the sand particles blowing in the air. Tess guided them to her private home, a hut located to the back side of the camp. It was massive and draped with a beautiful deep blue cloth.

She ducked under and answered, "I'm the one who started the Resistance. I left my city years ago and over time I have gathered more and more people to join me."

She pointed to a couch to their left and said, "please have a seat." Desti and Tate took a seat on the plush fabric couch. Tess was in her kitchen grabbing some water. "Would you like some water?" she asked Tate while handing Desti a glass.

"Yes please. Thank you," he said.

It had been a while since Desti was able to drink clean water. Back in the city of Mors, their water came from a single well, located at the center of the town. It was hard work getting enough water for the day. It was always slightly off colored and smelled foul. She closed her eyes as she sipped the crisp liquid. This water was different. It tasted pure on her lips.

Tate sipped his in silence, waiting for Tess to take a seat. She leaned forward with her hands cupped over her knees. "So, you found the Resistance. What were you guys doing out of your city if you weren't searching for us?"

Tate shot Desti a glare. His eyes asked, *should we tell her?* She thought about it for a second. *Should we tell her?* Even though Desti didn't like Tess, she hadn't shown her a reason to not completely trust her yet. Her eyes glared back at Tate and said, *yes*.

Tate was the first to speak. He leaned forward and said, "I left the city looking for the lost Lux of the angels." Tess lifted her eyebrow curiously.

"The light of the angels? That is just a myth, you know?"

Tate was passionate about finding the Lux. It's what Desti loved about him the most. That he could find something to look forward to in such a desolated world. "But what if it's not just a myth. I have something. Look," said Desti. She reached into her pocket and pulled out the small leather book that she had kept tucked away.

"Is that—" Tess trailed off, grazing her fingers along the leather exterior.

"The Holy book," finished Tate. His voice trailed off, "but how?"

Desti had realized that she didn't get a chance to show Tate what Crazy Joan had given her. "But these are forbidden. Where did you even get this? I heard that all of them were destroyed during the Era of the Damned."

Tess was trying to take it from Desti's hands, and so she pulled back, shoving it back into her pocket. "My source will remain unnamed." Tess seemed intrigued. She bit her lip and arched her brow. "And you think that the two of you are going to what? Save the entire world?" Tess's voice rose. "Our world cannot be saved. Your only option is to build a life good enough to live out here."

"My parents were overheard talking about promising my soul to the demons of Hell, when I turn twenty-one."

It felt like a jab in the chest, admitting that out loud. Her whole life, she had never felt love from anyone besides Tate. Her parents were more like strangers to her. She recounted memories with her mom and dad. The only thing that resonated with her was the pain she'd feel from her father's calloused knuckles and the absence of her mother's comfort. But that's just how it was in the city of Mors. Love was forbidden. Desti used to think it just meant romantic love, but maybe it went deeper than that. The demons that controlled the world didn't want us to feel any happiness. Only suffering.

Her eyes glossed over and went blank. The gentle touch of Tate's hand on her shoulder brought her focus back to reality.

"I know it's a cruel world and all but damn—" Tess sat back and crossed her arms across her chest. Then Desti asked, "were your parents—kind?" There was a true curiosity in Desti's voice. Sadness.

Tess was quiet for a moment, but then answered, "I wouldn't know. I was abandoned when I was a child. I grew up under the control of the leader of our city. So no, I was not shown kindness either. It's why I left searching for something better."

Tess threw her hands up as if she were holding something on her shoulders. "This camp has been a true blessing and I have found happiness here." Tess brought her arms back down and said, "so, you are searching for the lost Lux of the angels. Do you know where to even begin?"

Desti's eyebrow arched. She had no clue where to begin. She had never even been out of the city before, let alone masterminded a plan to conquer the world back from the demons. She seemed to be in over her head. "I don't know. I don't what to do."

"We start simple. Start with what we can. Like your book. It must have some clues in there," said Tate.

"I know what we can do." Tess shot up. "We can start with battle practice." *Battle practice?* Desti had never battled anything before. She and Tate gave each other the same sideways look as they stood up too. Tess walked off in the distance and yelled, "come on! I'll take you to our arena."

***

They had walked all the way toward the back of the camp, into a cavern buried within the canyon walls. The sunlight was no more as they hunched their bodies inward the dark, vast hole. Desti paused just before entering.

"Uh—are you sure?" She glanced back at Tate. Going into a dark cave was the last place that she wanted to be. *This is where the demons live.* Her hands trembled as she clasped on to the edge of the opening.

"Don't worry Des. I'm here." The touch of Tate's hand gently pushed her forward, following Tess. It was cold and the only noise that she could hear was the sound of her heart slamming against her chest. There was a glowing light ahead. As she crept forward, things became clearer about what was in front of them. Her eyes shot open. Mouth dropped low. "What the—" She was interrupted by Tess's voice echoing toward her. "Welcome to the arena."

Desti's body reached the end of the cave, and soon entered a vast arena embedded deep in the Earth. "Tess, what is this place?"

"This is where we practice."

As soon as Desti entered the arena, her senses were assaulted by a cacophony of sounds. The sharp clinging of swords and thuds of mangled bodies being thrown to the ground reverberated through the air like thunder. There was screeching that felt like icepicks jamming into her ears. She threw her hands over her head to block out the alarming noise.

She stood above on a large ledge that encased the arena below. In it were dozens of soldiers, covered in blood and guts, fighting *demons*. Desti reached for Tate's hand and held it close to her. He stood by her side in the same statue-like manor. Her eyes locked with his. He looked frightened too. *I don't like this,* they spoke.

Tess walked over to a wall that held a handful of weapons. She yanked one of the swords off the wall and tossed it to Tate. "Come on. I know you'd love to get some revenge on one of those vile things." Tess spat on the ground. "They deserve it!" As she yelled, it was as if she unleased a sea of echoes, chanting in rhythm, *they deserve it*. Desti wanted to back out. *These people are crazy*, she thought. She tossed Desti a knife from the wall and took one of the spears that were left. "This one is my favorite," said Tess. She licked the tip of the spear, spilling a tiny drop of her blood on the blade.

"Tess, what the Hell is this? Those people could die down there."

"I know they could, but this is how we learn from the demons. This is how we learn how to kill them." Her eyes turned black. Soulless. Desti was frightened to even look at her. She cupped the knife in her hands and thought about jamming into Tess's heart. *We could kill her and run. And get far away from whatever this is*. But she didn't. She hesitated. This wasn't who she was. *Killer?* She couldn't be.

"Oh, come on. Don't look so scared. We have the demons chained up. They can't get away."

Desti glanced back down and saw them; the slithery, leathery, slimy creatures from the depths of Hell. And Tess was right. They were chained. But chains could be broken.

"Desti, you don't have to do this. We can go back to the camp." It was Tate. His voice was always so soothing and peaceful. It was the only thing that could break Desti from her fears. She thought about it for a minute. Why was she scared? There was no reason to be. Desti turned around and said, "no. Let's stay. Maybe we could learn something." Staying would give her a chance to learn more about the demons, but also, she would learn more about Tess.

Tess kicked a pebble to her side and ran down the spiral of stairs swinging her spear around in the air. "Oh my God, she's crazy," Desti said to Tate while walking down the stairs. They shared a laugh before focusing their attention on the arena before them. "You ready?" he asked. "No." Desti laughed, shoving down the fear into her chest.

There were four vile, slimy demons chained out there. Their teeth were sharp as razors, nipping at anyone who dared to get too close. One of them had a tail like a scorpion, shoving its stinger into the ground, trying to stab anything that wasn't inhuman.

Desti squinted. *Who is that?* A woman wearing black leather pants and black tank top, front flipped off the ledge and onto the back of one of the demons. She rode it like a bull, holding onto its horns for support as it tried to fling her off. "Woohoo!" she yelled.

The woman took out a knife stuck in the back of her belt and shoved it into the demon's neck, slicing it through the throat. Black acidic blood poured from its body, melting away the sand beneath it. A unanimous roaring of the crowd cheered as she jumped off its dead oozing body.

"Who is that?" asked Tate.

Her blood red hair hung down her back, delicately twisted into a braid. She approached, threw her knife down to the ground and said, "sup. I'm Rebecca."

Desti stood there like a deer in headlights. Tate reached out his hand and shook hers. "Hey, I'm Tate. This is Desti." Desti was still silent. Probably in shock at what she just watched. She blinked and then reached her hand out. "Hey, I'm Desti. It's nice to meet you."

"You too. So, Tess tells me you guys came in with Elijah." Rebecca held both her hands on her hips. "Well yeah, we rescued him from our Master's chambers and ended up finding this place."

"Lucky you. This place isn't easy to find." Rebecca was right. Finding the Resistance would have almost been an impossible task if they didn't just accidentally stumble upon it.

Desti was so curious about this place. About the people in it. She lifted her chin. "So, Rebecca, how do you guys catch these demons? I've never heard of anyone catching a demon before."

Desti recounted the long hours stuck in her class listening to Ms. Clyde rant about how demons could never be overpowered. That we all were just prisoners under them. Maybe she was wrong. Maybe the demons aren't as powerful as Desti thought. She glanced back up. Rebecca was about to answer, when Tess jumped into the conversation and said, "we have our ways of capturing them. Our soldiers train every day and are the best of the best." Tess was covered in silt and blood. Her face was painted like a warrior. The spear in her hand dripped a thick, black goo onto the ground.

"Is that—" Desti reached for the spear. Tess pulled back, "you don't want to touch that. Demon blood is very potent."

The howling of the remaining demons grasped the attention of the group. The giant worm-like creature was covered in spikes, slithering its way around the arena. *It looks hungry,* Desti thought. Desti was snapped out of her daze studying the creature by Tess shoving her spear in her face.

"Do you want to try?" she asked Desti.

"Oh—I can't. I don't think—" Desti couldn't finish.

"I thought you said you wanted to try." *That was before I got a closer look,* she wanted to say. She hated to admit that she couldn't do it. That she was scared to go into the arena. It was stupid and dangerous, she wanted to say. But she didn't. Desti took a step back and grabbed Tate's hand.

"I've changed my mind. Maybe we should go get something to eat and drink Tate." Desti yanked Tate's hand and pulled him back toward the cave that brought them into the arena. The white sunlight ahead lured Desti forward. She couldn't wait to get far away from that place. Once Desti burst out from the canyon, she hurled over in a panic.

"Desti, what's wrong? Are you okay?" Tate held his hand in between her shoulder blades. His touch sent a comforting energy through her.

"I'm sorry. I just couldn't do it. Something doesn't feel right."

His face squinted. "What do you mean?"

Desti inhaled and stood up. When she turned around Tate stood chest to chest with her, resting his hands along her forearms. He never lost his focus on her. His touch melted her body. His eyes stole her worries from her mind. She didn't respond, only peered into the iris of his eyes. *I see you.*

Desti leaned into him as she felt the slight brush of his hand grazing the side of her cheek. She closed her eyes. Safety. That was what Tate gave her. He was the only person who could make her feel safe in such a cruel world. His voice was a melody that sang to her deepest desires.

"I've got you. You're safe with me," he whispered. His touch was like magic. His scent, like a drug. *I'm addicted to you.* She could feel his body leaning closer to hers. The sweet hint of his breath brushed against her lips. Her mouth opened slightly, and she inhaled, tilting her chin upward.

"We can't—" she pushed him back. "It's forbidden Tate. I'm sorry. We can't." A flood of sorrow and regret streamed through her veins. Desti ran away leaving Tate standing there in her dust. She wanted him. She wanted him more than she had ever had him, but her fears of being caught ravished her desires and turned them into dust.

It's forbidden.

10: Discovery

A FEW DAYS HAD PASSED AND DESTI WAS seemingly isolating herself from the others. Most of her days were spent lying on her bed, counting the holes in the cloth ceiling above. Thoughts of the unknown clouded her mind with an intrusive feeling of despair. Her arm lay across her chest and one of her legs was slightly hanging off the bed. *My parents. What are they doing? Are they searching for me?* The fear of her parents finding her tore at her chest. It felt like a blanket of lead crushing her with every passing thought.

There were probably so many people after her. Ms. Clyde, the Master, her parents. All of which wanted to probably feed her to the demons of the Wastelands. She thought about running away, but where would she go? Then she thought about Tess. Something wasn't right with her. Maybe her whole life, she was programed not to trust people, and so that's what she did. Maybe she was being unreasonable. Desti sat up and gasped. "I need to talk to Elijah. He would know how to handle this."

***

Desti reached the tent where Elijah was being held. There weren't many soldiers around at this time of day. Daylight was their training hours. Most of the soldiers' had gone into the arena to fight and practice slaying the demons. Desti looked toward the auburn sky. *How do they get those demons?*

Desti realized that Tess still hadn't fully explained how they did it. She shrugged it off and ducked into the tent. There was Elijah laying in the bed farthest against the wall. He looked powerful. Strong. It's not how she remembered him. "Elijah." She walked up with a carful stride. Her eyes went down, noticing his bare chest and exposed tattoo. It was a tattoo of a broken cross. Her eyes studied it for a moment until she heard, "Desti. You came to visit."

"I wanted to come check on you. It's been a few days since I've seen you." She sat down in a chair next to him. "How are you feeling?"

"Much better. Thank you." Elijah pulled up the blanket covering his leg and showed her his wound. The purple oozing skin was no more and was now healed over, leaving a slight scar where the demon's razor-sharp tongue penetrated him. Desti reached for it and placed her fingers along the scar. "Does it hurt?"

"Not anymore." His hand gently pulled her hand off his scar and up to his chest. "You saved me Desti. I am forever grateful for that."

Elijah was a kind soul. She felt safe with him. Like how she felt when she was with Tate.

"I couldn't just leave you there to die." She was silent for a moment. "I'm actually here for a reason Elijah. Tate and I left our city looking for the Lux of the angels. It's the only thing that will be able to save us when the Master finds us."

Elijah leaned forward. "What do you mean, finds you?" Desti sighed. "You don't think he was just going to let me steal you and Tate away from him, do you? He is probably searching right now for us or has an army of demons searching for him. Along with my parents who want to sacrifice me."

At that moment, Desti felt so alone. So in over her head. Tate had been off sword fighting with Tess and Rebecca while she had just been isolated in her sleeping corridor. Elijah reached for her hand. "Desti, you are safe here. They won't find you, or Tate." She huffed out, blowing a strand of hair out of her face and stood up. "You don't know that, Elijah. They could be only a day away from us and we wouldn't even know it."

She began to pace from side to side. Her hands flailed in the air. "And I don't even know what is up with Tate. He's been acting like a zombie ever since we—" she paused. *Kissed.* She turned around, whipping her hair behind her, facing Elijah. "Look, the point is that we are not prepared for the what ifs. This place is great and all, but haven't you noticed that everyone seems a little off?"

Elijah lifted his eyebrow. "What do you mean?"

"You know, like hypnotized or something. Why does everyone seem to follow whatever Tess does? I think she is hiding something." Desti threw her hands on her hips. "Desti, you can't be serious. I've known Tess for years. She's been nothing but a great leader to this Resistance."

Desti grew passionate, throwing her arms up. "Tell me then, what have you guys done that has made a difference, except catching a few demons and fighting them? Why haven't you freed some of your cities?" It was as if her mouth had opened a dam of her most intrusive thoughts, spilling out like word vomit. Elijah sat back and listened as Desti ranted some more.

"And every time I try to ask about how you guys catch the demons, she changes the subject. She is hiding something, and I know it."

"Look Desti, I think you are overthinking everything. But if you would like, I can show you around. We can take a closer look at Tess's living space. How does that sound?" Desti rested her arms to her side. A calmness had now swept over her. "You would do that for me?" she asked. "Of course. You did save me from being eaten. It's the least that I can do."

Elijah had just finished pulling on a pair of black cargo pants. He wore a green military style belt around his waist. Desti tried not to stare but couldn't help but notice the decoration of scars that scattered across his side and chest. In each chiseled muscle, there was a mark, as if it were telling a story. She didn't say anything. Elijah grabbed his shirt and threw it on, and just before his head popped through, Desti turned around, not wanting to be noticed.

A burst of shivers ran through her body when she felt the gentle touch of his hand placed on her shoulder. She closed her eyes and inhaled. "You ready?" he asked. Her eyes opened and she turned toward him and said, "yes. I'm ready."

***

The sweltering heat from the desert air felt like she was being baked alive. Desti covered her eyes as she walked outside, blocking the sun's brutal rays from blinding her. To her right, there was the door. The entrance that she and Tate had so helplessly ran through. *We almost died.*

Desti slowed her pace, staring at the entrance door. If it weren't for the Resistance, they would have been eaten. She must owe them some kind of gratitude.

"Come on. Tess sleeps over here." Elijah waved his hand for her to follow.

Judging by the sun's position, it was about three in the afternoon. That meant that the soldiers would be done with their training soon. "We should hurry," Desti said.

Her feet scurried swiftly to catch up with Elijah. They had reached Tess's tent, which was draped with a beautifully detailed curtain. Inside, it was clean and organized. Her lip curled downward, "hmmm." *This looks like it would be her tent.* Elijah stepped forward, opening her drawers, and rummaging through her desk. Tess had a collection of old artifacts on the top of her desk.

Desti walked forward and picked up a cracked silver mirror. She couldn't remember the last time she had seen her reflection. Desti held it up, revealing her true self. Desti's skin was tanned from the brutal sun, leaving her complexion with a mixture of sunspots and freckles. Then she looked into her eyes. There was wisdom in them. Like as if they were trying to tell her something.

For a moment, she got lost in her own eyes, until Elijah, clearing his throat, snapped her back to reality.

Her hand fell, placing the mirror back where she found it.

"What did you say?" she asked.

"I said there is nothing here. See I told you. You have nothing to worry about." Usually she trusted her gut feeling, but Elijah was right. Tess had absolutely nothing in her room.

"Right. Well, thank you for bringing me here. I appreciate it."

"Anytime," he winked. Elijah held open the canopy of curtains to let Desti out. She leaned through the curtain, spilling forward her strands of hair like flowing water. *Maybe I was overreacting*. Desti felt defeated. Embarrassed. The Resistance had only shown her kindness and yet there she was searching through Tess's things as if she didn't trust her. *Is this all in my head?*

The loose string hanging from the side of her pants had been completely ripped off by this point. A feeling of guilt and nervousness took control. Desti held the string from her pants in between her fingers and twirled it into a little ball. She was silent for a moment.

"I think I will probably go find Tate now." She cupped her hands together and paused for a moment. Elijah's eyebrows lifted; he was about to speak when Desti embraced him with an awkward hug just before taking off to find Tate.

***

The people of the camp began to pool out of the cavern hole like a swarm of fleeing ants. Her eyes darted back and forth, desperate to see Tate. *Where is he?* Clara and Tilly were decorated with an abundance of cuts and bruises, and yet they came out giggling amongst themselves, as if it were just a normal day to them.

Desti ran forward. "Clara!" Clara and Tilly stopped in their tracks, still carrying their bloody swords in their hands.

"Desti! Why haven't we seen you in the arena? Tate has been doing so awesome." Desti slowed her pace and was now gradually walking up. The orange rays of sun peered through the cracks of her fingers that covered her face.

"So, Tate is with you guys?" Clara turned back, and as she did, Tate ducked out from the cavern hole. His beautiful jet-black hair dripped with sweat and blood. *Where is his shirt?* Desti got caught up staring at his glistening bare skin. It was as if the world had slowed down the moment she saw him. But why did it? She had never felt this way before. It was becoming impossible at times to ignore her true feelings that were trying to burst through the surface. He was her best friend. She had seen his bare chest before, but this time it *felt* different.

Desti shook her head. Maybe it was because she had been so isolated from him the past few days. Being alone truly made her crave the things that she was missing. *Him*.

"Tate! Hey—" she trailed off. Usually conversation flowed naturally between them, but this time, her mind went blank. Tate was different too. As if he was a stranger walking out of that cave. He gave Desti a slight nod and kept walking, talking to Matt.

Desti's head slanted, and eyebrows narrowed. *Why didn't he stop and talk with me?* This wasn't like him. Since she can remember Tate and her were inseparable. She knew his darkest secrets; he always made time to talk to her. Desti recounted the night he told her about his parents. About how they would punish him. His scars along his chest were so raw, so new then. The pain that she saw when looking into his eyes that night was the most vulnerable, she had ever seen anyone be. The city of Mors was a dreadful place filled with hateful people, but that's all there ever has been. She and Tate knew they wanted to be different. That's why they were best friends. He got her, and she got him.

So, why was he acting like a stranger? Desti ran forward but this time reaching for his arm. "Tate. Did you not see me? We haven't talked in like three days."

When Desti grabbed his arm, she could feel the rage within him flow into her veins. She let go, her eyes glossed over. "I'm busy," he said. His eyes were lost. Empty. She didn't see that special glimmer like she usually does. There was something off about them. Tate kept walking and caught up with a group of soldiers, as they all reenacted their battles from the arena. Like a pile of dust dispersing through the wind, everyone had left Desti standing there alone. A rageful confusion festered in her mind. Something felt off. Her finger rested on the tip of her chin. She had been acting differently too. It wasn't just Tate.

A brutal sandstorm was starting to blow through the valley and was picking up speed. It felt like tiny needle pricks when her hair whipped against her skin. Desti hurled forward as she ran, only seeing a few feet ahead through her squinted eyes.

The run back to her tent felt like she had run through miles of treacherous land. Her hand reached through the curtain door and pulled it aside. When she walked inside, everyone that was sitting at the table eating stopped, and glared right at her. Desti stood at the front of the curtain door, sandy, sweaty, and exhausted. *Why is everyone staring at me like that?* And there Tate was too. Giving her the same judgmental look. He sat next to Clara and Tilly and in front of Matt and Tess. There they were scarfing down whatever creature they had killed and made into soup, laughing. Then Tess nodded her head, and with a full mouth of food asked, "Desti. You want to come eat?" There was a smugness to her tone. It threw Desti off. Her lip curled down and scoffed. "No thank you. I am going to get cleaned up."

***

Desti lay there on her bed, feeling fresh. It felt good to get cleaned up. Her damp hair left a slight water stain on her pillow as she rolled over. Her small Holy book, that Crazy Joan had given her, was shoved away inside her pillowcase. She thought *we hadn't really tried to find any clues yet.* Desti twirled her hair around her finger, and then pulled the book from under pillow and held it in her lap. The tips of her fingers traced the stitching of the leather binding. It felt weird to be holding something so forbidden. Even though she wasn't in the city of Mors, she still felt as if Ms. Clyde would be bursting around the corner any second to drag her off to the Master for such a crime. Desti huffed out a large breath she didn't realize she was holding in her chest. She opened it up, to a page where there was a fold.

And in the darkened shadows, emerged the beasts of Hell. Unleashed from blackness, arose the veiled depths of the evil shroud. For those who suffer, in their peril dwell, enslaved by the beasts for their souls to sell.

Desti's eyes were locked onto the scripture. *What does that mean? Why would someone save this page?* She tried to make sense of the paragraph she read, repeating it over again in her mind. She kept reading, hoping that it would start to make more sense. Her finger ran along the page.

Fear not, for he who finds the Lux shall hold the light of the angels, power from the angelic beings, ability to shred the demonic bindings.

Her eyes went big. *The Lux of the angels. This is it.* Her first reaction was to find Tate and tell him that she found the scripture about the Lux, but the more she thought about it, the more it sounded like a bad idea. He wasn't acting like himself.

So, for now, she kept it to herself. Desti kept her knees bent and feet in the air as she lay on her stomach, reading through the Holy book. Without realizing it, Desti succumbed to a deep slumber, until she felt her body sway back and forth from Tate rocking her.

"Desti, wake up," she heard.

Her eyes cracked open. She rubbed the crust from the corner of her eyes and looked up. There Tate was holding a bowl of soup. She could still see the steam rising from the bowl.

"You missed dinner. Are you hungry?" he asked.

He looked at her with that cute smile of his. The one that she remembered from back home. The one that she grew to love.

"Tate?" She sat up on her bed and Tate sat next to her.

"Yeah, I got you some soup. I figured you were hungry." This wasn't like her. She was awkward. It was Tate. Why was she being awkward?

Desti grabbed the bowl of soup and slurped a few sips down. She closed her eyes, enjoying the warmth running down her throat and wiped the excess drips from the corner of her mouth. "Thank you. I was hungry."

When she looked up, she noticed Tate staring off past her, to her right. She looked over and realized that her book was still laying out. "Oh, Uhm—" she didn't finish.

Tate interrupted, "is that your Holy book?" In her mind, she was racking around what to say. She hesitated at first but then replied, "yes. I found something that could be a clue to find the Lux." Tate grabbed the book and peeled back the pages to where she had left off.

Desti watched as Tate read through the passages that she had read through. His beautiful green eyes swayed back and forth, emerging in the scripture. He then looked up. "I think we need to go search for it Desti." In her mind, she was reluctant. Where would they even begin? Desti reached for the book and asked, "why? Did you find a clue to where to search?" Tate cocked his head to the side and said, "sort of. Look." He traced his finger along the next page and read out loud.

"And so, it may not be where you seek, for he who finds the Lux shall hold the power of the true light, look not where you can see, but follow where darkness runs free."

Tate looked at Desti with a look as if he had discovered a new species. "What does that mean?" Desti asked. "I think it means that the Lux is not where we think it is but where we are least expecting it to be."

Desti huffed out a breath and said, "and where do you think that would be? The Wastelands are huge if you haven't noticed." A short smirk tugged at the corner of his lip.

"We just need to keep reading. There has to be a clue as to where we need to look." Tate ran his finger along the crème page and read aloud again.

"Where truth's radiance unveils, upon darkness' very edge prevails, to find the light, it shall be found in a realm that is not there, for darkness emerges everywhere."

Tate closed the book, keeping one finger inside the page he was reading. His golden-green eyes glimmered. Desti knew that look. *He figured it out.*

"I know what that means. It is saying that the Lux is hidden in the darkness of our world." Desti's eyes went big.

"And so—" she raised her hands and kept going, "our whole world is darkness. That could be anywhere." Tate threw the book down and grabbed her hands. His firm grip on her fingers sent a wave of chills up her arms.

"Where is the one place that people do not want to go? Where do they get sent to when they break a rule?" Tate asked. It took Desti a minute to think about it. She sucked in a gasp once she realized it and said, "the Master's chambers?" Tate stood up and paced around the floor. "I think the Lux is hidden down there. The Master must be hiding it."

"But how are we going to get down there without being noticed? That place is swarming with demons. Not to mention, the Master is probably really pissed since I broke you and Elijah out."

"Desti don't worry. This is what the Resistance is for. They are trained to kill demons. We can set up a team to take us down there."

"Why have you been acting differently? You seem like a different person at times." Desti's eyes shimmered with desperation for an answer. She bit the corner of her lip, wondering if she should have even asked him that. Tate glanced up, looking into her eyes. She expected to see annoyance or anger, but instead, it was Tate. The Tate that she grew up with looked back at her this time. He inhaled.

"I'm sorry. I have been feeling off lately, and you have been so isolated the past few days, that I thought you didn't want to speak to me."

Desti sat back on the bed, leaning onto her elbows. "Honestly, this place has been giving me off vibes too. I'm sorry too. I want us to stay united." She smiled at him, and at that moment, they had locked eyes. Tate mirrored her expression, smiling back with a softness in his face.

This was the Tate that Desti missed. The charismatic, optimistic guy. The guy whose eyes glimmered when he spoke about anything he was passionate about. Just for a second, she had almost forgotten about how weird everyone had been acting.

She bit at her lip and said, "okay. Let's talk to Elijah and Tess about it tomorrow. Okay?" Tate's midnight curls bounced as he nodded his head. He sat on his bed and said, "goodnight. I'll see you in the morning."

"Goodnight Tate."

Desti slipped her legs under her covers and closed her eyes. The distant noises of chatter and chirping insects slowly echoed away as her mind drifted into a deep slumber.

11: The Hunt

"DESTI?"

The sound of a familiar voice softly echoed through the darkness of Desti's subconscious mind. There it was again. "Desti?" Desti's mind began to succumb to waking up, as this familiar voice pulled her mind forward. "Desti, wake up." Suddenly, Desti sat up and gasped, frantically looking around. She looked to her left and now she was able to make the connection to whose voice she was hearing.

"Elijah. What are you doing here? What time is it?" Desti glanced around her. Tate was still sound asleep in his bed. It was still dark out. Judging by the moonlight, it was probably about three in the morning. Desti curled the blanket under her nails as she pulled it up to cover her chest. She waited for Elijah to answer.

"I'm sorry for intruding like this, but there is something that I think you need to see." A swirl of emotions ran through her body. Anger. Confusion. Curiosity. "Why do we need to see it now? What time is it?" Elijah seemed desperate. Desti tilted her chin up as she analyzed him. His eyes were big, and his body movement was shaky. "There is no time to talk, please just follow me. I need to show you something." Elijah held out his hand for her to take. She quickly glanced over to Tate sleeping. *Will he be mad if I sneak out without him?* They did everything together. Desti couldn't help but feel as if she were betraying him in a sense. A slight sigh pushed out of her chest as she threw her blanket off her body and took Elijah's hand. "Okay, I'll come see whatever you need to show me, but let's make this quick."

Elijah led Desti out of the living corridors. Now they were outside, under the milky moonlit canyon. The echoing sounds of distant screeches and howls made Desti tense up. Elijah looked back with a calming expression. "Don't worry Desti, those demons are far away. The Wastelands carry their howls through the winds at night. They may sound close, but they aren't." Desti gripped onto his hand even harder and whispered, "good to know. Thanks."

"So where are we going?" she asked. They were walking toward the back of the camp, past all the tents that were set up. When Desti looked ahead, the canyon looked like a tunnel of darkness, just waiting to swallow her up. She stepped back and hesitated. "I don't think we should go any farther Elijah." She wasn't scared. She was smart. Growing up in a place like this, it was known stupidity to travel anywhere so dark. So secluded. *Why would Elijah be taking me over here?* She questioned. Elijah turned around. He was so close that Desti could feel the warmth of his breath touch her cheek as he spoke. "I found something. After we checked Tess's tent, I just had a feeling that I needed to keep looking for something. She has been acting weird toward me too. Everyone around here has."

"Well, what did you find?" Desti asked, as she leaned slightly forward. She felt a slight tug on her arm pulling her ahead. Elijah's voice softly spoke, "just follow me. We are almost there," as he led her into the darkness.

There was what looked like a large crack embedded in the side of the canyon. Elijah held up a small torch and lit up the surrounding wall. Desti reached out her hand and touched it.

"What are these markings here?" Elijah touched the markings too. "I don't know what they mean, but I do think that they are a marker for this entrance," he said. Desti looked over at him. The warm orange glow from the torch outlined his face. "Well, what is in there?" she asked.

"I don't know. I haven't gone in yet. I just found this a few hours ago. I waited for everyone to fall asleep before coming to get you."

"You don't think we are actually going cave exploring, do you?" Elijah tilted his head to the side and lifted his shoulders. "Elijah, there is no way I am going into an uncharted, dark, mysterious cave without proper preparation or backup. We need to think this over. Okay?"

"We might not get another chance to see what this is," he pleaded. Desti rolled her eyes. She was too tired for any of this. "It's too dangerous. Tate and I are going to search for the Lux. We were going to tell you today. I can't be going off into dangerous situations right now. How about, when we come back, me, you and Tate will try to see what is in this cave. Okay?" Desti felt Elijah let go of her hand. He stepped back. "I'm sorry. You are right," he said.

***

They had probably walked about an extra two miles away from camp and so the walk back took about thirty minutes. Desti didn't say much on the walk back. Maybe it was because she was so exhausted. The more she thought about it, her whole life had always been survival. It was bound to take a toll on her. She pulled away a sweaty strand of hair that was sticking to her cheek and tucked it behind her ear. All she could think about was getting back to her bed and getting a few more hours of sleep. She felt the gentle touch of Elijah's hand tap her arm. "Here we are," he said. He had left her standing in front of her tent and walked off the other way.

Desti tiptoed her way back into the tent where the rest of the Resistance members were sleeping and snuck past their sleeping bodies until she was able to make it to her bed. She knew she had about another hour or so to sleep, and so that was what she did once she slipped her body under her covers.

11: Journey to the Unknown

THE DISTANT SOUND OF SOFT CHATTER ECHOED ITS way into Desti's subconscious until it broke her free from her deep slumber. She inhaled a huge yawn and stretched her arms over her head. As she sat up in her bed, she picked off the crust in her eyes and blinked.

"Good morning."

Desti glanced up to see Tate sitting on his bed, staring back at her. *He looks rather cheerful this morning*. After the long night she had, there was no way she would be able to match the energy Tate was giving off.

"Hey," she groggily replied.

"What? You didn't sleep well?" he asked.

"You could say that." Desti tried to crack a smile from the corner of her cheek.

"Are we going to search for the Lux today? I have already recruited a team to take us through the canyon."

Wow. "Already? Isn't it only like seven in the morning?" Desti asked. Her eyebrows narrowed to Tate giggling at her question. "No, it's almost noon. You slept in pretty late."

"Oh wow. I didn't realize that I had slept in so late." Desti paused for a second. "You said you gathered a team to take us to the Wastelands?" Tate's dimple appeared as he smiled. Desti leaned forward and started getting dressed. "Who did you get to come with us?"

There was a silent pause. Desti's eyes widened, and head tilted to the side. *Please don't say Tess.* Tate threw Desti a dark green jacket and said, "Tilly, Clara, Tess, and Matt." *No Elijah?* She tried to hide the fact that her face was full of disappointment. Tate didn't know the extent of her distrust of Tess. She swallowed and forced a smile on her face. "Great. What did they say? Do they think this is something that they can handle?"

Tate was bent over, putting on his black boots. Desti got stuck gazing at his perfect hair dangling over his face. "They all seemed excited for the opportunity to go out there and try to make a difference."

"What about Elijah. Is he coming with us too?" Tate paused just for a second before answering, "no I don't think so. I haven't seen him around." That seemed odd. Only because Desti was just exploring with him a few hours ago. She couldn't help but to think that something didn't add up. Before Desti could respond, she heard a call from outside their barracks.

"You guys back here? Let's go!"

Before Desti could ask who, it was, in popped a familiar and equally unsatisfying face. "Tess. I see Tate has recruited you. I hope you guys know that this is a very dangerous mission."

Behind Tess followed Clara, Tilly, and Matt. They all wore their best combat attire. Mostly cargo pants, crème or green colored, loaded with pockets. They each were decorated with an array of tools or weapons along their belts. Tess lifted a belt loaded with its own set of tools and weapons and threw it to Desti.

"We know. That's why we agreed to come. We have been waiting for an opportunity like this for years."

Desti held her belt in her hand, dangling it in front of her face, studying the weapons that they gifted her. Her eye was particularly caught by the shimmer from a small hatchet hooked through one of the loops. She could almost see a blurred reflection on the blade. Desti ran the tip of her finger along the edge, accidentally slicing a little too deep. "Ouch!" She pulled her finger to her mouth and sucked the drop of blood that was seeping from her cut.

"So, what's the plan?" asked Matt. Desti's eyes glanced up at him as she pondered what to say. *Plan? I haven't even had a chance to discuss this with Tate yet.*

Matt had such a desperate look in the glimmer in his eyes. When she looked into them, she could sense his desire for adventure, his yearning for purpose. She then glanced over to Tilly, and then Tate. They all too had the same desperation. She could feel how much this group had wanted to help her *or help their egos*. Tess, though, had a look of pure aggression, as if she were ready to take revenge on those who had crossed her. *Maybe we really can do this.* For the first time, Desti started to feel hopeful that everything would work out.

She snapped out of her thoughts and turned her attention towards Matt. The tips of her fingers clutched the leather bounding of her Holy book as she held it up. "There is a passage in here that we think it is leading us to the Master's chambers."

Tilly's eyebrows lifted as she stepped forward. "You mean the place that you rescued Tate and Elijah from?" She had a look of fear in her eyes. Not something that was common among their group.

Desti stood strong and said, "Yes that place. The book says that the Lux is hiding where we would least expect it. Somewhere dark and evil. Where else would that be?"

There was a unanimous look of hesitation that seemed to bounce off their faces before Tess stepped forward. Her voice was like a dagger, jabbing into her group and taking hold of their thoughts. "Look! We can do this, and we can truly say that we are warriors, or we can let them go alone and be cowards. Are we cowards?" Tess yelled. A cacophonous roar emanated across the room as the rest of the group answered, "Hell no!" It was at that moment that Desti realized how much power Tess had over her people. They looked up to her because she was fearless.

Tate stood off in the corner finishing up putting on his weapons belt. His peculiar smile was just barely hidden underneath his silky locks. He lifted his head and locked eyes with Desti. She smiled back at him. It had been a while since they locked eyes like that. She knew him so well. She knew the look in his eyes and what he would want to say. They had their own language that didn't need to be spoken. Tate grabbed a backpack from the side of his bed and handed it over to her. "Here. It should have everything that you will need." Desti gave Tate a nod and tossed the strap over her left shoulder as Tate did the same. The rest of the group followed, throwing their backpacks onto their backs as well.

"Well, we should get going while we have some sunlight," said Tess. Desti watched her walk out first, with such a prideful stride. She decided to fall back and walk next to Tate as the others tried to keep their pace with Tess.

***

The group trudged for miles, leaving the safety of their camp behind, venturing into the ominous uncertainties that loomed within the Wastelands. Every howl of the wind that blew past Desti's face made her fear creep a little closer to the surface. Desti held the hatchet in her fist, ready to attack anything that may leap out at them. She didn't want anyone to notice but somehow Tate did. The gentle touch of his fingertips touching hers distracted her from her intrusive thoughts.

"What?" she asked.

"I said, are you okay?"

Of course, I couldn't hide it from him. She smiled. "Well, I don't know. I am just—"

"It's okay. I'm nervous too. I know they don't seem like it right now, but I am sure that we all are thinking the same things." Tate nodded his chin forward, directing Desti to look at the group.

On the surface, they did look fearless, but he was right. Maybe they too were trying to hide their doubts from her. Desti's eyes squinted trying to block out the beaming white rays from the sun. The Wastelands sure were the epitome of Hell. As she pressed forward, each step resonated with the crisp crackling of the arid desert floor beneath her boots, intensifying the relentless thirst that clawed at her. Desti reached for her water bottle but there was only a little bit left. She didn't dare drink all her supply just yet. She tucked her bottle away and kept pushing forward, wiping the beads of sweat from her cheek.

The canyon that had kept her safe was now like a mirage in the distance, fading away with every step. Dusk was nearing soon. As the sun dipped below the desolate horizon, casting long shadows that stretched across the barren wasteland, an eerie stillness descended.

"Tess," Desti called out. The group stopped and turned. Tess didn't reply. Only nodded for a second. "It's getting dark. We need to find somewhere safe for the night." Tess held out her hand, pointing a dagger to her left. "Over there," she said. Desti squinted, trying to make out what she was looking at. There was a group of boulders off in the distance. "We will set up there. I will keep watch."

Desti let the weight of her shoulders drop with a breath of relief. She never thought that a boulder would make her feel so safe.

Now that the fading light was almost engulfed by hues of ashen gray and deepened shadows, an eerie otherworldly tension began to grow thick in the air. Amid the oppressive silence of the night desert, a haunting symphony unfolded as the demonic howls reverberated through the land. The air itself seemed to quiver. Desti jumped to the side, almost knocking Tate off his feet. "Did you hear that?" The group all stood in silence. She knew they heard the howls too. No one said a thing. They didn't dare. Tess swiftly picked up her pace toward the boulders and whispered, "Come on. Hurry."

The last bit of daylight was now fading into the abyss of the desert night. The group had managed to crawl into the crack between the boulders, using it as their barricade. There was just enough space for them all to huddle around, with their backs up against the cold stone wall. Tess sat at the front of the entrance, just barely within reach of the outside. Desti could hear the quivering in her shallow breathing. Her heart felt as if it were going to explode out of her chest. She reached her trembling fingers to her left, grabbing Tate's hand and holding it tight. He leaned in closer to her, wrapping his arm around her body as he pulled her in. She closed her eyes. The warmth from his body sent a feeling of security through her, melting away some of the fear that was weighing her down.

"I can hear them getting closer," whispered Tilly. Desti glanced to her right but could only make out the shadowy silhouette of her face. Matt expelled a deep chuckle, almost mocking the fear that surrounded the cave. "Ha, we will be fine Tilly. How many demons have we killed?"

"That was different Matt. We had the advantage. Out here, we are in their land—" Tilly's voice trailed off as a horrifying, gut-wrenching screech stabbed through the Wastelands. Desti threw her body back in fright. *Demons.* Their otherworldly howls cut through the silence like serrated blades. A panic began to fill the air.

Suddenly there was a glowing light that began to blind everyone in the cave. Desti squinted her eyes, trying to see where it was coming from. "What is that?" she asked.

"Shhh—"

"Everyone be quiet," Tess ordered.

She pulled out an orb, about the size of her two hands cupped together, and she placed it at the entrance of their cave. The light was nothing like Desti had ever seen before. It resonated with such purity and power. *Why do I feel power?* Desti's head tilted as she studied the orb. She wondered, why could she feel a power coming from this light. What was it? She had never seen anything like it before. It drew her in. Captivating her like a moth attracted to a lamp. The moment the white light emitted its radiance from the cave, Desti heard hissing and screeching coming from the demons that were hurtling toward them. It seemed to repel them, burning their disgusting rotten flesh with its light.

"Woah." Desti looked over to Tate and he too had an expression of wonder and fascination plastered across his perfect face.

"Tess, what is that?" Desti asked. Tess didn't answer. Another thing that annoyed Desti to the core. *Why does she have to ignore me?* She asked again, but this time with her chest. "Tess! What the hell is that?" The group sat back in silence. Tess turned her crouched body toward Desti. She almost let out a snarl as she curled her lip in fury.

"If you must know Desti, this is Holy light. I harnessed it. It will keep us safe in the darkness. Is that okay with you?" Desti threw her head back in confusion. *Holy light? How the hell did she get that?* Before Desti could speak, Tess said, "Look, we don't have time for twenty questions. Okay? We need to stay quiet. They are attracted to sound." Desti's shoulders relaxed, and her chest pushed out a sigh. "Okay."

Tate's hand never let go of her. She pulled him in closer and leaned her head onto his shoulder. Something that felt so distant now. She and Tate used to have sleepovers all the time, watching the sky from his window. Just his presence sent comfort into her soul. He was her best friend. That's what best friends were for. As Desti glanced up, looking through his tangled hair, she whispered, "Let's try to get some sleep." Tate cracked a smile and nodded. "Agreed. Sweet dreams Desti."

As the night progressed, the group huddled around, waiting for the warm orange rays of the rising sun to make their appearance, drifting into their unbothered slumbers.

12: Knocked Off Course

"DESTI! WAKE UP! THEY ARE GONE. THEY ARE ALL GONE!"

As if she had been punched in the chest, Desti sat up and gasped. "Tate? What do you mean they are all gone? Where did they go?"

"I don't know."

The sun was now illuminating its radiant glow throughout the horizon, so she knew that it was safe to leave the cave. Desti dipped her head forward, crouching through the crack that had given them shelter and security, and emerged into the vast emptiness of the Wastelands. Tate's silhouette stood in front of her as he peered from side to side, looking for any sign of where their group had gone. Desti stepped forward and placed her hand on his shoulder.

"Do you think they got cold feet and decided to go back to the camp?" Tate was holding something in his hands. Desti saw a flash of silver peaking between his fingers.

"What is that?"

Tate turned and held out one of the daggers that one of their group members had. "I don't think they went back to the camp Desti. Look." As Desti studied it even further, that's when she saw it. Blood. Blood streaked onto the cold sharp blade that was supposed to keep them safe. Desti stepped back in disbelief.

"Whose blood is that?"

"I don't know."

Tate was quiet. It was something he did when he was stressed. Desti knew not to pry too much. She too was stressed and trying not to panic, but panicking was difficult to suppress at a time like this. Desti began to pace, kicking the rocks and sand into a twirling storm around her feet. "Do you think they are alive?" Her arms unwillingly flailed in the air as she tried to make sense of what was happening.

"I don't know. I don't know what happened, but I don't think it's good," he replied.

"Well, we have to go look for them, Tate. They can't be too far, right?" Desti's voice cracked with desperation. The last thing that she needed was to be stranded in the Wastelands. Tate's eyes had a glimmer of bravery. She locked eyes with him, just for a moment before he began walking heavily in the direction of the mountains.

***

Under the relentless gaze of the scorching sun, Desti trudged wearily through the vast expanse of the unforgiving desert. Her body ached with every heavy step. She licked her lips, trying to give them the last bit of wetness her mouth had.

"Tate, how much farther? I don't think I can go on any longer."

Desti reached out her hand and tugged at Tate's shirt. His sweat had soaked through the fabric, making it difficult to grasp onto him. Tate suddenly shifted his weight and halted.

"Are you okay? It's not much longer. I think we are almost there." Tate held up the blood-covered dagger and pointed to a mountainside, sharp and serrated. Even from afar, it was intimidating.

With a heavy breath, she asked, "Is that Rotten's Crude?" Immediately there was a pit in her stomach. She clenched her shirt and hunched over just thinking about it. The last time she was in Rotten's Crude was when she was almost eaten by the Master's horde of demons. That horrid memory swept its way through her mind, causing her to pause in a moment of hesitation.

Tate opened his bag and reached for his canister. "Here, you have the rest of my water." Without hesitation, Desti gulped down the rest of the water that Tate had in his canister. Her eyes shut and chin tilted as she indulged for just a moment. "Oh, that was so good. Thank you."

"No problem. Are you ready?" he asked. The wind carried his hair in such a way, that even in those relentless conditions of the desert, he still looked majestic. Desti smiled and answered, "Ready as I'll ever be. Do you really think they are in there?"

"I hope so."

***

There it was. Rotten's Crude. The cave system Desti so perilously escaped. *I can't believe we are going back here.* The jagged rocks framing the entrance seemed to echo the haunting whispers of their recent encounter with the demons. The air hung heavy with an ominous stillness, and a cold breeze wafted out from the depths of the cavern. Desti slowly reached for Tate's hand, wanting to feel a sense of comfort, and familiarity. He squeezed it tight and looked over. "You ready?" he asked.

"Mhmh," she nodded. They stepped into the blackness of the cave, being engulfed by the pitch darkness of the unforgiving Rotten's Crude.

12: The Unforgiving Rotten's Crude

THE AIR WAS THICK AND MUSKY, MAKING EACH inhale feel like a reluctant surrender to the unknown. Desti reached for her flashlight from her bag and turned it on. She was grateful that the Resistance had salvaged them. Flashlights were a thing of the past, of the time before, but somehow, they found some *and* got them to work. The only sound she could hear was the occasional drip of water falling from the stalactites hanging above. She raised her light upward, staring face to face at the cave's razor-sharp rocks. Each inhale became heavier with every step deeper into the cave.

"You, okay?" Tate asked. There was something so calming about his voice, something that always seemed to bring Desti back down to her true self.

"Yes. Just try not to make too much noise. I don't want anyone to hear us," she whispered. "Does any of this look familiar to you, Tate?"

"Not really, but the last time we were in here, I wasn't really paying attention to the décor of the cave." Even though it was dark, Desti knew that Tate had a stupid smirk on his face. He always loved to poke fun at her.

***

Before she knew it, hours seemed to pass by.

"This cave just keeps going. Do you see any openings or other passageways?" she asked. Tate stopped moving and stood in the center, with his feet just barely in a small puddle of water. "Shh. I think I hear something."

Suddenly Desti's heart began to pound. She heard something too. The sound of not-so-distant chatter. It sounded like it was getting closer.

"Tate, quick. Hide!"

Desti yanked on Tate's shirt and pulled him behind a boulder off in the corner. The light switched off, leaving them in complete darkness. The echoes from the distance soon became so close that their deep rumbling voices reverberated around them. Desti felt the heaviness of their tones penetrating her ears.

She squirmed, realizing that the voices she was hearing were coming from demons. They had their own language. Unknown to her and most of the rest of the world. Her back sat firmly against the cold stiff boulder as she held her breath, nervous to make any kind of sound that would draw attention. *I wish I knew what they were saying to each other.*

Desti gently reached for Tate for a sense of comfort. Suddenly a dim orange glow appeared from the far end of the cave. Desti peeked her head carefully around the corner from where she was hiding and watched as those vile creatures dragged her friends into another opening. *It's them!* She wanted to shout. Desti wanted to leap from the darkness and take the demons by surprise, but she held back. That would be a suicide mission. She had to think clearly. Come up with a plan. *Where are they taking them?* Desti and Tate waited until the cave was once again a chamber of darkness. She let out a sigh, releasing all the pressure that she held in her chest.

"Tate, did you see that? I saw them. They were being taken somewhere."

"Where do you think they are taking them?"

"I don't know but we need to go follow them." Desti crouched down and quietly went into the tunnel where she watched her friends get dragged as Tate followed behind her.

"Shh. I can hear your footsteps from all the way over here."

"I'm sorry Des. I can't see the ground very well."

"Well, why don't you keep up that wat you can be closer to my light then?" Tate scoffed. "Sure, okay your highness." Tate playfully shoved Desti's shoulder as he stepped closer.

"Shh. We don't have time to goof off. Now come on. They went this way."

There was a sharp turn up ahead. Desti reached out her hand and grabbed Tate's, not wanting to lose him. She knew there could be anything around that corner and holding Tate's hand gave her a sense of security. An orange glow illuminated from around the corner as she approached.

"There is someone there," she whispered. Desti cautiously scurried along the cold stone wall, letting the rough texture scrape against her palms as she pressed forward.

Desti peered her head around the corner slightly, trying to see what was around the bend. Her chest was tight. Holding her breath made her feel like she was going to pass out. There they were. Standing along the wall. Tess, Clara, Matt, and Tilly. *What are they doing?*

"They're here," she whispered.

"What are they doing?" Tate asked.

Desti took one more glance at her friends. She was confused. They all looked like mindless robots. No chains or restraints, and yet they weren't trying to escape. *What is going on?* Desti looked back at Tate, staring into his dimly lit eyes.

"They are all just standing there. But I don't see any demons." Tate took hold of his knife and Desti did the same. She didn't have to speak to know what Tate was going to say. *Ready?* His eyes said. With hesitation, she gave him a nod and ran into the room to save her friends.

"Guys, it's us," she whispered. Desti frantically glanced around the room, terrified that something was going to attack her from behind. Tate ran to Matt first and grabbed him by his shoulders.

"Matt, it's me, Tate. Come on let's get out of here." Matt seemed lost in a daze. They all did. Desti took a step back as tears began to gather. "Tate, something isn't right. Look at them." Desti waved her hand in front of Tess's face, and yet there was no response. "What is wrong with them?" Tate asked. Desti didn't know how to answer. She had never seen something like this before. "I— I don't know. They all seem hypnotized or something."

Desti tried a more aggressive approach and slapped Tess across the face. *That felt good*, she thought. Nothing. It was as if she and Tate were talking to a group of statues. The cave was so dense, so muggy, that every inhalation felt like her lungs were grasping for air. Desti coughed into her arm, as she struggled to breathe, but as soon as she finished, she froze.

"Desti, that was loud. Do you think they heard that?" Before Desti could answer, she was blinded by a bag being forced over her head. Fingers dug in deep into her arms as she was dragged off. "Tate! Tate! Where are you?" she screamed.

"Desti!" Tate yelled back. Their screams echoed through that cavern as they were dragged away.

***

With a heavy thud, Desti and Tate were thrown onto the dirty floor. She heard the clinking of a metal door slamming shut. Her trembling fingers reached for the cloth over her head and yanked it off. It was in that moment that her whole world came crashing down on her. She sucked in a gasp, unable to hold back the shock of what she was seeing.

"Elijah? What is going on?" she cried.

Tate took his blindfold off too. Desti looked over at him with bloodshot eyes, only to see the same expression smeared across his face. "What the Hell Elijah? What are you doing here?"

His eyes were black. Cold. Soulless. His voice even seemed to change. "You two are so stupid. Look at you now. Back right where we first met." Desti glanced around the cell. Each corner and wall were littered with insects and mold. *He's right. This is where I found him.*

"Elijah, I don't understand. Why are you doing this?" The tears were almost too powerful to hold back as they streamed down her cheek. There was a moment of silence before he answered. "Don't look at me like that Desti. You know how hard this world can be. I was tired of living in the shadows, scared of when I might be the next sacrifice. It was time I took control and did something. Change something," he growled.

Tate spat on the floor. "You're crazy man." Desti thought maybe she could get through to him. She stepped forward, wrapping her hands around the cold metal bars. "Elijah, what do you mean? You had the Resistance. Why would you turn on them?"

Elijah's voice got louder. "You think I wanted to spend the rest of my life hiding away in that canyon? I took control. I was granted power. Protection. All I had to do in return was turn the Resistance and make them see my vision. For the Master." It was as if an ice pick had stabbed her in the chest. She trusted him. How could he do this to her? "The Master? Elijah, you can't trust the Master."

From the corner of the room, Tate interrupted. "How?"

"How did you turn them? What did you do to them?"

Elijah snarled, flashing his sharp teeth. "It was easy. Demon blood. I put it in the food. It changes people slowly. They forget who they are and are easily controlled. But what I don't understand is why you two weren't affected."

"Demon blood? Are you serious? You have been poisoning us with Demon blood?" Desti felt an overwhelming rush of disgust run through her body. How could she not see through his act? She thought about Tess. Desti knew that she didn't trust her, but she couldn't help but to almost feel guilty for judging her so quickly. *It wasn't her fault.* Desti snapped herself out of her thoughts. Anger was building in her eyes. "That is how you were able to get those demons down in the arena. Because they were working for the Master, and you were working for him too. You used the slayed demon blood to poison us."

Elijah began to clap. He paced back and forth with an evil grin gripped to his face. "Congratulations. You figured it out. But what I can't figure out is you two. It should have had an effect on you by now." Desti looked back at Tate. She reached for his hand. His touch is what she needed. The fear and anger were becoming too much for her to bear. "You Tate. I almost had you. You were changing, but what happened?"

"Elijah, this will never turn out the way you want it to. The Master can't be trusted." Elijah slammed a knife against the cell bars. "Silence! We have a plan. He can see my vision. With our new army of people, we will be able to infiltrate every city and take control of those who look to undermine us." Elijah was too far gone. Too deep into his delusions for Desti to be able to reason with him.

"But we found you locked up in *here,*" she cried. "I don't understand."

He glared at her; his piercing eyes just visible through the metal bars. Elijah smiled. "That was a misunderstanding. The Master can be ruthless at times, and I failed."

"So, why on Earth would you go back to him Elijah? Why?"

Elijah slammed his fists against the bars, standing dangerously close now. Desti could feel the warmth of his breath seep out between his crooked smile. "Because, in this world, you are either a master or a slave and I will be no one's slave. With the Master, I have *power*. I have an *army*. I shall not fear anymore."

She tried to hold back the tears but couldn't resist anymore. Desti fell back into Tate's arms as she cried helplessly on his shoulders. Elijah stepped back, seemingly bored that Desti had given up. He scoffed, walking away, fading into the shadows of the cavern.

"Desti, he is gone," Tate whispered. Chills crept down her back from the touch of Tate's fingers running through her hair. He had never held her like this before. Not with such passion. She didn't want to let go. Her fingers clenched deeper, holding onto his arms. "What are we going to do Tate?"

"We just need to figure something out. Don't worry. We will figure this out." Desti pushed off, facing toward him. "But how? We are literally trapped in a cell underground surrounded by demons. How will we get out of this?" Desti cried. Tate looked as if he wanted to reply but words wouldn't come out of his mouth. She knew that he was feeling the same way. "See, you know I am right. We are going to die down here, Tate." Tate pulled Desti into his chest as he embraced her. She squeezed tightly around his body and buried her head under his arms. The only sound that lingered was the occasional dripping of the stale water coming from the cave ceiling. It dripped onto Desti's face. She glanced up and opened her mouth, letting the water drip into her mouth. When she finished, she placed her head back into his chest. "I'm so tired."

"It's okay Desti. Close your eyes, I will keep watch." The heaviness of her eyes took over. She couldn't fight it any longer. Desti closed her eyes succumbing to her exhaustion.

13: No Way Out

"DESTI. DESTI. WAKE UP," TATE WHISPERED. HIS voice danced its way into her head until she groggily opened her eyes. For a moment, she was peaceful, that was until she remembered where she was. "Hey. How long was I asleep for?" She picked herself up and sat against the wall. "If I had to guess, maybe a few hours. Time is different down here." Sweat seemed to keep pouring from her pores. She pulled away a strand of hair stuck to her cheek. "Has Elijah come back at all?" she asked. "Not yet. Maybe now is the time to think about how we can escape."

Desti scoffed. "Psh – Yeah okay. I don't see any way for us to get out of this Tate." Tate pulled out his knife and placed it into Desti's hand. "We have weapons. Don't give up so easily." She played with the blade, dragging it along her fingers. "Okay, so let's say that we attack whoever comes to grab us. Then what? We stab our way out of here?"

"It's better than not having a plan at all. I will protect you until the end of the Earth. You are the only thing that keeps me going." Tate lifted Desti's chin. She had refused to let herself get too close. To allow herself to feel those urges. Why did it matter anymore? Who was she trying to obey? Desti leaned into his touch, placing her hand over his. "Tate?" She paused. "You have always been the only one who has kept me going too. In a world like this, you made it worth living." The tension was almost too strong to ignore. Desti bit the side of her lip. Her tongue flicked across the bottom of her teeth. She could feel the heavy pounding of his chest the closer he leaned in.

The warmth of his breath gently caressed her bare neck. He leaned in closer, gently kissing her until her body began to tremble. The moment she felt the softness of his lips touch her body was when an explosion of ecstasy ran through her. She gasped. Her back arched as she pulled him closer. "Kiss me," she whispered under her breath. Her fingers grasped the curls of his head as she pulled his face onto hers. In that moment, there was nothing but them. The world seemed to stop, encasing them in their own pleasurable reality. For once, her mind had been swept away from the horrors of her world, catapulting her into somewhere worth living.

Their dreamy fantasy was suddenly shattered by a gut-wrenching screeching. Desti threw her body back. "What was that?" Tate stood up, holding his knife in his hand. "I don't know."

The horrific sounds grew louder as they echoed. "They're coming for us Tate. What do we do?" Desti stepped behind Tate, trembling.

A snarl pierced its way into her ears. That was no demon. It was too sophisticated. "Desti," the voice tailed off. She had never heard her name said in such a way. Such horror. Desti sucked in her breath, trying to stay still. "We've been searching for you," the voice trailed off again. *Me? Why me? Who is that?* Fear seemed to be crawling its way over every nerve in her body. "Tate?" she cried in a whisper.

From around the corner, there he appeared. She never thought she would ever see him again. His towering dark body stood over them like a growing shadow. He dragged his claw-like fingers across the wall, piercing their ears with a sharpness. Desti and Tate threw their hands over their heads in hopes of muffling the sound. She stood cowering behind him. The Master. Desti tried to speak but couldn't let go of the clutches of her terror. "Mm—Mas—," she couldn't say it. Master. She could barely breathe. Tate stepped forward, pushing Desti even farther behind him. He held his left hand behind his back, clutching onto a small knife. "I'll protect you," he said softly. Maybe he truly meant it, but Desti knew there was nothing they could do. She sobbed silently, knowing that there was no way to escape.

"You are a difficult one to track down. I don't like it when people disobey me. There are consequences you know?" Hate and anger festered in her. "Yeah, well I don't like it when my friends are held captive," Desti spat on the floor, nearly hitting his hooved feet. The Master snarled. His glare was striking. Like a dagger to the face. With the swift force of his arm, he ripped the metal door with one yank, tossing it behind him. Tate threw his body backward onto Desti's. She could feel him trembling. Tate always tried to hide his emotions. He was always tough. But this was something even he couldn't hide from.

The Master stomped forward and grabbed Tate by the head, digging his claws into his scalp. Desti cried. Watching as her only meaning to survive was dragged off into the darkness. "Tate! No! Please don't take him!" she cried helplessly. Desti fell to the ground. Her finger soaked in the reminiscence of his blood. As she tried to stand up, to run after him, she was smacked in the face with a heavy hit.

***

Blackness swirled around like a relentless storm. Desti reached for her throbbing head and touched just slightly above her ear. Her head felt wet. More wet than it should be. *Is that blood?* Desti brought her red soaked hand in front of her face. It was too dark to see fully but the smell alone gave it away. *What did they hit me with? Where am I now?* Her ears perked up to the sound of something in the darkness. *What is that?*

Ravished by fear, it was difficult for her to focus. Ahead, a large fire emerged from a pit. That was when she saw it. The room she first had laid eyes on the Master. But this time, she was the one who was helpless. Desti glanced to her left and found herself staring at a large boulder. The blood stains seeped down until they tarnished the ground. Desti's eyes grew big. That was when she realized. *This is where he ate that guy*. Heavy breathing took control. She wished that someone would come to rescue her like she did for Tate.

The fire emitted an eerie orange glow. Dark shadows began to emerge from the cracks of the cave. She focused her eyes and gasped. Demons, everywhere. Disgusting creatures. Desti thought back to the days she was in school. Learning about the demons never fully painted their true picture. They were hideous and equally terrifying beings. Their sounds alone would give children nightmares. They would crawl their way into their minds like a parasite. Planting their evil harmonies until it would drive someone mad. She was scared. More scared than she had ever been. "Where's Tate?" she whispered to herself. Desti felt desperate to find him. Just as she went to take a step to the side, she was pulled back. "Ugh, what is this?" She reached down and touched something heavy and cold. In her hands, she held a rusty chain that was wrapped around her ankle.

It wasn't long before her attention was grasped by a familiar voice. "Where is she? Where did you take her?" Desti gasped. *Tate.* A sense of relief rushed over her. Tate was across the room, hanging by his arms between two posts. Desti frantically searched for something, anything, that could release her from her chains.

"Desti is the last of your worries, boy," snarled the Master. His voice disgusted Desti to her core. There was something about it. Tears pooled in her eyes as she helplessly watched Tate from across the room. "I have to help him. I have to get out of these stupid chains." Desti's voice was a mere whisper. She couldn't help herself.

Tate spat on the ground. His face was dirty and defeated. Not a look that she was used to seeing on his face. "You won't get away with this," he said. Tates voice cracked with anger. She glanced around some more. Along the walls of the room, there stood the rest of her friends, trance-like. *Come on guys. Someone do something. Please.*

Once again, the Master snarled. "It is time."

Time for what?

As if Desti had been sucked into a horror novel, she watched helplessly as the Master began to chant. Surrounding him were his vile minions. The demons she so intensely despised. They were speaking another language. Something that Desti had no clue how to decipher. Suddenly her heart sank. She knew something terrible was about to happen.

"The time has come, boy. Your punishment," the Master growled. His voice was deep. Evil.

They couldn't possibly still want to punish Tate for the rules that he broke, she thought. Desti watched as the Master raised his razor-sharp claw-like fingers and with one swipe, slashed across Tate's ribcage. His skin tore so easily, like a hot knife cutting through leather.

Desti couldn't just stand there and watch her best friend get mauled. She started digging through her pockets, looking for anything that could help free her. *Where is it? Where is it? Where is my knife?* It must have been snatched when she was knocked unconscious. Something small and cold brushed the tips of Desti's fingers as she rummaged through her clothing. She lifted her hand, staring at a small cross necklace. *I forgot. I had this with me.* Desti put it on – for good luck. She kept looking. For anything. Suddenly her hand reached down grasping onto a large rock. Desti didn't have time to think. Just act. With all the strength she had left in her body, she began smashing the side of the chain until it cracked.

Yes!

Desti stood. The demons paid no attention to her. It was as if they too were in a trance. The Master had gotten a few slashes in, ripping Tate's body to a state that she had never seen before. There was blood everywhere. She was running out of time. Tate was running out of time. The Master lifted his hand once more. Desti knew that he was going to kill Tate. She ran as fast as she could. "No!" she screamed. And as the Master's hand came crashing down, Desti jumped in front of Tate, taking his claw to her face.

14: Hidden

EVERYONE WAS BLASTED WITH A WHITE LIGHT, and what once was a room filled with danger lurking at every corner, was now a room covered in ash. It took a moment for Desti to succumb to the reality of what had just happened. She scurried backward. The pebbles on the ground felt like tiny pricks on the palms of her hands.

"Tate?"

Tate was behind her. "Desti. I'm okay—" his voice was frail. Weak. Not something she was used to hearing from him. "What happened?" she questioned. Desti glanced around the room. All the demons— gone. Incinerated. *But how?* She looked around some more. It looked like permanent shadows decorating the floor. But the Master— he was nowhere to be found.

"I don't know, but can you get me down from here?" It took Desti a second to realize that Tate was still hung up. She found the lever around the back and pushed it up, releasing him. "Oh my God. Tate. You're hurt badly." The blood running down Tate's abdomen outlined every muscle. To Desti, it only made him more enticing, but thinking about his perfectly chiseled abs was something she didn't have time for. Her concern right now was to get him better. She shook her head and refocused. "Come on. We need to get back to the Resistance."

"But what about everyone else? Elijah?" asked Tate. "I don't see Elijah anywhere. We can deal with him when the time comes. As for them, let's take them back to camp and try to undo what ever Elijah did to them."

***

It had taken what seemed like hours to find their way out of Rotten's Crude. Desti glanced back at the cave system that had almost taken Tate's life. Her life. "I'm never going back there again." Tate looked back and scoffed. "Me either." The rest of the crew trailed behind. Zombie like. They dragged their feet, eyes bloodshot, coming out of whatever trance they were under. Tate reached for Desti's cheek and said, "your cheek—" Desti reached up. "What? Is it bad?"

"No. Actually the opposite. It's almost healed."

"What? But how?" A simple cut was all that was left. Under the stroke of her fingers, it felt like a leftover scar. A story for another time. The tips of her fingers slowly fell to her sides, and she glanced over at Tate. "What do you think that was in there?"

"What? That light?"

Desti nodded.

"I don't know. Maybe it was some kind of energy from the Master. I mean he disappeared, so maybe it was him flashing away?" Tate tilted his head, trailing off, squinting his eyes to the sky above.

Desti realized that daylight was soon ending. "Hey guys? It's getting dark. Are we close to your camp?" Tess looked up from her zoned-out daze. "What? I'm sorry, my head—"

"It's okay. I asked if we were close. It's getting dark quickly. We will be sitting ducks out here."

"There is nothing around," Matt chimed in. "Yeah, I don't see any demons," said Tilly. Desti rolled her eyes. Maybe this was their true personalities. Annoying and naive. "I don't know what Elijah did to your heads, but do you not remember how stupid and dangerous it is to be out here when it is dark?"

"Especially now," Tate pushed in. Tate was right. Especially now. Especially after Desti broke his prisoners free— again. *There certainly must be more coming for us.* Desti racked her brain trying to make sense of what happened. It didn't make sense. And the Master, Elijah, where did they go? Are they dead? Matt caught up with Desti and Tate. "Come on guys. We will be fine. I've personally killed, I don't know, like a hundred of these things," he over confidently puffed out his chest and continued, "I will protect us."

"Yeah okay, Matt. Like how you protected me from whatever Elijah was doing to us? I mean I still feel weird," Tilly complained. "That's not the same. How was I supposed to know we were being slowly drugged with demon blood?" Desti shivered in disgust. Demons were already gross enough, but the thought of ingesting their blood for any reason really made her skin crawl. "You guys really had no clue what you were doing?" Desti picked at her pants nervously. She still didn't fully trust them. How could she?

"Enough. Desti, I know that you never trusted me, and maybe you had a good reason not to, but what I do know is that we would never work with the Master." Tess was quiet most of the way, but she must have finally needed to put her two cents in. Desti sighed. It was hard for her to admit that Tess was right.

There was a pause.

"Tess, you're right. I'm sorry. But, let me just ask this, do you remember everything that you did while under your spell?" For a moment, everyone stopped. Desti felt the slight tug of Tate's hand pulling hers before he realized that she had stopped too. Tess for once looked defeated. Depressed. It was not what she was supposed to be. She was strong. A leader. Desti waited for Tess to respond.

"I remember most of the things. It was like I was watching a movie of myself doing whatever he needed me to. My mind believed that I needed to be a certain way. Act a certain way," Tess trailed off, "but that isn't me Desti. This isn't us. We don't enslave people—"

Enslave people? What could she mean by that? Desti didn't remember seeing anyone physically held hostage at the Resistance or someone who resembled a slave. Before Desti could speak, she was interrupted by a haunting familiar sound. "Did you hear that?" She held on to Tate's hand tight. Demons. But not just a few.

"I heard that," said Matt. "It sounds like a lot more than what I usually hear." Everyone seemed on edge. The hairs on the back of Desti's neck perked up. Her adrenaline was pumping. Preparing for something. "Yeah, like hundreds of them—" Desti's voice softly let go. Tilly stepped forward in a frantic panic. "We need to go now! There is no way we can take on even two demons out here, let alone hundreds!"

"Yeah, I'm with Tilly on this one. I am going to try to get back to the Resistance before they catch up to me."

"Matt wait," Tess called. "What? You'd rather stay here and fight? I'm with Matt and Tilly on this one, Tess. Come on, we need to run. Fast." In a split second, Desti yanked Tate's arm and pulled him forward, sprinting off in a race against the darkness.

15: The Battle

THE SHIFTING SHADOWS ACROSS THE CANYON seemed to contort with the dimming light. "There! Ahead," Tilly called. Matt had almost surpassed her in their marathon to the camp. Tate was not too far behind. Desti ran closely behind, admiring, studying. *Even when I am in imminent danger, I can't shake him from my mind. Now is not the time,* she told herself. Desti arched back just enough so Tess could hear her yell, "come on! We need to hurry!"

"Desti! The lights." An unnerving tremble came from her voice. Desti saw the lights, the mysterious glowing orbs that were supposed to keep the camp safe, but now, they were dim. Almost gone. "Tess what's wrong with them? Are they not working?" She called back. With the camp approaching everyone slowed their pace just before reaching the entrance. "Did I just hear you right, Tess? We don't have anything to keep those things out now?" Matt seemed furious. Frightened to his core. "I don't know, Matt. They should be brighter than that. It must mean that they are almost out of their source."

Desti tilted her head slightly. *And where did this power source come from?* She never truly got an answer to that question. Desti was snapped out of her thoughts by a familiar warming voice. "Desti, come on. Let's get inside."

***

Sirens were blaring. People were panicking. It was total chaos. "Tate, here!" Tate was almost smacked in the face with a sword as Tess tossed it over. He glanced over and flashed Desti a smile. He always found a way to make her laugh. Even at the worst times. Desti ran up to the arsenal that was in their stash and yanked off a metal spear from its rack. "I think this should do. Don't you think?" She held it next to her, firmly gripping the leather center. "I think you look pretty badass in my opinion," Tate joked. "Tate come on, it's not the time for jokes."

Tilly and Matt looked how Desti remembered first meeting them. All geared up in their armor, carrying their battle weapons. "I hope we can do this. We need to do this." Desti's voice was uncertain. Vulnerable. But who could blame her? No one was prepared for a battle. Not yet anyway. Her eyes were drowning in feelings of loneliness and uncertainty. *What if this is it? Where do we go after here?* She almost lost herself until a familiar soft touch brought her back.

Her chin was guided up toward the only thing that could ground her. *Him.* It's always been him. Her savior. Her night and shining armor. Her soulmate. Best friend. "Tate?" He didn't say anything. His eyes instead said it all. *Don't speak.* She knew that was what he wanted to say. She could feel him leaning in. She desired for him too. *Maybe just one last kiss before we die.* She leaned in. She wanted to feel him press the soft texture of his lips onto hers, and so she did, pulling his head forward, embracing every ounce of him like it was the last time she would ever feel him. Truly feel him. And maybe it was the last time. "Desti! Come on, let's go!" someone screamed as they ran past her. She stepped back, tears streaming down her cheek.

It was time. The demons had found the Resistance. The holy glow that kept their camp safe was slowly dwindling away. Desti gasped. There was a sea of slimy, scaly, creatures making their way through the entrance. Screams from some of the members tore away at her. The terror. The pain. It was all too real. Just like her friend Nash back at school. "Tate, what do we do? They are getting in?" she cried. "There's too many of them."

16: Hidden Horrors

TATE'S HAND YANKED ONTO HERS. "DESTI, COME ON. We need to go." Her eyes were burning from the tears. "But where?" she cried. There was nowhere to hide. Fire had burned its way over most of the tents. Bodies were piling up. People screaming in flames. "I don't know but we can't stay here. Move. Now!" Tate pulled Desti even farther back into the canyon. Back to the outskirts of the camp, and then past it, until they were looking into an endless canyon of unknown. Desti stopped running, pulling on Tate's arm. "Wait."

"Desti, we can't stop. We need to keep running. They are after us." She remembered something. Something that Elijah had shown her before. "I know where we can go. It's over here somewhere." His eyebrows narrowed as he asked, "what are you talking about?"

"Elijah. He brought me to this hole in the wall. He tried to get me to go in there the night before we left. We can hide in there." It was like searching for a needle in a haystack, but she didn't give up. "What the heck are you talking about? You went off somewhere with him, alone, in the dark?" Desti rolled her eyes. Tate was right though. It was dangerous. She knew that was what he wanted to say to her by the tone of his voice. But how was she supposed to know what he was doing this whole time? Ignoring his question she yelled, "there! I see it!"

She ran forward. Her hand caressed the strange markings on the stone. "This is it." She turned back to look at him. She expected to see anger in his eyes. Or disappointment. But instead, his eyes were calm. She reached out her hand and he took it. "I trust you," he quietly spoke.

***

Familiar and heavy air filled the dark room. Desti waited for Tate to step through the slim hallway leading to where she was standing. Her light was running low. "You're almost through. It opens up once you get past here."

"This was probably easier for you to fit through." Tate always had broad shoulders. Desti loved that about him. She loved the fact that she had to stand on her tip toes just to see past his shoulders. He made her feel safe. She held out her hand so she could pull him through. "You can fit. Just keep going."

"Well, it definitely looks like someone has been down here before. Look over there," Tate said while walking over to a stone table. "What are these markings?" Desti asked. It was the same markings that she saw on the entrance of the cave. They resembled some sort of alphabet. Sharp lines intertwining and curving like ancient runes etched by the hand of some long-forgotten civilization.

As Desti traced her fingers along the intricate patterns, a shiver ran down her spine, a primal instinct warning her of the danger that lay hidden within the cryptic symbols. Each stroke felt as if she were that much closer to an answer.

"Woah— Do you feel that?"

"Feel what?" asked Tate. Desti placed his hand onto the symbols. "You feel that energy, right? Like it is trying to tell us something." Eyes wide and curious, he replied, "yes. I do. What do you think it means?"

"I don't know, but look, the cave goes deeper. I see a light coming from the end of the tunnel." Desti focused her attention walking toward the tunnel. She stopped and sighed. "Tate? What are we going to do? Everyone out there is probably dead." Tate reached for her hand.

"We will make it through this." He looked past her. "Whatever is back there, we should go see." Venturing deeper into the cave seemed like a dumb idea, but Desti knew that it was either there or outside where they didn't stand a chance. She blew out a sigh. "Okay. Let's go see."

The cave opened up again. Around was a smaller room with no more secret passages or tunnels. A dead end. Desti wasn't prepared for what she saw next.

17: Hidden Secrets

"OH MY GOD. LOOK!"

Desti ran over to a young boy. Chained. Bloody. Bruised. Desti kneeled next to the boy and stroked his hair. She leaned in closer and listened for the slightest hint that he was breathing. "He's alive." Desti jerked her head back to look at Tate. There was a single tear forming in her eye. "Who would do this?"

"Elijah. It had to be," Tate answered as he walked up closer.

"But why on Earth would he lock up a little boy?" Desti reached for under his arm and said, "Tate, come on. Help me sit him up." Tate did just that. Together they propped the boy's body against the wall.

"Hey. Wake up," Desti said while trying to lightly pat his face. "You have to do it a little harder than that." Tate opened up his hand and swung it across the boy's cheek. *Was that a little too much?* She thought but then the boy mumbled. Tate stepped back to give the boy some space and Desti did the same. He looked frightened. Hopeless. "Hey, it's okay. We won't hurt you. What is your name?" asked Desti. At first, he didn't answer. Desti thought why should he anyway? Why should he trust them? But then— he spoke.

"My name is Anthony." Desti wanted to lean in. Wanted to hold him in her arms and tell him everything would be okay. But will it? Instead, she held back, leaning against the stone table. She studied him. The way he looked. Covered in ash and dried blood. *What did they do to you?* Desti got lost in the thought of the torment he must have endured. Her fingers ached from gripping the table behind her. She took a deep breath and then let go.

"Anthony," she said. "What happened to you? How long have you been down here?" This question burned a pit into her stomach. It made her head ache with the thought of what he was going to say next. She kneeled next to Anthony and got closer.

"I don't know how long I have been down here. I lost track—" he continued, "it must have been years since I was first brought here, to the Resistance. It wasn't long after that when I was taken and locked in this cave." Desti reached for Tate's hand. She needed something to help her hold it together. She didn't know what she was feeling. Sadness. Rage. Guilt. All her emotions seemed to be having a battle, leaving her feeling helpless and drained.

"Do you know why you were taken down here?" asked Tate. Anthony coward away as if he were scared to say. "It's okay Anthony, we aren't going to hurt you. You can tell us."

Desti waited for him to answer. His hesitation only made Desti more curious. *Come on. You can trust me.* "He said it was because of my blood. Something that I had in me," Anthony began to say but Desti jumped in unable to control herself. "He who? Elijah?" When Desti said Elijah's name, Anthony's eyes went wide. Consumed with fear. "How do you know Elijah? Is he coming back?"

"Anthony don't cry. Don't be scared. He isn't coming back. I won't let that happen. Okay?" Desti held out her hand and Anthony grabbed on tight. "Why did Elijah chain you up? What was he using your blood for?" In her hand she could feel the trembling coming from Anthony. He was scared to speak. Scared. Period.

"He uses it for protection. Against the demons. It lights up those glowing orbs that hang out front of the camp entrance." *Your blood protects him from the demons?* Now Desti was left with more questions than answers. She looked to Tate for some reassurance, but he too had the same confused expression. "How does your blood protect the camp?" asked Tate.

"My—" Anthony trailed off as if he was too scared to continue but Desti and Tate kept their eyes locked in, waiting until he continued. "My blood protects the camp because I have something in it that is more than human." *More than human. What could he mean by that?* Now Desti for sure was entering a rabbit hole of unanswered questions.

"What do you mean more than human? Are you—" Desti paused for a moment, she almost didn't want to say it. *Cambion. Is he? Is he part demon?* She cleared her throat and asked again. "Are you a Cambion?" Getting that word off her chest felt equally good and terrifying. If he was a Cambion, could he be dangerous?

"What? No, I am not half demon. I am actually the opposite." What did he mean opposite? Desti looked over to Tate. He looked just as confused and intrigued as her. "Opposite meaning?" asked Tate.

"I'm half angel. Nephilim," answered Anthony.

18: Nephilim

NEPHILIM? DID HE JUST TELL US THAT HE IS HALF *angel?* Tate had a look of shock on his face.

"Nephilim? Tate, I thought they were just a myth. I didn't think that they were—" she paused, "real."

"I thought so too. Are you sure?" Tate asked Anthony. He leaned in closer now, touching gently on his shoulder. This time Anthony didn't seem scared. He seemed as though he finally let down his guard. "Trust me. I'm sure. Otherwise, I wouldn't be chained up."

"Well, how did you find out that you are—Nephilim?"

"Little hints here and there. I would heal much quicker than others. I wasn't so easily influenced by the demons in my city or the people who ran it. My mom saw this in me. She knew and so she told me to run as far as I could until I found the Resistance. People like me are being hunted and slaughtered. She had heard stories of this place. They called it a sanctuary."

Desti reached for Anthony's hands, holding on tight. "Oh my God, I can't believe you are real." She looked back. "Tate, we need to break these chains somehow. Find something to smash them."

The cave was dense and dimly lit, which made it difficult to search for something to break Anthony free from his chains. Desti started on one side of the cave, searching for anything that could be of use, while Tate took the other side. Only a few minutes had passed when there was a gasp. "Look!" Tate was holding up what looked to be a stone hatchet. "Okay, Anthony, just hold still. He is going to get you out of here."

***

The sounds of distant screams and fighting echoed its way to the cave entrance. Desti stood there, frozen, almost too scared to exit the cave. "Desti, it's okay. We will keep running the other way. Away from the demons." She felt the gentle touch of Tate's hand grab hers. She closed her eyes. For a moment, the world fell away. It was just him and her. How she wished it could be. "Okay. Let's go." She took the first step forward.

The camp was far away. Far enough that it was a mere shadow on the horizon. Desti turned to escape in the other direction. "Come on, the coast is clear." One by one, they exited the cave and took off into the valley.

They had walked about a mile before slowing their pace. Anthony followed closely behind Tate. "Why did you stop?" asked Tate.

"I don't know. Look," she pointed. Where are we supposed to go? This place goes on for miles." Desti turned around and was now facing him. "We can't just keep running Tate. The Master has a whole army out there looking for us. We pissed him off and his is coming for his revenge." Tate didn't answer. It was as if Desti took the words from him. "You know I am right. What are we going to do?" She felt helpless. Hopeless.

"We will fight until the very end. Okay? I will protect you, and Anthony. We will find the Lux and defeat the Master and his stupid army. Just like we had planned." Tate had grabbed a firm grip on Desti's arm. She didn't want him to let go. *I will protect you.* Those words resonated with her. *Will he? Can he?* She thought of Anthony too. He was just a young teen. Now she had to keep him safe too.

"Where do we go from here?" Desti was desperate. Desperate for someone else to take control. She was exhausted. Survival was her entire life, and it was time for that to end.

***

Desti and Tate had spent most of the night curled against the side of the canyon, protected by the straggling rocks that protruded outward. Anthony was curled under Tate's arm. In the other hand, he held the hatchet. "Tate, wake up. We fell asleep." Tate's eyes shot open, bloodshot, and drained. Desti wondered if she also looked like that. They had been up half the night keeping watch. "How long did we sleep for?" he asked. "I don't know. Most of the night, maybe. Look," she pointed. "The sunrise."

Even during such dooming times, she still found peace and comfort in the beauty of the blood orange and pink sky. "Anthony, look." Desti shook Anthony from his slumbers. It had probably been years since he had seen any kind of daylight. She watched his face light up. "It's beautiful," he said. Desti pushed off the wall and stood up. "We should get going." Tate and Anthony followed, brushing the dirt from their clothes.

"You see the smoke?" asked Tate. He was pointing in the direction they came from. Toward the camp. Clouds of smoke swirled above the burned and withered camp. A reminder of why they were running and what they were running from. Desti gasped, cupping her hands to her mouth. "All those people—dead." Her eyes burned from the tears that gathered. Too many collected until they ran down her cheek. "Do you think anyone made it out?" she asked. Desperate.

"I hope so."

"Where do we go now? We need supplies. Water. Food." Desti asked. What came from Tate's mouth next shook Desti to her core.

"We go back to the city of Mors."

19: City of Mors

DESTI, TATE, AND ANTHONY HAD SPENT THE NEXT agonizing two days traveling back to the city. Not much of a city to say the least but it's where she grew up. Going back there was the last thing that Desti wanted to do but she was right. They needed water. Food.

On the horizon, under an ash filled sky appeared their desolate town. Something that made Desti cringe at the sight of it. So many horrible memories there. She clenched her fingers into her palms. "I can't believe we are going back here."

"We will be okay if we lay low. And besides, I am pretty good at sneaking around." Tate cracked a smirk trying to provoke an unintentional smile. He had his ways of bringing out the best in her. She felt the muscle in her cheek pull at her lip until it curved. "Yeah, okay whatever. But seriously, Tate, we cannot be seen. By anyone. We are fugitives now."

"So, what did you guys do to become fugitives anyway?" asked Anthony. Desti had almost forgotten that he was so clueless to their situation. On their journey back to the city she didn't mention her life back here in the city of Mors. Tate shot Desti a look. *Should we tell him?* His eyes asked. It took a moment for her to think if it was such a good idea to tell Anthony why they were fugitives. The last time she trusted someone, well, he tried to kill her.

Desti huffed out a breath and said, "fine."

"Tate got sent away to the Master."

Anthony arched his brow. "Oh? Why did he get sent to the Master?" Desti was hesitant to give Anthony the full truth. Her trust in people had significantly diminished. She pulled a strand of hair away from her lip. There was silence. A few seconds passed until she gave in. "Tate went looking for the Lux— to save me."

"The Lux? I've heard the rumors growing up. What was he trying to save you from?"

Desti had almost forgotten why their entire mission existed in the first place. Her birthday was coming up. It felt like an icepick to the chest when she thought about how her parents were planning on promising her soul to Hell. *Selfish,* she thought. Her parents were never loving, but to sell her soul— she didn't think that they would be *that* evil.

"My parents—" her voice became frail, "they wanted to give me up, to the demons in exchange for riches and protection." Desti thought about Tate's parents too. Were they planning the same thing? Is that what he heard that one night? She felt an urge to look over to Tate. A yearning to be close to him. He must have felt the same way too because when she glanced over at him, he was staring right back at her. She could get lost in those eyes of his. Growing up, she never knew love. It was forbidden, but maybe she just didn't know what love felt like. Was this it? Was this love?

Anthony didn't seem shell shocked when Desti told him about her parents. Maybe his city was just as bad, filled with people just as bad as this one. He continued forward, almost reaching the outskirts of the city now. "There it is. It doesn't look much different than where I came from," he said. For all Desti knew, the whole world looked like this. Just a land filled with decay and sorrow. The air began to emit a stench of rotting flesh. Carcasses of dead stray animals, demons and who knows what else littered the perimeter of the city boundaries. Desti threw her arm over her mouth as she involuntarily gagged. "Ugh. It smells." Tate and Anthony did the same. Desti coughed as she tried to inhale the thick musky air. It was much different than the air out in the Wastelands. "I didn't miss this."

"So where are we going now?" asked Anthony.

Everything about this mission was dangerous. Who could they trust? Was there anyone who might not have an alternative motive? Those thoughts danced so dangerously into her mind. Desti froze. "Wait." *Anthony is right.*

"Where do we go now? It's daylight. Someone might see us," she said, but Tate always had something clever up his sleeve.

"Don't worry. I have a plan."

20: The Mission

WHEN TATE SAYS HE HAS A PLAN, IT USUALLY WAS never a good one. Desti has learned not to trust in his "plans" over the years, and this one by far was the riskiest.

"I don't know Tate. Are you sure you guys know what you are doing?"

"Don't worry. I've got this," Anthony said in full confidence.

Tate had Anthony standing on his shoulders as he was lifting him up to one of the windows leading to the school cafeteria. That was his big plan. Break into the school and steal some food and water from the cafeteria. I mean, it wasn't terrible, but Desti thought about the what ifs. What if they get caught? She thought about Ms. Clyde. Desti shivered as her brain flashed images of Ms. Clyde's ash gray hair and bristled chin hair. She shook it off. "Okay but hurry up."

Anthony was flung with full force through the window, followed by an echo of crashing.

"What was that?" Desti asked. That was loud whatever *that* was. Her eyes darted all around, afraid that someone might have heard. "Don't worry. It wasn't that loud," Tate said. He had a gentle touch on Desti's hand. She pulled back and said, "Just throw me in."

Once inside the school, Desti wasn't sure what she'd expected to find. An army waiting to capture them. Ms. Clyde ready to throw them to the Master. But what she didn't expect was this. Nothing. No students. No teachers. The school was empty.

"Where is everyone?" she asked. Her voice seemed to get hung up on that question. Tate was brushing the dirt from his very ripped pants. "Maybe we came on an off day. Lucky us, huh?"

Kids were forced to go to school until they turned twenty-one, but only for four days a week. The rest of the week they were slaves to their parents and whatever else kind of commitments they had. Many of the kids were forced to labor when not in learning. Desti broke her focus from her thoughts and said, "yeah. Really lucky."

Everyone slowly took their own corner of the room, scoping out what they could use. Desti picked up a book. One titled "History of the Era of the Damned." She rolled her eyes. When she was younger, she remembered learning about the Era of the Damned. One hundred years ago people walked this planet and were free. She thought about life back then. What was it like? Then her mind went to Crazy Joan. *She lived free. Before.* Suddenly Desti turned around and yelled, "I know where we should go next."

***

Crazy Joan's house ran along the perimeter of the town, nestled in between the rotting bodies of dead things and half crumbled in houses. Desti, Tate, and Anthony had spent nearly three hours meticulously dodging and weaving through shrubs and bushes to get across town without being seen. By the time Desti had reached Mayberry Lane, she was covered in filth and sweat.

"Is this where you found her?" Tate was asking. Walking down Mayberry Lane again brought Desti back. It seemed so long ago that she had learned that her best friend was dragged away to the Master or that she went off to find him and somehow, she found *her*. Crazy Joan. *Without her, I would never have gotten the clue to find the Lux*. Desti blinked and looked back. "Yes. Her house is down a little farther." She walked past the old houses overgrown with vines and shrubs, stepping over the mounds of trash that seemed to obliterate the street. *We are getting close.*

From the left, there it was. Crazy Joan's house. *She has to help us. She helped me before.* Desti couldn't help but feel— hesitant. She had been gone for so long. Would Crazy Joan even remember her encounter with Desti? Had the Master gotten to her and convinced her to turn against them? These thoughts ravished any sense of security Desti was feeling, but she didn't show it. She couldn't. *I have to be strong. For Tate.*

Desti was now standing at the front of Crazy Joan's door. "Should I just knock?" she asked. She turned back for reassurance. Anthony and Tate both shrugged their shoulders and gave her a friendly nudge. "You know her, Desti. I don't," said Anthony. While holding a breath in her chest, she knocked.

To Desti, it felt like seconds were minutes as she so nervously waited for the door to open. Her fingers had nearly been picked raw at that point. She wanted to abort. But just as she was about to turn away a familiar voice rang in her head. "You girl." Desti finally pushed out the air that held in her lungs. Relief embellished over her body. "Craz—" she cleared her throat, "I mean, Ms. Joan?" Desti stepped forward toward the door. Ms. Joan had it cracked just enough that she could see the flow of her skirt dancing along the floorboard.

"Yes? What do you want?"

Before Desti could answer Ms. Joan stuck out her chin and said, "Ah— I see you found your friend." And like that, the door swung open. Desti looked back to see

Tate and Anthony equally as shocked. She shrugged her shoulders and waved for them to follow.

Her house hadn't changed a bit, Desti thought. There were still cobwebs where the walls met the ceilings and the floor looked like it hadn't been swept in a century. Desti found herself being ushered over to the sitting room where she first had met Crazy Joan.

"Sit," Crazy Joan insisted while poking Tate with her cane.

"So, tell me girl, why have you come back to my home?" Her voice sounded frail and rigged, just like any hundred-year-old lady would sound. Desti got closer to her. She reached into her pocket. Desti guided Ms. Joan's hand to hers until she placed the Holy book into her palm. "We need your help."

For the next hour, Desti had practically done a charade for Crazy Joan, explaining their exhausting and exciting adventure, catching her up to where they all were on their journey. "And you say they are after you, girl?" She knew how this sounded. Like they were in over their heads.

"Ms. Joan," Desti leaned forward, "I know how this sounds. I know you probably think that we can't win, but we have to." Her throat tightened around her words. "If we don't defeat their army, then we are good as dead." It hurt to admit that. All her life, Desti grew up around death. It didn't bother her back then, but now— now coming so close within death's touch, it truly felt surreal.

Tate must have felt the need to comfort Desti. She didn't know that she needed it until she felt his touch. She leaned into it, blew out all the emotions that lingered in her chest, and let go. Like a stream of water, her stress flowed off her until she was collected.

"Well, young lady, I don't know what you think I can do for you. I'm nearly one hundred years old. I can't move around much."

Anthony jumped in, "Ms. Joan, if I may, we really just need a place to lay low and stay until we can figure out our next plan." Desti shot Anthony a look. "Anthony, we haven't really discuss—"

Before Desti could finish, Crazy. Joan stood from her seat. "All right, but no funny business. Lord knows it's about time someone stand up to those awful creatures."

21: The Plan

NIGHTFALL ENVELOPED THE SKY LIKE A RIVER OF darkness, drowning out the last bit of light.

"No stars." Desti was looking out the window of one of Ms. Joan's rooms. "I forgot how the smog blocks them out."

"It's weird being back here, right?" Tate asked. He placed his hand on her shoulder. Desti glanced back at Anthony asleep on a dusty chair, and then focused her gaze on Tate. She danced her fingers along his forearm.

"Yeah, but at least I am here with you." She turned to face him now, only inches keeping their bodies a part. "You are the only thing that matters to me in this world. You are my best friend. I don't know what I would do if I lost—" Desti's voice cracked. She couldn't say it. *Lost him.* Tate reached for her cheek with such a gentle caress. Desti placed her hand onto his.

"I'm not going anywhere."

Tate lifted her chin ever so slightly and kissed her. His lips were electrifying. The world fell away into insignificance, and it was only her and him. The warmth of his skin was sensational, sending a wave of comfort and pleasure throughout her body. He felt so good. She pulled him in closer as his hand studied the curves of her back. She had pushed down these feelings for so long, but she couldn't hold back anymore. For the rest of night, it was just her and him. Together.

***

Dawn snuck up on Desti too soon. Light from the sunrise spilled onto the floorboards until they crept their way up to the walls. Desti rolled over, halfway snuggled under Tate's arm. She sat up.

"Tate, wake up," she whispered.

Tate rolled closer to her and then sat up. "Woah," he stretched his arms above his head. "That was the best sleep I had in a while."

"Yeah, me too actually. This floor was pretty comfortable," Desti said.

Anthony must have heard them waking up because he stretched out his arms and belted out the loudest yawn. "Good morning you guys." Desti was slipping her legs back into her pants and looked up. "Good morning to you too. Did you sleep well?"

"Yeah. I can't remember the last time I got to sleep on a cushion. Thank you for that."

"Well, I think out of all of us, you probably deserved the chair the most. You know, with being chained up and all."

"So," Desti rose to her feet, "we need to figure out what we are going to do. The only way we even have a chance at defeating Elijah's army is by finding the Lux." A sigh escaped her throat. "But I feel like we aren't even close to it."

"The Lux?" Anthony's brow furrowed. "My mom sometimes would talk about the Lux, before she—"

Sent him away. Desti thought about Anthony and his mom. His mom sent him away because she thought it would be safer for him. To protect him. But Her's, they were trying to send her to Hell. Desti scoffed. "Oh, sorry I didn't mean to," she walked toward Anthony, "It's just that my parents wanted to send me away too but for something else." Desti let her voice linger just a little long on that sentence. It pained her to admit and to think about.

"Anyway, what did your mom tell you about the Lux? Maybe it's something we don't know." Anthony was fixing his mangled bird's nest of a hair. "Well," he stood up, "from what I can remember, she would say that not everyone can find it. That you had to be special." Anthony shrugged his shoulders. *Special?* Desti got closer. "What did she mean special?"

"I'm not sure, but she told me that I was special."

Desti cocked her neck just slightly, thinking deeply about what Anthony said.

Silence.

Desti's brain scavenged for answers. Anything. And then it hit her. "You have to be Nephilim," her eyes grew big. She said it again, but this time she was almost yelling. "You have to be Nephilim."

"Anthony. Thank you!" Desti ran over to Anthony and hugged him. She turned towards Tate. "Don't you know what this means? Anthony can find the Lux." Tate looked over at Anthony with the same expression painted onto his face. "Desti." He grabbed her hand. "We can't get ahead of ourselves now."

"I'm not. We aren't. He is our missing piece." This time tears began to gather in her eyes as she turned toward Anthony. "Right?" Anthony at first was quiet, but he got closer too. "Desti, I am not going to leave. Not now, but I think we need more answers before we go back out there. We need to be prepared."

It had been two hours since Desti realized that only Anthony could find the Lux. He was half angel. Nephilim. She sat in Ms. Joan's kitchen, or what used to be, and brainstormed the best plan that came to her mind.

"Okay." Desti paced back and forth, stirring up dust with every stride. "I say that we gather up our own army. We go back to Rotten's Crude, and we kill them all." At this point Desti had worked up a sweat, and continued, "The Lux has to be down there. I just know it is. And once we kill Elijah's army, we will be able to search the caves." She sucked in a large breath as if she had just finished running a marathon.

Tate stood. "I mean, it isn't half bad but where do we find our army?"

22: Gathering

GATHERING UP AN ARMY SEEMED EASIER SAID THAN done. Desti and Tate agreed that if they were going to do this, they would do it his way.

"Are you sure about this, Tate?"

"I'm never fully sure about anything," he replied while shooting Desti a flirtatious smirk. Desti was crouched down behind him, and Anthony behind her.

"These bushes aren't very bushy. Someone is going to see us."

"Just trust me. Okay." Tate had a way of getting what he wanted. Desti sometimes couldn't resist. Maybe it was his confidence in the way he talked, or maybe the way he made her feel safe. She blew out a huff of air and kept quiet, crouching behind a mound of bushes.

"Whose house are we at again?" Anthony asked.

"My friend, Brandon," Tate whispered. He refocused on crawling to Brandon's window. Tate stopped and crouched. "I know him from school. We can trust him."

"How do you know we can trust him?" asked Anthony.

Tate glanced over his shoulder and said, "because, he has been running a secret club, training people on how to fight." Desti's brow narrowed. "What? How would you know that?" she asked. Tate seemed hesitant but then answered, "I used to sneak out and join them sometimes. Trust me, he can be trusted."

So that was what he was always up to, sneaking around the school grounds. She huffed out a laugh.

Desti didn't have to question Tate. She knew Brandon from walking the halls. Troublemaker was what he was. But that was good news for them. She needed troublemakers. Anyone who broke the rules, even just a little, might be willing to start a revolution.

The pinching sound of Tate tapping a small rock on Brandon's window nicked at her ear. She peaked through the leaves of the bushes hiding her, making sure that no one was around to hear. Suddenly, she heard the window open.

"Tate?"

"Hey man. Long time."

Brandon stuck his head slightly out the window and looked down at Tate. "Where have you been? Ms. Clyde and everyone have been looking for you— and Desti." Once Desti's name escaped his tongue, she poked her head up and said, "hey Brandon."

Brandon shot Tate with a look of disappointment. She knew that look all too well. "Do you know what will happen to both of you if someone sees you?" She knew what would happen. The worst kind of punishment. They were outlaws now. Rejects. Fugitives being hunted by the worst kind of creatures she could possibly imagine. Brandon's comment seemed to roll right off Tate because he didn't answer it.

"Listen, we need your help. Can you let us in?"

And just like that, Desti was yet again inside another house. She watched as they pulled Anthony through the window, and then continued studying Brandon's room. "Where are your parents?" she asked. Her hair whipped around her face as she turned to look at him.

"It's Thursday. My parents work at the bazaar on Thursdays."

"That's good. We won't have to worry about sneaking around them," Tate added.

Anthony had stuck himself on Brandon's bed. He was focused on feeling the pleaded blanket rather than her conversation. She walked up to Tate and took his hand. Her touch was gentle. *This is wrong. This feels wrong*. She wanted to say. *I don't want anyone else to die because of me.* Those words burned into the pit of her stomach, but she couldn't bear to speak them. She clutched onto her shirt as if the pain became physical.

"Tate do we even know if he wants to become a part of this?" She poked her head around Tate and looked Brandon dead in the eyes. "Do you want to be a part of this?"

"I know why you guys left. I know why everyone is looking for you. The Master has people all over the city working for him. I know what I am getting into, and yes, I want to help." Brandon had a life and yet he was willing to give it up for her. To find the Lux.

"We need to find everyone that we can who is willing to join us. We must, or we won't stand a chance," Desti argued.

She thought about it. Maybe tearing these kids away from this city wasn't so bad. They were slaves here. Slaves to their own desperation. There was no future here. None anywhere for that matter.

Maybe they could start a new city.

Anthony walked to a cupboard and pulled out a small book. "What is that?" Desti asked. Anthony got closer and held it out. "I've got a test later," he rolled his eyes, "on the Era of the Damned. What better place to recruit and army than a school full of rebellious teenagers?"

Tate's eyes had a hunger in them, as if he had been fueled with the desire to burn the whole city to the ground. "We leave tonight. You get us an army and I will get us out of the city." He walked over to the window and pointed. "You see that street? Follow it until the end. We will be waiting just before sundown."

That was the same path Desti took to sneak out of the city herself. Not many of the residents went to that part of the city. It was dangerous. Decayed.

Brandon clutched his book under the wing of his arm and went to walk out his door. He stopped just before and said, "try not to get caught while I'm gone." And like that, he had dispersed beyond the door. "So where do we go now?" asked Anthony.

***

It must have been midday judging by the sun's position. The heat had always been exceptionally horrid that time of day. Desti covered the peak of her forehead with her palm, peaking through the cracks of her fingers at the blazing sky. "Are you going to knock?" Tate nudged. Desti was standing back at Crazy Joan's front door. Most kids would be scared to even be in the vicinity of this neighborhood, but Desti somehow found a weird comfort there. "Yeah, I am. Just give me a minute."

She took two steps forward and clenched her knuckles into a fist. Crazy Joan's door felt like it would give her a splinter with the slightest shift in angle. But she knocked.

The door opened.

"You are back. I see your plan didn't work out too well, huh?"

"Actually," Desti stepped forward some more, "it did. We need to borrow your home. Just for today—please." Crazy Joan peered around her, shooting a glaring stare at Tate and Anthony. A small grunt expelled from her chest. "I guess you should come in again then." She pulled open the door and got out of the way as Desti, Tate and Anthony went back inside.

"You are doing what now, my dear?" Crazy Joan asked.

"We are gathering up friends, to help us. They are meeting us down your street tonight." Desti answered. She was playing with the splits of her hair, pulling, and twirling it around her fingertips.

"And how do you plan on keeping you and all your little friends safe out there? Those demons will smell ya from a mile away," she slammed her cane, "gone! Eaten, just like that. Is that what you want?"

Desti sucked in a gasp. She hadn't gotten that far yet. Crazy Joan did have a good point though. How would she protect them? Before she could answer, Anthony barged in.

"With me." Desti shot Anthony a confused look. "What? How?"

"I can show you. They did it to me all the time back at the camp. You saw them. The glowing orbs. I can make us some." Anthony talked with such a calmness to him. He must be numb from all the torment he experienced, Desti thought. Her chest tightened. "But I thought that they tortured you to do that." Desti was almost fighting back tears at this point. She could never do that. Not to anyone.

"They did a ritual. I can recreate it. I can harness my *angelic* powers and bless some of our things. Light. Weapons. It will help." Desti looked over at Tate. *Say something. Say no.* Tate leaned forward, resting his elbows on his knees. "I think if he wants to help, we should let him."

And just like that, Desti was about to perform a ritual. The same one, that was the reason for Anthony being locked away for so long. It felt wrong. In every bone her body it felt sinister.

***

"Do you have a knife?" Anthony asked while clearing a large enough spot on the floor. It was now only a few hours away from sundown. Desti and Tate had helped Anthony with the setup of his "torture" chamber. She rolled her eyes. "This feels wrong, Tate." Desti was merely whispering, trying not to be heard. He didn't break his gaze from his hands in front of him. "I know, but we need to do this." Desti glanced back at Anthony. Crazy Joan had carried away what rubbish was left from her sitting room and left him to do the rest.

"What is that? Desti asked as she slid her knife from her pants and handed it to him. "This," he said while crouching down, "is how we invoke the powers." Anthony smiled, putting finger quotations around the word powers. "Those symbols— they look like the ones in the cave." Desti walked toward him. To the center of the room. She was standing in a circle, carved into the wooden floor and every few inches, a symbol broke that circle.

"That's because they are the same symbols. They are demonic." Anthony finished the last symbol, completing the circle and stood.

"How do you know they are demonic?"

"I remember hearing Elijah talk about them. I watched him perform the ritual so many times, that I could do it in my sleep now." The way Anthony talked about his torture as if didn't bother him was sickening. How could he not want to cry or scream? Desti's gaze became locked in on the symbols, feeling a twisting pain in the pit of her stomach. "You ready?"

She blinked, breaking her focus. "What?"

"I asked if you are ready," Anthony said. Tate had finished setting up their medical area. Desti insisted. A bucket filled with water, three clean cloths, and some old tape Crazy Joan found hiding deep in her cabinets. Tate got up and said, "I'm ready." He gave Desti a nod. All eyes were on her. Even though she wanted to yell no, wanted to scratch away those symbols, she didn't. Desti bit her tongue and replied with a smile.

23: The Ritual

IN THE DIMLY LIT ROOM, THE AIR HUNG HEAVY, crushing Desti with its oppressive weight. She couldn't breathe. Every breath felt like it was clawing its way to her lungs. *I can't do this. We can't do this.* Glancing around the room, she sought for a sign, anything, to stop this ritual from happening.

Anthony sat in the center of the circle, legs crossed and hands resting loosely beside his waist. Tate held the knife in his right hand. "So, what am I supposed to say again?" he asked.

Anthony chanted out loud, *"exite, o tenebrae, adferte mihi potentiam quaero. Vobis, dabo infirmos."*

"What the Hell does that mean?" Tate shot Anthony *the* look.

"It pretty much sums up to *give me powers and I will give you blood."* Anthony ran his fingers down his forearm. "You are going to cut here and chant that. Okay? I will pour my blood on our weapons and lights."

"This better work."

Desti couldn't bear to watch. Her fingers clenched the seams of her jacket as she closed her eyes. Without sight, her sense of hearing was particularly picking up all sounds. It started with Tate chanting. *"Exite, o tenebrae, adferte mihi potentiam quaero. Vobis, dabo infirmos."*

His chanting grew louder, drowning out Anthony's quiet moans. Then—

Silence.

Desti opened her eyes. In horror, she gasped at the amount of blood pouring from Anthony's arms. "Tate! Do something! He's losing too much blood." Desti ran for the rags that were lying on the counter. Crazy Joan had grabbed the bucket of water and brought it closer to them. Anthony's moans started strong but as the minutes went on, he became less aware, falling more and more unconscious. "Hand it to me!" Tate yanked the rag from Desti's hand and tied it tight around Anthony's arm.

"Come on."

"I'm trying, Desti."

Desti ran over to Anthony and sat underneath his head, resting her arms just under his neck. "Anthony, I'm sorry. We shouldn't have done this." Guilt ravished through her veins. *How could we do this?* Anthony's head lay motionless in her lap, but there was still a glimmer in his eyes. "Stay with me. Don't go to sleep," she cried.

Tate had finished tying the rags on Anthony's arm. Blood pooled around them on the floor, the grain of the wooden planks becoming stained with red. Desti held him tight. She didn't dare to move. Not now. A single tear dropped onto Anthony's cheek as she helplessly cried over him. *Stay awake. Stay awake.*

Minutes had passed, and silence filled the room. Crazy Joan sat in the corner, leaning on her withered cane. Tate was kneeling on the ground trying to wipe up the blood that stained him and Desti held on tight. She thought he was dying. Losing that much blood, he had to be close to death, but then something happened.

The cuts on his arm began to heal. What should have taken days, took only a mere few minutes for him. Desti reached down and ran her finger gently across his forearm. "Tate, look."

Tate glanced up. He stopped wiping up the blood and untied the rags from Anthony's arm. "Desti, his cut. It's almost healed."

"But how?"

A slight mumbled interjected. "I told you; I am half angel." Desti gasped. A wave of relief rushed over her nerves. "Oh, thank God," she leaned in closer, "you are okay."

"I didn't realize that you could heal that quickly. You lost so much blood. I thought—" her voice croaked, "I thought you were dead." Anthony lifted his chin, looking up at Desti. "Don't worry. I know what I was getting myself into." She could hear the strength returning in his voice. Anthony sat up and pointed to the counter. "Hand me that cup. We need to collect my blood."

Tate did as he asked and grabbed the cup sitting on the counter and handed it to Anthony. Desti watched as he let the excess blood drip, filling about halfway. "This should now give us the power that we need to protect ourselves. I have to drip it onto our weapons."

Desti gathered the weapons that they had. A knife, currently in Tate's hand, a small sword, generously gifted to her by Crazy Joan, and a small hatchet. She put them in the center of the circle, next to Anthony, and stepped back. "Now what?" A slight smirk tugged at the corner of his pale cheek. "Watch."

It was like magic happening right before her eyes. Growing up, she had heard myths about many different things, but power filled weapons was not one of them. With each drop of blood, Anthony was whispering something under his breath, his eyes gently closed. The metal on the weapons went from a dull shine to almost luminate. There was a type of glow that surrounded it, almost like a force field. When he finished, he handed Desti her hatchet. "Here. Do you feel the difference?"

The weight was the same, yet there was more to her hatchet. The power radiated from it, electrifying her senses with every touch. "Yeah, it's different. And this will work?"

"It should. Here we need some light. Give me that lantern." Crazy Joan grunted and shuffled her way to a small table nestled in the corner of her room. On top, lay a lantern. It looked antique. Flakes of rust encrusted the once silvery metal and the glass stained with reminiscences of smoke. "Here, boy." She handed it over. Anthony poured his blood onto the lantern until it turned red. He gave it to Desti. "When we light it, it should keep us safe. Like a barrier between us and the darkness." Desti let the lantern dangle from her grasp. Almost as if the lantern had hypnotized her, she became stuck gazing upon its eccentric beauty. The hopefulness that she had for it to work pulled her in like a current sweeping her away. "This must work." Desti let her eyelids fall shut as she whispered to herself.

She knew what this lantern meant for her. It could be her greatest protection or her worst disappointment. She turned to Tate. "If this fails, all of us—" her voice lingered, "are dead."

Tate walked close, close enough that she could feel the rise and fall of his chest pressed against hers, close enough that his breath ever so slightly blew away the stray strands of hair that tickled her face. He was her comfort. Best friend. *Love?* Desti let her guard squander, leaning into him. His hand gently pressed against her cheek as he guided her gaze to him. "It will work. We have to have faith."

Their energy was electric. Kinetic. Passionate. Desti couldn't resist him, and so she let go, leaning into him until her lips touched his. When she pulled away, it was just her and him, staring into his eyes. "Even if we don't succeed, I'm happy that my last moments will be fighting along your side." Her whole life it had always been her and him, together, best friends. He was the only thing that gave her peace in this destructive world. In a world designed to tear you apart, he was her glue, piecing her broken soul back together. Desti was then interrupted by the poke of Crazy Joan's cane into her side.

"See, I told you girl. You love that boy. That's forbidden you know?" Crazy Joan playfully joked. Tate and Desti stepped apart with reminiscence of a smile on her lips. "Okay, we need to hurry. Look it's almost sunset," she said while pointing to the warm glow peering in through the window. Anthony grabbed what he could carry and Desti and Tate followed suit.

They finished one last sweep of the house before stepping out the door. Desti stopped just as her hand touched the doorknob, fingers playing with the cross charm that hung just at her collarbone and turned back to Ms. Joan. She pulled the necklace over her head and gently placed the cross necklace back into her palm. "Keep this safe for me and thank you, for everything."

Ms. Joan lifted her cane and cheered, "you go kick those demons' asses."

24: The New Resistance

THE END OF MAYBERRY LANE WAS WHAT YOU'D expect out of a horror story. Desti shivered, grabbing the sleeves of her shirt. Her skin was decorated with an array of fading bruises and healed scars. As she glanced around, the houses almost seemed to grow with their everlasting shadows. She pulled herself closer to Tate. "This place always gives me the creeps."

Tate didn't say anything, but instead she found his arm wrapping around her, holding her under his wing. The sky was almost dark now. Only hints of daylight clung to the horizon. "Where is everyone?" Anthony asked.

"Don't worry. Brandon will come," said Tate.

Desti held their lantern slightly above her shoulder and her hatchet in the other hand. Every step she took seemed like one step deeper into her nightmares. A wall of darkness was coming, overshadowing everything in its path. She knew that the demons wouldn't be far behind. When Tate stopped, so did she. "Why did you stop?" she asked.

"This is far enough for now. He will find us here."

They waited for a few minutes and just when Desti was about to give up hope, she heard something in the distance. "Psst."

"Tate, did you hear that?"

"Yeah, hold on," Tate answered while pushing back toward the street. "Brandon, is that you?" His voice was merely a whisper at this point. She heard it again but this time a little louder. "Psst. Tate?" *That must be him,* she thought. Desti blew out a sigh of relief and walked toward the noise.

Out of the bushes appeared Brandon, hanging a satchel over his shoulder and a machete stuffed into the loops of his belt. "I told you I would make it." *Where are the rest?*

It was just him. Desti ran up to Brandon in frustration. "Where is the rest of your group? Did no one else want to join us?" Brandon had a smirk plastered onto his face, which threw Desti into a heightened state of annoyance, but before she could get a word in, she was interrupted by Brandon saying, "you think I would come here and not deliver?" He turned around and waved his arm. "You can come out. Coast is clear."

One by one, Desti counted four students, friends from school, crawled from the shrubs that surrounded her. Brandon stepped in front of them and introduced them. "Desti, I believe you remember my friends; Kaelen, Renzo, Lyra, and Seraph." When Brandon called their name, they gave Desti a slight tilt to their chin, never breaking their gaze.

She recognized them as the group that Brandon would always sneak around with, but as she traced her gaze along the group, she only grew more frustrated.

"Desti, what's wrong?" Tate asked.

Desti shot a glare at Tate and yelled, "four. Really? You could only get four people to join our resistance?" She was now directing her attention to Brandon. Brandon stiffened and took a step forward. "Desti," he said. "I only had a short amount of time to do this, plus these are the only people that I truly trust. Anyone could be a spy for the Master. We must be careful."

Tears began to well up in her eyes. "How are we going to defeat the Master with such a small group? What if—"

"Desti," Tate said, placing his hand on her shoulder. "We have to do this. If we don't, all of us will be as good as dead. And with Anthony, we have a chance at this." How does Tate do that? How does he always know what to say? He was like the sunshine that could blast away a dark storm, and she was that storm. Desti let out her breath and closed her eyes.

"You're right. I'm sorry. I should appreciate them coming." Brandon still stood a few feet in front of her, waiting patiently with his hand slightly pressed against his weapon.

She walked closer. "Do they know what we are doing? Are they okay with this?" The first to interject was Kaelen, a beautiful blonde bombshell she remembered all too well. Kaelen was the *it* girl. "He explained everything. I'm fine with it. They are too." She gestured her hand toward the rest of her group. Kaelen wore black pants, with two large side pockets. There was a knife hanging from her belt loop and a small backpack thrown over her shoulder. The rest of the group pretty much dressed in the same, dark clothing, pants with pockets, and backpack of some sorts.

"Thank you." Desti cleared her throat. "Thank you all for coming here, for me. It truly means a lot."

By now they were standing in complete darkness, with the only thing emitting any kind of light was the lantern she held in her hand. "We should go, before someone sees us," Tate said.

Desti carefully stepped over the overgrown bushes and trash, making her way out of the city boundaries. The rest of the group followed behind her. "So where are we going?" asked Renzo. Desti looked back. "We are going back to Rotten's Crude."

***

They had now walked miles away from the outskirts of the city boundaries, with the only thing keeping them safe was the hues of light radiating from the lantern that Desti carried. "Your lantern seems to be working," said Seraph. Desti glanced back at him. His dark brown hair almost blended in with the midnight sky. "You can thank Anthony for that," Desti said while flashing a smile at Anthony.

The wind blew heavily this cold and brutal night, carrying the guttural growls of the demons that lurked nearby. Lyra gasped, sucking in a breath, to the screeches that echoed around them. "Did you hear that?" she asked.

"Just keep walking. Sometimes they sound closer than what they are." Desti kept her pace forward. Her mind was set on one thing. *Get to Rotten's Crude. Find the Lux. Defeat Elijah's army of demons.* Shouldn't be too difficult. She took a deep breath. Thinking of everything that has yet to come felt like a crushing weight against her chest. *We can do this. We can do this.*

Hours passed and now the moon hung high in the blackness of the sky. Out in the Wastelands, the stars twinkled like shining diamonds. Desti caught a glimpse of the beauty of the sky. She found herself gazing under the milky moonlight. It took her mind to somewhere peaceful for once. She was getting tired, and thought that if she was losing energy, then so must her group. Desti stopped, standing just a few feet from a withering tree.

"We should take a moment to rest," she said.

The first to plop themselves onto the ground was Lyra. Her jet-black hair was stuck to the sides of her face. Sweat dripped from her rosy cheeks. Seraph sat next to Lyra, and then one by one, the group huddled up under the skeletal tree.

***

The air was crisp, like a winter storm had rolled through. That's how it was in the Wastelands, brutal heat during the day and freezing air in the night. Desti set the lantern a few inches in front of her feet. There was just enough heat from the fire radiating from the lantern to keep them warm.

"You guys get some rest. I will stay up and keep watch," said Brandon.

Desti rested her head on Tate's shoulder and closed her eyes, letting her mind succumb to a peaceful sleep.

25: Chaos

"HELP!"

The screeching sliced through Desti's slumber like a jagged blade, ripping her from her tranquility. Her eyes shot open. Adrenaline flushed through her veins, every heavy breath in unison with the slamming of her heart against her chest. She reached next to her and shook Tate awake.

"Tate. Wake up." He shot up just as fast as Desti did. She could see him frantic, a panic in his eyes.

"What's going on?" he asked, but before Desti could answer, there was another scream, this time a man's voice.

"Where is Brandon?" Desti glanced around and noticed he was missing. Tate did the same. "And Lyra?" he asked. Kaelen and Anthony sat up, followed by Renzo, and Seraph, clutching their weapons in their hands.

"Desti what is going on?" Seraph asked.

"Brandon is missing. So is Lyra."

Desti stood, knees half bent, hatchet in her hand, ready to attack. "I think we are under attack." Desti looked down at her lantern. The dim light still fluttered its orange glow. *Did it not work?*

There was a putrid stench of rotting flesh that emitted in the air. Desti almost gagged at the horrid smell. She threw her hand over her mouth. "Tate? You smell that, right?"

She was now back-to-back with Tate. Kaelen and Seraph stood back-to-back next to them, and Anthony and Renzo did the same. "I smell it," Tate answered. *Demons must be near*. "Do you see anything?" asked Desti. The wall of blackness seemed to overshadow any silhouettes that might be in the distance. "I can't see anything. It's too dark," cried Kaelen.

"Tate!"

Desti gasped. "Where are you?" she yelled. She helplessly tried to see Brandon in the darkness. Hearing his cries only made her tremble even more. "What do we do?" Desti asked Tate.

"We need to go find him and Lyra."

"Alright," Desti instructed, "we move as a unit. Do not break our circle. Keep an eye out for Brandon and Lyra, and if you see a demon coming, give it everything you've got."

The first step was the scariest. Desti felt so vulnerable, how anyone would in that situation, but the weight of her hatchet beneath the clutches of her fingers somehow gave her a little bit of a sense of security. "Follow the noise."

One by one, they began to call for Brandon and Lyra.

"Brandon!"

"Lyra!"

Their muffled cries danced around them like a storm in the desert. "That way," Desti pulled to the left. Lyra's cries grew louder in that direction.

"Lyra? We're coming for you," yelled Kaelen.

What Desti came across next, she couldn't have prepared for. Blood. The smell of blood lingered in the air, like a mixture of iron and sweetness. Desti's bottom lip quivered the closer she walked forward. They slowed their steps, standing in something wet.

"Is this blood?" asked Anthony. Kaelen sucked in a gasp. "No, it can't be—" she trailed off. Desti kept her gaze forward. "Keep moving," she ushered. A few more steps forward and that's when she saw it. A piece of skin slabbed onto the ground, mangled, bloody, and torn from someone's body.

"Oh my God," Tate whispered. He stopped and held out his arm, stopping Desti from going any farther. "Desti, don't." Desti shoved his arm down. "We can't just leave them out there, Tate. We must get them back."

She turned to face the rest of the group. "If you want to stay here, that's fine, but I am going to get them back."

Renzo spoke up, stepping into the dim light and said, "I want to stay here. I'm sorry." He hung his head as if he were shameful. Seraph placed his hand on Renzo's shoulder and said, "there is no shame in that. I will go ahead; you stay here with Kaelen, Anthony and Desti."

Desti wanted to object. She needed to find Brandon and Lyra. If she didn't, the guilt alone would eat her up inside. She went to speak, but Tate held up his hand to her mouth. "Desti will stay here with Renzo, Anthony and Kaelen, and you and me will go after Brandon and Lyra." *Don't leave me. I can't do this without you.* She wanted to say, but she held those thoughts in.

Tate took a torch and lit it with the fire from the lantern and followed the trail of blood. His body was slowly engulfed by the darkness the deeper he descended into the unknown.

26: A War too Soon

WAS IT HOURS? MINUTES? IT WAS HARD TO TELL HOW much time had passed since Desti watched Tate disappear. She clung to her lantern; Anthony clung to her. It was silent now. No cries or screams. Silence was almost more terrifying than the noises that they were following. She felt alone. She felt helpless. Guilty. *This is my fault. I'm going to get us all killed.* Desti pulled Anthony closer and cried. "I'm sorry," she whispered to him.

Anthony glanced up. Never once did he seem angry with her and yet she felt as though he should be. "Don't be sorry." Desti had to be tough. If she wasn't then what good was her *resistance*? She didn't respond. Instead, she just tucked her chin into Anthony's shoulder.

Renzo was clearly having a moment of panic. His body rocked back and forth, clenching his knees into his chest. "Renzo, you are going to be okay. Desti will protect us. Her lantern will keep us safe," Kaelen said.

Desti's ears picked up her conversation. *Will it? Will it keep us safe?*

Desti couldn't help but to think that maybe their ritual didn't do a damn thing and that she walked them out into a certain death. She held that thought in. What good would it do to frighten them?

Peering into the midnight surroundings, she yearned to see anything remotely *human.* "Do you see anything?" she asked.

Kealen darted her head, first to her left and then to her right. "No, nothing yet." Renzo was too busy trying not to implode on himself and Anthony hadn't seen anything either. Desti stood.

"Maybe I should go look for them."

Anthony yanked onto Desti's arm. "I don't think that is a good idea, Desti. We should wait here. We seem to be safe here." Desti wanted to pull away. How could she feel safe without Tate? Knowing he was out there and possibly in danger made her feel like she was going to puke. "I'm sorry. I have to go. I can't just wait here knowing that they are out there." She paused for a moment, looking Anthony in the face. "You keep them safe while I'm gone. Okay?"

"Of course," he replied.

Desti took another torch from one of their bags and lit it. "Okay, I'll be right back," she said as she too descended into blackness.

***

This was the time where she was truly alone. It was a feeling indescribable. Fear pinched every nerve in her body, and every movement felt as if she were pulling against a weight. Her body wanted to turn back, but she knew she had to keep pushing forward. Along the ground, she followed a trail of blood, passing by the chunk of skin that lay just beneath her feet.

Desti quivered as she sucked in her breath. She thought of Lyra, and then of Brandon. Whose skin was that? Were they dead? Desti shook her head and banished those thoughts from her mind. "I can't think like this." *Just keep walking. You will find them.*

There was a sudden heaviness in the air that seemed to linger above her. This shift in energy only told her one thing. Demons were near. *So, where is Tate?* Slowly her nose began to pick up subtle hues of the demons' stench. It smelled like a noxious blend of sulfur and decay. It was hard to breathe. Every inhale ripped through her lungs with a burning sensation. Desti coughed, and when she did her eyes grew big, knowing that that was a bad idea.

Hissing and growling suddenly surrounded her. Her heart palpitated with a heavy uneven beat. With the hatchet in her hand, she held it up, preparing to fight.

"Where are you?" she cried. She didn't know who she was yelling out to at this point. The demons? Tate? Lyra and Brandon? She yearned for anyone to come and get her out of this mess.

Without warning, Desti was swiped onto her back, expelling every ounce of air the filled her lungs. She gasped to breathe. Her body ached from the sudden attack. There was no time. She had to get up or she would be good as dead.

Desti jumped onto her feet and that's when she saw it. A grotesque shadowy figure lurking just within her reach and when it stepped closer, she fell back. Its soulless black eyes bulged from its sockets, and its mottled gray flesh was stained with freshly devoured blood. Desti gasped. She grasped at the ground pulling herself backward, trying to get up onto her feet.

Her voice was stolen from her by the sheer terror that ravished through her. She couldn't scream. Wouldn't. It might attract more of *them*. The demon shifted and lunged forward, protruding out a razor-sharp tongue. Desti twisted, just escaping the vicious attack.

Its tongue recoiled back into its snarling mouth, oozing, and dripping with thick salvia. She stood, firmly grasping her hatchet. *This better work.* If her hatchet didn't possess any angelic powers, then she might as well not even fight.

Desti's eyes watched the demon's movements, it swaying from side to side. It was playing with her like a cat would play with a mouse. The demon flashed her a vicious smile, licking its dagger-like teeth. *I'm coming for you;* she heard in her mind.

Almost too fast to see, the demon lunged forward again, belting out a screeching growl as it tried to take a bite out of her. She screamed and swung her hatchet with everything that she had in her.

"Help!"

"Tate! Please!"

A sharp pain radiated up from her leg. When Desti reached down to touch it, she felt something warm and wet. *I'm bleeding.* Tears started to gather in her eyes. This was not how she imagined her last moments would be. *Alone.*

Desti lost control of herself. She swung her hatchet using the momentum of her body and didn't stop. Around and around. Around and around, hoping that the demon would give up, but then something struck her to the ground and wrapped itself around her ankles.

"No, please," she begged. Desti was being lifted by the snake-like tongue, dangling her head over its vile rotten mouth. The heat alone that seeped from its throat was painful to feel. She closed her eyes, tightened her chest, and braced for the pain of being eaten alive.

27: Old Enemies

JUST BEFORE HER HEAD REACHED THE TIPS OF ITS pointed teeth, Desti was knocked out of its grip. She flung to the ground, hitting it with incredible force. The suddenness to everything confused her on what really just happened, but when she looked up, peering through the strands of her hair, that was when she saw him.

"Tate!"

Tate had a tear up his sleeve, his arm was dripping with blood, and he was limping. Desti watched as he held out his knife and stabbed the demon in its eye. Its screeches caused Desti to cover her ears. The demon tried to fight back, lunging at Tate, attempting to swallow him with one bite, but failed as Tate took another jab at its throat.

Desti's fingers curled into the dirt beneath her as she sat there and helplessly watched. *You can do it.* Black tar-like blood oozed from the demon's neck, pouring onto the ground. With every drip, the dirt burned like acid being poured onto metal. Desti inhaled and found her strength to stand. She grabbed her lantern and her hatchet and ran over to Tate.

The demon coward on the ground, convulsing and melting away. Its body slowly dwindled until it became a gross blob of tar-like blood. "Don't touch it," Tate said while holding out his arm. "It might burn you."

He was breathing heavily, his hair had been matted, and his face bruised and scraped. "What happened to you?" she asked while reaching for his face. Just the tips of her finger brushed his skin before he pulled away. "I'm fine."

"Your arm. It's bleeding. How bad is it?" Desti went to take a look, but Tate wouldn't let her. "My arm will be okay, but you need to come with me. Now."

There was an urgency in the tone of his voice. Something didn't feel right. Something was wrong. Tate grabbed Desti's hand and pulled her to follow him. After a few minutes, he turned around and grasped her by her arms, kneeling slightly just so that he was at eye level with her. "I'm going to show you something. It's not good. We must stay quiet. Do you understand?" Those words cut into her deeper than her physical wounds. *I'm going to show you something. It's not good.*

Desti prepared herself. She followed Tate forward and that was when she saw it. Not it, but who? She saw her. A gasp forced its way into her lungs as she froze in terror.

"Is that Lyra?" she whimpered.

In front of her, there lay a body, or pieces of one. Lyra had been torn limb from limb. Desti was looking at what was left of her torso. Lyra's knife was still hitched to the side of her pants. She could see where the chunk of skin had been ripped off from her.

Desti's voice cracked, but then she remembered to keep it under control. "What happened to her?" she cried. Tate held his finger up to her mouth. "Shhh. They can hear you," he whispered. He lifted his knife, pointing in every direction around them. She knew who he meant by *they*. The demons of the Wastelands.

It smelled of blood. So much blood that it became unbearable to breathe. With tears falling from her face, she asked, "where is Brandon?" She braced herself, expecting the worst. Tate gently grabbed her hand and led her even farther into the darkness. Desti held up her lantern, giving just enough glow to see where her feet would step.

A shoe appeared from the shadows, then legs, then a body, until she was standing over Brandon. Not dead but injured. He was bleeding and unconscious. "Is he okay?" Desti knelt down feeling for a pulse. It was faint but there. "I found him like this after I came across—" he couldn't say it. He couldn't say her name. *Lyra.*

"This is my fault, Tate. We should have never asked for them to come out here with us." She wanted to cry.

She wanted to scream or kill or something. All the emotions that ravished through her felt like a storm that was never going to let up.

"This is not your fault. Our world is full of evil. We can't keep living like this. I would rather die trying to fight against them than endure anymore, and I know that she felt the same way too." Tate's eyes were fearless. It scared Desti at times to see him this way, so full of fury and power. Desti interlocked her fingers with Tate's. She needed his touch to bring her back to reality, but suddenly she gasped.

"The others! Anthony!"

***

Desti and Tate had carried Brandon all the way back to where they had left the others, his body flung limply over their shoulders. The weight pressed against her neck made her collarbone start to ache. She didn't have much farther to go.

"Is that them?" she asked. Her eyes squinted, trying to clearly see the silhouettes in front of her. Tate didn't have to answer. She knew she had found them again. Her light slowly illuminated, shining over Anthony. But something was off.

She ran forward, leaving Tate to carry the full weight of Brandon. "Anthony, I'm back. It's me—" but when she stood at his feet, she froze in sheer terror.

"Daddy?"

Flashbacks of Desti's dad rushed into her mind. The beatings she would endure from him, his vicious words, the way he would look at her like an insect. She tightened her knuckles, digging the tips of her fingers into her palms.

"Hi Sweetheart. I've been looking for you."

Those words slithered from his lips like a viper striking her wounds. He was devoid of any kind of empathy, a cruel and selfish man. The tips of her fingers brushed against her left-over scars. *Daddy did this*. Desti gazed back at her father and then noticed what she hadn't noticed before.

In the clutches of his calloused knuckles was a wad of Kaelen's hair, her head helplessly dangling from him. She looked unconscious. Next to her lay Anthony and Renzo. Desti jolted forward but stopped –

"Ah ah ah." He wagged his finger. "Don't take another step my darling." Tate caught up behind Desti and she could practically feel the anger fuming from him. He didn't say a word, he knew better. She looked back, back at Tate. She needed guidance more than anything right now. He didn't have to speak. Their unspoken language was enough. His eyes said it all. *Attack.*

Tate dropped Brandon to the ground and chucked his knife, slicing through the side of Desti's dad's sleeve. Kaelen hit the dirt, stirring up a cloud of dust around her. Soon, Tate and Desti's dad were face to face. "What are you doing out here Mr. Anderson?"

"So nice of you to ask Tate. I see you've been spending a lot of time with my little girl. Thank you for bringing her back to me." Mr. Anderson flashed a sharp smile. Tate snarled, curving his lip downward, and then spat on the ground. "Whatever you are doing out here, consider it over. We are leaving, without you."

Desti was kneeled, crawling toward Anthony. There were splatters of blood scattered around him. "Anthony?" she whispered.

When she touched his leg, she could practically feel his shivering through her body. "I'm sorry," he cried. "I tried to stop him." There was no stopping her dad. He had always overpowered her since the day she'd been born.

"No," she leaned in closer, "you don't have anything to be sorry for. I am sorry. I should have never left you, or even brought you out here." Guilt filled her body. It was becoming unbearable. *This is all my fault.*

Desti stood, hiding her hatchet behind her back. "Daddy, how did you find me?" she cried. Her voice cracked, aching for an answer. She held her breath. In the darkness of the night, he was even more terrifying. As he stepped closer, she took one step backward.

Mr. Anderson cocked his head to the side. "You really want to know Sweetheart? I saw you and your little friends sneaking around town." He played with a knife, twirling it between his fingers. "You ruined our plan when you and Tate decided to run off." *Your plan. Your plan to give my soul to Hell.*

Tate had warned Desti about his plan. It's why they ran away. Her memory recounted that conversation. *I overheard them talking about sacrificing you*. Those words burned into her memory. Everything was okay before. Manageable. Anger began to fester.

She stepped forward and yelled, "I know what you were planning on doing to me Daddy. Do you think I would let you and Mom do that to me?"

Tate had made his way behind Desti and took hold of her hand. "I won't let you take her Mr. Anderson. Go, before you make me do something that I might regret." Tate's voice never quivered, never stuttered. Looking up at him, he seemed— powerful.

She thought that she had won. Mr. Anderson was outnumbered now. There was no way he could fight all of them off, but just as she let her guard fall away, Tate was yanked from behind. As she heard him scream her name, before she could look his way, something hit her on the back of the head. She fell to the ground, slowly fading into darkness. The last image she saw was her father's crooked smile.

28: Your Worst Nightmare

AN OPPRESSIVE WAVE OF DARKNESS SURROUNDED Desti as her mind slowly regained consciousness. The stench of sulfur and blood violated her senses with every attempted breath. She could hardly breathe. The air was thick and muggy, and with every breath, it felt as if she were drowning.

Agonizing screams reverberated throughout the stone-cold walls, twirling their way around her. Desti sucked in the air around her. *Where am I?* As her vision returned, that was when she knew, she knew where she had been taken.

With a sinking heart, Desti curled into herself. *This can't be. Not again.* Before her stood a group of shadowy silhouettes outlined by the flickering torchlight. Interjected into her mind was a voice, a voice so sinister it made Desti want to cry. *At last.*

Trembling, terrified, and hopeless, she slowly traced her eyes upward until she was staring right into his soul-sucking eyes. *The Master*. Desti felt the pressure in her chest trying to explode. She was too scared to breathe or think. His hooved feet scraped the rocky terrain as he strode toward her, reaching out his razor-sharp claws. Her hair twirled around his claw-like fingers. He was smiling. The kind of smile that would frighten anyone who dared to stare.

"At last," he said.

Desti was silent. Fear had ahold of her tongue. The only thing her body would do was tremble. Her body recoiled in disgust with every touch she felt from him. The stench of old blood encrusted his skin, imbued into his pores. She finally found the strength to speak.

"What do you want with me?"

The Master flashed a wicked smile and belted out a heinous chuckle deep from his chest. "I want what I have been promised." *What does he mean by that?* Desti searched her mind. Was it her? Did her father promise her soul to him? All she wanted was Tate. *Where is he*? It was too dark to see every corner of the room. She wanted to cry his name, but she didn't dare.

And just like that, from the depths of the shadows emerged her father. "Daddy? Why?" she cried. She hung her head, silently sobbing, tears splashing on her knee. Her wrists burned from the rope holding her hostage. Mr. Anderson walked into the light.

"Oh Honey, don't cry. You knew this was coming. Your mom and I have planned for this for a long time." His hands fell beside his hips as he dangled a dagger.

Desti's eyes went straight to the dagger. Wide in fear and unsure of what was to come next, she lost control. All the strength she held in her had been swept away and she could no longer take it anymore. She screamed a bloodcurdling scream, wishing and praying for a miracle to come and rip her away from this dreaded nightmare.

There was a sudden flash of orange light emitting from somewhere in the room. The ground shook with incredible force, ripping apart right in front of her, emerging a molten pit of flames and terror. Desti squinted her eyes until they adjusted and that was when she saw them. Her friends that she yearned to save. Anthony and Kaelen, Brandon and Renzo, and Tate, all tied up, lying on the ground, and blindfolded. She sucked in a breath and held it in. *I have to save them*. The restraints on her wrists and ankles were too tight, too difficult to break free from, as she tried to wiggle her way out.

"Let them go!" she demanded. The rage burned in her eyes. They were like fire, but the Master stepped forward and matched her energy. His enormous body shoved through Mr. Anderson and with incredible force yanked up Renzo by his ankles.

"No!" Desti screamed. Tears poured down her face as she helplessly begged. "Please don't." She pleaded and begged for mercy. With every passing second, her fear grew and then another familiar voice stabbed her ears.

"Oh Desti."

When she saw who she was looking at, it sucked the breath right out of her lungs. *It can't be. Elijah.* "I thought you were—"

"Dead?" he finished. "No, quite the opposite. You see I have been granted special power. Power in exchange for something valuable." Elijah twirled his finger in the air and gently caressed the side of her cheek. Desti's eyes went straight to the Master, standing off to the side. His grotesque silhouette was outlined by the torchlight behind him. "And you promised him me?" she asked but kept her gaze on the Master.

The Master stepped forward. "I have been promised the souls of young flesh. Innocent flesh, and I shall receive what is owed to me." Desti whimpered in the presence of the Master. Ash and steam ejected from the fiery hole. Her eyes went to it. *No. Please don't.*

"What are you going to do to us?" she asked. Anything to distract him. Anything to stall. At this point Desti was trying to break free from the ropes that confined her, picking away at the fibers meticulously.

There was that deep rumble of laughter that shook her to her core. "I'm going to feed you and your friends to the portal to Hell," he growled. That was when she knew, she knew what she was looking at. The hole in the ground wasn't just a hole. It was a portal to Hell. To actual Hell.

She frantically picked at her ropes. It felt as if the tips of her fingers had been cut and mangled from the hoarse fibers. She looked back at her dad, eyes full of tears. Maybe he wouldn't follow through. "Daddy, please," she cried. *Maybe he will see me. Maybe he will save me. Daddy please.*

The Master stepped in. "What's done is done. What's promised can't be taken back."

Desti's eyes burned. She couldn't even pinpoint what she was feeling swirling around her. Rage. Fear. Sadness. Guilt. It was too much to bear. She looked at Elijah, feeling the guilt of all the lost souls because of her. "Where is Tess. And Matt. And—" her voice gave up.

"How do you think the Master granted me my power?"

"You didn't." She didn't want to believe that he would betray her and them. For power? How could he? "Elijah, please tell me you didn't do what I think you did."

"What? Throw them to the pits of Hell?" His sharp smile sliced through her like a razor.

Hope was lost. Desti knew it. What could she do in this situation? "I'm sorry," she cried to herself. To all the people who lost their lives because of her. The Master, still holding onto Renzo said, "let's get this over with," and tossed him into the fiery pit.

Desti hurled her body forward in dismay. The Master picked up Kaelen next and tossed her in. Each friend lost, threw her more to the ground in physical pain. *This is my fault*. Then he yanked Anthony by his ankles.

"No," she sobbed. He had been through too much. He deserved better and she couldn't save him. He was too innocent. Too young. Desti couldn't bear to watch. But she knew Anthony had been thrown in when the sound of his body hit the flames. Tate was next. She didn't want to believe it. This one pained her the most. She would do anything to protect him. But confined to her restraints, she could only sit there and watch.

Desti lifted her chin and met the gaze of the Master. It was as if he were waiting for her to look at him. He smiled, with Tate dangling from his claws. Tate's head hung over the flames, he was unconscious and unaware of what was about to happen to him. Maybe it was better that way. Tears streamed down her cheeks because she knew that time was up.

"Any last words?" The Master hissed.

Nothing came out. She couldn't bear it. In a split second, he was gone. Thrown into the pits of Hell. Her best friend, her whole world, everything that she had grown to love over her twenty years of life, gone in the worst imaginable way. And now she was alone.

29: Into the Pit

DARKNESS. EVERLASTING DARKNESS. WAS THAT what she was about to experience? *Is that what Tate was experiencing?* The flames grew brighter and larger with every sacrifice, as if it were feeding on their souls. Desti curled her fingers into the gravel beneath her knees. One last touch of the Earth. One last touch of anything before being burned alive.

"Just do it already," her voice whimpered. There was no more strength within her. Desti had been drained of any hope that may have coursed through her veins. As she stayed there, kneeled in the bloody gravel, she gave up and accepted her fate.

Mr. Anderson yanked on the ropes that held her down, forcing her to fling forward, smashing her face at the feet of the Master. She looked up at him. From down there, his body seemed to go on forever. Her lips parted as if she were going to speak, but only a slight cry escaped when she was snatched up by the roots of her hair.

Desti was eye level with the Master, closer than she ever would want to be. His complexion was perfect, but once she looked into his eyes, that was when he changed. Those were the kind of eyes that would suck the breath right out of you. His eyes pierced through her like a dagger in the chest.

"Just. Do. It," she said through gritted teeth.

As Desti was tossed into the burning flames, her life flashed before her eyes. Memories of her and Tate gave her one last bit of peace. But there was one in particular that brought her soul the most. *Their first kiss.* Her entire existence played out like a movie, giving her one last show before there would be no more. She sucked in one last breath and closed her eyes.

***

Unimaginable terror violated every nerve in her body as she was hurtled into the abyssal maw of a portal to Hell. The world she once knew dissolved away, melting into the molten flames, as she was sucked into a swirling vortex of despair and darkness. It felt as though her body was being pulled apart at the seams as the forces of the infernal realm clawed its way into her soul.

She thought the terror and pain would never end, just continuously falling for eternity, but to Desti's surprise, she hit something with a hard thud. The air in her lungs was ejected out with the initial hit. She gasped, clenching her fingers into her chest.

Her head was fuzzy, her vision blurry, and her body ached with unimaginable pain. *What happened? Where am I?* Desti blinked and slowly regained her sight. Above her there it was, the swirling Hellfire vortex. *Am I dead?* Desti patted her arms and elbows trying to *feel* if she were really there.

A shroud of doom enveloped Desti as she gazed at her surroundings. The air smelled of death and decay. Fire burned at every corner and the ground was hot to the touch. Distant screams carried through the thick air, tempting her terror with their agonizing calls. Being scared was an understatement. She was terrified.

Tate. Thoughts of him flashed into her mind. *He would know what to do.* It didn't take long before Desti pieced together what was truly happening around her. The fire. The screams. The decay. Her eyes went big once realization struck her in her face.

Hell.

"I'm alive and I'm in Hell—" she lingered onto those words, almost unable to believe them. She said it again. "I'm alive and I'm in Hell." Desti crossed her arms across her chest and held herself tight, walking forward through the unforgiving terrain.

Every decaying tree that she passed, sharp boulder, and shadowy figure in the distance made her slowly shrink into herself more and more. She stopped. Overwhelmed, Desti dropped to her knees, burning them on the sweltering gravel. She clawed the sand between her fingers and chucked it across the terrain and screamed.

She screamed with everything she had in her, all her hate, all her guilt, and all her despair, and when she was finished, she sat there for a second in silence.

It didn't take long before a spark of hope appeared in her mind. *If I'm alive, then maybe the others are too.*

***

Minutes felt like hours and hours felt like days. Time was an illusion. It was endless. A small dark path took Desti farther into the unknown, and even though every nerve in her body wanted to turn around and hide, she pushed forward, because the only thing keeping her going was the possibility that she might not be alone down here.

30: Endless

IN THIS FORSAKEN REALM, TIME LOSES ALL MEANING. The suffering was endless. The path Desti was following was endless.

What am I doing? I'm never going to find them.

She began to lose hope, wandering aimlessly. The torment in her mind almost overpowered her physical pain. She was trapped in an unending assault. Desti clung to the threads of her sanity. She squeezed her arms into her chest. *You will be okay. You can do this.*

As Desti continued farther into the darkness, the very fabric of her reality began to distort around her. Whispering growls wisped past her ears. She could feel the hot breath brushing her skin. She recoiled in terror. She was surrounded, surrounded by demons. Desti was in their territory now.

Suddenly a sharp pain shot up her leg, knocking her to the ground. The palms of her hands burned as she tried to catch herself. Trembling and shocked, Desti lifted her pant leg, and that was when she noticed that she had been bitten.

Oozing red blood trickled from the punctures, creating a stream of a sweet metallic scent. Her eyes darted around her. *Where is it?* She knew that the demon wasn't far. Then Desti remembered, back to when she had cut herself. *They can smell blood.* Her eyes shot wide open.

A cacophony of hisses and snarls reverberated around her, riding through the harsh gusts of wind. Chaos ensued. She had no time to react. Suddenly the ground shook, vibrated with incredible force and that was when she saw it. A wall of black silhouettes charging her way. Desti gasped and stood. She ran as fast as she could away from the horde of bloodthirsty demons as the darkness threatened to consume her.

"Tate!"

She cried for him so desperately. She knew that he was probably gone, but his name just slipped out. She cried again, but this time louder. Her heart palpitated with every rugged breath. *I have to hide.* She looked around her. To her left, a river of lava. To her right vast deserted wastelands. Hope was diminishing with every passing second, but then she noticed something ahead in the distance.

Desti ran with everything she had in her, her leg still aching from the initial bite. She darted and ducked behind a massive boulder and crouched.

"Please God. Please make it stop." Desti found herself beginning to pray, something that she had never done before. Growing up in her world, in the city of Mors, praying was forbidden, but it's as if a river was flowing freely, spewing words without her even thinking. She closed her eyes and tucked her head into her knees. *This is it. I'm going to die.*

When all hope had dissolved, a familiar voice ignited a spark in her once again.

"Desti?"

31: Hope

DESTI LIFTED HER HEAD, TREMBLING, TERRIFIED, BUT that was when she saw it. *Him.* His jet-black hair that hung so freely on his face, his sharp cheekbones that seemed to catch even the faintest of light, and those eyes that she could get lost in for days. Desti reached for him and pulled him into her.

"Tate. Oh my God, I thought you were dead," she cried.

Tate reached his hand forward, brushing his finger against her lips. "Shhhh," he said. "They will hear you." Desti watched his eyes glance up, but not once did she see fear in them. He was frozen, locked in on something. After a few minutes Tate let his finger glide down her lips, gently brushing the side of her cheek, until he was pulling her in. Tate wrapped his arms around her as she buried her head in his chest. She missed this. She missed *him.*

"They are gone now," he said.

Tate pulled Desti to her feet and then pushed her back against the boulder. During the midst of it all, of all the chaos and all the terror, he kissed her. The feeling of his body pinning against her, or the way his lips pressed her just right, melted away all the fear that had been ravishing her. She pulled back just for a second and let her words escape. "I missed you."

"I would never leave you," he said going in for another kiss. She didn't want it to end, she didn't want *this* to end, but she pulled back, locking eyes onto him.

"We need to get out of here."

***

Tate had Desti by the wrist, pulling and weaving through the Hell-ish terrain. She didn't know where she was going but anywhere with him was better than being alone. They came across a mountainside that seemed to stretch beyond her comprehension, and above it was clouds that looked like something out of a nightmare, swirling black and red mist that seemed to emit its own fire. There were bird-like creatures flying through them, exploding its gaseous shape as they flew through.

Desti looked up in terror. "What are those?" she asked. Tate followed her gaze but guided her chin back to him. "Don't worry. I've noticed that they don't bother the things on the ground much."

Tate had found a cave, tucked away in the mountain. It looked almost identical to Rotten's Crude.

She recoiled, fearing that something may be lurking inside, but Tate flashed a smile and pulled her in.

It was dark at first. Pitch black and so the only thing she could do was follow Tate's voice. "It's this way," his voice echoed. "Just a little farther." Suddenly a spark of hope appeared. A light. Not the kind of orange light that emitted from fire pits of Hell, but a gentle glow that seemed to draw her in. *Anthony?* The glow was the same kind that the Resistance used to scare away the demons.

When they passed through the doorway, that was when it all clicked. Desti lunged herself forward embracing Anthony with a hug. She sobbed relentlessly, holding Anthony in her arms. "You're okay," she cried while brushing her fingers through his hair. "I'm so sorry. This is all my fault."

"It's okay Desti. It's not your fault. We are okay."

Desti sat back in realization. "Where is Brandon and Renzo and Kaelen and Seraph?" If Tate and Anthony were alive, then they must be too. She then felt someone's hand touch her shoulder. When Desti turned around, she saw Kaelen standing behind her. Seraph and Brandon were there too. A gasp forced its way into her lungs as she could hardly believe it. They were alive. She didn't kill them. Embracing Kaelen with a hug, she cried, "I thought you were gone." She stepped back, eyes looking past Kaelen. "All of you."

But then she paused, noticing that something— someone— was missing. "Where is Renzo?" Her voice trembled, noticing that he wasn't there. Desti looked at Tate. "Where is he?" she asked again. The silence in the room was almost deafening. It spoke when no one could speak up. "He's dead, isn't he?" she asked. Her voice quivered over those last few words. Tate stepped forward and reached for her.

"He was attacked." He glanced back at Kaelen and continued, "trying to save her." Kaelen almost shamefully bowed her head. So many emotions wreaked havoc on Desti's mind— fury, rage, and confusion, all seamlessly tore away at her until she felt raw. Numb. Once the initial flush of emotions wore off, she focused her attention on Kaelen.

"It's not your fault." *It's my fault*, she wanted to say. Why didn't she just let her dad give her up? Then none of this would have happened. Everyone would be safe. The heaviness of guilt crushed her as she tried to breathe. I have to be strong. I can't give up now. Desti shook away her feeling of despair and readied herself to come up with a plan.

***

Hours passed as they all huddled together. The sweltering heat was relentless, attacking every sense in

Desti's body. Desti lifted her hand to wipe away the strands of hair sticking to the sides of her face.

"Okay so let's go over this again. You think you saw a castle, in the distance?" Desti asked Serpah. He was propped up against the stone wall, arms crossed against his chest. Seraph pushed off, striding forward as he spoke. "I *know* I saw one."

Memories of the literature that was forced down her throat when she was younger surfaced. She remembered learning about Hell. It was ruled by three kings, split by regions. She wondered what region they were stuck in. Each person condemned to Hell was forced to live out their eternity in specific regions based on their torment. Some souls suffered psychological torment, others, physical. The demons supposedly roamed free, given permission to wreak havoc on the souls that were trapped, but she wasn't trapped. Not like the other hopeless souls. Does that mean that they could escape? Would she find answers in the High King's castle?

A shiver flushed down her back at the thought of all that suffering. She crossed her arms against her chest and held herself tight. Desti glanced at Tate, who was standing somewhat off in the distance. "What do you think? Do you think there is a way out of here?"

Tate stepped into the soft light, highlighting his sharp features. "There has to be. We are alive. We still have our souls. If the Master and his demons can enter as they please, then there must be a way out of here."

"Should we try to go back the way we came in?" asked Kaelen. That thought had crossed Desti's mind, but she questioned how they would climb up that pit of fire. "I don't think it's possible, Kaelen. We fell down a fiery pit. Could you climb all the way back up?" Desti witnessed Kaelen fold into herself. *Exactly.*

"Maybe the Lux is in Hell. Think about it, this place is the darkest place in existence. The Holy book implies that Lux hides within the darkest realms." Tate came closer to the circle and continued. "Maybe it was never in Rotten's Crude, in the Master's chambers, but what if it is actually hidden in the High King's castle?"

The High King's castle. A castle so evil that it is rumored to devour and shred the very fibers of your soul. Desti matched a gaze with Tate. He was telling her something, with his eyes. Those wonderful, dreamy eyes. She knew what he wanted to say. *Let's break into the High King's castle. Let's look for the Lux*. A smirk tugged at the corner of his lip.

"No way, Tate. There is no way we can pull that off," Desti said.

The rest of the group blankly glanced around. "What?" asked Anthony. Desti rolled her eyes and said, "Tate wants to break into the High King's castle because he thinks that the Lux will be hidden in there and that is how we will be able to return home."

"How did you know th—"

"We have an unspoken language," she interrupted, giving Tate the side eye. The room was silent for a moment. Probably because everyone was soaking in the fact that they might be adventuring into the most dangerous place in existence.

The first to break the silence was Tate. "So, what do you think? If we don't try, then what will become of us? We will be stuck here for the rest of our lives."

Looking around the dimly lit room, Desti could still make out the expressions on everyone's faces. Most of them had the expression of total fear, but a hint of excitement lingered underneath. "I think Tate is right. I would rather die trying to find the Lux and get home, rather than die wasting away in this cave," Desti added.

One by one, they each held out their hands, invoking a group handshake. Kaelen. Anthony. Seraph. Tate. Then Desti.

One unit. One group.

"We can do this. We know how to fight the demons and we have Anthony," she said while glancing over at him. Anthony was her secret weapon. With him, they stood a chance. She held out her hand and grabbed his tight. "Because of you, we have hope."

"So, what is next?" asked Kaelen.

Desti huffed out a breath and said, "Now we break into the castle."

32: Journey Through Hell

"HOW LONG DO YOU THINK WE HAVE WALKED?" Kaelen asked. Desti looked back at her, sweaty, fragile, and exhausted. *She wouldn't last alone out here.* Desti glanced past Kaelen, looking back at the cave they emerged from. It seemed so far away. *How far have we walked?* Time was an illusion in Hell. Was distance too?

"I would guess at least five miles. It seems as though we have been walking for hours," Desti answered.

No one had their weapons anymore. They were probably collected and hoarded by the Master and Elijah. Tate had made a makeshift knife by sharpening pieces of broken stone. But sharpened pieces of rock could be just as effective. It slapped against Desti's leg with every step, as it hung by her pant loop. Desti reached for it. For comfort. Knowing that Anthony blessed her weapon made her feel way more at ease.

The castle seemed to grow farther away the closer they seemed to get, almost as if it had a mind of its own, playing a sick trick on their sanity. Ahead, Desti's eyes lay upon what looked to be a dark forest, with withered, decaying trees that seemed to twist and contort like broken bones. She sucked in a breath. The very thought of going in there shot an impending doom feeling throughout her body.

She reached for Tate. "I don't want to go in there." He glanced back, taking her hand into his. "There is no way around. It will be okay." *Will we be, okay?* She played on that thought in her mind. What creatures could be lurking, waiting for them? Everyone else continued forward. Leaving the deserted wastelands of Hell behind them and entering the forest of torment and terror.

***

Horrific howls carried through the ashy gusts of wind that wisped past her ears. Desti swiftly turned her head. "Did you hear that?" Her heart was racing, pounding all the way into her throat. She tried to swallow but each attempt felt like sandpaper. Kaelen and Serpah stopped. "I heard that," she said.

"What was that?" asked Desti.

"A demon. What else could it be?" Tate answered while pulling out one of his makeshift daggers. He held it in his hand so perfectly. Desti felt his back brush up against hers in a stance ready to fight. Desti instinctively grabbed her knife from her pants and held it out too.

Again. A snarl violated Desti, growing louder. She gasped. "It's getting closer." *Not again.* Desti brushed her fingers against the wound still healing on her leg. It still ached from the other attack. She should have been dead. Most demon bites were lethal, but maybe the venom didn't go into her bloodstream.

Suddenly an ear pitching scream reverberated across the forest. *Kaelen*. Desti shifted her view toward her. Kaelen was face to face with it. A demon too big to fathom. Protruding from its overly large mouth was a set of razor-sharp fangs. Desti squinted as she watched its acid-like saliva drip from the tips. Kaelen was frozen. Petrified. Everything happened so fast and yet it felt as if she were moving in slow motion. Desti went to throw her knife but before she could release it from her grip, Seraph slid underneath the demon, stabbing his sharpened rock into its belly, spilling its guts onto the forest floor. Black oozing tar burned the grass beneath it, melting away everything that came in its path.

With a heavy thud, the demon slumped onto the ground, withering away into a pile of gooey mush. Kaelen stood trembling over the dead body.

"Kaelen, are you okay?" Desti asked. There must be more in the distance. Desti wondered how many were stalking her, waiting for the perfect time to pounce.

Desti reached for Kaelen and touched her shoulder, feeling the trembles vibrating through her arm. Kaelen looked over at her and said, "I'm okay. That was just—it just took me by surprise."

"Keep your eyes out for more. Where there is one, there are plenty," said Tate. He kept his dagger in his hand. Desti did the same as she continued forward deeper into the forest.

The shadows seemed to stretch beyond the tree lines, engulfing any and all light that tried to make its way in. First Desti had to endure fiery pits of lava, burning gravel, and relentless heat, but now, she was facing a new danger. Darkness.

It seemed that the deeper they traveled, the darker it became. Anthony followed somewhere in the middle of the group, holding up a torchlight that he had made. "Anthony?" Desti asked. He made a quick jolt of his chin, acknowledging her question. Desti played with the tip of her knife, poking the tips of her fingers. She thought about whether it was sharp enough to slice through the hide of a demon. Would she be able to think fast enough to do it? Then she asked, "that torchlight that you are carrying, did you— you know, bless it?"

The thought of what Anthony had to do to give their weapons power, to give them protection, sickened her to her stomach. She felt guilty for even asking. She held in her breath, waiting for him to respond.

"I did. Before you found us, Desti, I did the ritual. My blood is on all our weapons, and this torch." He held it up as if she couldn't see it.

"Are you sure that the ritual actually works? Why do you think that demon attacked Kaelen?" Seraph asked. Tate shot Seraph with a glare. What Seraph was asking was valid though. *Why did that demon attack? How could it if we had the protection of the light? Were some demons immune to the power?*

Blackness surrounded them at every corner, seeping its way into places that Desti didn't think it could, like oil spilling in water. In the forest, the air was different. Cold. Freezing actually. Shivers ran up the surface of her arms as she pulled herself closer to Tate.

"It's freezing. How?" she asked.

Tate's body against hers was the only thing keeping her from collapsing. His hand gently found its way to hers. He pulled her in and then wrapped his arm around her. "It's just one form of torment," he added. "Unbearable heat, and now unbearable cold. It's meant to mess with our minds. With our bodies."

"How much farther?" asked Kaelen. Her voice was almost unrecognizable because of the chattering of her teeth. Desti tried to see anything in the distance. She looked for the castle, but there was nothing but endless darkness.

"I don't know," she answered. Desti stopped walking and pulled on Tate. "We should stop. I think we are lost."

"Lost?" Kaelen huffed out a breath of disappointment and fear. "We can't be lost. We haven't gone any direction but straight. Right?"

"Right, but down here, what if normal laws of physics don't apply? Maybe us walking straight took us farther away from the castle."

Seraph stuck his knife in the trunk of the tree in front him, crossed his arms, and asked, "So what do we do now?"

33: Darkness

SERAPH WAS RIGHT. *WHAT DO WE DO?* THEY COULD continue forward but was Tate, right? Would staying on their path take them farther away from the castle? Desti glanced around, searching for any clue to guide them out of the darkness. An everlasting weight was crushing Desti and every decision she had to make put their lives in her hands. There was no way that she would let the others notice her crushing pressure, instead she welcomed silence as she pushed it down, inhaling deeply.

Nothing.

Desti pushed out a breath and said, "we have a few options. We can continue forward, or we can send a scout to try to find the way out." Tate's brow furrowed. He was thinking. Kaelen and Anthony stood with blank stares smeared across their faces. No one spoke up.

"I think we should keep going forward," Kaelen said, finally breaking the silence. She came closer and continued. "Splitting up is a bad idea. What if someone gets lost, or—"

Eaten?

Like Renzo and all the others. Did Matt and Tess, and Clara and Tilly get eaten too? An uneasy feeling engulfed Desti, creeping its way down her body, like a spider stalking its prey. She hated thinking of the fact that so many people were dead. She didn't necessarily like Tess, but she still felt guilty for what happened to her.

"She's right. We shouldn't split up," a slight tug in Desti's neck directed her attention to Tate, "we don't need any more people – friends – dying for us."

A harsh gust of wind blew through the canopy of twisted branches that towered above her, sending an even colder air to attack her senses. Howling and whistling bled into their conversation as the trees contorted above. A quick glance up and that was enough to send a shuddering wave of despair through her spine. Desti hugged herself tight, trying to keep warm. If she didn't find a way out soon, they would be good as dead, and stuck in Hell for eternity. She pondered on the idea of the path and which way she should lead her friends. Going straight could mean certain death, or it could be their way closer to salvation.

"Desti—" Tate trailed off, pulling her off to the side, eyes flickering with sorrow—defeat. "Let me go ahead," he said, the muscles around his chin sharpened, "I am fast, I have a weapon."

Letting go of those strong, calloused hands of his, and stepping back, Desti could only feel regret, fear, and guilt lurking through her veins. *What if you never come back?* She wanted to say, gazing into his eyes as if it were going to be her last time, but if risks weren't taken, in Hell, then Desti and all her friends would be as good as dead. They needed to get out, so instead she nodded and then pulled herself into his chest.

The sound of his breathing, the rising and falling of his chest pressed so firmly against her face, warmed her, comforted her, and eased her. Desti closed her eyes savoring this one last touch, not knowing if this was their final goodbye. She inhaled, trying to remember the scent of *him*, rustic, Earthy. "Be careful," she whispered, stepping back. One last look into his eyes. She could get lost in those eyes of his. There was curiosity in them, excitement, *love.*

Tate ran his fingers through his midnight hair and leaned in. His lips ever so slightly pressed against the side of Desti's cheek, she inhaled as if he were going to take her breath away. One kiss. One gentle, soft kiss, and it was all she needed in that moment. Tate's fingers traced their way up to the side of her face, stroking back the strands of hair that dangled, and whispered, "I love you," and took off into the wall of darkness.

34: Lost

"I DON'T KNOW, DESTI, IT HAS HAD TO HAVE BEEN AT least a few hours by now," Seraph said. He paced back and forth between the trunks of two rotting trees.

"I know, but we should wait for him to get back, to show us the way out." She glanced back at Anthony. "Right?" Anthony didn't speak at first, instead his head hung in silence.

"Desti—" he said. "We can't just sit here. We need to get out of these woods."

Kaelen was propped up against a tree, knees curled into her chest, shivering. Each breath in was as sharp as ice, as Desti tried to breathe, think. Every moment spent in those woods was a moment too long. They were too vulnerable left in the dark. At any moment, another demon could try to tear them to shreds, and another was inevitable, it was just a question of when.

They weren't alone. The echoing of snarls and growls told Desti that much. They were lurking, stalking, watching her moves. The only thing she wanted was for Tate to come back with some good news, something to give her hope, but it had been too long, and she couldn't wait any longer.

Desti pulled a half-broken branch from one of the trees, snapping it off, and wrapped a piece of her ripped undershirt at the end. Using the flame from Anthony's torch, she lit the tip of her stick.

"You're right. We are as good as dead if we just sit here," Desti glanced around and continued, "we should go in the direction that Tate went in, and hopefully he will run into us on our way out. Stay alert and move fast."

Desti lead the way, gripping the end of her branch until her palms were sore. She stayed a good few steps ahead of everyone. Anthony followed right behind, then Seraph and Kaelen. The darkness seemed endless, seeping into every corner of the forest and the only thing that gave her any sense of direction was the flickering flame she held in her hand.

Like a ghostly footfall, whispers echoed in her mind, leaving traces of secrets that only she could hear. Desti stopped, jerking her head in every direction. "Did you hear that?"

"Hear what?" Anthony asked.

There it was again. Desti jolted to the side as Anthony placed his hand on her shoulder. She turned around almost completely out of breath. "You don't hear that? The voices."

The look on Anthony's face said enough. *What voices?* Her hand cupped the side of her head as she slowly stepped back. *Am I going crazy?* Suddenly, the voices grew louder, until they were blaring inside. Desti dropped to the floor and screamed, rocking, praying for it to stop.

Anthony and Seraph ran over to help but their voices were muffled out by the attack inside Desti's head. "Make it stop!" she pleaded. It was too intense, too loud for her to make out what they were trying to say, but then it was just one voice left inside her head, screaming for help. Lifting her head, eyes wide open, that was when she realized whose voice was in her mind.

"Tate."

"It's Tate!" she stood to her feet in a panic. "We have to go help him," she cried. Tears relentlessly streamed down her cheek as she took off running. Anthony's distant voice faded in the background as he yelled for her to slow down, but she couldn't. Wouldn't.

"Tate!" she called for him desperately. It was only when her own breath became too hard to take, that she stopped and kneeled forward. Adrenaline ripped through her body like lava from a volcano.

"Desti!"

Desti threw her head back, glancing over her shoulder, her hair falling over her shoulder like a waterfall. Out of breath she tried to answer, "Tate. I heard Tate. In my head." Anthony, Seraph, and Kaelen slowed their pace as they approached her.

"What do you mean you heard him?" Kaelen asked. Before Desti could answer, Seraph dropped to the floor, screaming, thrashing, like someone who was being tortured. Kaelen kneeled and touched his shoulder, but as soon as her fingers grazed the texture of his shirt, she hurled herself into fetal position, cupping the sides of her head.

"Desti, what is going on?" Anthony asked. Desti could see fear in the flecks of his eyes. Anthony glanced back down and then up, and that was when she saw the shift happen to him too. It started with the light in his eyes, dulling until there was no life left in them, and then he too was forced to the ground.

"What is happening?" She cried but no one could hear her. "Tate, where are you?" Could he hear her voice carrying through the winds? Was he okay? Desti fell into one of the withered trees and clawed her fingernails into the bark trying to keep sturdy. The air was heavy, crushing her chest with every forceful breath. The screaming wouldn't stop and that was when she started hearing Tate's voice again. He was screaming for her. Begging for the pain to end. She could feel his agony within her head, seeping its way down her nerves.

The tips of her finger dug in deeper until she felt the shards of bark penetrate underneath her fingernails. "It's the forest. It has to be." While still holding one side of her head, Desti reached for Anthony and yanked him to get up. "It's not real! It can't be." Anthony crawled forward, stumbling over the roots of the trees.

"Keep moving," she called. Serpah and Kaelen blindly followed, barely shuffling their way forward. Through the cracks of her bloodied fingers, that was when she saw it, the way out of their never-ending darkness.

"I see something," Desti called back towards Anthony. It was only about ten trees away, an opening, leading into another part of Hell, a way out of the forest. The screams rippled through her mind like a stone tossed in a river, overlapping to the point where Desti couldn't understand what he was saying, but only that she knew it was Tate's voice.

Keep running.

Keep running.

Almost there.

Only a few more steps and Desti could be free from that Hell of a place, but before she broke out, her face was hit with an incredible force, knocking her body into one of the trees. Dazed and throbbing, Desti tried to get up but couldn't fully control her body. She wanted to puke from the pounding pain that ached inside her head. Desti held it tight, curling into her fingers, but once she came to, and sat up, that was when she saw what had knocked her off her course.

"Desti," it hissed, exposing its venom dripping teeth. It lingered on her name as if it could taste her with the lick of its tongue.

Desti sucked in her breath. The small hints of light that peered through the edge of the forest exit outlined it just enough to where she could see what was standing in front of her. She met its gaze. Its vile and cold eyes never broke their gaze while staring into her soul. She wanted to run, but where to? Desti glanced to her left, then to her right. It was just woods and trees, and nothing, surrounded by cold blackness just waiting to chew her up and spit her out. The only thing she could do was stare back and pray for a miracle.

35: Fight

DESTI'S THOUGHTS FADED INTO SILENCE, PLUNGING her mind into a vast emptiness. The shock and horror that she felt swallowed her whole, until she curled into herself. *Not again.* She was so close to finding a way out of the pitch-black forest. So close.

She couldn't move, paralyzed with a trembling fear coursing through her. *This can't be. I need to kill it before it kills me.* As stealthily as possible, Desti fidgeted her hands, searching for her weapon.

"What do you want?" she asked. Anything to distract the demon from what she was trying to do. Her finger slowly inched their way to the sides of her pants.

"You. I want you," it hissed. The demon came closer, so close that she could feel the hot, stench of its breath caressing her face as it spoke. She turned her head to the side, holding her mouth closed so tight that the muscles in her face strained. The first pocket on her left leg, empty, nothing but flecks of lint.

"What do you want with me?" she dared ask.

Its viper-like tongue whipped around its massive head, licking the thin line of its lips. "Don't you know? I'm hungry. For your suffering—"

Desti gritted her teeth. After everything that she had been through, this was not how she would go. *Keep him busy. Stall.* Her right hand fumbled into the other pocket, but it too was empty. *Where is it?*

"Why is it my suffering that you want?" Realizing that she must have lost her weapon, her hands then retreated to the ground around her, searching for anything that she could use. She held her breath as she waited for it to respond. Knowing why it wanted her to suffer sent a shudder down her spine. She braced herself, still searching for something, anything, that she could use.

"I can smell it on you," it said. The demon's eyes rolled to the back of its head as it lifted its pointed jaw and sniffed, as if it was getting a taste of her. "Your blood…it's—"

With a swift swipe, Desti flung a handful of gravel and dirt toward the demon's face, shattering its vision with tiny shards of rocks. It screeched, thrashing around. *Run.* Desti shot up and ran as fast as she could, she looked back, the demon clawing at its face, as if it were trying to gouge out its own eyes to save itself from the pain. Then, she saw something in the distance, coming closer and closer.

"Anthony! Seraph!" she yelled. "Hurry!"

Facing the exit, Desti fueled all her strength into her running, running as if her life depended on it. Because it did.

Passing the edge of the forest, Desti fell to the ground in exhaustion. The palms of her hands burned as she kneeled forward. Each inhalation she took was like a gasp for air, filling her lungs with the fiery, ashy air that surrounded her. She coughed, expelling whatever gunk had made its way into her lungs. The sweaty strands of her hair fell forward, sticking to her cheek. Focused and breathing, Desti almost didn't hear the screaming coming from behind.

It was Kaelen. And Serpah.

She jolted back, staring back at that horrible forest, and between the rotting trees, there it was. The demon, slashing its claws, trying to knock down Kaelen and Seraph. Desti's eyes darted around. *Where is Anthony? Where is he? He was just there.* She couldn't see him. She tried not to imagine the worst, but how could she not, in a place like this?

Just as Desti thought things couldn't get worse, a horrendous symphony of growls reverberated about the treetops. What looked like to be skeletal birds, flew out from the tops of the trees, screeching and soaring past her, as if they were trying to run away from something. She could feel something was wrong.

Something was worse than what was happening right now. She could feel it in her gut.

Ahead, hundreds of slithery silhouettes emerged from the shadows like cockroaches, swarming the fresh scent of blood that was now lingering. Desti gasped. She knew they stood no chance of fighting off the horde that was now hurtling toward them. Desti didn't hesitate, didn't think, she only took off back to where she so desperately escaped from.

Every beat of her heart slamming against her chest only fueled her more and her breath, heavy and fast, didn't seem to slow her down. *Just twenty more feet.*

Ten.

Five.

Each inch closer to the darkness was a second closer to inevitable danger. Desti sprinted past the outskirts of the forest and was now running toward the fight. Seraph and Kaelen were swinging large sticks around, standing back-to-back, as they tried to fight off the demon that she had escaped. A quick glance around, and she knew that time was running out. They were surrounded. She was surrounded. She didn't think this far ahead. *How am I going to fight these demons?* She questioned as she realized that she was outnumbered by hundreds. Hundreds of black, leathery bodies that could probably crush her in one hit.

"Kaelen!"

"Seraph!"

When Desti yelled for them, the demon suddenly turned its vicious eyes onto her, almost winking with a smirk. Its sharp serrated teeth flashed as it opened its mouth to howl, sending a shockwave knocking her to the ground. The air was sucked from her lungs as she hit the dirt beneath her. Dazed and disoriented, it took a moment before Desti realized that the demon was running headfirst toward her.

"Desti, look out!" Seraph called.

There was no time to react. The demon lunged forward, snapping its jaws at her, but she ducked and rolled just seconds before it touched her. She stood quickly, knees bent, and ready.

"Come on, you nasty creature," she spat.

The roaring of the sea of demons was now inching its way in. Without glancing away, Desti called out to Seraph and Kaelen.

"The treetops!"

She didn't break her gaze. It smiled at her with those evil eyes, looking like it was getting ready to pounce again. She had only one shot to make this work. One shot, and if she missed, she was going to be gone, in a raging mosh pit of demons. From her peripheral Desti could see them climbing to the top of the trees. Maybe the demons could climb too, but she was hoping for the latter. If she was right, then she might have just found her way out of there.

One.

Two.

Go.

Desti hurtled herself toward the nearest tree with every bit of strength she had in her, screaming, climbing, and clawing her way up.

Up.

Keep going.

Don't look back.

It was only when she reached the top of the withered twisted branches that she dared to look down, and with a breath of relief, realized that the demons could not follow her up. Breathing was difficult, heavy, and the adrenaline that rushed her made her feel like she was going to puke.

"Seraph? Kaelen? Anthony?" Desti called. *Did Anthony make it out?* She glanced at her surroundings, at the top of the forest, but it was dense and full of darkness. *Where are they?* But then she heard it, someone calling back.

"Desti?"

"Anthony? Is that you?" she cried.

"It's me. I got separated. I didn't know where to go, so I went up."

Desti could have cried happy tears if her heart wasn't pumping so damn hard. She called out again, "where are Seraph and Kaelen?"

"We are over here!" This time it was to her left. She couldn't see them, but she could hear them, and being at the top of the trees, she had an advantage, and could see the edge of the forest.

"We need to climb out of here. Go to the edge!"

Desti started crawling, crawling through thorns, sticks, and branches. Every inch she was either being cut or poked, bleeding from every attempt to get out, but none of that mattered. Desti kept her head down, focused, and kept forward. Looking down was like looking at a sea of monsters, with their open mouths and sharp teeth just waiting for her slip and fall. Desti sucked in her breath and shivered at the thought of those jaws crunching down on her bones. It could break her bones so easily.

Suddenly the air grew thick with the acrid scent of smoke. Desti began to cough, wheezing with every breath as she tried not to pass out. Towers of black smoke billowed upward suffocating any air that might have been left. It was all darkness now, surrounding her. She only knew that she needed to keep climbing through the branches. Straight. Then she would be out.

Tendrils of fire hungrily flicked at the underbrush, burning everything that stood in its path. Desti could see it now. Light. A small sliver ahead in the distance. *There. That is my way out.* She tried to look around for the rest of her friends, but the smoke was too thick. If she wanted any chance at surviving, she needed to focus.

You can do this. Her arms ached, burned, with a fiery sensation that radiated throughout her body. All Desti wanted was to collapse from the exhaustion, but she didn't succumb to it. "Almost there."

"Keep going." She called out to herself, to keep herself focused. "Just a few more feet."

Desti screamed as she fell forward, releasing herself from the clutches of the tormenting treetops. She fell hard, hitting the ground with an incredible thud. Coughing and gasping, she clenched her fists into the dirt beneath her as she tried to expel the smoke from her lungs. Her arms were shaking. Blood oozed from every part of her body, cuts and scrapes covering her head to toe.

"Desti," a weak and familiar voice called out.

Trying not to collapse onto the ground, Desti turned her gaze to her right where she saw them. Her friends. *They made it.*

"Anthony," she called, trying to wave her hand over her head, but she collapsed and rolled over, just staring at the auburn burnt sky. It was only moments before Seraph, Kaelen, and Anthony had rushed over to her. They looked just as beat up as she felt.

Desti reached her hand up and held on to Kaelen's. "You look like shit," she laughed. Kaelen sat her up and responded with, "so do you," while giving her a friendly smirk.

"Where did the fire come from?" asked Desti.

Anthony stepped closer, covered in ash, and burnt bark. "That was me. I threw my torch at one of them and it caught the tree on fire. Before I knew it, it started spreading," he continued, "the demons don't like fire, not like that, and so I just climbed until I saw you."

Desti pulled back the hair that was sticking to her mouth. "You saved us."

Anthony pulled Desti to her feet and that was when she took the time to really study the forest behind her. The darkness was no more, and flames just now ravished the trees that once stood there. She could hear screeching from the demons caught inside the fire, burning to a crisp. Desti spat on the floor as she glared at it one last time.

"Come on. We need to keep moving."

36: Relentless

HOURS. DAYS. WEEKS. IT WAS HARD TO TELL anymore. Time was different in Hell. It moved slower, faster, and everything in between. Desti couldn't tell how long she and her friends must have been trudging through the wastelands, but it was long enough to cause her legs to shake. How would she get past them? Defeat them?

Touching the tops of the smog filled sky, swirling with charcoal clouds, was the tip of the castle. It reminded Desti of the stalagmites back in the caves, sharp and pointed. It wasn't the kind of place that she wanted to go. Desti tried to imagine what dangers could be lurking in the castle.

"We've been walking for hours, and it still looks like we haven't moved," Kaelen whined. She looked pretty brutal. Kaelen was covered in thorns and had spent the last hour trying to pick the rest of them out of her skin.

Everyone was covered in something. Thorns, scrapes, ash—just a few of the many sufferings she knew were inevitable. There was no sun in Hell, but a relentless scorching heat that seemed to light the sky as if in a perpetual summer. Desti wiped the sweat from her head and inhaled thick air. She couldn't help but worry about Tate. *Where did he go? Is he okay?* These questions tormented Desti as if she were stuck in her own mental Hell.

"Do you think Tate is in there?" Desti asked while nodding her head toward the castle. Seraph's eyes were empty. Desti looked at Kaelen and she too had nothing to say. "You think he is dead, don't you?" Desti's voice was brittle.

"I don't know. We barely made it out of the forest alive, Desti. Look at this place," Kaelen answered. She waved her hand around and Desti did look. She was surrounded by death and decay. Rotting carcasses, broken boulders, and brittle trees were all that stood. This whole place was meant to suck you in until your own despair consumed you.

"Maybe he made it out." Desti stuck up her nose and held her chin high. She couldn't, wouldn't, let her mind go to that conclusion. Tate was alive. He had to be. Seraph and Kaelen kept a few steps ahead. Desti glanced back just to make sure nothing was sneaking up behind her and slowed her pace to walk closer to Anthony.

"Did I ever tell you how Tate and I met?"

Anthony looked up and met her gaze. There was maturity in his eyes. Years of torment and fear burned deep within them. He was too young and was forced to grow up too fast and the thought of him being alone, chained up, in that cave twisted Desti's stomach into knots. She clenched her fingers into her stomach as if she could feel the aching for him within. Anthony slightly nodded his head and said, "yeah. You met down the street. Right?"

"He was your neighbor?" Anthony kept his hands curled into a fist.

"Yeah, he was, but he was so much more than that," Desti inhaled, and continued, "he saved me from a dark place." She lingered on those words, taking her back to all the abuse she endured as a child, as a teenager. It never let up.

Moments must have passed because Desti realized that Anthony was staring, probably because he wanted to hear more. She laughed and pulled her hair out of her face. "My parents," she corrected, "our parents were very abusive and unkind. They would beat me, beat me down so hard that I wouldn't want to get up. My dad would always say, *I'll give you something to cry about*." She paused for a moment, marinating on those memories, and then took her gaze to the ground and scoffed. "Tate found me one day in the bushes down the street, crying. I had just had a beating and so did he, and we just held each other until we felt better—"

A single tear gathered in the corner of her eye, but she blinked it away.

"And you guys have been friends ever since?"

"Mhm— he has always been there for me when I needed him, which is why I *need* to find him. He doesn't deserve this. All of this. All of this that he did was to save me, from them." Those words coming out were like venom on her tongue. *This is my fault.* Desti tried to shake away the pain and the thoughts, but it was building inside her like a stream ready to burst through a dam.

"From them? You mean your parents?" His eyes flickered.

Desti paused for a second. It was difficult to admit such horrors coming from her parents, but then she nodded. "Yeah—"

"They— uh," she cleared her throat, "they were planning on sacrificing me on my twenty-first birthday to the Master in exchange for riches and protection." Anthony must have had a look of utter disbelief when she told him because she then quickly leaned in closer and asked, "doesn't your city do that too?"

"Isn't love forbidden? Our parents never loved me, but I just assumed it was because they didn't know how to love. No one does in the city of Mors," she said. She flicked back the hair that was sticking to her neck and said, "people in my city are paired together. Chosen by the leader of the city. No one has a choice. I'm sure people have fallen secretly in love, but my parents, they weren't like that."

There was silence, just for a second, before Anthony answered. Maybe he was thinking back to his memories with his family and friends. Did he suffer the way she did? The glimmer in his eyes faded away as he tilted his chin, cocked his head, and said, "actually, my mother was never unkind," he lingered on those words as if he were savoring the memory with his mother. "All she ever did was try to protect me. That is why she sent me away, because she knew what kind of danger I would be in if I stayed, but my city was no different than yours. Love was forbidden, but my parents, after their arranged marriage, they secretly fell in love, and when they had me, that love extended to me."

"I always wondered what that kind of love must have been like. It must have been nice—" Desti said. Her mind flashed through memories of them, as if she were trying to see any reminiscence of love in their marriage. "My dad was an angry man, and my mom," she paused, "well she was isolated and pathetic." Those words hurt coming out, almost worse than the beatings she had endured.

Desti flicked her gaze at Anthony and said, "remember the good memories with your mom and don't let yourself forget what that kind of love feels like."

And just like that, Desti was called from ahead, breaking her focus and attention from her conversation. It was as if she had somehow walked thirty miles in a matter of minutes and now was coming up on the outskirts of the castle. Kaelen and Seraph stopped in their tracks and gazed upon it, blocking the brutal light from their eyes coming from above. Desti slowed her pace, came to a halt, and held out her arm to stop Anthony from walking any farther.

"What is that?" asked Kaelen. She was pointing to a massive wall of thorns and vines, and it seemed to stretch on for miles around the castle.

Desti walked forward, standing closer to Kaelen. For a moment, the sight of what she was seeing almost took her breath away. "Uh— I'm not sure what that is. It looks like a wall made of thorns."

The air was thick with a stench of decay, floating around like an ominous cloud. The thorns that protruded from the vines were massive and like no other Desti had ever seen before. Sharp, serrated edges twisted and wound like some sick bondage knot. Seraph went to touch one of the thorns, but Desti jumped forward screaming, "don't!"

His hand pulled back, mere inches away from the edge of the thorn. It was almost bigger than his forearm.

He turned back, eyebrows furrowed and asked, "what's wrong?"

"They might be poisoned. Look over there," Desti said, and nodded her head in the direction of a row of decaying carcasses that lined the perimeter. She continued, "they look like they all came in to contact with the wall. I wouldn't touch anything down here if I were you."

Seraph backed away and put his hands into the pockets of his leather jacket. "Okay, so how do you say we get through? If they are *poisoned*, then climbing is out of the question."

A smirk pulled on Desti's mouth. "You see that over there," she nodded, "it looks like an opening."

Kaelen, Anthony, and Seraph focused a few feet down the wall and there it was, an opening, almost as if it were waiting for them to come. Kaelen turned around with a look of regret and fear smeared across her face. "So, we should go through there, is what you are saying?"

"What? Do you have a better idea? Why don't we just sit here and wait until something comes and eats us?" When Desti saw Kaelen's eyes flick with a hint of anger, she realized that maybe she was being…offensive. She pushed out a breath and said, "I'm sorry, that came out wrong, but look, what other options do we have?"

Miles. Desti had walked miles in the sweltering heat, ducking and dodging being pecked by skeletal birds flying above and worrying about demons coming to eat her like a snack. She was ready to get out of the vastness of whatever desert she was walking through and go somewhere with less vulnerability.

No one answered, not for a minute or so. Anthony was too busy prowling the perimeter, carefully not touching the thorns, and Seraph had gotten a closer look at the entryway, which stood about ten feet taller than him. Kaelen, Desti could tell, was scared shitless. Desti closed in on her, held out her hand, and said, "come on. You can hold my hand," and smiled.

Slowly, cautiously, and one by one, they entered under the arch and walked into the unknown that lurked behind the wall.

37: Labyrinth

AS DESTI STEPPED THROUGH THE THRESHOLD, behind the wall of coiled thorns, it was as if she had been sucked through another portal, catapulted into another realm of terror. Twisting swiftly to glance back from where she came stood no entrance or exit, but rather a towering wall of vines. Her eyes went wide.

"Guys? Where did the entrance go?" Desti turned back to face her friends, but they too seemed preoccupied with their owns confusions. As Desti peered to her left and then to her right, she realized that she was trapped in what seemed to be a labyrinth. Endless hallways of poisonous spikes protruding from the walls, with the occasional small crack, just large enough for one person to slide through.

Seraph had walked down one of the paths to get a better look, while Anthony took off in the other direction to check out the maze. Desti stood centered, picking at the seams of her pants. Kaelen stood next to Desti and seemed to be in a daze, confused and terrified, as she stood in silence.

"You, okay?" Desti asked.

Kaelen blinked as if she were resetting her mind and coming back to reality. "Yeah, I just— I just have a bad feeling about this place."

"We're in Hell. This whole place gives me a bad feeling."

Kaelen scoffed. "Yeah, well let's just hope that whatever we need to get home is in that castle."

Desti nodded her head slightly to the left, inviting Kealen to follow. "Come on." She strode down the path to her left and called for the rest to follow. If they were going to get through this, they first needed to prowl the perimeter.

***

So far, from what Desti could gather, the labyrinth was a cylinder wall, surrounding, protecting, the castle that lurked within. On the outskirts, the only thing that seemed to pose any kind of threat were the poisoned thorns that stuck out like broken shards of glass. She had come across a few openings, doorways, within the wall, but had yet to make her way through. Assess the perimeter first, then face whatever dangers may be waiting. Ash filled sky blanketed over the castle like a shroud of suffocating darkness, making the air unbearably difficult to breathe, almost as if it were taunting, toying with Desti.

She missed home. Never in a million years would she think that she would wish to go home. Back to the chaos. Back to conformity. Back to it all as long as she could be back with Tate. There was a gaping, aching hole in her heart that yearned to see Tate, to know that he was alive. Tate was her home, her everything, and now she didn't even know if he had made it out of the forest.

A single tear began to form in the corner of Desti's eye. She blinked it away, only leaving a slight shimmery streak down her cheek. The tips of her fingers dug into her palm as she clenched her fists tight. She shot Anthony a sharp look and said, "you ready?"

Ready to go into the maze of mystery and misery? Ready to probably risk your life again? Anthony nodded, followed by a silent ripple from the rest of the group. Desti went first, stepping and squeezing her way into the passage as she carefully twisted her body—bare skin— away from any thorns. She had merely inches between her and the razor-like tips. One wrong move and she would be good as dead. She wondered if it would be a slow agonizing death. Would the poison ravish her body slowly to make her suffer? Desti held in her breath, scared that a single breath could throw her off balance, and kept shuffling.

Almost through.

There was an opening ahead, now only a few feet away. Desti broke free from the twisted hallway and called out for the others to follow. "I'm through!"

Anthony went second, his prepubescent body barely visible through the towering wall. The twisting shadows that lurked beneath the vines engulfed his silhouette as he inched closer. Desti bit the side of her lip in a nervous tick. One wrong move and—

She exhaled a breath as Anthony finally made it through. "Good," she said, "okay, Kaelen, be careful."

It felt like an eternity, watching her friends barely scrape by almost certain death. One prick, that's all it would take. Just one prick and scrape of their skin and they would be gone in probably a horribly agonizing death. She held her breath as she waited for Seraph to pass through, but relaxed her shoulders knowing that he was the last one that needed to do so.

"Ah, crap!" is all Desti heard Seraph yell before she ran forward, fear beating through her veins. She stopped just at the edge of it all, peering down the passageway, but she couldn't make out what was going on.

"What happened?" Desti called back.

"One of the thorns," his voice went ragged, "I – I think it got me."

No. No. No. This is all my fault. She shook her head in disbelief. In utter guilt that ripped her apart at the seams. She turned her gaze to Anthony and Kaelen, her eyes already stinging from the salty terror smeared across her face. Kaelen and Anthony looked equally terrified. Anthony ran forward and called out to Seraph. "Are you sure it got you?"

"I don't know man. It hooked my shirt, ripped a huge gash in it. I can't tell if I'm bleeding or not."

"Just keep coming our way. Careful."

Seconds stretched to hours. Heavy panting echoed around her now, not only from her ragged breathing but from Anthony and Kaelen as well, taking shallow, terrorized breaths."

Desti could see him now, appearing within arm's reach. She reached out her hand, palm up, and waited for him to take it, then pulled him through with one swift yank. Seraph collapsed onto the ground, knocking Desti to the ground with him. He was on his knees, palms down, and head facing the shadow beneath him. Desti grazed a gentle touch on his shoulder and asked, "are you okay? Did you get cut?"

It took a second, but when Seraph came to, he quickly twisted his torso, pulling at his shirt, searching for the inevitable cut. But when he pulled back the cloth that had been ripped to shreds, he did not find a single scratch on him. Desti took a second look, just in case, but she too found nothing. A heavy breath of relief escaped her chest, and she bowed her head.

"I think he is okay. It must have missed his skin."

Kaelen, with a gentle, playful smirk on face said, "you're one lucky bastard."

That indeed he was.

***

The labyrinth stretched for miles, twisting, and turning with a cunning sense of humor, leading Desti always back right where she started. She had spent nearly three hours now searching through the maze only to go in full circle.

"I don't know what we are doing wrong," she breathed heavily. The muscles in her legs screamed for a break as she wobbled her way to sit down. Kaelen plopped down beside her, expelling a sigh.

"We've tried every path," she said.

Anthony sat on the other side of Desti and added into the conversation, "There has to be something we are missing. This maze is here to keep things out, obviously. They wouldn't make it that easy to navigate. Maybe the rules are different down here."

An epiphany hit Desti, as she stood up, arms gesturing toward the vines. "I have an idea." She carefully reached for one of the dagger-like thorns protruding from the wall of vines and with a swift snap, cracked it off. She turned around, grin smeared on her face, and said, "now we have a knife."

If traveling through the passageways only brought her right back to the beginning, then maybe she was supposed to find a different way through. Straight. Seraph and Kaelen stood with blank stares in their eyes, but Anthony smiled slightly, stepping forward and snapping a thorn off for himself too.

"If the passageways aren't taking us where we need them," she cut through the first layer of vines, and continued, "then we make our own passage."

Carefully Desti sliced and cut forward, very delicately snapping away any thorns that stuck outward. Anthony was behind her, slicing away until there was a clear path that led to another part of the labyrinth.

"It's working," Kaelen yelled.

Seraph followed suit and took a thorn for himself, and then yanked one off for Kaelen. "Here, just in case you need some protection," he said, coolly.

"You better keep that thing pointed in that direction," Kaelen joked, nudging Seraph.

Desti made it through the thick mass of vines and thorns and was now standing on the other side. "I made it through, come on," she yelled. When she turned around, she could have sworn that her gut hit the floor in disgust. She gasped, cupping her hands to her mouth, tears stinging her eyes. Anthony stood next to her in silence, but she could feel his disgust.

"What is that?" His voice cracked.

She could barely get the words to come out of her mouth. "I—," she paused, took a deep breath, and continued, "It looks like some kind of torture arena."

A tide of despair washed over Desti as she stepped forward, clenching her stomach in utter disbelief. Her breathing became shallow, uneven. Terrified. As she inhaled, she could almost taste the metallic tang of blood in the air. It took everything in her not to gag at the putrid stench of rot and decay that lurked beneath. Anthony stood just as she did, frozen, petrified, unable to speak.

Before she could speak, Seraph and Kaelen popped through the passageway and stopped in their tracks. "Ugh, what is that smell?" Seraph almost gagged.

Desti slowly turned her head to Seraph, tears coating her eyes, and the only words she managed to get out in a mere whisper were, "we are not alone."

38: Fight or Die

DOZENS OF SLITHERY SILHOUETTES FLICKERED in the cracks of the arena. Towering stones pillars rose like twisted spires, etched with the same symbols that Desti had found in Anthony's cave. She glanced down, staring at rotting bodies and rusted chains laying on the blood-stained sand. Desti took a shallow breath. That I when she heard them, their vile wretched growls attacking her mind.

"We've been waiting for you," they hissed.

There was no way out, besides the way they came from, but even then, she would be trapped. This was bad. Really bad. Desti still gripped the massive thorn in the palm of her hand, careful not to squeeze too tight. Her eyes darted around the room, looking for any way to escape.

Suddenly, one by one, the demons began to emerge from the shadows, with their twisted smiles and venom dripping teeth. She dared not stare at them in their soulless black eyes. Desti was surrounded. In the center of the arena, there was a body, slump, purple and black from what seemed to be blunt force trauma. This is what people endured down here. Suffering. Torment.

"What do you want with us?" Desti asked. She held her breath, terrified of what might come out of their vicious mouths.

This time, it spoke out loud, for everyone to hear. "We want your suffering. We want to feed off your fear. We want to taste—" the demon's eyes rolled to the back of its head as it intimately licked its thin lips, and continued, "your blood." Its eyes met Desti's, almost taking the breath from her lungs with its intensity.

This was not good. She needed to find a way out or come up with a plan to escape. She felt cornered. Trapped, and that was exactly what the demons wanted. A flicker of movement shifted on her right, then on her left. They were closing in, and that was when she met the gaze of Anthony, Seraph, and Kaelen, knowing that without speaking, they all knew they had to fight.

Kaelen acted first, ducking, and rolling to her right as she stabbed the demon closest to her in the leg, and that was when chaos ensued, bodies attacking and flailing, screams of suffering and pain. Kaelen was flung across the room, body smacking into a concrete pillar. Desti was too occupied to see who was screaming. The largest demon lunged forward slicing its bear-like claw at her, but she jumped to the side, dodging its attack.

"You think you can win, girl, but we are power, we are the dark and the twisted, and you will not defeat us." Desti cringed at the evil emitting from its hoarse voice. She held up her thorn and said, "well I think you are underestimating me."

She didn't think, only acted as she dodged and lunged past the demon, climbing her way up to the top of the centered pillar. It stood about fifteen feet high, higher than the demon could reach. *They can't climb*. The view was chaotic and terrifying as she helplessly watched her friends fight for their lives. Anthony and Seraph were back-to-back, taking on a pair of alligator-like demons, their long ravenous snouts snapping at every movement they made. Kaelen was surrounded by two demons, who seemed to be tasting her, licking her body as if they were testing out their midday snack.

"You can't hide up there forever, girl," it hissed.

They were losing, bad. She had to think quickly, think of something, anything to buy them more time. Kaelen screamed from the top of her lungs as she was dragged by one of the demon's claws. Anthony and Seraph were running out of time. She was running out of time. Desti held a firm grip on her thorn and too quick for the demon to react, she jumped down, straight on top of it, jamming the thorns straight into its eye socket. She shoved it so deep, that its eye popped, oozing out a thick tar-like liquid as it dropped to the ground.

Desti turned around, running after Kaelen, but just before her fingertips could grasp on to her, Kaelen was pulled into a pit of darkness, screaming until her voice faded away. Desti froze, not in fear but in total utter despair that she had failed her. Everything was happening so fast. Too fast for her to react.

"Desti!" cried Anthony.

When she turned around to help him, the last thing she saw was the massive snarling face of a demon before everything went black.

***

Slowly, painfully, consciousness began to seep its way back into Desti's mind. A slight groan escaped through her clenched jaw as she tried to open her eyes. Every beat of her heart pulsated in the veins in her head. *What happened?* Desti went to lift her arm to her head but instead was met with the clicking of metal that encased her wrists. *Chains?*

That was when she knew, she knew that after all her fighting and all her perseverance, she had been captured. Probably captured to be tortured for mere amusement or to be the next meal. Once her vision was back to normal, she gazed at her surroundings, realizing that she must be inside the High King's castle.

It wasn't what she expected. Not the blood-stained stone and rotting corpses she was used to coming across, but in fact, this place was— beautiful. Marble floors stretched across the foyer, intricately swirling with shades of gray and gold. It was empty, no one in sight, but the slight echo of footsteps told her that someone was coming.

Desti's heart yearned for just one more touch, one more kiss before she was killed, because that was what this had to be. Her execution. *Where is he? Is he alive?* Memories of Tate flashed through her mind as she hung her head in shame. There was no way out, not when she was chained to the stone wall.

"Ah, at last. I've been wanting to meet you," a voice said.

This voice was not like the others, not vile and cold, but smooth, suave, as it echoed louder in her ear.

"Who is there?" she said, trying to see the face behind the voice.

"Oh, surely you have figured it out by now. You are smarter than you portray."

The voice was closer. She could almost feel the hot breath caressing the back of her neck. And then around the corner emerged a man, a man so beautiful, so clean, that it took her by surprise. His jet-black hair curled up with a smooth swoop, exposing his sharp perfect cheekbones. The corner of his lip curled, flashing his pearly whites.

"Who are you?" Desti asked through the strands of her hair.

He stepped closer, standing directly in front of her now. He wore a fitted suit, embroidered with blood red thread. The man leaned in, lips almost touching hers, as he said, "I am the High King of Hell, my name is Amaros."

It was hard to focus on anything other than his emerald eyes. She could have sworn she saw a glimmer of humility in the flecks of his irises, but instead of lingering her gaze she spat on the ground.

"Where are my friends?" she demanded.

"Ah, yes, your group of wanna be heroes."

"Where are they?" Her eyes were cold, anger filled.

Amaros tskd as he wagged his finger, "that isn't how you should talk to the High King of Hell, now is it?"

"I don't care who you are," her words like venom.

Amaros smiled, precisely to tick her off even more. With a snap of his fingers, the doors across the room flung open, as she watched Tate being dragged across the floor.

Desti could hardly contain herself as she dropped to the floor sobbing. "Tate!" Desti sobbed into her palms, tears streaming through the cracks of her fingers.

Without lifting her head, she asked, "what did you do to him?"

Tate tried to lift his chin but seemed too weak to even meet her gaze. He was filthy, covered in dried blood and black dirt. His clothes have been torn to mere shreds, looking as if he fought hard with whatever had taken him. She wanted to reach for him, wanted to touch him. Tate had always been her protector but now… she needed to protect him. It will be okay, she wanted to say.

"Your friend has had quite an adventure before I found him," Amaros stealthily strode across the floor and continued, "I think you have it all wrong, my darling. You see, I saved him." Desti narrowed her brow, meeting the gaze of Amaros. There was a wickedness in his voice, something that told her not to trust him.

"Then if you are not here to hurt us, then let us go. Let us *all* go. Send us home."

"I can't do that." He picked a strand of hair from his shoulder and flicked it.

"Why can't you just let us go?" Desti's voice cracked. Fear and sorrow ravished though her like a flowing river of lava, burning up every bit of life in its path. She glanced back at Tate. He was still so beautiful, so strong, even now.

"I believe that you have something that I need," he said.

"I don't have anything," she cried, "Everything has been taken from me. Everything." That realization hit her like a freight train. This was the moment that she truly felt alone. Her body began to tremble, as she clenched her fingers into a fist, dried blood now cracking underneath her nailbeds.

"What more could you possibly take from me?" her voice grew louder, "I have risked everything, given all of myself, and for what? To be your next tortured entertainment?" she cocked her head to the side and scoffed. "I've failed and I have nothing more to give."

The room fell silent, blanketed with a shroud of despair. She knew Tate could feel it by the way he shifted his body toward her. Maybe it was pity or maybe it was calculated but Amaros snapped his fingers, unleashing the chains that clutched to Desti's wrists. The room echoed with the loud thud of it hitting the marbled floor.

She held out her trembling hands in disbelief and looked over to Amaros. He nodded his head toward Tate and said, "go to him."

Desti didn't hesitate. As if a burst of life had just run through her veins, she catapulted herself forward nearly knocking Tate over in the process, wrapping her arms around his neck and buried her head into his shoulder as she cried relentlessly. She lifted her mouth to the edge of his ear, just barely brushing his skin, and whispered, "I love you, Tate."

He hugged her back, pulling her body into his, swirling strokes down her back with his finger, then crept them up until he was stroking her hair. "I love you too," is all he said back.

"So sweet. True love," Amaros flashed a smirk, playing with the cuffs of his jacket. He strode forward, never breaking his glare on Desti and said, "now, I thought that love was forbidden in your world. Hmmm?" He cocked his head to the side.

Desti scoffed. Like spitting venom she hissed, "it's none of your business what I feel toward anyone."

Tate seemed too weak to get up, but Desti knew by the shift of his weight, that he wanted to royally kick Amaros's ass. She held her hand on his forearm, comforting him, but that didn't stop her from getting up and giving him a piece of her mind.

She stood, now charging at Amaros, the blood drained from her face as she yelled, "it's your fault we are even in this mess. We shouldn't have to be scared to *feel*, or to *love*, or do anything for that matter. But our entire lives, we have been deprived of pleasure and joy, all because *your* kind infested our world." The muscle in her jaw tightened as if she were trying not to bite off his finger, but her eyes could have done as much damage if looks could kill.

Amaros's face was stone cold as he stood inches away from Desti, smirking at her with pure amusement. "How about this? I give you what you want, and you give me what I want."

Desti's brow furrowed, and she took a step back almost tripping over her own foot. She reached into her back pocket, hoping that she still had one of her knives hidden in there, so she could stab him in the neck, but nothing. "What do you want from me?" is all she said.

39: Promises

IT HAD BEEN DAYS SINCE DESTI HAD SEEN OR smelled food, days since her lips felt the crisp kiss of fresh water. The hunger that ate away at her gut was too much to ignore when being offered such desires. Every nerve in her brain wanted to scream and run away but she was no fool and knew that eventually, her body would succumb to death if she didn't fuel it, and so she sat there at the King's table, and ate.

The sweet aroma of the apple meat almost made Desti quiver in sheer ecstasy. It was so good. So, so good, but she didn't dare let Amaros see the satisfaction on her face, instead, her face was stone cold. Amaros sat at the head of the table, stretching at least ten feet wide.

Amaros had Tate sit next to him, dangling his power at Desti, taunting her, showing her that he still had them under his control. The color seemed to rush back to Tate's face as he drank his tea and ate his meal. She eyed him closely, watching every flicker of movement that he made.

Keeping her gaze aggressively on Amaros, pushing her food around her plate with her silver fork, she asked, "so what is it that you want from me exactly? I'm assuming that was why you haven't killed us yet."

Amaros sat back in his seat, twiddling his fingers for amusement. "Don't you want to enjoy your meal before we get down to business?"

"I'd rather know what it is you want now," she said flatly.

Desti cocked her head to the side and asked, "but first, I want to know what happened to my friends, and how did you know I was here? I mean, you said that you were expecting me."

The energy shifted in Amaros's face. His wicked smile turned down, as he scowled. Tate stopped eating and looked over to Amaros, waiting for an answer. He probably was curious too.

"You mean your friends who dared to burn my forest to the ground and break into my castle grounds?" he toyed with his glass, swirling his wine in even circles, and continued, "let's just say that they are indisposed." His emerald eyes, oh so wicked they were, met Desti's, and for once she truly was terrified of what powers he possessed.

Her throat tightened as she tried to speak. The thought of any more people getting hurt because of her was like a dagger to her chest. She shook her head and leaned forward, saying, "where are they? What have you done with them?"

"You know, you ask a lot of questions for someone in your position, I would be careful how you speak to me." Amaros stroked his chin in one motion. "Let's make a deal, shall we? You have something I want, and I have something you want," he tilted his chin upward as if he were examining every bit of Desti across the table.

Something about his tone, his demeanor, shook her to her core. She was silent for a moment, capturing the sorrowful gaze of Tate's empty eyes. They were filled with tears. She knew what he wanted to say. *Don't. Don't make a deal with him*. Tate shook his head, never breaking his gaze with Desti, but it was too late, she made up her mind, and if she had to give something of herself in exchange to get her friends back, then so be it.

"May I ask what our deal is in exchange for my friends' safety?"

"You must simply accept or deny, the terms of our arrangement will be made clear afterwards."

A simple nod.

A simple nod and she had sold herself to the King of Hell. Amaros simply smiled, flashing a sharp and jagged smirk, and snapped his fingers. Wooden doors flung open, and two servants came through shoving Anthony, Seraph, and Kaelen to the ground. Desti's eyes burned, she wanted to run to them, but when she tried to get up from the table, she had been tugged back by a chain that now held her hostage to her chair. Anthony was the only one not crying. Maybe enduring years of neglect and solitude in that dark cave was enough to break his soul, but Kalen and Seraph clung to each other and sobbed. It shattered Desti's heart seeing them like this.

"Let them go," she said.

"Now the terms of our arrangement," Amaros stood from his ivory chair and stalked toward her, "you and your friends will become bound to me, to do as I wish." A guttural chuckle escaped his chest as he came closer. He stood only inches away, stroking her hair with his calloused hands. Desti didn't dare look him in the eyes. Her pure disgust might just send her hurling on the floor.

"You said that you would let us go," she growled through her gritted teeth.

"No, Desti darling, I said that I simply would not harm you. I have much more amusing plans in mind, and you asked how I knew you were here, well…"

Amaros snapped his fingers and in less than a heartbeat appeared Elijah at the table.

The sheer shock took Desti's breath away. It took everything in her not to pounce across the table and rip his throat out. *How was he here?* Desti searched in her mind for answers. And then she remembered a simple conversation that she had, remembering someone telling her that the Master was rumored to be a High King of Hell. It must be true then. *Elijah is working for the High Kings of Hell.* A wave of disgust fluttered through her body. Desti couldn't believe that she had trusted him. That he had deceived her so easily.

Before Desti could say anything, Amaros snapped his fingers, binding Desti to silence. Rage. Utter rage was what she felt in the depths of her soul. Desti thrashed and flailed trying to break from her chains, but that only seemed to tighten the magical grip on her more.

Amaros must have noticed the horror in Desti's eyes, grinning. "Oh yes, you know Elijah, don't you?" He held his hand up and said, "no need to answer, Elijah has told me everything about you. You are quite fascinating."

Desti shot a look of terror at Tate with glazed eyes. She wanted to scream, wanted to break every damn thing in this place.

The table nearly broke in half as Tate slammed his hands in it and demanded Amaros to let her go. A snarl escaped his gritted teeth, one noise that Desti was not accustomed to hearing.

"Oh, I see I have upset your friend. We can't have an uprising just yet."

And just like that, with a snap of his fingers, Amaros bound Tate to total silence, as he continued to speak. "You and your friends shall not be killed by me or any of my servants in my realm, however, there is a game you shall play," he continued, "if you and your friends can survive it, I just might grant you your freedom."

"Take them to the dungeon," he flatly said. One by one, Kaelen, Anthony, and Seraph were dragged back through those wooden doors, sobbing, and begging to be let free. Amaros snapped his fingers, releasing Desti and Tate of their chains. Desti cupped her mouth, realizing that the magic that gagged her must have vanished.

"You are a sick bastard!" she spat.

Amaros waved his hands. "Take the rest of these kids to the dungeon. I want some peace."

Two more servants appeared from nowhere and dragged Desti and Tate away from the table, toward the wooden doors. Just before she was pulled into a room of darkness, she yelled, "you never told me what it is that you want from me. What the Hell could I possibly have that you want?"

As the doors began to shut, a simple answer was all she got.

"Your blood."

40: Wicked Truth

IT WAS COLD. SO COLD.

Desti grasped for the damp stone wall as the last servant shoved her in. The only light that gave any visibility were the flickers of a small flame across the hall. The air, thick and suffocating, hung heavy over Desti like a shroud of inevitable despair. Trickles of stale water dripped, one after another, enough to drive any sane person mad. *Where is Tate? And—*

"Desti," a soft voice said from the shadows. That voice was so familiar, but she couldn't quite put a face to it, until that person emerged from the wall of darkness and strode forward.

"Desti?" she said again.

"Tess?" A question of pure shock and surprising relief.

"I thought you were dead," Desti cleared her throat, "I mean…you know, when the camp was attacked."

Tess was nothing like Desti remembered her to be. Not hard and intimidating, no. This Tess seemed to have been shattered from that shell and revealed what she probably hid underneath, a timid fragile thing.

Desti stepped forward and reached out her hand. "Are you okay? What happened?" She wanted to know everything. *What happened at the camp. What happened to everyone else? What happened to damn you down to here?* Dried blood crusted in the knots of her hair and cheeks, staining her face with red streaks. The clothes that she wore were barely hanging on, as if they had been shredded with a pair of sheers.

Tess quivered and lunged forward, wrapping her arms around Desti, sobbing relentlessly. "I never thought I would see anyone ever again."

Desti held her, her touch so foreign to her body's senses. Desti asked through muffled cries, "Tess, what happened. With you, with the camp, with everything? How did you get here?"

Once Tess's tears ran dry, she sat down and patted next to her. Desti took a seat and listened. Tess explained everything. How Elijah had been poisoning the camp with demon's blood. How he had betrayed the resistance for power and how he had offered her soul in exchange for that power. She continued on about how Elijah went crazy with the idea of power and alliance with the Master. It was like a poison, slowly seeping into his soul, turning him evil over the years. He had betrayed everyone and everything he knew for it.

After she finished explaining her side of things, Tess's breathing became ragged and uneven. It must have been difficult to relive such horrible things. Desti gently placed her hand over Tess's and asked, "how long have you been down here?"

Tess scoffed. "It feels like years. Who knows really? Time is different down here, you know."

She nodded her head and said, "so how did they get you? From what I remember you are a feisty little thing." A slight laugh pushed from Desti.

"Well, we escaped the attack on the resistance and hid in a cave and went back to the city of Mors to recruit more people to join our new resistance. We almost made it back to Rotten's Crude, where we thought the Lux was, but we were attacked and taken as prisoners back to the Master," she continued, "he was pissed that I had broken Tate free from his cave, among other things, and was promised me and my friends by my father and Elijah."

The memory of her father, that stupid smirk he had on his face when she realized what he had done, haunted Desti, made her sick to her stomach. She clenched her core in disgust at the thought of him.

"Anyway, we were all thrown down some kind of portal to here. Tate found me and saved me, he saved my other friends too, but we got separated, and that is when—" Desti trailed off for a moment. She inhaled. "That is when I was tricked by Amaros to make a deal with him. Our freedom for something in return."

"Well, what does he want from you?"

Her mouth almost wouldn't voice the words. *My blood. What could he possibly want with that?* Utter horror hit her in the chest at the thought. Realizing that Tess was still waiting for her to finish, Desti huffed out a sigh and said, "Amaros wants my blood."

Distant chattering broke Desti from her focus. She twisted her body, now facing the edge of her cell. "Who is there?" The voices grew louder until they came up just around the bend of the wall.

"In here," a sharp voice demanded.

"Keep walking," another one said.

It took almost every muscle in her body to hold herself back from lunging toward the door as Tate and Anthony appeared from the shadows. The servant opened the cell door and shoved them in, slamming it shut behind them.

"Oh my God, Tate," Desti cried, embracing him in her arms. She pushed back for a moment and cupped the side of his face. "I'm so sorry," she said, pulling him back into her chest.

"This is all my fault."

Once Desti felt the warm embrace of Tate, savoring his warmth, his scent, his touch, she let go and turned her gaze to Anthony, that witty, strong thirteen-year-old boy who had stolen a different part of her heart. Her bottom lip quivered, barely unable to hold back the sobs that were about to roar to the surface.

"I'm so sorry," she cried.

He was so dirty, so frail. Desti held Anthony in her arms and stroked his hair, slowly. "I am going to get us out of this, okay?" She looked deeply into his eyes, and he stared back.

A quite cough from the edge of the cell broke her focus from Anthony. Anthony too looked over with furrowed brows. "Who's there?" he asked. Tess had stepped forward out of the shadows.

Before anyone could react, Tate shoved his arm in front of Anthony, pushing him back against the wall. "You stay away from her. She is one of the reasons why we are in this mess in the first place."

Tate must have hit a nerve because Tess's eyes glossed as she gasped. Stepping closer she pleaded, "please, Tate, I wasn't myself. I'm sorry for what happened. Elijah drugged me. He drugged all of us."

"How do I know you weren't in on it, and you being down here is just some other way to keep us prisoners?" Tate's voice was cold.

"Please," she begged. "I'm stuck down here, just as you are."

Desti placed a gentle hand on Tate's shoulder and stepped in between. "Please, this will only make things worse. We can trust her, okay?" Her eyes begged for him to stand down, for him to break down his wall that he had built. She met his gaze, staring into those daring eyes, and held it. "We all need to find a way out of this. Out of this agreement and find a way out of Hell. We need her on our side."

With his irresistible cockiness and charm, Tate flashed a smile and said, "your wish is my command."

41: Alone

IT HAD BEEN, WHAT SEEMED LIKE, DAYS, ROTTING away in that cell. The only foreign sound beside her friends' voices was the constant dripping of water from the stone ceiling above. *One. Two. Three.* She counted. Over and over in head.

Occasionally a servant would shove a tray of some stale food and water through the door, not at any certain intervals. And so that was what their torment had become. Not knowing when their nourishment would come, the constant, relentless sound of that dripping water, and darkness, never ending darkness.

It seemed Tate had let go of his grudge towards Tess because now they were off sitting in the corner, chatting away. Tess had a chance to truly get to know Anthony the past few days, learning about what Elijah put him through and more about his Nephilim lineage. While the company of each other seemed to hold them above the depths of sorrow, Desti found herself sinking deeper into it.

"You didn't eat the last feeding," Tate said.

Desti didn't answer, only kept her gaze upon the flicker of the torchlight. She wondered if the light went out, would they bother to re-light it? Her fingers picked at the rust flaking off the metal poles on the cell door and sighed.

"Here I saved you some food. You need to eat." Tate slid over the tray of a half-eaten sandwich and some broth, but Desti didn't even flinch.

"We are going to be trapped down here forever," she finally spoke. She turned her head, only half of her face lit by the orange glow of the flame and continued to say, "he tricked me, and now we are bound to him. How will I get us out of this?"

There was no life in Desti's voice as she spoke, only pure despair grasped her vocals. Before anyone could answer, distant steps from down the hall stole the attention. Anthony, Tess, and Tate stood with their backs against the walls, but Desti remained at the door.

"You're coming with us today," said one of the servants. His eyes looked as if they'd been gouged out with daggers. Empty blackness was all that remained. He grabbed Desti's arms and yanked her forward and slammed the door shut before Tate could reach for her. Desti tilted her head back, for one more gaze, before she was dragged off, disappearing around the corner.

***

"I heard you aren't eating," said that familiar wretched voice.

"I'm not hungry," Desti flatly replied.

Amaros gestured for her to sit down at the wooden chair in front of her. He sat in another, cozied up against a blazing fire. "Sit," he demanded.

Desti sat with the urge of the servant's hands shoving down on her shoulders. "Is that why you brought me out here, to tell me that I need to eat?"

"There are a lot of things that I am going to tell you."

Amaros snapped his fingers and appeared one of his servants carrying in a limp body, unconscious, laying over their forearms. He didn't say anything as the servant sliced a deep cut into their neck and poured the squirting blood into a golden goblet. Amaros swirled it around and took in a long sensual sniff before shooing away his servant and the body. Desti recoiled in disgust, curling her legs into her chest. A trail of blood was smeared across the marbled floor as they passed through the doors.

"Mhmm." Amaros touched his lips to the edge, never breaking his gaze with Desti, and took a sip. "It tastes so much better when it is fresh," he said as he set down his cup.

"So that is what you wish to do with me? Kill me and drink my blood?" Her eyes dared to break focus just once as she slipped a glance at the blood smeared on the floor.

"You are getting ahead of yourself, my Dear." There he was, dressed in a pressed suit, golden cuffs, hair so majestically perfect. It took everything in Desti not to scoff at the sight of him. "You seem to have a distaste for me. I don't expect you to understand just yet what your purpose is."

"It would be nice to know what kind of torment I should be expecting. You said you wanted my blood," she glanced down at the golden cup and continued, "why? Why mine?"

And there he flashed his wicked smile, as if he were waiting for Desti to ask, savoring the anticipation on her terrified face. His fingers interlaced, he leaned forward, and replied, "Because, my Dear, you are Nephilim, and your blood might be exactly what I need."

Nephilim. *Did he just say Nephilim?* Desti shook her head in utter disbelief at the words that just came out of his mouth. "No, you are wrong. I am not...Nephilim," she almost couldn't bear to say. Her chest felt like it was going to cave in, adrenaline coursing through every nerve in her body.

"My darling, did your parents not tell you anything about your past?"

"My parents?" she growled. "My dad was an abusive, narcissistic alcoholic who beat his wife into silence. And my mom, well, she was weak. A coward. Neither one of them bare the blood of the angels, I know that for certain." Desti crossed her arms, digging her nails into her skin, finding any way not to leap at Amaros and gauge his eyes out.

"Your mother..." his lips lingered on the words, "had a secret. A lover. Your true father."

"What?"

"What? You don't believe me?" Amaros stood from his chair and fixed the cuffs of his sleeves. "Have you ever wondered why you would heal so quickly after your father would beat you? Or how you never were able to be controlled by the authorities of your city?" He twisted around and clapped. "Or, ah yes, or how the demon blood seemed to have no effect on you when all your little friends became mindless zombies at the hand of Elijah?"

Desti shot him a sharp glare and shook her head. "How do you know that—"

"I have my acquaintances in your city," he interrupted, crossing his leg over the other and leaning back into his chair.

Desti shook her head, her breathing shallow. "It can't be. I mean—" she trailed off. "How could you even know all this?" Amaros stepped close, too close for her liking, she could almost feel the heat of his breath kiss her mouth as he spoke. "I know many things and can inquire what I please," his lip curled, "you could say that we are not so different, you and I."

Desti tilted her head, brow lifted. "How so?"

"I wasn't always a king of Hell you know. Before I was casted down, cursed to these insufferable realms, I lived somewhere so incredible, your eyes wouldn't believe what they would be seeing," he strode toward the fire and with a long stroke of his finger, caressed the mantle above the fireplace, he continued, "your blood, my blood, come from the same heavenly source."

Silence.

Either Desti was too overwhelmed or too tired to reply, instead she blinked.

Desti inhaled. "We are both Nephilim." Not a question. More of a statement of realization. She watched as Amaros's eyes glimmered with a hint of excitement.

"Yes," he said.

"If you are Nephilim too, then why do you need my blood? What does my blood do for you?" Desti twisted her fingers around the arm of her chair in utter fury. Rage coursed through her. Rage toward Amaros, but also rage towards her parents. How come her mom never told her? But then again, her mom moped around like a ghost, only around when it scared her most. Desti searched her brain for answers, clues, anything from her past that could solidify what Amaros was speaking of. If her *true* father was out there, somewhere, then where was he now?

Fingers snapping broke Desti out of her daze, and Amaros cocked his head and smiled. "There you are. Did you get lost for a moment?" He straightened his body and took another swig of his cup of blood, red dripping from the corner of his mouth. As he wiped it away, licking his finger, he continued, "my blood is no longer pure. The moment I was cursed, cast down here," he scoffed, "it did something to me. Changed me. My blood. It must be pure."

Amaros took a seat, crossing his leg over one another in one smooth swoop. All this information…Desti inhaled, holding it in her chest. Everything came crashing down. Fear. Rage. Confusion. Was he trying to corrupt any sense of reality that she had left? It was lingering now, holding on by a sheer thread. Desti glanced once more at the goblet of blood and then back into those sharp eyes of his. She gulped. "So, you want to drink my blood?" Tears gathered in her eyes.

Amaros cracked a wicked smile as if he knew she had figured it out. "My, Dear," he said. "Your blood might just be able to break this curse of mine."

Her head shook. "No, I can't. It won't work," she cried. She didn't realize that she was clenching the arm of her chair, until her fingers were met with a sharp pain, as the tips of her nails snapped. Amaros huffed out a wicked chuckle, stroking his tie, and said, "your blood is the missing piece that I need." With another snap of his fingers, doors flung open, and through it walked another not so dead servant carrying something in their hands. Something that seemed to glimmer, refracting the light of the fireplace with a sheer sparkle.

About this size of a small dagger, lay a pearly translucent sphere in the palms of the servant's hands. The sheer shimmer gleamed brighter than the brightest stars in the night sky. The power radiating from it was electric. She could feel the pulsating vibration caressing her skin. Goosebumps rose up her arms.

Before Desti could speak, Amaros took the sphere in his hands and walked it over to her. "I believe this is what you have been searching for," he purred.

It can't be.

Desti reached out her hand, brushing the tips of her fingers along the smooth surface, and in an instant, sucking in a breath, knew what beheld in front of her.

A mere whisper escaped her throat. "The Lux."

42: Unforeseen

TINY HAIRS ON THE BACK OF DESTI'S NECK SPIKED AS the air turned frigid. The sheer power emitting from the Lux pulsated through her fingertips. She closed her eyes and breathed. After all the pain, all the failures, she had found it.

The Lux.

Amaros snatched it back into his chest, stroking the surface. "I can't let that power go to your head now."

Desti still held her hands out, and turned palms up, trembling. "I can't believe it," she glanced up. "It's real. This whole time, I wondered—" she trailed off. *Wondered if it was all for nothing.*

Her voice caught in her throat as she tried to ask, "what are you going to do with me?" Thoughts of her being tortured, or worse, flooded her mind, splattering gruesome images as if she were watching it head on. Breathing became shallow. She waited for Amaros to give her an answer but instead was yanked away by one of his servants. Her arms being held tightly to her sides.

Desti kicked and screamed, "what are you going to do to me?"

Her voice cracked, the chair she was sitting in kicked over, as she panicked. Again, she cried, "you Bastard! Tell me what you are going to do to me. To us!" And as she was hauled out of the room, the last image burned into her mind would be of Amaros and his wicked smile, licking the excess blood from the corner of his mouth.

***

It burned.

The jagged stones scraping the palms of her hands raw as the servants threw her to the ground. Each heaving breath became a struggle as she tried to draw air into her lungs. The cell air was stale, stagnant, leaving a sickening sensation of nausea that crashed through her body. Desti hurled over. She clenched her stomach and sobbed.

She was trembling but a gentle touch from Tate on her shoulder eased her. "Desti," he said, calmly. "Are you alright? What happened?" She could hear the concern in his voice. The trembling that he tried to mask.

In between breaths she said, "he wants my blood," she glanced up, through her matted hair, "the Lux…he has it."

Tate wrapped his arms under her and pulled her forward, sitting her against the stone wall. Her throat felt like sandpaper, aching for a sip of clean water. Stale water leaked down the stone wall like a trickling river of temptation. Tate brushed the strands of hair that were stuck on her face back and tucked them behind her ears. Anthony and Tess stood silently in the background, looking curious, but knowing not to interrupt.

Tate cupped the sides of her face gently and said, "okay. Tell me what happened."

Those eyes. Those dreamy, perfect eyes stared right back at her, glimmering with what Desti could describe as sorrow. She raised her hands and interlocked her fingers with his, still held to her cheek. "Amaros," she cleared her throat, "he said that my blood is Nephilim." Desti's gaze shifted toward Anthony. He was Nephilim too. How come Amaros didn't ask for his blood?

"Nephilim?" Tate cocked his head to the side.

"He told me that my mom had a lover. A man who had angel blood."

"And you believe him?" Tate asked.

"Well, I don't know, Tate. He knew quite a lot about my life growing up. Why would he make that up?" She scoffed. "I think he is going to eat me, drink my blood,

I don't know." It was as if something had squeezed her throat at those last few words, almost unbearable to admit aloud. Terrifying.

Desti continued, tears now pouring from her eyes, "he…he drank someone's blood like God damn wine, right in front of me. Toying with me. It was…" she shook her head. "It was horrible. I couldn't do anything besides watch."

Tess came closer. "We need to find a way out of here." She kneeled, placing her hand on Desti. "Desti, we won't let him do that to you."

From the dark corner, Anthony asked, "why does he want your blood? Because you are Nephilim?" There wasn't much strength left in her, and all she could muster up to say was, "his blood is like ours, but tainted. He thinks that my blood can cure his curse and purify his blood somehow."

An aching, throbbing headache pulsated without remorse. Desti scrunched her face in utter pain. She needed rest. Tate must have seen the discomfort on her face because before she knew it, he was pulling her into his lap, stroking her hair. "It's okay," he whispered. "We will protect you. Rest."

As she closed her eyes, her mind was pulled deep into the black abyss of sleep. Peaceful sleep.

***

"Desti, get up."

"Desti," Tate whispered again. It was only when a slight shove against her shoulder broke her from her slumbers. Groggy and dazed, she propped herself up, halfway leaning on her elbows. "What's wrong?" she asked. A simple nod from Tate was all she needed to see to tell her that it wasn't good whatever it was.

Anthony and Tess stood flat against the back of the room; fingers clenched into the rock behind them. When Desti turned her gaze toward the door, she knew, she knew why everyone had such a frightened look plastered on their faces.

Standing before her, through the rusty poles, was a creature unlike anything she had ever lay her eyes on before. Not like the demons she had encountered out in the Wastelands, or even some of the ones down here in Hell. No. This thing, its very essence screamed death. Desti sucked in a gasp, holding it into her chest. "What the Hell is that Tate?" she breathed.

She didn't dare break her gaze, and from the lack of response, she assumed Tate was too terrified to answer her. It stood, still as death, contorting its jagged claws around the poles of the door, and it stared, right at her. Eyes so dark that she knew that was where nightmares were born from. Lips so thin and teeth so sharp, even seeing it sent a wave of pain to her gut.

It breathed, heavy and hard, and within that ghastly breath, it spoke her name. "Desti."

Her fingers traced the cracks of the wall until they met with Tate's, grabbing him ever so carefully. She didn't know what to say. What to think. What do you do in that situation? Her lungs begged for a gasp of air, screamed for the burning to stop, but she held her breath in fear of moving.

The thing snarled, reverberating an ear wrenching screech into her head. Desti threw her hands over her ears and hurled forward.

"It's time," it growled.

Before she could do anything, the door flung open, and the beast stepped forward. Desti tried to turn back, reaching for Tate, but its claws jammed into her thighs, yanking her away, her fingers barely touching Tate's as she screamed for him. This was it. She was going to die. She was going to die.

***

Desti must have fainted from her undeniable fear because she awoke somewhere else entirely without remembering how she got there or how much time had passed. Her head throbbed and nothing seemed to come into vision as she blinked.

Where am I?

When she went to take a step forward, a sharp tug on her ankles yanked her back. It was dark, almost too dark to see what was holding her in place, but she knelt down and when her fingers brushed the familiar cold rough texture, she knew what it was. *Chains.*

Realization hit her like a spear in the gut. *Where the Hell am I? What is this?* Surrounding her was darkness, a darkness so black that not even light could escape, and what lurked within it was something she knew she didn't want to get close to.

She could hear them though. The guttural growls and slithering whispers of the abyss. Swirling around like a storm of nightmares waiting to chew her up and spit her out. Terrified was an understatement to what ravished through her. All Desti could think about was Tate, and Anthony. Were they okay? She hung her head in a silent cry, but it was that familiar voice that snapped her focus into clarity. The arrogance poured from the tones of him. She could practically feel him sneering from wherever he stood.

"It's time for us to have a little fun now, my Darling."

She didn't answer.

Amaros's voice grew louder with every heartbeat. "I told you, that I wanted you to play a little game." She heard a snap, and then instantly fire exploded from every corner of the room, illuminating her surroundings with an eerie orange glow.

There she stood, chained to a stone slab in the middle of some kind of arena. A single knife lay at the edge of her feet. Desti took it in. The putrid smell of tangy blood that seemed to imbue itself in the air, the sweltering heat that emitted from every pore of the cavern, and the realization that she was in some serious shit.

Ahead, embedded in the walls of the cavern were what looked like cells, and in them, creatures and monsters of all sizes lurked behind. *That was what those sounds were.* Some had wings, large enough that they scraped on the floor as it walked. Others resembled snakes, with their serpentine features and elongated snouts. But then there was one in particular, one with eyes so dark, so evil, that she couldn't break the gaze between them. She knew that creature. It had stolen her from her cell, however long ago that was, and throughout all the screeching, growling, and hissing, there was that deep guttural voice that her ears could not help but to hear as it said her name.

"Desti."

Even without it physically touching her with its grotesque mottled skin, its essence seemed to have a grip on her soul, paralyzing her with undeniable fear. She darted her eyes to the side, stuck, and noticed a flicker of movement to her left.

43: Arena

IT TOOK A MOMENT FOR DESTI'S EYES TO ADJUST, BUT when they did, utter horror blanketed her. She was surrounded. Surrounded not only by a horde of demons that looked like they couldn't wait to taste her flesh but also by hundreds of tortured souls. Their shadowy translucent silhouettes hung up like a sick and twisted decoration. But what really made Desti want to curl into herself, and cry were the sounds of their anguished cries for help.

It was a symphony of unrelenting torture that ravished through the stagnant air. Desti was paralyzed. There was no time to process the horrors that struck her before Amaros began a torture of his own.

His stride toward her was stealthy, slow, as if he knew that drawing out the suspense would make her quiver even more. And he was right. Desti's knees buckled under the resounding anxiety and fear that took control. She caught herself, palms touching the stone slab, and that was when her gaze shifted to the dagger just a few inches away.

"Go ahead, take it," Amaros dared.

Desti didn't hesitate. She snatched up the dagger into her hand, clutching so tight that her knuckles turned white.

"What is this?" she asked.

Amaros lifted his arms in a cheery gesture and said, "this is the game. I've been quite bored down here all these years." His wicked smile made Desti want to hurl. Her eyes burned with anger as she glared him down every step he took. Closer.

Closer.

Just a mere few feet away, Amaros stood from her, taunting her with his smirk. If only she could reach him and jab that sharpened tip into his neck, but she didn't dare move. Not while she was chained. There had to be a smarter way out of this.

"You tricked me," she said.

"I'm the High King of Hell, my Darling. What did you expect when making a deal with me?" Amaros lifted a brow. In a swift motion, he turned his body, now walking adjacent to her. Desti peered to the side, watching.

It was like his voice was everywhere and nowhere all at once. In her head and around her. She could feel the wisps of wind kissing her neck with every word he spoke. It sent a river of chills down her back at the thought of anything of him touching her.

His voice cold as ice, sharp as talons, ripped through her once more. "It's time for the fun to start." And with his wretched chuckle, he stepped away slowly, turning to another part of the arena.

That was when she saw them.

Her friends.

Shackled to a slab just like hers, stood Tess and Tate, the look of pure terror plastered on their faces. They were standing the closest to Desti, but as Desti's gaze crept forward, she saw more. Then there was Seraph, Kaelen, and…

Brandon?

She thought Brandon was dead. After what happened in the Wastelands…

Desti shook her head trying to keep the images of Lyra's torn body, limbs, and all, from violating her mind. The memory of that sent a rush of sickness to her gut. It was her fault, she felt. Her fault that Lyra was now dead. Desti had just assumed that the same thing happened to Brandon when he had disappeared, but now, now she had a chance to save him.

An uncontrollable wave of despair crashed into her, clogging her throat with sobs and tears. Her eyes burned from the salty streams that now fell down her face. But there was one missing. Her eyes went wide when she realized…

Where is Anthnoy?

"Tate?" Desti cried, tears now pouring from her eyes. Did he know where Anthony was? But he didn't speak. Something was wrong. That heinous laugh swirled around the arena like a violent storm of torment. Then Amaros spoke. "He can't hear you, but nice try."

"What did you do to them?" she snarled. "Where is Anthony?"

Amaros stroked his chin, slowly, and said, "nothing that can't be undone. And your little friend, well I have other plans for him. Now for the fun to begin." His stride now crept closer to Desti. Her body naturally wanted to recoil from his presence, his arrogance, his…

Evilness.

So close. He was standing so close now, that Desti could see every flawless feature on his evil face, yet his eyes…

His eyes, devoid of any human compassion, any warmth, just sucked the essence of life from her. His gaze had a grip on her soul, draining any bit of hope she may have had left in her, and when he was done, his smile, contorted with such darkness, left her dropping to her knees.

"For your first challenge, my Dear, you will have a choice to make. You may use the dagger in your hands to save your friends," he stroked his chin, "but…let me warn you; my demons are hungry. You might be able to save a few of your friends, but all…." Amaros tsked and shook his head, and continued, "there is no way you will be able to save them all."

"No…Please." Desti wept on the ground, tears splashing against the stone slab. Her ankles ached from the rusty chains that held her hostage. She lifted her head, eyes glaring at Amaros. "Please don't do this. Let us go." Her voice cracked, shattered at the disparity that lay at her fingertips. How could he make her choose? To choose one of her friends to perish would be damning her soul. Damning *their* soul.

Then Desti's attention was briefly swept away by the anguished cries of sorrow that radiated from the cavern walls. From the souls who were stuck down there for eternity. She didn't want that for anyone. For her friends. There had to be a way out of this.

"I will unleash one entity at a time. Kill the demon, or let it kill your friends. Up to you." Amaros shrugged his shoulders and made his way up a walkway, taking a seat to watch. Desti spat on the ground. She gritted her teeth, breathing heavily.

There was no way out, she realized, and so, Desti gripped her dagger, and prepared herself to fight. Amaros snapped his fingers, and her chains broke free. Before she had time to think, she lunged into a sprint from the stone slab she was standing on and ran headfirst at the demon that was released.

The serpent. That's what she would call it. The demon that slithered like a contorted, jagged snake, with its razor-sharp teeth and tongue that could snatch her up with one swipe. She ran right toward it, aiming herself right in its line of sight. If she could hit it first, surprise it, then maybe she would have a chance at killing this thing.

The only sound that she focused on was the drumming of her heavy heartbeat, taking in gaps of air in tempo with it. *Run fast. Hit first. Attack.* She repeated to herself, anything to keep her mind focused. Only five feet now. One more step and she would be right on it.

It began to open its jaw, preparing, probably to swallow her or slash her with its tongue, but she knew what it was doing, and so Desti ducked and rolled, just missing its attack, and jabbed her dagger right into its thigh. Black oozing blood squirted onto her hands and ground. It screeched from the initial stab, falling backward, giving her just enough time to make a run toward Kaelen first.

Her eyes glanced down, noticing the chains on Kaelen's ankles. Desti held up her dagger and knew that she would have to break them off with it somehow. Kaelen couldn't speak, maybe it was a spell that Amaros put on her, but Desti could see it in her eyes, what she wanted to say. Her eyes spoke, *please. Save me.*

Desti kneeled down, taking the tip of her dagger, and pushing it as hard as she could into the lock of the chains, twisting and twisting. Desti looked up just once, but that was when Kaelen's expression changed slightly, her eyes now looking behind where she was kneeled. Desti looked over her shoulder and had only a few seconds to react.

The demon lunged full force at her, smashing into her and Kaelen, knocking them off their feet. She hit the ground with an incredible thud, losing her dagger in the process. Her hands curled into the dirt under her as she staggered back from the Serpent that now plodded toward her. Saliva dripped like honey from the tongue that slashed around in the air. Its eyes set right on her, taunting her with a sinister stare. Desti sucked in a sharp breath as it inched closer. The gray and black mottled skin looked like leather, leather that had been beaten and worn. It would take incredible power to slice through that.

Where is my dagger? Desti's fingers fumbled for it, but she realized that it had slid away from the force of the hit. She had to think fast. Think of a way out of this. The closer the Serpent came, the more she felt her body shutting down. Fear was a powerful thing, and when you let it take control of you, that is when you lose, but she slipped one last glance at Tate, his eyes yearning for her to get up and fight. She could see it in them. The love that he had for her. The friend that she didn't want to lose. And while she had those few seconds to have one last look at him, Tate mouthed to her, *"fight Desti."*

That was when she remembered. It all clicked in that moment. She remembered back to the forest and what had helped her get away then. Desti curled as much sand as she could into her hands, closing her fingers into a fist and quickly threw the sand right into the Serpent's eyes. Then the other hand. The Serpent growled from the pain, staggering back, and thrashing around. Desti threw herself forward into a sprint and ran as fast as she could to Kaelen. Her dagger lay just a few feet away from the slab that she stood upon.

With a swift motion, Desti grabbed her dagger, and this time jammed the tip into the lock even further, twisting and twisting.

Come on. Break. Please.

The Serpent huffed out a snarl that sent a shiver down her back. She glanced over her shoulder to see it now running again full force at her. The weight of its massive body rumbled onto the ground with every step. The power of that thing was unfathomable.

"Come on!" Desti twisted one more time and heard a click.

The lock opened and Desti gasped with relief, releasing Kaelen from her chains. There was no more time to think. React. Desti threw herself on to Kaelen, shoving her out of the way from the Serpent, landing entangled on the ground. Shrouds of dust swirled around her face as she breathed.

"Desti, get up. It's coming back," Kaelen said.

Desti met Kaelen's eyes. "You can talk."

"Yes, hurry. Your knife." Kaelen pointed to Desti's hand that held the dagger. When she turned her body around, laying on her back, the Serpent was in the air, full lunge, toward Desti and Kaelen, and so she held out her dagger and closed her eyes.

It was like a massive explosion had hit her with a force that could only be described as thunderous. The wind sucked out of her lungs with the initial hit. Blood covered her, every inch, but as Desti scrambled to her feet to react, that was when she realized that her dagger had gone exactly where she wanted it to, and as she stood over the carcass of its bleeding body, she came to realize that she had killed the Serpent.

Desti pulled Kaelen into her arms and held her tight. Every huff of breath blowing the strands of her hair over her shoulder. And in the midst of the embrace Kaelen whispered, "you did it. Thank you. Thank you." But that feeling of peace, that feeling of relief was quickly washed away from the sound of Amaros's clapping.

He strode down the steps but stopped at the final one before touching the ground, his hands lingering in the air. "Bravo, Desti."

Desti's eyes glanced over Kaelen's shoulders and met his. One look at him and she knew this wasn't over. This was just the beginning. Desti gently pushed back from Kaelen, keeping her glare on Amaros.

She didn't speak.

"What? You didn't like my game?"

Desti didn't want to answer him. What she wanted was to stab him in the neck with her dagger. She envisioned how easily the knife would penetrate his buttery soft skin, or how his blood would pool down his shoulder and on to the ground. She imagined him choking on it and her standing over his body as he struggled for air. Her fingers tightened ever so slightly on her dagger at the thoughts.

"I saved her. Let her go," was all she said.

Amaros stroked his chin, flashing a smirk. "The fun has just begun for you." Amaros snapped his fingers and in a heartbeat released the next monster lurking in the dark.

44: The Beast

THE BEAST. THAT'S WHAT THIS ONE WAS.

Desti had merely a couple seconds to study its grotesque features before hurtling herself into another sprint, her eyes traced its features as she ran, its body covered in jagged spikes. Unlike the Serpent, who moved freely, slithering, the Beast had a different approach. Its body tremendously built, muscles flexing with every movement, stomped with a heavy thud as it lifted its trunk-like legs before slamming them into the ground. Desti knew that killing this one was going to be...difficult.

Desti tossed her dagger to Kaelen and yelled, "free the others! I will distract this one."

Kaelen only nodded and then ran off to Seraph first as Desti ran again straight toward this massive monster. She didn't think or plan this far ahead. There wasn't time to. Desti had to improvise. Without her dagger, she was merely defenseless. How could she kill the Beast with no weapon?

Every step she took kicked up a swirling storm of dust. The closer she got to the Beast, the more she could feel its footsteps stomping and rumbling into the ground. Her mind thrashed around ideas of what she could use to injure or kill the Beast. Looking around, she searched for *anything* to use as a weapon.

Then in the corner of her eye, a flicker, a glimmer, shining under the dim glow of the torches that surrounded her. A shard of something. Desti shifted her direction, just for a second to grab whatever lay on the ground.

She had seconds at best, before the Beast would notice her change in direction.

Good.

She needed to draw it away from the others so Kaelen could free them. Desti didn't dare sneak a glance over at them. It would cost her precious time. And her plan had worked, drawing the Beast farther away from her friends. Desti was running toward to the outer boarders of the arena now, shard of metal in her hand, and the Beast did exactly what she wanted it to. Chase her.

She had a plan. It had to work. It had to, or else…

She shook away the thought of her failing. Being eaten and crushed by those massive teeth that hid in its mouth. The sheer thought of the pain…of the terror that would come with that sent a shiver down her spine. Is that what all those souls were feeling? Forever tormented by unrelenting pain and terror. Their screams that reverberated around the arena were almost loud enough to drown out the sound of her heartbeat.

The Beast was charging straight for her. Its snarling mouth curved upward in a wicked smile as it inched closer. Desti sucked in a sharp breath, almost automatically recoiling in fear, but she had to push through that fear. Her stance was strong, feet shoulder width apart, and she was ready for it.

A thunderous snarl punctured through the air and hit Desti with a force almost strong enough to knock her to the ground. The Beast licked its lips, preparing for the taste of her. And with its massive trunk-like legs, it pushed off the ground, now in a full leap, hurtling straight for Desti. She had to time it right. One second before the Beast's titanic body came crashing down on her, but she shifted out of the way just before it hit.

The crashing boom that rumbled the ground sent a shockwave outward, knocking her even farther out. Her legs were wobbling as she tried to stand up right, heart beating incredibly fast. When the Beast realized it had missed, it turned its head, shooting a deathly stare toward her and growled. She could hear it in her mind.

I bet you taste so good, its voice lingered on the word. As if it were savoring it, tasting her just from its imagination.

"You're not fucking tasting anything from me," she spat.

Maybe that wasn't such a good idea to piss it off, but Desti didn't care. *She* was pissed off. Raw power rippled through its muscles as it hurtled itself into a full force run. The only vulnerable part that she knew of was its eyes. She was aiming for that. Desti went to jump, to reach its eyes and stab the dagger in but the Beast was too fast. Too big.

Her body was crashed into, hit with such force that it knocked the air from her lungs. She might have felt a rib crack and as she inhaled, she cried from the sharp pain that radiated down her chest.

Desti lay on the ground, broken and beaten, and the Beast now plodded toward her. Slowly. Savoring the fear and anguish that poured from her cries. She still held the shard of metal in her hand as if it would do her any good now.

It stood over her, towering like those twisted trees from the forest. She tried to speak but only whimpers escaped through her gritted teeth. It took everything in her not to gag from its putrid stench emitting from the hot breath of its mouth that was now only a few inches away from her face.

The dirt beneath her fingertips clung to her nailbeds as she tried to stagger backward but failing at that. The Beast took its left leg, pinning down her right arm against the ground. Then the left one, pushing that shard out of her fingertips. She was breathing shallowly now, maybe it was from the pain in her chest or maybe it was from fear. A single tear slid down her cheek, leaving a path through the matted dirt and debris that was caked on her face.

She waited.

Waited for the crunch of her bones to snap between its massive teeth. She could see them now, now that the Beast was standing so closely, like broken shards of tree trunks protruding from its mouth. The pain and sheer power to be eaten by those things…

Desti didn't let herself think that far. But now she was stuck.

The Beast inhaled, pulling her scent in, tasting it through its orifices, its jet-black eyes rolling into slits. It was tasting her. Tasting her fear and sorrow, but then it stopped, and was staring right at her.

A snarl escaped its chest. "Your suffering, it tastes," it inhaled again, and continued, "so good." And as it savored the last word, it opened its mouth, preparing to swallow her whole. Desti expelled a mixture of a scream and a yelp in utter fear. She couldn't move and she was going to be eaten.

Just before its teeth sunk into her flesh, she felt something pull it back, releasing her arms from the pressure that held them down. It all happened so fast. Too fast to realize what had happened, but when Desti sat up, that was when she realized who had come and saved her.

"Tate."

But not just Tate. All her friends were free from their shackles. Desti had forgotten that Kaelen went to free them during the midst of her fight with the Beast. Desti stood, brushing the dust from the palms of her hands, and then realized what Tate had done.

They must have broken one of the chains that held them prisoner because Tate had lassoed it around the Beast's neck and body, trying to pull it to the ground. Seraph was on the other side about to throw another one across its back. And that was when Desti snapped back into it, running toward the danger, toward the Beast, to help bring that motherfucker to the ground. She breathed through the sharp pain in her chest, pushing it aside.

"Desti, grab the other side and pull hard!" yelled Seraph.

Seraph tossed his chain over the Beast and right to Desti. She pulled tight trying to pull the Beast to the ground, but this was harder than she imagined. It was like trying to wrestle a bull, with its thrashing body, kicking and stomping at any given moment. The guttural roars that rumbled from its mouth were nothing short of monstrous.

"Pull!" Tate screamed.

His chain had been thrown and wrapped around the head of the Beast. Kaelen stood behind him, dagger in hand, waiting for the right moment to attack. They were aiming for the eyes. If they couldn't kill this thing, then blinding it would be the next best thing. Tess dangled a broken chain from her hands, like a whip, and stood in the back as if she were there to stop it from escaping.

Brandon was on the other side, standing shoulder to shoulder with Kaelen, and he had something in his hand too, not a dagger, but sharp enough to puncture. Desti pulled. She pulled with all the hate in her heart, all the memories from her abuse growing up, but most importantly, she pulled from all the love that she had grown, because love was what kept her alive. She knew it now. The feeling of love. And so, all those thoughts and fears came rushing to the surface. Desti screamed as she pulled hard, and when she looked over, she saw Kaelen and Brandon in motion, aiming for its eyes.

It was only one second before the screams ripped through the air around them. The Beast flung its body backward, thrashing its head side to side in a frantic panic, and protruding from its eye sockets, were Kaelen's dagger and the shard that Brandon had held.

Everyone stepped back, creating space between them and the Beast. It was injured but not dead. Not yet. And in the chaos, in the relentless storm of fear and doubt, there was one thing that brought Desti back to herself. She closed her eyes in that split moment when Tate's hand carefully slid into hers and squeezed tight. His touch melted her fears. Blasted away any doubts she was being consumed by.

Tate gently pulled Desti back, stepping away from the danger. The Beast still thrashed around in a frenzy. But all her good moments seemed to come to an end quickly, just as this one did when that vile chuckle slithered its way to her, ripping her away from her moment of peace.

"Well, well, well. That was quite entertaining," Amaros said, clapping slowly.

Again, he strode down the steps that he sat on and walked closer to her. Desti had forgotten he was watching. She had forgotten that this terror was purely for his sick entertainment. Her face recoiled in disgust with him as she watched him come closer. Tate pulled her into him, wrapping his arm around her shoulder. His lips pressed slightly and gently against her ear as he whispered to her, "I will protect you."

Amaros cocked his head to the side. "What? You didn't have fun? I thought it was quite genius to blind my little friend," Amaros stroked his chin.

Desti glanced back at the Beast, the massive body that was rolling and thrashing behind her, but Amaros's voice pulled her focus back in. "I didn't think you and your friends would have been able to pull this off. You did quite the damage on him." There was a flicker in his eye. Amaros glanced up, past Desti, and lifted his fingers.

He snapped. And in a heartbeat, the screams that echoed from the Beast were now silent. Desti heard the sound of a crack and a thud, and when she looked back, the Beast was lying lifeless on the ground, black blood oozing from its jaws.

"You killed it?" Desti said.

"*You* injured it. What good would it have done me now?" Amaros flashed his teeth.

Tate held his hand firmly on Desti. She leaned into his touch. Behind her, she could feel Brandon, Seraph, and Kaelen hovering. Tess stood just a few feet from Tate, still carrying the chain in her hands. Their fear lingered like a hue of something rotting in the near distance. Desti straightened her back and held her chin up and said, "we defeated your monsters. Let us go home."

Amaros didn't speak. Not yet. His eyes just glimmered with a hint of aggression, his mouth curving upward. "You think you can tell me when you can leave?" He stepped closer, his voice now growing louder. "You are mine. I will say when you can leave."

That was when Tate stepped forward, gently shoving Desti behind him. "You tricked her into making a deal with you, and from the looks of it, I would say that you appreciate a fair fight," he said, while glancing Amaros up and down. Tate continued, "give us back Anthony, let my friend's go home, and I will stay as your prisoner."

"What?" Desti interjected. She tugged on him, pulling him away.

He couldn't be doing this. This was not the way. There had to be a different way out of this. It was as if the world had come crashing down on her chest the moment her ears heard him say *prisoner*.

"Tate, no. You can't." Her voice cracked.

"Desti, it's my turn to save you. Let me."

Desti held Tate's hand tightly. More than she had ever before as if it would keep him close to her. And as she finished studying Tate, savoring *him*, she glanced back up, staring right back at Amaros, at those pit-like eyes. *What is he thinking?*

His expression was impossible to read, his face stone cold. Desti could hear the silent whimpers and gasps from behind her, from her friends as the realization was setting in. Amaros stroked his chin, looking her up and down, then stepped only a few inches away from Tate.

"Interesting," he said.

Tate didn't respond.

"You would give up your soul, your freedom, to save your friends," Amaros continued, "but it would seem as though she would do the same for you." A quick nod toward Desti.

Desti felt Tate's hand tighten against her own. The silent affirmation that he was to keep his promise to her. *I will protect you*. The words still danced in her head, keeping the storm that was building at bay. She waited. Waited for that awful chuckle to escape his mouth.

Waited for a demon to come up and snatch her, but none of that happened. Instead, Amaros now stepped toward Desti, studying her.

"I have one last deal to offer you," he said. "Play a game for me, and your friends will be sent home, no longer under my control."

Desti inhaled. She felt Tate push into her, as if his body was trying to tell her *no*, but she didn't listen. She would do anything to protect her friends, and so she locked eyes with Amaros and said, "if I play this game, you will send all my friends home? Safe? No one dies?"

Amaros nodded. "Do we have a deal?"

Tate shot a sharp glance at Desti, his eyes burning with passion and fear. *Don't. You can't trust him.* She knew that was what he was trying to say. She glanced back at her friends.

Desti inhaled.

"You have a deal."

45: Trickery

AFTER THE ARENA, DESTI WAS SHOVED BACK INTO her cell, along with the rest of her friends.

The aroma of body odor and who knows what else lingered in the air. The first thing that she noticed when being brought back to her cell was Anthony curled up in the shadowy corner.

"Oh my God. Anthony," Desti gasped. She ran forward cupping his face between her palms. "What did they do to you?" she cried.

There was no longer life in his eyes. It had been replaced with what she would describe as brokenness. Sorrow. Despair. That's what they wanted down here. In Hell.

Anthony's skin was caked with dried blood and dirt. He had half healed lacerations all over his body and when Desti went to touch him, he recoiled.

She repeated herself. "Anthony, are you okay? What did they do you?"

It took him a moment for her words to register in those blank eyes of his, but when he came to, and looked up at her, that was when she saw it. The fear. Anthony grabbed onto her wrists and squeezed.

"Don't let them take you," he whispered.

Tate kneeled next to him asking, "why? What did they do to you?" Tate kept his hand rested on Anthony's shoulder and waited, patiently.

"He wants our blood." Anthony was now looking right at Desti and continued, "did he tell you that he is Nephilim too? He is cursed. Tainted. That is why he wants ours. To drink it and purify his own."

"But why does he need to purify his blood?" Desti asked.

"He has the Lux you know. Not everyone can use it. You have to be pure, of angel blood, and even then, it requires sacrifice."

Tate glanced over to Desti with those emerald eyes. She knew from the look in his eyes that there were questions dancing behind them. Desti's brow narrowed. "What does he want with the Lux? Why does he need it?"

Behind her she could hear Tess and Seraph, and Kaelen and Brandon rustling around. Pacing, as if standing still would be the death of them. She glanced back at them, knowing that they were listening too. The look of fear was smeared along their faces.

"Did he say what he plans to do with the Lux?" Tate asked.

Anthony inhaled, shaking his head. "It's supposed to lift his curse, so he can go to Earth. He wants to have total control of Earth and Hell. He would be *the* High King of both realms."

"Is that what he was doing to you? Cutting you? Drinking your blood?" To ask those words almost made Desti want to hurl. Imagining Anthony having to endure any more torment, was just…

She shook her head, wiping away the tears that gathered.

Desti stood and faced everyone. "This is why I have to do it. Just one more game and he will send you guys home. I can figure out a way to kill him. But knowing that you all are safe, is all that I want."

Surprisingly, Tess spoke first, face full of sorrow. "Desti," she said. "I can't let you sacrifice yourself for me. After how I treated you," Tess shook her head. "You don't have to do this."

"Tess is right Desti. We can find another way. Break out of this cell and find a portal back home." Tate was now gripping Desti by her shoulders, firm, with passion. She could see the burning desire building inside him. That broke her the most, to see him that way. She gently pushed his hands from her shoulders, hanging her head in sorrow.

"It's already done. I already made the deal with him. I will find a way to kill him, and I will come find you when it's over."

***

Hours slipped by as Desti waited for something, anything, to happen. The first hour was full of crying and begging for her to find another way, but she stood her ground. They all gave up eventually, accepting the fact that she was going through with Amaros's game.

Distant shuffling echoed from the outer parts of the chambers, in the shadows, growing louder with every heartbeat. Someone was coming. Desti was sitting, back against the wall, but now stood as she waited for the unwelcome visitor. Tess and Kaelen sat in the corner, only lifting their heads with the realization that someone was coming down the hall. Seraph stepped in front of Anthony and Brandon, who were sitting on the opposite side of the cell and stood strongly next to Tate.

The last time she was in this cell, that *thing* took her. Shivers flooded her body at the sheer thought of it. The evilness that just leaked from its essence seemed to seep its way into every sense that she had. Desti held her breath, hoping, praying that it wasn't that thing again. But as the silhouette approached, she realized that it was Amaros's servant.

"You are to come with me," he said, flatly, opening the door.

"What about my friends? Amaros said that he would send them home." Desti turned her head, locking eyes with Tate before being yanked from the cell. She thought that was it. Her final goodbye. But to her dismay, the servant reached in with his other hand and pulled Tate forward too.

"Wait. Why are you taking him too?" she yelled. Her voice ricocheted off the stone walls. Tate was trying to pull his body out of the servant's grip, but his hands were latched on too tight.

"Let us go!" he yelled.

"You are supposed to send them home. You are supposed to send *him* home!"

The servant, stone cold, didn't respond. For his merely average size, he sure had incredible strength. Desti and Tate thrashed around, trying anything to release his grip, but to no avail.

And as they were ushered away from the darkness, away from their friends, Desti cried, "I'm sorry."

***

The room was white.

Empty.

In it, in the center, sat a stone table and two chairs. One on each side. Desti was shoved in, along with Tate. Her body hit the table and hurled forward from the force of the push. Her fingers gripped the edge firmly. Every breath, every heartbeat, mimicked the intense fear that ravished her mind.

"Tate, what is this?" she asked through the sweaty strands of her hair that hung over her face. Tate didn't answer. Not at first. Maybe he was in shock too. She felt his hand touch the small of her back.

"He promised to send you home." She was now facing Tate, tears burning her eyes.

"Whatever happens, I am here, and I will keep you safe." Tate reached for the tears now streaming down her face, wiping each one away. "It's always been you, Desti. My best friend, the only person who knows me. I will give anything to protect you." He leaned in and pressed a kiss against her cheek. Desti closed her eyes and took in that moment. The safety of being held by him. She opened her eyes and met his gaze. "I love you. I know that now."

"I love you too, Desti."

Suddenly the door creaked open and Desti leaned into Tate as he pulled her into his chest, wrapping his arms around her.

Amaros always made the air feel frigid. Every hair on Desti's neck stood up as he strode inside the room. He stroked his chin, glancing Desti up and down, slowly. A chuckle. More like a slap in the face.

"You promised," Desti began to cry, "you promised that you would send my friends home." She was now out of Tate's grip, and now standing face to face with Amaros.

"I kept my promise. Your friends are being sent home through one of my portals as we speak."

Desti spat at his feet. "You fucking liar," she growled.

There was silence.

"You must be wondering why Tate is still here in this room with you. Am I right?" Amaros began to pace back and forth. "But from what I recall, you asked for me to only to send your *friends* home. You said nothing about lovers."

And there it was. That heinous chuckle that Desti hated so much. The sound. The pure evil that poured from his mouth. And in that moment, she knew that she had been duped. Tricked yet once again trying to save the ones that she loved most.

It was as if the room was spinning, total fear and horror just sweeping her off her feet. Desti grabbed onto the table to keep herself from falling over. Glancing up, through the stands of her hair, she watched Tate step in front of Amaros's face.

"We will play your little game, and when we get out of here, I will kill you with my bare hands."

"Is that so?" Amaros said.

There was no glimmer of fear in his eyes. Desti looked for it. Prayed that she would see something hidden behind the black pits of darkness, but there was nothing. Nothing but total evil. Desti took a seat at the table to keep herself from dropping to the floor. Amaros only nodded his head toward the other seat, waiting for Tate to follow. The game was going to happen, whether she wanted it to or not.

46: The Game

THE GAME WAS TO TEST THE STRENGTH OF THE MIND. Or that was what Amaros said as he explained it to Desti. She tried to think of what to expect. Ever since she had stepped foot into this horrid place, all she had encountered was absolute terror at every corner. There must be some kind of trick coming. She knew it.

Amaros left her alone with Tate after his initial appearance. Tate seemed just as perplexed as her, a growing expression of confusion and fear now lingering on his face. His eyes glanced up at her, reminiscence of tears gathered in those glossy eyes.

"Desti, I'm sorry."

She leaned forward. "Why are you sorry? I should be the one apologizing."

"No. This is all my fault. I shouldn't have broken one of the forbidden rules. I should have told you what I heard our parents talking about before just leaving the city." His voice was hoarse now. Desti studied Tate's perfect face. His strong cheekbones, jet-black hair that hung just slightly in his face, and his eyes, so full of strength and bravery. She didn't want to lose that. Lose him. She listened as he continued. "We could have escaped the city together. Instead of you having to rescue me from the Master. I was stupid and acted irrationally."

Desti reached her hand to his. "It's okay. I don't blame you for any of this. We lived in a shit world and sooner or later we would have been thrown into this whether we wanted it or not."

There was silence for a moment. A moment of clarity between them. Desti savored his touch as she met his gaze. Even if it was just a moment, she would hold on to the feeling he gave her for eternity.

Suddenly, a noise drove Desti to swiftly turn around. "Did you hear that?" she asked. When Desti turned back around to look at Tate, what she saw made her gasp so hard that it threw her out of her chair.

When she refocused, that was when she was able to see it. The *thing* that lurked in the darkness. The thing that whispered her name and savored every syllable. The darkness that took her from her cell. She remembered the way it looked at her in the arena and the way it spoke her name with such hatred.

Her body froze, unable to think or move from her petrified fear that took control. She wanted to scream, but it was as if something had her throat in a chokehold.

All she could do was watch in terror as the Shadow hovered over Tate.

Tate must have noticed the fear in Desti's eyes because his expression changed swiftly to concern. "What's wrong?" he asked. Desti couldn't answer, but her eyes lingered on the Shadow, and that was when Tate turned around to see for himself.

There was a gasp and then it was as if the sound had been sucked from the room. The Shadow was now forcing its way down his throat like a swirling vortex. Tate didn't yell, but slight moans and gags escaped as he helplessly took in the Shadow. Desti wanted to scream. In her mind she was yelling for it to stop. Begging for the Shadow to let him go, but nothing came out as she was forced to watch.

Tate's neck twisted back, and his mouth was pried open as he sucked the blackness in. His body convulsed, shaking so violently she thought that he was going to fall out of his chair. And then it was over. The Shadow had disappeared, and Tate sat up right, staring at the ground.

Desti was no longer under the clutches of the Shadow and so, she leaned forward, gripping the table and whispered his name.

"Tate?"

He didn't respond, not at first. Tate sat slumped in his chair, focused on the ground. But then a noise, a chuckle, that made her body shiver from the sound echoed around the empty room. A snarling growl rumbled from the depths of Tate's chest and as he lingered on it, he turned his head, now facing her.

Desti sucked in a sharp breath.

Gone were his emerald eyes that were filled with love and bravery. And now she was staring back at two dark, soulless pits. He smiled at her. But this smile was contorted and evil. Tate gritted his teeth as he breathed heavily, keeping his gaze right on Desti.

"Scared?" he growled.

Desti could only nod her head slowly. She couldn't muster up a word even if she tried. Through every nerve, every pore in her body, there was undeniable fear seeping its way in. Her breathing was shallow and all she could do was sit there and watch in horror. The tips of her fingers ached from how hard she was gripping her chair. This was really bad.

Desti thought about her father. How he would beat her and about the fear that she felt in his presence. She used to think that was total terror, but compared to this…

Her lip quivered, realizing that she had no idea what *real* fear was until now. A stream of tears was now pouring down her face, she realized this was what Amaros wanted. He wanted her to suffer and what better way than to watch the one you love become lost to the darkness of Hell?

Tate tilted his head back and stretched a wicked smile across his face. "His fear," he licked his lips, "is delicious." Tate now glared back at Desti again as he savored that last word.

"Tate?" Desti whimpered.

Tate wasn't there. That *thing,* the Shadow, had taken over. And as she cried his name all she got in return was an evil smirk.

She cried again. "Tate, please," she begged. "I know you are in there. Please come back to me." She reached for him, not even thinking, just her body naturally yearning for his touch, but soon she realized that that was a mistake.

He slapped his hand down, ricochetting a vibrating thud through the concrete table, pinning her hand to it. Under his grip, he curled his fingers around her wrist tightly, not breaking his gaze with her. "Tate let go."

He didn't. He gripped tighter until Desti's face crinkled in pain. "I said let go!" But instead of doing just that, he snatched her arm up, pulling her halfway across the table, and took a bit from her forearm, sinking his teeth into her softened flesh.

Desti screamed a searing yelp as the pain of his teeth came down on her flesh. Blood trickled from the open gashes where his teeth had penetrated. Tate still had her in his grip, and he smiled at her, licking the tangy blood from the corner of his lip.

"What is this?" Desti was now in a full cry. Tate shoved her arm back into her, making Desti fall back into her seat. "I thought we were supposed to play a game. What kind of game is this?"

"If you wish," he snarled.

Desti's cries faded to whimpers as she held her bleeding arm to her chest. She sat silently now, listening. Tate fingers gripped onto the stone table, so hard she thought that his nails might snap.

"If it's a game you want, then it's a game you'll get."

47: Imposter

THE AIR IN THE ROOM HUNG HEAVY AND THICK EVEN as the frigid tension felt like shards of ice on Desti's skin. Her head throbbed from all the crying she had done, and her arm ached, pain radiating all the way to her shoulder as she held it closely to her chest.

She was to play a game of the mind. That was what Amaros had said. And as she sat there and listened to Tate, the Shadow, explain the rules, everything became much clearer. His voice, *its* voice, lingered in her mind. That cruel guttural growl will forever be burned into her memories. As the evilness of the lingering voice carved a path through her mind, she felt even more violated when the Shadow had pried into her memories and then into Tate's. Every emotion, everything that made her and Tate who they were was no longer theirs to share. It had been ripped from the crevices of their minds so violently. She felt naked. Exposed. Vulnerable.

He explained, *you are to test the strength of your connection. Your* love. Desti remembered the distaste on his face as he spoke the word love, as if it were poison to him. His face had recoiled into a look of utter disgust as the word had touched his lips.

She was waiting now, waiting for the game to start, if you would even call it that. Her chest rose and fell heavily, giving up the illusion that she was not fearful. Because she was, even if her face was now stone cold.

With a swift motion of his wrist, Tate swung his hand across the table, leaving a trail of dark shadowy mist behind. Slowly, a small dagger appeared in front of him, etched with the same symbols Desti had once seen where Anthony had been held prisoner. She squinted, studying the swirls and letters that she recognized, as if she would suddenly be able to read them. Horror traced its way down her spine as she sat there in front of it. *Why would he need a dagger*, she thought.

He must have noticed the terror on her face. She couldn't hide it anymore. Her eyes darted down and then up, staring into his pit-like eyes. He was smiling, but this smile took the very breath from her chest. It was no longer Tate staring back at her, instead she looked upon the essence of evil itself.

"Oh, no need to worry about that," he glanced down at the dagger, "it isn't for you."

"Then who is it for?" But as Desti finished asking that question, she realized that it was for Tate. He must be in there still. If he could feel, then maybe he was still able to hear her, *see* her. Her eyes burned.

"Please don't hurt him."

His fingers traced idol circles around the dagger that lay on the table. "I will test your knowledge of your lover. If you are right, then maybe I just won't hurt him. But if you are wrong, well," he smiled, "then you know what will come of it." He picked up the dagger in his hands and played with it, taunting her.

There was nothing she could do, except play. She held in her breath for a moment. Everything was too much to bear. But she couldn't let it take control, wouldn't. She held her bleeding arm close to her, leaned forward and said, "okay then, let's play."

"Excellent," he hissed.

"I'll make the first question easy." He played with the tip of the dagger as he spoke. "Tell me," his voice was low and guttural, "when did your precious Tate receive his first true punishment?"

Desti sat back in her chair, crossing her arms at the thought. She tried not to think about their punishments back in the city of Mors. She remembered hers clearly. Desti reached her fingers and ran the tips along the scars scattered along her skin. She was seven when she received her first punishment. Her father had taken a hot piece of metal and burned the scars onto her arm. The pain almost resurfaced at the thought. Then her mind went to Tate. He didn't like to talk about his punishments. Always tough, always protecting others, but there was a vulnerability to him that he hid deep beneath.

She closed her eyes, envisioning that moment Tate had opened up to her about the punishments he would receive. She knew of the whippings along his back. The scars that now decorated the peaks of his muscles. But how old was his first? Did he tell her that? Desti pushed out a huge sigh. If she answered incorrectly, Tate would ultimately suffer.

Desti cleared her mind. Cleared it of the pain searing down her arm, cleared the throbbing ache in her head, and pushed away the crushing pressure of the consequences she might face. She thought back to when they first met. She was just a child then, young and learning the harshness of their world. Her mind played the kindling of her friendship with Tate clearly, tracing every detail, every conversation, until—

Her eyes opened.

She was hesitant at first. If she was wrong…

"He was seven when he got his first punishment." Desti's shoulders tightened, tensed, as she waited. *Please don't be wrong. Please don't be wrong.*

Tate's eyes were lacking any humanity, and instead were replaced by the evilness that now leeched onto them. The curve of his lip twitched. He danced his fingers along the dagger that lay in front of her and Desti felt herself almost lunging forward, but then she stopped as his hand fell to his lap.

"Well…that was too easy. Don't you think?" he said.

"What kind of game is this?"

"You don't like my game? Shall I just kill him now then?"

Desti shook her head with regret. "No, I'm sorry. Please don't hurt him."

Tate took the dagger into his clutched fingers and held it against his exposed chest. "Tell me, what is the thing he fears the most?"

Desti watched as he held the sharp tip just below his collarbone. Thinking back, Tate had always been brave. He never showed fear, not even as a child. *This must be a trick question,* she thought, and so Desti straightened up and spoke. "Nothing. He fears nothing."

Desti bit the corner of her lip, waiting for a reaction. Tate's eyes flickered with a hue of aggression and then excitement. His grip tightened on the dagger as he said in a low growl, "wrong answer." And as he finished those words, he drove the dagger into his chest and downward, slicing a huge gash into Tate's bare chest.

Desti jumped over the table, reaching for the dagger in his hand but was slammed face down onto the table with his other free hand. He now held the blood dripping dagger above her face. Trickles of blood dripped onto her cheek and into her mouth as she lay there under the crushing pressure. "Please," she begged under muffled cries.

"Please stop this."

In less than a heartbeat, Tate had lifted her from the table, clutching the edge of her jaw with such force that the sheer power thrusted her against the wall, his face only a few inches from hers.

Desti tried to cry through her gritted teeth, but only silent sobs streamed down her face. Tate inhaled, tasting the scent of her fear, pressing his body against her chest.

"Is this what you want?" he asked. His voice was predatory. Aggressive. "It's what he wants," he groaned. "I can feel his desire for you pulsating through his body."

A deep groan escaped the depths of his throat as he slammed his body against hers, the hotness of his breath coating the surface of her skin. Desti whimpered. Every pore of her skin recoiled in fear and disgust of the evil that poured from him.

"Please stop," she cried. But her voice merely came out as a pathetic whimper.

"He wants you." And as Tate finished speaking, he flicked his tongue, licking the droplets of blood that still stained her face. "Aghhh, you taste better than I imagined." The white of his eyes took over as he rolled them back in pure ecstasy.

Desti's hands were pinned beneath the pressure of Tate's demon possessed hands, the dagger still dangling between her hand and his fingers. The coldness of the dark metal sent shivers up her arm. She imagined the pain of being stabbed by that thing. It must be coming. There was no way to live through this. She was trapped and she knew it.

Desti almost gave up. Almost gave into the relentless sorrow and despair that held her hostage but then there was a spark of something powerful within her. A voice.

Fight.

Desti listened to the voice. If the Shadow was in a human body, then maybe it was vulnerable to pain. She thought of what to do that could hurt him without harming Tate. With a swift jolt of her knee, she kicked up, jamming her knee right into the center of his crotch. Tate dropped the dagger and hurled forward, growling in agony.

Desti took off running, heading for the door on the opposite side of the room, but when she reached it, to her dismay, it was locked. She banged on the door until the palms of her hands ached and throbbed. She screamed in terror.

"Let me out. Please!"

She glanced over her shoulder, Tate now straightening up, fists clenched tightly. He looked pissed. And with only a few steps, he cleared the room, coming up on Desti. She gasped and braced herself for the pain. She knew it was coming. As her body curled into the door, she waited for him to hit her. Beat her. Tate cocked his loaded fist back but just as he went to swing at her, the door opened.

48: Hostage

DESTI FELL TO THE GROUND SOBBING.

She didn't have to look up to know who had opened the door. She traded one miserable situation for another one. There was that horrid voice she despised so much, followed by a cackle of pure mockery.

"Well," Amaros said, "that was interesting to watch. I always love to be surprised by my demons."

Still curled on the ground, Desti glanced up to see Amaros peering down at her, smiling. "What did you say?" she growled. Desti was furious. What was the point of all of this? She clenched her fingers into the ground and breathed.

Amaros leaned forward and repeated himself. "That was interesting to watch. You know, I thought my dear friend was just going to torture your poor Tate. But taking over his body—" Amaros stroked his chin and yanked Desti up from the floor, and continued, "well, that was clever." His voice savored that last word, as if he were drinking in the suffering from the air.

Desti glanced back, blood still trickling down Tate's chest. His eyes were set on her. He watched her like how a predator watches its prey. She felt the tight grip of his hands take control of her arm. Amaros gave him a smirk and then snapped his fingers. Tate obeyed and began to pull Desti down the hall.

"Where are we going?" she resisted.

Desti thrashed, clawed, and screamed, but Tate's hand was too tightly secured. "I played your game. Leave him alone! Let us go!" Her voice echoed down the dimly lit hall as she was dragged off. The last of the words that echoed through the chambers was her screaming Tate's name.

***

He was throwing her back into the dungeon, alone and in the pitch darkness. Desti was terrified. Not only for herself, but for Tate.

"You can wait in here until it is time," he said flatly, shoving her in her cell.

But Desti wanted to try something, before the window of opportunity ceased, and so, just as Tate's hand was about to release its grip from her, she turned and pulled him into her, pressing her lips to his with a fiery passion. She pulled back just barely and whispered, "I love you, Tate. Please come back to me."

Her hands gently gripped the sides of his cheeks and just for a second, she saw a glimmer in his eyes. They were no longer soulless and evil, but instead, they looked at her. They *saw* her. The way Tate used to see her.

"Desti?" he whispered.

She gasped and pulled him into her chest. "It's you. You came back to me?" She was now looking back into his eyes, searching for anything that might be lingering under the surface. "Is it gone? Are you okay?" she laid her hand on his chest where the knife had cut, blood still oozing down his chest.

Tate suddenly groaned and hurled forward. His grip suddenly clenched into her arm, sending a searing pain up to her shoulder. "Tate?" She called but he didn't answer.

"Tate, please," she begged, but then her heart sunk into her chest once she heard that sound that solidified what she knew was happening. He was laughing. That evil kind of laugh and as he lifted his head, she could see in his eyes were the soulless expression she had seen before. "No," she whimpered, staggering back.

Tate tilted his chin slightly. "Your little game won't work on him. I'm too strong and he is too weak," he hissed. Tate paused, smiled, and reached for Desti's face, tracing the lines of her face and lips aggressively. "You'll have to kiss better than that next time," he scoffed, "I like mine fierce." As he finished speaking, he shoved Desti back, causing her to fall to the ground.

Tate left. The only reminiscence of him was the lingering sound of his footsteps.

Desti stayed there, kneeled in a dirty puddle of water and rocks. Tears splashed beneath her as she sobbed. The whites of her knuckles poked through as she gripped a handful of muddy pebbles. With all the aggression, all the sorrow, that now was building in her chest, she belted out a blood curdling scream, ripping through the air as she threw the handful of rocks at the wall. She screamed again. And again, splashing and kicking the water that lay stagnant in her cell. Once Desti was done screaming at the ground she flung herself to the wall, punching and kicking with all the aggression that had built up inside.

"Why? Why is this happening?" Desti turned and sunk to the ground in defeat. She covered her face and cried a horrible cry, tears seeping through the cracks of her fingers.

***

Time was no longer something that seemed real. It was foreign, distant, like a mirage taunting someone in the desert. It had broken Desti until she was nothing but an empty shell. They had left her there, in her cell, for what seemed like days. Her sense of reality had warped into a shroud of unrelenting despair. She had given up.

Four thousand and fifty-two. That was how many stones made up her cell. There were twenty rusty metal bars that made up the door that kept her prisoner. Desti sat on her knees, not caring about how badly they ached, and rocked back and forth, humming a soft melody under her breath. Memories of her life on Earth drifted back into her mind. It seemed so distant now. She thought about her friends who had burned when the Resistance was attacked, how her friend Nash was sacrificed for Tate's rule breaking, and how she would probably never be able to go back to her normal life. It was crazy to think about everything that had happened between then and now. She never thought in a million years she would have wished to go back to before that day, when Tate was taken. It was a miserable life, but it was all she knew. And at least that life had *some* normalcy. It had Tate.

The thought of him almost undid her. That *thing,* the Shadow, took him from her. The worst part was not knowing though. Not knowing if his soul was suffering, if he was trapped behind those eyes, watching that thing use his body however it pleased. Thinking of that ate at her soul the most. She felt helpless and all she wanted to do was to save him. And she failed. Desti stood from the ground, wobbling from her aching knees, and again screamed at the tops of her lungs until she could hear her voice carried down the dark hallway that led to her cell.

Desti walked toward the metal bars and clung to them as if they were the only thing keeping her knees from buckling. She almost went mad at the solitude, but then she heard something coming in the distance.

"Who's there?"

That voice.

A cringe forced itself onto her face at the sound of it. She knew who was coming.

"Leave me alone."

"What? I thought you could use some company. It's been quite pathetic watching you sulk in your cell all this time," Amaros said.

"What do you even want with me? If you're going to kill me, just do it already," Desti said. Her voice was devoid of any emotion as she spoke, as if the very life of her had been lost as long time ago.

Amaros stepped closer, his body now being highlighted by the warm hues of the torchlight. The shimmer of his finely pressed suit flashed with his subtle movements. "Your death is not what I am after, my Dear."

"Then what the Hell is it that you are after? I'm tired of this. You have taken everything from me." Desti loosened her grip on the rusty metal bars and staggered back slightly. She went to turn away, but Amaros had said something that caught her attention.

"Your power," he said. "Your power is what I want. I know you are what I have been looking for. Your blood is the key to my cure."

Desti scoffed. She cocked her head and said, "how do you even know that about my blood? You know—that I'm Nephilim? I didn't even know it."

Amaros closed his eyes and inhaled, as if he were tasting the delicious sweetness that coursed through her veins from the air. "I can smell it on you. That's how I knew that the stories of you were true. But you have done a good job at hiding that power. You know what they do to your kind up there, don't you?" Amaros looked up at the ceiling above them, gesturing his reference to Earth.

Desti just glared and didn't say anything in return. She could feel the fiery anger that pulsated behind her pupils. But she listened as he continued.

"They slaughter your kind. There are armies up there that hunt down any human with a hint of angel blood. You are a dying species, and that makes you worth a lot more to me than you could guess." He started to pace back and forth with a steady stride. "My blood is cursed, but yours is pure. Untouched. If I can somehow figure out how to—"

"Why do you think I would do anything for you after what you have put me through? What was the point of that? Of all of this?" she raised her arms in the air as she yelled.

"I had to test your strength! I had to see if you were worthy of what I have been planning for," his voice simmered, "your battling skills impressed me. I did not expect you and your friends to slay my demons, and yet, you did." Amaros stroked his chin as he continued. "You were too powerful with your group. I couldn't risk it and so I sent them home."

"Not all of them," she hissed.

"Oh, you mean your beloved? Tate, is it?" He stepped close again, his face only inches from hers. "I had to test your mind. I had to try to break your soul, see how far I could push you. Taking away your true love surely did a number on you. You see, I needed your power to be strong, and bringing out that festering anger in you will grow your powers, that way when I take your blood, I will have the best chance of ridding myself of this curse."

Strong. That word resonated with her more than she wanted to admit. She didn't feel strong, but maybe there was strength that lingered in her somewhere. Her eyes were now focused back on Amaros. "And tormenting me will somehow make my *powers* stronger?

That's why I had to endure all of this?" She shrugged her shoulders.

"Trauma. Pain. Suffering. Those are all things that will make any person stronger," he savored the last word, then continued, "if it doesn't, of course, break you. I just have one final test in mind."

"I'm not doing anything else for you," Desti spat.

"Oh, don't worry, this test won't require anything from you." Amaros let out a heinous laugh that taunted Desti to her core. He seemed to get pleasure out of her suffering. She was a game, a toy, and he was a bored king unleashing years of his pent-up boredom. Before Desti could speak, Amaros had lifted his finger and in a single heartbeat, snapped his fingers and vanished, leaving only a trace of black smoke in her presence.

49: The Last Test

DESTI HAD SAT IN HER CELL NOT KNOWING WHEN Amaros was planning on snatching her up for his final test. Maybe he wanted the anticipation to fill her with fear and anxiety before taking her away, but it wasn't long.

She had been curled into herself, knees to chest, when Amaros's servant came for her. His cold, clammy hands pressed firmly against her wrist as he dragged her down the dimly lit hall. Desti had fought and screamed the entire way.

She was thrown into a room; the same one she had sat in when Amaros showed her the Lux. Desti peered through the loose strands of hair that dangled in her face and studied her surroundings. To her left was a fireplace and at it sat three masterfully carved wooden chairs. To her right were the same doors she remembered his servant had dragged that body through. Red, crimson blood had coated the floor. Coated Amaros's mouth as he drank it for pleasure. Desti turned her head and shook that memory away.

She didn't want to think of what was probably going to be happening to her.

She glanced around the room, eyes tracing over every detail, every possible exit to escape through. Maybe the portal back home was in this room, she thought. Her body was still, obeying the orders that were given to her, but in her mind, she was planning a way to get her and Tate out of this. Maybe if he wasn't in Hell anymore, the demon would be forced to leave his body and stay where it belonged.

Amaros's servant pointed to the wooden chair in front of her and said, "sit." She obeyed and sat down. Not even a second later a loud creak echoed through the room as the doors opened, and out came Amaros and Tate. There was a large metal chain that was wrapped around Tate's neck as Amaros dragged him across the room like a dog. Desti sucked in a shallow breath.

"What is this?" she asked.

Amaros locked the chain to a bolt embedded into the ground and stood next to him. "This, my Dear, is your final test." He flashed a wicked smirk and Desti knew the moment she looked into his eyes, that this was not good, whatever it was. Something inside her was festering. Maybe it was anger. Maybe grief. She didn't quite know yet, but she could feel it getting stronger.

"I told you that I don't want to play anymore of your games."

"And I told you, that this one doesn't require anything from you." Amaros snapped his fingers and suddenly Desti felt the hands of his servant gripping her shoulders, holding her back into the chair. She tried to yank herself out of his grip, but he was too strong.

"Let go of me!"

Amaros tsked and wagged his finger, stepping closer to her. "We need you to stay where you are for this one. It won't be pleasant for you." A slight smile smeared across his face for a second before a ripple of pure evil took over him. He walked over to a small stone table and grabbed a whip that lay on it. It was leather, decorated with shards that staggered all the way to the tip. Desti thought of the labyrinth and all those thorns that covered it. Her eyes went big the moment she realized what it was for.

"This will be fun," Amaros said while twirling the whip through his fingers. He lifted his hand and with an incredible whack, struck Tate across the chest. Desti screamed at the sound of his ripping flesh. She tried to run forward but was pulled back by Amaros's servant. Tate screamed and dropped to his knees.

Amaros circled Tate slowly. "I made sure to let him feel the suffering his body will be going through. He just has no control, but I can assure you, he is suffering."

He was in there. She knew it. If she reached Tate once, then maybe she could reach him again. Amaros lifted again and whipped. And whipped. Flesh ripped and split, blood gushed to the ground, pooling around his weakened body. Every whip, Desti screamed, wishing it was her instead of him. There was so much anger in her chest. So much despair coursing through her veins, and it weighed heavy as she tried to inhale.

Her sobs almost drowned out the cries that escaped from Tate's clenched teeth. But she couldn't take it anymore. She couldn't just sit there and watch her best friend, her love, be brutally tortured, and so Desti turned her head and bit down on the servant's arm until her teeth had sunken deep enough to draw blood. He yelped and let go. That was her moment to escape. She shoved herself away from the chair, Amaros's hand was in motion to whip again, but Desti was faster. She lunged forward, hurtling her body over Tate, taking the whip to her back. The crack of the whip hitting her skin sounded like booming thunder in her ears. She screamed with incredible pain, but suddenly a burst of energy emitted from her.

A white light.

For a moment she couldn't see. The only thing that was visible was the glowing light that filled the room, but as that light dimmed and faded away, she noticed Amaros laying on the ground. A quick glance over her shoulder, *where is the servant?* He too was on the ground.

Desti faced Tate, cupping the sides of his face with her palms.

"Tate?"

She stared into his empty eyes, praying to see that glimmer she had once seen before.

Please. Please come back to me.

She brushed his jet-black hair back and kissed his cheek. "Tate, it's me. I'm here." She kissed the other side. "Please hear me. You are stronger than that thing. Fight." Desti peered into his eyes again, waiting. But then she saw it, that flicker of life and he was now staring right back at her.

"Desti," he whispered.

Tate sat forward, interlacing his fingers with hers. She closed her eyes and breathed a sigh of relief.

"We need to get you out of here," she cried. Blood still leaked from his open wounds. Desti slipped a glance at the chain that was locked around his neck. It was shattered, destroyed, as if it had been melted by literal Hell fire. As Desti tried to lift Tate, he whimpered in pain. "What happened to the Shadow? Is he still in you?"

"I don't think so. When that light hit me, it felt like something got pushed out of me." Tate looked up at her. "What was that?"

"The light?" Desti shook her head. "I don't know. It's the same thing that happened in the Master's chambers. I didn't know that that was me last time. Maybe it was my angel blood thing doing its magic." A muffled sound of groans broke Desti from her focus. It was Amaros and the servant coming back to consciousness.

"We need to hurry. There must be a portal somewhere. The one he used to send our friends home." Desti lifted Tate and threw his arm over her shoulder. She practically dragged his heavy body to the doors, trying to leave before Amaros completely woke up.

"I—I know where it is," Tate struggled to say.

"What? The portal?" She felt Tate trying to nod his head. He lifted his finger and pointed to his right. Desti took a sharp turn at the hallway to their right and shuffled her way down. "How do you know where to go?"

"When that thing was inside me—" he groaned in pain, "I could feel his thoughts." Tate nodded his head. "Turn left." Desti complied, taking a left.

At the end of the hall were three doors. A fiery ache radiated up her arms as she struggled to drag Tate any farther. *Almost there. You can do this.* Desti took a huge breath.

Suddenly, a raging roar echoed down the hall, sending an electrifying shiver down Desti's back. She gasped. "Did you hear that?"

"He doesn't sound happy," Tate replied.

"We need to hurry. Which door is it?"

Tate pointed to the red door on the left. Desti opened it and threw herself and Tate inside. The room was warm. A crackling fire was lit in the fireplace in the corner. She traced her eyes along the walls of the room, taking note of what surrounded her.

A table.

The fire.

The—

Desti almost gasped audibly. "Is that the Lux?" she asked in disbelief. But she remembered that pearly translucent orb that Amaros had shown her. He had told her it was the Lux. And there it sat, perfectly secure on another table on the opposite side of the fire.

Tate had kept walking toward the back of the room. "Desti, the portal, it's over here. We have to hurry." Tate was standing over a black depthless pit. He glanced back and held out his hand. "Come on. Trust me." He smiled at her, and it was that smile that could melt all her fears away. Desti hesitated for a second.

"Real quick," Desti grabbed the Lux, holding it cupped between her hands, and nodded. "Okay, let's go."

She took his hand, held it tight, and took one last glance over at him. He did the same and they smiled at each other. "I love you," he said, and jumped in. Desti was only a second behind him as she fell feet first into the black endless pit.

50: A New Earth

FALLING DOWN THAT PIT WAS AN ALL TOO FAMILIAR sensation of pure terror and anxiety. Desti wasn't sure how long she had fallen but it felt like hours. The burning in her throat had finally subsided from her screaming. Tate looked over his shoulder and shouted something to Desti.

"What did you say?" she yelled.

Tate pointed down and Desti looked. "We're coming up on something," he said.

Beneath her feet, an opening was ascending. She could see a bright light growing larger with every passing second. Desti closed her eyes and braced herself for the impact. Suddenly, she was no longer falling in darkness, but hitting solid ground with a hard thud. A groan escaped her throat as she pulled herself up to her knees.

The Lux was still in the clutches of her fingers, but she nearly dropped it when her eyes locked in on something unusual.

"What is this?" she said softly.

Her fingers were now grazing the ground beneath her. Soft, green blades of grass tickled between her fingers. She was in a trance. Tate was off to the side groaning from the initial hit but then she heard a slight gasp.

"Is this grass?" he said.

Desti looked over at him with curious eyes. The green in his irises seemed to match the bright color that danced between her fingertips. She looked back down at the blade she had plucked. "How? I thought grass like this was killed off a long time ago…" her voice trailed off.

"It was…" Tate replied.

Desti was now standing. Tate too. But it was when she stood up that she fully saw what was surrounding her. Not just a patch of green grass but an entire forest of lush vegetation. Bright sunny skies and fluffy white clouds floated above, gracing them with moments of shadows.

"Tate." Desti reached for Tate with her right arm, still holding onto the Lux with her left. He leaned into her, touching the tips of her fingers with his, but did not break his gaze from what lay ahead.

"I see it," he simply replied.

What could he say? Desti too was speechless. Her entire life she was taught that the world's resources were scarce. Almost all of the vegetation had been burned away from the war against the left-over humans and demons at the begging of the Era of the Damned. That was what she was taught anyway. She had grown up in a wasteland, and the only crop she had ever seen was the potato farm a few miles from her city. Grass like *this* didn't exist anymore.

"I don't understand how this could be…real?" Desti continued forward with a slow stride. The crunch of grass crackled beneath every footstep. Whispers of wind and trills of nearby birds flowed between the branches above. Even the air tasted better. Cleaner.

Desti twirled around with a smile plastered across her face.

"I never thought I would ever get to see so much…life." Before she could say anything more, her eyes focused behind Tate. She pointed and said, "the portal is closing up. Look."

Tate turned around and watched the swirling black vortex that just barely hovered a few feet off the ground vanish into thin air. "Well, looks like we are stuck here. Wherever this is," he said.

"Tate look." Desti had run off to the edge of a nearby boulder. "There is blood. Here." She pointed to red smears on the boulder. And just beneath it in the dirt were footprints. Lots of them.

"You don't think…"

"It has to be them," Desti interrupted.

"Which way do they lead?" Tate asked.

Desti pushed back a shrub and called out, "this way!"

***

They must have spent a couple hours tracking the blood smears and random footprints that hid in the forest, but Desti soon realized that Tate was trailing behind.

He groaned and dropped to his knees.

"Let's rest. Here let me help you." Desti staggered back and slowly helped Tate take a seat on a nearby log. "Let me take a look. I'll be gentle." She pulled back the blood soaked and torn shirt and what she saw made her suck in a gasp. She cupped her hands to her mouth to try to mask the horror on her face. "This is bad. Why didn't you say something before?" She gave Tate the stare that said *we could have fixed this a long time ago if you wouldn't have to be so manly.* Desti ripped a piece of her shirt off and pressed it against his chest. The moment the fabric touched his wound, Tate whimpered in agony. She pulled back. "I'm sorry. I didn't mean to hurt—"

She stopped, realizing something, remembering that whip that had slashed across her back.

Wait. Why don't I feel any pain?

"My back. Take a look." Desti spun around until Tate was now looking at her back where she should be bleeding. "Well. Do you see anything?"

"No— It's healed." He looked up at her. "You're healed."

Desti kneeled in front of Tate, holding the Lux in between them. Her palms grasped each side of the orb. "The Holy book said that I would hold the powers of the angels, right? Maybe that means that I can heal you."

Tate didn't say anything but the glimmer in his emerald eyes said enough. *Do it.* "Okay, place your hands on it," she said.

"How do you know what to do?"

"Shhh. I don't. I'm guessing. Just trust me, okay?" Desti closed her eyes and let blankness overcome her mind, flushing away all the negative that had built up in there. She thought about white light. The sound of the gentle breeze that blew through her hair. She thought about the feeling she got the first time she had kissed Tate. And then in her mind she prayed. She had never prayed before. It was forbidden, and yet it came so naturally to her. She prayed to the angels. *Please angels, if you can hear me, heal my friend. Take his pain and make him strong again.*

It was silent and at first, she thought that nothing was happening but just as she started to lose hope, she felt something. A warm tingling sensation under her fingers. She gasped. "Do you feel that?" she asked.

Tate didn't answer. His eyes were still shut. She watched his beautiful jet-black curls dance in the wind as a glowing translucent light began to shift up from his hands and down his chest. Tate expelled a huge breath. One by one, the gashes that decorated his chest had sealed up and disappeared as if they were never there. The only reminiscence of his injuries was the torn fabric of his shirt.

"Oh my God. It worked."

"What did you do to make it work?" he asked.

"I don't know. I just prayed in my head." Desti said.

Tate reached for Desti's hand. "Can you believe it? After everything we have been through, we finally found the Lux." He matched her gaze. His eyes spoke during the silence. *I'm proud of you.* The corner of his lip curled up. A gentle wind blew Desti's loose strands of hair around her face. With a gentle touch, Tate tucked the hairs behind her ears, holding his warm hands on the side of her cheek. His touch was electrifying. It was pure ecstasy in a world of madness. Desti inhaled, holding her gaze on him.

Seconds passed between them and then carefully Tate leaned into her. The warmth of his breath caressed the edges of her mouth. One second, they were just being, and the next Tate had pulled Desti to him, embracing her with a passionate kiss. Her tongue flicked behind her teeth as his lips danced with hers. She was breathless, pulling his body to hers until she could feel the heavy rise and fall of his chest. It was as if a dam had broken free, and all their desire, all their passion for each other, could no longer be held back.

"We shouldn't—" Desti breathlessly spoke. Tate now had leaned her back, lying on a soft patch of grass. His fingers played with the pads of her lips. He didn't speak but, in his eyes, there was a feral look in them. Predatory. As if a lion had finally found its mate. Her whole life she had been trained not to love. Not to touch. It felt so foreign to her, but she had made it out of that terrible place and was now somewhere beautiful. Somewhere that felt *safe.*

Tate's lips kissed down the edges of her neck and Desti moaned from the pleasure. She interlaced her fingers into his hair and pulled him into her. He nibbled gently as he reached just above her collar bone. She felt as if her body was going to explode. Desti lay there as Tate's hands grazed the curves of her hips, then her thighs, playfully kissing and licking his way down along with them. The moment he reached in between her thighs was when the predator came out.

His hands grasped the meat of her thighs and Desti was practically begging for more. She arched her back, inviting him to continue. Only seconds and Tate had ripped her pants off, spreading her wide for him. "Please," she managed to beg. Her entire body was quivering, begging for more.

Tate's hands reached around grabbing the sides of her hips and he pulled her into him as his tongue gently flicked the pulsating wetness between her legs. Desti sucked in a pleasurable moan as she endured the pure electric ecstasy that coursed through her body. She felt the warmth building within her, until control was something foreign. Her body quivered as she exploded, and then after the climax had slowly faded, she was left panting as she cupped her mouth in disbelief.

"I didn't— know— that was what that felt like," she said breathlessly.

Tate giggled and gave her a gentle kiss on her exposed thigh. "I've only heard rumors of the pleasure, but you made it look way better than it sounds." Tate sat up and tossed Desti her pants. She quickly pulled them on and sat up.

Silence soon enveloped over them. Tate was sitting next to Desti, and she had leaned her head on his shoulder. "Do you think Amaros is still after us?" she asked.

"I don't want to be the downer here but yes, I do. We probably should keep moving. If we hurry, maybe we can catch up with whoever left these tracks."

For a moment, Desti had forgotten that they were tracking bloody trails. She hoped it was her friends. Just to know that they were alive would be enough to take away the guilt that laid heavy on her chest. "You're right."

Tate stood first and lent out a hand, pulling Desti up. The forest was unlike anything she could have imagined. She felt as if she could stay there, on that grassy patch, forever. Tate ducked off through the greenery and Desti followed.

51: The Lost Ones

"IT'S UP HERE," TATE CALLED FROM A DISTANCE.

The sound of running water echoed through the canopy. It took her a moment to realize what sound she was hearing, but when her eyes laid upon the rushing river, that was when it all clicked. Back in the city of Mors, there was no such thing as running water. The water there was barely clean, but it was all they had.

It had been at least two days without a good drink of water, minus the occasional sip she got with her dreadful meals in her cell. Desti hurtled forward, almost completely diving in as she gulped and gulped. Tate had jumped in, looking like a god under the glistening water droplets. Desti saw his clothes piled along the riverfront and decided to do the same.

Once the crisp wetness hit her body, she felt alive again. "I've never seen this much water before," Desti called out. Tate smiled at her and slowly strode out of the river to retrieve his clothes.

"Me either," he said while slipping his shirt over his head. Desti had followed suit, leaving the water to get her clothes. She knew that they didn't have all day to spend swimming and admiring wherever they were.

"Do you think we will find them? Our friends?"

Tate walked over to Desti and held out his hand and said, "I know we will. Now, follow me. I think I saw which way the tracks were leading."

***

Desti trailed about another three miles before Tate had crouched and slowed his pace. She got down on one knee and peered through a bush. "What do you see?" she whispered.

Tate gave Desti a quick glance and smiled before turning his gaze back to what was in front of them. "Look," he said.

A fire.

"Did someone camp here?" Desti asked.

"Looks fresh. The coals are still glowing."

One second Tate was kneeling behind the bush, and then the next he took off running, straight toward the camp. "Tess!"

Did he just say Tess?

She was right. Tate was running because he had done it. He found their friends. Once Desti realized whose camp they came across, nothing could hold her back from making a run for it. To see Anthony again. Seraph, Brandon, and Kaelen. And Tess.

"Tate?" Tess called out. Her gaze then looked passed Tate as she yelled, "Desti! But how? How did you find us?"

"Desti broke us out and we found the portal back to Earth. It was either jump or be captured and tortured, so…"

"So, we jumped," Desti interrupted.

Tess had looked the best she ever had. Her face lit with such a gleeful expression, and she truly looked—happy. Her eyes then narrowed, focusing on what Desti held in her hands. "Is that the Lux?"

Desti clutched it tight against her chest and nodded. Tate was the first to answer. "Yeah, we found that too. Just in time before getting the Hell out of there."

She still couldn't believe that after all that time planning and searching, and *dying*, she had finally found it. Even holding the orb in her arms sometimes didn't feel real. Desti let her gaze graze across the camp. She was searching for the rest of them.

"Where is Anthony? And the rest?" she asked.

"Over here." Tess waved her hand for them to follow as she led them to an area with a makeshift house made from things from the forest around them. Desti's eyes went wide when she saw it. It was almost nicer than some of the houses back in the city of Mors. Most of those were covered with mold and dead things.

"You built this?" Tate asked.

"Yeah. With the help of the rest of the group. They are inside."

Tess ducked into an opening and went inside. Tate followed, but Desti was cautious to follow so quickly.

She had learned that open trust had only gotten her in terrible situations, but it was the cheerful tone of Tate's voice that pulled her in.

The moment she walked through, a wave of relief flushed through her. "Anthony!" she yelled, practically knocking him over as she hugged him. Her hands poked and grazed his face, looking to see if he was okay.

"Are you okay? Are you hurt?" Tears almost started to fill her eyes, but she wiped them away.

"No. I'm okay now."

"I honestly wasn't sure if Amaros had followed through with sending you home."

Then it hit her. The realization that she was somewhere new and foreign. *Where are we exactly?* Desti focused back on Anthony and his expression was curious. "This is home, right?" she let her hands fall to her sides. "I mean, I don't remember any place looking like this back home," Desti said while looking around.

Tate was off in the corner talking with Seraph, Kaelen, and Brandon. Desti stood at the other side feeling more confused than ever, and that was when she heard something that she never in a million years would have expected.

It was Tess, coming from the side. "Desti, I think we got sent to past."

52: Beginning of the Era of the Damned

"I'M SORRY. WHAT?"

Desti blinked but didn't fully register what she had just heard. Tate must have overheard because he had come running over to her with the same confused expression on his beautiful face.

"Tess, did I hear you right?"

Tess simply nodded and it was Seraph who came running over to explain. "That's right. We have been here for days. There are some things that we have seen, and we realized that we *were* sent back home, just to a different time."

"Are you sure?" Desti tilted her head then glanced at Tate. His mouth was slightly parted. "How do you know this?"

Kaelen appeared from the back and explained that she and the others had found other people in this forest. They had asked where they were and how to get back to the Wastelands. Apparently, the people looked at them like they all had three heads.

"So, they told us that we are in a state called Oregon," Kaelen finished.

"What the heck is a State?" asked Anthony.

Oh right. He had been sent away so young from his city. He probably never learned about the history of the time before. Desti remembered being in school and learning about some of the history. The schools didn't allow the students to delve into it extensively because learning about the New Era was more important, however Desti had learned enough to know that she lived in a place that once was a state called Nevadah. All states and even countries had been eradicated by the demons that walked the Earth, thus leading to the creation of the cities. All named after something somber and depressing. Desti's city was the city of Death if you translated it to English.

"The point is," Tess interrupted, "that we are now living in the time *before* the Era of the Damned." Her eyes flicked to the Lux that Desti was clutching. "And now I think that we might just have a way to stop this war from happening."

Acknowledgments

I would like to thank my wonderful family for all their support and help with this book. Writing City of the Damned has been a labor of love for me and I have enjoyed every minute of it.

Thank you to my sweet loving husband for supporting me throughout my writing journey. I would like to thank my aunt Kathryn for supporting my book and believing in me and my writing.

I am so grateful to be able to do what I love and share my stories with you. Thank you for reading my book and I hope that you enjoyed it.

About the Author

Kay Marrie lives in central Florida with her three young

children, two cats, and husband. When she is not juggling playtime with her kids, she spends her time dedicated to working at a charter school. Her true passion is writing and storytelling, and she has found a way to pursue her dreams of being a writer in her busy life. When she is not changing diapers or typing away, you can find her nestled up with a book, enjoying the warm Florida sun on her front porch.